P9-DKF-735

Also by William H. Gass

FICTION

Cartesian Sonata

The Tunnel

Willie Masters' Lonesome Wife

In the Heart of the Heart of the Country

Omensetter's Luck

NONFICTION

Life Sentences

A Temple of Texts

Tests of Time

Reading Rilke

Finding a Form

On Being Blue

Habitations of the Word

The World Within the Word

Fiction and the Figures of Life

Middle C

Middle C

A novel

WILLIAM H. GASS

ALFRED A. KNOPF · NEW YORK · 2013

THIS IS A BORZOI BOOK
PUBLISHED BY ALFRED A. KNOPF

 Published in the United States by Alfred A. Knopf,
a division of Random House, Inc., New York

www.aaknopf.com

Library of Congress Cataloging-in-Publication Data

Gass, William H., [date]
Middle C : a novel / by William Gass
p. cm.
"A Borzoi book."
ISBN 978-0-307-70163-3
1. Music teachers—Fiction. 2. Self-presentation—Fiction. 3. Austrians—
Ethnic identity—Fiction. 4. Identity (Psychology)—
Fiction. 5. Psychological fiction. I. Title.
PS3557.A845M53 2013
813'.54—dc22 2012017087

Jacket design by Gabriele Wilson

Manufactured in the United States of America
First Edition

For Mary

never more so

When I am laid in earth,
may my wrongs create
no trouble, no trouble
in thy breast.
Remember me! remember me!
but ah! forget my fate.

—HENRY PURCELL AND NAHUM TATE,
Dido and Aeneas

ACKNOWLEDGMENTS

Earlier versions of some chapters in this novel have appeared as fictions in *Conjunctions,* a magazine for whose loyalty I am deeply indebted through all of its history and much of mine. "The Apocalypse Museum," in no. 37, 2001; "The Abandonment of the Family," in no. 40, 2003; "The Piano Lesson," in no. 44, 2005; "A Little History of Modern Music," in no. 47, 2006, as well as in *The O. Henry Prize Stories, 2008* (New York: Anchor, 2008); "Garden," in no. 49, 2007; "Professor Skizzen Gets the Word," in no. 53, 2009. I have pilfered a few lyrics from some old-time tunes from a quaint book called *Songs That Never Grow Old* by Anonymous (New York: Syndicate Publishing, 1909).

Middle C

. . . it repented Jehovah that he had made man . . .

I

Miriam, whom Joey Skizzen thought of as his mother, Nita, began to speak about the family's past, but only after she decided that her husband was safely in his grave. His frowns could silence her in midsentence; even his smiles were curved in condescension, though at this time in his absence, her beloved husband's virtues, once admitted to be many, were written in lemon juice. He had a glare to bubble paint, she said. Her recollection of that look caused hesitations still. She would appear alarmed, wave as if she saw something gnatting near her face, and stutter to a stop. Joey was helped to remember how, at suppertime, for only then was the family gathered as a group, the spoon would become still in his father's soup, his father's head would rise to face the direction of the offending remark, his normally placid look would stiffen, and fires light in his eyes. His stare seemed unwilling to cease, although it probably was never held beyond the lifetime of a minute. But a minute . . . a minute is so long. Certainly it continued until his daughter's or his wife's uneasy expression sank into the bottom of her bowl, and the guilty head was bowed in an attitude of apology and submission.

When the soup was a clear broth, as it often impecuniously was, Joey could occasionally see his face floating in a brown dream, and he thought of his mother's real self submerged in a brown dream too, beyond the reach of life. His father sent his spoon to the bottom, and they could hear it scrape as he ladled, faster and faster as the level dropped. He was a noisy eater because he felt noise signified relish and appreciation. Whenever a meal was especially skimpy, Yankel, as he insisted he was, slurped his soup, he sucked his teeth, and he exclaimed Aaah! after a set of swallows. When they had bread, he would strenuously rend it just above the surface of the soup so that flecks of crust would fall as snow might on a pond. Then he'd allow the torn piece to follow after, his hands aiming it somewhat like a bomb. His father would watch the hunk slowly tan, gradually sog, and finally sink. Joseph knew he had to finish his bowl, whose basin would have to seem licked, but he hated to put his own implement down there in the dream and see it thrust through his own moist eye or quivery cheek because down there his thin bit of all-purpose tableware suddenly became his father's wide one, ready to scoop up his nose or chin and inhale him spoon by spoon the way, later, he read that the Titan who was called Saturn had swallowed his children.

They had reached London by then, where Joseph was born Yussel, and where his father finally got a job printing leaflets for the army; leaflets that were to be dropped on the Germans to threaten or cajole. Yankel was proud of the errors he had caught in the texts. He laughed the way stout Austrians would laugh at anything inauthentic. He often described the leaflets for the family, demonstrating the size of the sheets, summarizing their messages, enacting the way they would flutter out of the sky. Heads will turn and hearts will fail, he said, spinning like a waltzer. Each littering page is hastening your father back from exile—thanks to the RAF and the government's printing offices—back to Vienna, perhaps even to Graz. His wide hands wavered for each leaf—a wiggle here, a wobble there—and then he would bend down to show, on the floor, how they'd land and even how they'd blow about the street. Already a bit of me is back, he bragged. They will pick up each piece. You know how neat we are. For the mayor he made a face that was puffed as a frog's; for the mayor he mimed a body bent to hold its belly from the ground; and, for the mayor, he pretended to read a quivering sheet in a quaking voice: Cit i zens of Graz . . .

The Fixels endured the Blitz as so many others did, huddled in cellars, but Joseph could bring back from those damage-filled days nothing specific now, only a nighttime world of noise and fear and fire. As well as the warmth of friendly arms. His sister, older by two years, also remembered with fondness hours of being held by one parent or other, though they both preferred their mother, who cradled them while gently rocking her arms, whereas their father squeezed them as if, any minute, they might break free and run away, when it was the squeeze that inclined them to scoot. The dents in their skins, they both vividly recalled, were made by his metal coat buttons.

A long way from Graz, his father would mutter many times a day. A long way. His head was close-cropped, already gray, his clothes simple to the point of penury. They made their lodging more in a pile of rubble than in a building, for one wall of the tenement was down, some stairs had collapsed, and many windows were broken. There is nothing here the Germans would want to bomb, Miriam remembered he often said when they sat at their single table in the middle of a ruined room to dine on dreams and reassurance. For their meals they set fires like tramps, and the shell of many a house in their sector was consumed by soup being warmed long before the incendiaries could get back to bomb them again.

Yankel, as he was officially known then, felt he had to keep the family's spirits up, especially those of Joseph's sister, who was inclined to mope and who simply refused to call or even think of herself as Dvorah, the name Yankel had picked out to harmonize with his; so, to do so, to keep their courage, he would uncase his cheap pinewood fiddle (as Miriam reminded Joseph, when they were both in a story mood) and scrape through a few jolly reminiscent peasant tunes. Ach, he was so bad he couldn't play gypsy, was the line she repeated when, in her tale, the fiddle's moment came. But she never referred to the instrument as a pinewood box while they were Jews because, as a Jew, Yankel was the head of the household the way, he felt, as a Jew, he ought to be: as completely in charge as any Austrian husband, but with the full backing, now, of Jehovah. All that Austrians have, he said sadly, shaking his head, all that Austrians have got is God; the Jews have Yahweh. Well, which is it, Jehovah or Yahweh, Miriam asked him once. Jews are not permitted to pronounce his name, Yankel said, so they are constantly changing it. I thought they had just one God, like most people, Miriam said, in receipt of a glower. Ha! just like you used to have when you were a Catholic, her husband replied angrily. Father, Son, Holy Spirit, Mother Mary, the Four Evangelists, Gabriel and an army of angels, perhaps the pope, all the saints, more than the mind can count. Miriam stuck to her guns: One God ought to be one God, no more, no less. Even busy as he was. With a reach wide enough to attend his chores. Worship Allah, then . . . Allah is one God, Yankel would answer, triumph in his voice.

Miriam was accustomed to domineering men—fathers, judges, generals, businessmen, bosses, all behind one beard, one fog of smoke, one vested chest. But the Rudi who had courted her was deferential, shy, calm, musical, not the stern bullyragging majordomo Yankel had become because he thought patriarchy was essentially Jewish. That's where his glare came from: the stage. Yet it seemed more genuine than the slow smile whose lips she'd first kissed.

Rudi Skizzen had barely reached manhood when he met Nita Rouse at a country wedding he had been hired to fiddle for. Rudi had ridden his bicycle when he could and pushed it uphill when he had to, traveling out from Graz on narrow grass-grown roads notable for the heads of rocks that poked through everywhere, so that he dared see no scenery but the ground. At eighteen he was a better fiddler than he was at twenty-eight, and Nita, herself fourteen, with great round black eyes not like raisins, rather like plump grapes in her round face, kept her wide eyes on him while he played, and the company tried to dance the country dances, although they had already forgotten the steps they had been taught as children. The old ways were wearing thin, Miriam said, and no longer kept anybody warm. But the new ways were worse, and hell was their deserving.

Nita's courtship, when the time came for it, was carried on in the country, too. The couple went for long walks on those same green lanes Rudi had earlier cycled over, hoping to achieve some solitude for themselves and their chaste embraces. Rudi remembered birdsong, because he had an ear for music and for poetry, while Nita saw flowers she knew well enough to name, and she frequently stooped to inspect those that forced their stems up between the many rocks to bloom yellow, blue, and white like bursts of pleasure, but she was careful to stoop without letting go of Rudi's hand, an attention that made her dawdling delightful for him.

I always knew we'd have a plain and simple way of getting on, Miriam said, for we were not privileged people, though we were not spared their worries. I was Nita then and could play cards and joke with men. I did hope to have a country life, away from hard roads, noise, and rancor, but Rudi wanted to be where he could use his music, and I thought him a fine fiddle player then, before I'd heard otherwise, and before his fingers grew foreign to the bow. The truth is no one could have squeezed a sweet tune from that soft cheap flimsy wood of his. What if he had had a decent violin? Maybe the opera in Vienna would have heard him, or in a café a gypsy—to his strains—whirl her skirts.

Nita's new husband found for his family a small leaky roof in Graz, and the printer's trade, learned from Rudi's father, put a modest living on their skimpy table; but Rudi Skizzen's talent lay nowhere near the typesetter's trays or music's page; he had two great gifts: first, he was a seer; he saw the future as if he were reading it on one of his broadsides; and second, he was born for the stage; he had as many colors as the chameleon; he filled roles like a baker; indeed, it was a Yankel he one day became, moving his family to an outskirt of Vienna and turning all of them but Joseph, who had not yet been born, into Jews simply by pinning a yarmulke to his hair with a bent wire and informing anyone interested that his name was Yankel Fixel. His wife heard this news without hearing. Was their name henceforth to be Fixel? Their name and the name of the boy who would be born, no longer under Bethlehem's star, was Fixel? Yussel Fixel? A clown's cap, Miriam thought. When the baby came he was circumcised, though the bris was as imaginary as the rest of life, and performed—who knew?—on the wrong day. Moreover, the mother of the recently brutalized child was now named Miriam. To her surprise. To her confounding.

The family didn't look very Jewish, but who, Yankel argued, would admit they were Jewish if they weren't Jewish? and why would they say they were Jewish in such uncomfortable times for Jews, when anyone who was Jewish and had any sense would put on Catholic habits in a thrice if they could get away with it, or twirl like a dervish, or leap like any Leaping Lena, if it would do the trick. Yet, as though Rudi had waved a wand and cried presto-change-o to impress a crowd, mass was now modified until it reached kosher. Although what was kosher confused Yankel. Jews were forbidden to see milk and meat on the same plate let alone seethe a kid in its mother's milk or drink and chew simultaneously. Jews were often thought to be otherwise than everybody, but who would want to mix milk and meat that intimately anyway? even bites of the same stew had to succeed one another. But by six hours? so they wouldn't have an intestinal confrontation? Well, he couldn't afford two pots for each person, two bowls, two dishes, two spoons. And every animal was unclean except those that resembled Satan—he of the cloven hoof—or those who looked silly, chewing their cud. And threw up. This was confusing. Fish without scales and fins were forbidden? who had ever heard of any? Did they mean whales? In addition, the Jews had special killers for their cows. Never mind, he was too poor to have much meat or too worried to practice rites in public and thereby advertise mistakes.

Nita claimed Rudi was especially comfortable in his role as Yankel when it came to the Jewish abhorrence of blood. They drained and buried the blood of the animals they killed, and they didn't hunt. His hatred of hunting, which his son shared, was certainly not Austrian. They were peace-loving, he thought, the Jews. All to the good. But why did they have it in for shrimp, lobster, mussels, clams? Being a Jew would be confusing; it would mean sacrifice; yet Yankel felt there was no time to lose, so the change-o must be presto, whatever the risk. Yankel Fixel had learned that there was a small underground organization smuggling Jews out of Austria to England. England was where he was bound, but he had no money in the pocket and person of Rudi Skizzen for the passage, so Yankel Fixel, a case for charity's mercies, he became.

It was Rudi Skizzen not Yankel Fixel who had the accomplished nose, and who could sense rot reaching a hazardous level. Rudi was not vastly lettered, but like most Austrians, he knew of Karl Kraus and of Karl Kraus's unpopular pacifist opinions. He had few beliefs he cherished, but one was that wars were always started by the powerful to be fought by the powerless who numerously suffered and died in them, though they were never better off whatever the outcome. He knew that of all the creatures God had put into this world, humans were the untrustworthiest and the meanest, another sentiment his son would share. In Eden, no snake had been needed. The Fall could be performed a cappella. He remembered how Karl Kraus admired dogs because a dog could smell shit a long way, though it be hidden in leather trousers, though it be squeezed from beauteous buttocks; but maybe it was not yet shit the dog smelled, but piss left in the pants, or a little blood released by a puncture, or pus from a wound long in service. Anyway, Rudi Skizzen smelled it—in the hunter-green coats, the embroidered blouses, the lederhosen, in the discreet farts from comfortable bellies, in the social rudeness of the properly positioned, and, above all, in good times: in the mug and on the platter, in raucous communal song, immersed in the smell of kraut, sausages, and beer. Austrians, he said, were both coarse and cultivated, and on the road between them was a stop called cruel. Cruelty came easy to engines of mastication, to people who didn't keep the door closed between milk and meat.

In those days, Graz was not so populated a place that Rudi could claim to have led an urban life. To be sure, hotels lined the Mur and just over the bridge the Weitzer cosseted its clients and flew its flags. Atop the burg the clock tower spoke its piece to the clouds while in the fall the leaves of the vines along the steep hillside turned a red rich as hair. The towers of the church had tried to be twins but settled for sisters. A metal Jesus admonished the town from the tip of a very tall stick. Even in the wind the figure did not waver. A fire-breathing lion remained nailed to the *Rathaus*'s courtyard door to guard and to sustain the authority of the city. In his mausoleum, von Erlach's statue stared at an elaborately coffered ceiling. Prosperous citizens patrolled the streets, burghers enjoying their capital.

Many years later, when Joseph was little and living in London, and his mother, Nita, grew certain her husband had disappeared for good or ill—and all between—she would laugh about what she called the Annunciation. Horror and history make a charming couple. One day, she related, your father came to me and said, The child that is getting you biggish is Jewish. He will be a nice Jewish boy and grow up to be a proper Englishman. And to stop her tears he said they would prosper in England, she would see, England was a country of constitution, of Magna Carta; but she couldn't see, blinded by weeping and in a state of confusion. She screamed at him, No Miriam me. Nita I am and shall remain, as I shall remain un-Britworthy and a proper Catholic girl. Nita you can be for me, Rudi said, but for everybody else you are Miriam now, and will remain Miriam until we are safely in London and out of the reach of reprisal. I see enemies in every direction, Miriam yelled at him. Yes. That is why we are making this adjustment in our selves. There are cowardly bullies and evil men circling our country, a country that has become a smelly corpse. To be an Austrian, now, is a calamity and will become a curse. We must leave. We cannot take the train so we shall harness a slower horse. Jews know something of such a life as we shall lead.

Miriam was dumbfounded by her husband's sudden hatred for the land of his birth. All Austrians dressed warmly, loved music, and, though they may have thought poorly of others, thought well of God. Now that the empire was gone, they lived happily by themselves and on their own. They toiled without complaining, but they also knew how to eat, drink, and have fun. They prided themselves on being overweight. Miriam smelled nothing foul when she sniffed, and sometimes a nice schnitzel.

I have no knowledge of this English language. No one will understand me, and I . . . I shall simply wander around every town like someone in a fog of foreign words. The change will be a good one, her husband said. But our families . . . our past . . . , Miriam began, and went on even when her husband cut her off. We will not hear Austrian again, he insisted, we will not speak Austrian again, not just because of what Austria has been but because of what it will become. We will not share its future, he shouted, we will not suffer its wicked nature or bear it forward one more step.

Her tears wet her chin and throat and ran between her breasts. What Rudi had proposed was crazy, unless he had never been a Rudi but had been a Fixel all along. By becoming a Jew now, he was hiding the fact that he had been one before. That thought occurred to Nita, and it would occur to Miriam too. The change was in a way romantic, because if Rudi had been a Jew from birth, he could not, as a Jew, have courted Nita, and certainly not, as a Jew, have married her amid the consternations of two families. Gradually, she did become Miriam, because whom had she wed? A Yankel? So what was she to do?

2

Miriam, watching a video, would see the cowboys' long coats and wide hats, and she would say, They—they looked like that: they wore long black coats hanging almost to the ground, wide-brimmed black hats, and showed faces full of solemnity and hair instead of other features. Five of them, five, she said, stood in a dark row before the opening—the hole in the house—where the Fixels camped. Caught unaware, flustered, Yankel held his yarmulke smashed against his head with one hand. The first figure said: You, Yankel Fixel, have never looked into—you have never been touched by—the Torah. Their long coats made them look tall, as if their shadows had been added to their stature. In a close row they formed a fence of black posts, each post surmounted by a stiff brim. Glares were all on their side. From Fixel not a glimmer. For this case, his power of stutter was lost. The second figure said: You, Yankel Fixel, have never seen the seal of God. The way they spoke made them seem wound up, their voices coming from far off like an echo among mountains. The third figure said: You, Yankel Fixel, are foreskinned as far as your face. (It was true.) Their pale visages, from which beards hung, appeared to be far away as well, their dark clothes a cave out of which a sibyl spoke. The fourth figure said: You, Yankel Fixel, have eaten unclean words; you have swallowed the poison of untruth. They each held a short black stick. The fifth figure was silent, everyone stood steady, and all were still. Finally, the fifth figure made a gesture that Miriam did not understand.

Yankel Fixel had been denounced.

This did not prevent him from enjoying the preferential treatment of a persecuted refugee. They—whoever the five Fates represented, a clutch of fanatical thugs, a row of wooden rabbis—had spoken to the false Fixel of their awareness and their displeasure, but they had not bothered to inform his boss or complain about him to anyone in the bureau that handled his affairs. So he had merely been confronted, not denounced. Denouncement might be in the offing. Rituals, he knew, proceeded by steps and stages. Perhaps Yankel should explain, he wondered aloud to his wife—she was, by his insistence, still Miriam—perhaps he should make plain the difference between his Jewishness and theirs: they had fled the ethically enviable condition of the victim, while he had fled the guilt of natal association, the animus of villainous authority. Might they understand, then, his plight? Was fleeing permitted only to potential victims? Might no one refuse the power and the privilege, the duties and indulgences, of the tyrant's role? the honey and the money of the profiteer? or flinch from the hangman's vengeance, the bigot's bile, the fat cat's claws, the smug burgher's condescension, and the swagger of the bully? Must the offer of evil, Yankel asked the sky, like some hospitalities, always be accepted?

In case his five calumniators returned, Yankel hurried to prepare some strategies. We'll admit we're not Jews . . . we'll admit it . . . but . . . but we'll beg to become Jews . . . yes . . . beg. Miriam said, He said "beg." I won't beg, she said. If a man wants to become a Jew, the Jews say to him, Yankel said he'd read, they say to him—how does it go?—they say, Don't you know that Jews are oppressed, prostrate, mistreated, undergoing suffering? and then we shall say, We know and we are not worthy of you. That's the phrase. We . . . are . . . not . . . worthy . . . of . . . you. I am, though, Miriam said. I am mistreated. Here . . . right now . . . hear how I am undergoing suffering. O weh! Well, I won't beg and I won't say I am not worthy. I am a woman. They wouldn't let me in their boys' club anyway. You beg, my husband, you dirty your knees, you say to them: I am not worthy of you. Go on. You say it, she said she said. But the five Fates never returned.

As the war wound down, Jews began leaking out of England and landing in America, at first a few drops at a time and then in rivulets and finally in torrents. Yankel could not hope that the leaflet business would continue to prosper during peacetime, so he too began to consider such a move. Miriam, during this period, was working at a laundry during the early evening, boiling sheets and napkins, aprons and towels, standing for hours in steam, breathing bleach and starch and soap, keeping herself clean of imposture, repeating to herself, I know I'm me, Holy Mother, I shall not beg to be another, I shall not say, I am not worthy, I'm me, dear God, you can see I'm me.

Professor Joseph Skizzen remembered how his mother smelled when she returned to their shattered flat, how her odor glowed as though she were a fumigation candle as she made her way amid the dark stench of wet burned paper, wet charred wood, the peppery bite of powdered glass, the reek of oil and rubber, of smoke-stuffed sofas. And his father was insisting that things looked grim for them again. In the world, affairs and facts smelled rank. To get to America as Jews they'd have to have papers attesting to their circumcised and wretchedly safe Semitic state, their exilic condition, and these bona fides they didn't have. They would need visas, no doubt, which they couldn't get. The Fixels were, in fact, fakes.

I am not a fake, Miriam said. You have made us fakes, she also insisted. You, a Yankel, have turned your children into liars, into Dvorahs and Yussels. Who are these folks? Abashed, annoyed, her husband would try to explain that people could choose to be otherwise than the selves that neighbors and the nation had shaped for them; that only an accident of birth separated Rudi Skizzen from Yankel Fixel; that she was Catholic because of her cradle; couldn't she take the cradle away and be . . . well . . . British? This line of reasoning was not persuasive. Actually, he, her husband, the man who thrust himself into her so reliably Tuesday nights, as well as Saturdays sometimes, when the week had not been too strenuous, performing the act of ownership with only now and then a few huffs that couldn't be helped so as not to disturb the children by moaning or threatening the thin mattress with his movements, was the same young man who had walked shyly along that rock-gardened country lane near Graz, steadily holding her left hand in his right and occasionally nuzzling her neck or nibbling an earlobe to hear her chuckle and chide him; he was the same because his convictions had not been revised; the heart that beat inside him kept up the same watchful rhythm as ever; he had no different a nose for disaster than before; and now the odor of the old order was overcoming him. He was a rare man, he told her, a wary man, a man of the middle, of leave-me-be, someone trying to stay out of moral trouble, a man of peace.

Gradually, a week at a time, the Rudi Skizzen who had wrapped himself in Yankel Fixel began to emerge as Raymond Scofield. He got a job in an offtrack betting parlor. He replaced his collection of Jewish jokes with quotations from music-hall songs and Gilbert and Sullivan. He left on his face a tentative slim mustache. He ate chips and tried to eat the fish. He spent more money than he should on movies. He bought a cloth cap. He practiced raising a finger to its bill. Not that he wanted to look touty. Not that he wanted to seem obsequious. What he wanted was to fade into the background, be a piece of household goods lost in the rubble of war; rubble from which the state summarily removed the family when it bulldozed blocks of bombed-out, burned-down, hovel-smelly buildings. This entailed considerable official confusion: Just who were they? Where should they be put? Confusion, especially among officials, his father said, was good, was promising, was an improvement. He told his wife she needn't have her head shaved as he had suggested despite her screams of defiance, so she wouldn't need the wig she refused to wear; that she could toss it down the broken stairs just the way she had already hurled it; and she'd never have a need to say, I am not worthy. Mary Scofield, he thought, should look for employment as a clerk. She should get rid of her accent by going to movies or listening to the BBC and then find safe work in an office. She should keep in mind that England was a class-driven society despite its constitution and its Magna Carta; a culture that could teach even the Viennese the importance of place and position. Stirring tubs of steaming dungarees was not for a Scofield who clearly had some social standing. Consequently they could claim to be only momentarily down on their luck.

Although his father could mimic British speech fairly well, his wife was unable to play the ape. Her accent could have held down papers in a wind. She refused, absolutely, to take on "Mary." She was too worshipful of the real Mary, sick of subterfuge, and wary of the English, who struck her as snobs before all else; so, in compromise, Miriam she remained. Miriam Scofield was possible, Yankel—who was now Raymond, Raymond Scofield thought. Yankel Fixel was a bottom feeder, with a carp's muddy name; Raymond—ah—Raymond Scofield would leap from the river to snap at the air. Calmed by the compromise, Raymond Scofield took a deep breath in order to think ahead. And from resentful, rebellious Miriam, Raymond Scofield stayed his hand, though she thought she saw it raised. The light was bad.

Infants and small children are sheltered from such changes, which take place at a level in adult life they hope, as they age, they will never reach. But the smells were different when they left the bomb-outs for simple bare rooms, institutionally disinfected, equal and anonymous; the look of their parents, the clothes they wore, the way they walked, the frowns they bore, were different, and to infants and small children the look of things, the sound and smell of things, the feelings, like atmosphere, that fill every emptiness, are all that life is. The warmth of their small stove was nothing like an open fire; they saw the world now through unbroken panes of greasy glass; they no longer had to pick their way among hazards, but the cream-walled room was cream walled night and day and all around them every way they turned. When Miriam came home, steamy and pungent, her smell seemed redundant in a room that was not a ruin, a room with a curtained corner for the commode, an uncovered corner for a stove, walls against which were pushed a small bed and two cots, no place where you could watch your pee fall through open floors for several stories. Miriam lay in Ray's arms more often than before because brooming the floor of the betting parlor was easier on his energy, and because in that bed there was room and reason finally to conceive.

Though, to her relief, she did not, which Ray put down to the slow and silent—almost insincere—thrusting that was required, as if the children, now both in public school, didn't know what their restless tossing and turning meant—to a degree, anyway. They are doing the blanket-bouncing business, they said. Ray urged Miriam toward another job. She felt clean as a creamery, of course, but he was sure his sperm could not live inside a womb so under the influence of soap.

Ray began to consider seriously what would be required, in terms of proper papers, friends, bribes, funds, to continue their journey to the New World, which now included Canada—indeed, Canada now looked easier. But they had no British papers, no Austrian ones, no identity, which the recently named Raymond Scofield should have found appealing, and indeed he would have, under slightly different circumstances, reveled in it, though he kept spelling his fresh name "Schofield," a mistake that was dangerous. The Fixels were on some bureaucrat's hands, the result of a national sympathy now silently regretted, and it seemed to Ray likely that those hands would be happy to release him from their responsibility. Release him, perhaps he thought. To be in the singular for the first time.

How is this possible, Miriam would frequently exclaim, she said, when trying to convey to her grown-up boy her husband's preoccupations, because Ray would treat her exclamation as a question, and then misunderstand its obvious import. When we left Graz, Ray would maintain, we undid our ties; we left our prior selves behind like old clothes on their way to rags; we joined the dispossessed, yet were not one of them, either; and lived among ruins, and were seen only by corpsmen, clerks, and firemen when the cracks grew large enough to make us visible: that is why I can become a Scofield; it is a world of opportunity; anything is possible for us. But for the Jews . . . Jews have to be Jews now. They can never be French or Polish or German again. *Opfer.* He used the German word. They will always be *Opfer. Opfer* forever.

What gave Ray moral weight was the news: of the war's victorious progress—or its calamitous outcome, according to Nita, who stubbornly retained her Austrian affections—news that justified his forebodings, that more and more stamped his harsh judgments with righteousness and made the family's bizarre move as prescient as the foreknowledge of a prophet. You may seem clean because you smell of soap, he said, but I am clean on both sides of my conscience; your hands may be wrinkled they are so overwashed, but mine are smoother and whiter than paper. He held up his palms. You can see right through. The work my hands have done need not be hid; therefore I cannot be Austrian; an Austrian's hands should slink back into its sleeves. And you too can enjoy an untroubled heart. Nita nodded without agreement. Her husband's Thanks to me was loud though unspoken. My heart has been kidnapped, she said, borne with my babies away into a world of wreckage. I could have lived in my village a quiet harmless life . . . and held my hands out to anyone. Ray made a face yet not one of denial. You would have shaken hands that made profits, he insisted, that made killing implements; that fingered folks for the police; that helped in roundups; that made murder: hands of an uncle who supplied a troop, hands of a cousin who drove a truck, a nephew who sold clothes. You would be unaware: of the neighbor's son who shot gypsies, homos, Jews, and the dentist who drew the gold from their teeth. There are so many slyboots, friends whom the Nazis fondled. You would have met on the street in Graz where you had gone to buy a hat—this one, that. You would have sat in a seat on the same train. You would not stare out the window but pretend to read as the train rolls past wire, cleared trees, a camp. You would have smiled at a man who had strung some of that wire, who had held a megaphone, who had taken advantage of imprisoned women. That would stain even well-washed hands and overcome nature's fondness for pale ones because even a Negro's palms are pink. Your graceful fingers would not be gnarled by honest work; they would slowly take the shape of claws. To desire an Austrian nationality is to accept the acts of assassins, tacitly to agree to—my God—mayhem and massacre. Now that you are no longer Nita, you are free of such disgusting contaminations. Don't let their sort be lichen on some forest rocks, unseen and unremarked, or taken for granted like the persistent damp of Vienna's stones, its postered kiosks, its gray streets. To the pure, to the stateless, my Nita, anything is possible.

Including . . . betting on a winning horse. Ray worked six months as a janitor at the betting parlor before he placed a modest sum upon the nose of a long-shot nag, not even in hope, more out of curiosity, and received immodest winnings, winnings which took him by surprise, took him aback, shook him up, shook him so he saw a solution in the sum he suddenly had in hand. This was the sort of shock Miriam later imagined her husband to have had: after a life of undeserving failure, a sudden unmerited success. Once you've placed a bet, you've made your bed, she said. Once you've been bitten by a bet and you're ahead, you're dead. Because bettors were mainly men of low principles, she was certain, often at loose ends, frayed in the bargain, men whose knowledge of the world was entirely set in terms of shortcuts, which, if you took enough of them, would allow your journey to zig in a ceaseless circle, to zag without seeing an end. Conceivably he could have lost his money in a game of cards and run shamefully away. To hide from whom, however? He could have gone from sin to sin, his appetites as sharp as razors, if he'd known what sin was or where sins were or how, even, to begin a stretch of sinning; but, though he could spot evil in a rubber stamp, he couldn't tell a streetwalker from a floor lamp. Eventually, both police and such parlor patrons as confessed to Ray's acquaintance concluded that he had secretly spent his money on documents, on plans, on bribes, on a steamship ride.

Rudi Skizzen would have said it was God's will, and certainly Yankel Fixel would have felt that it was Meant: that despite every likelihood he would find himself in just this job, where temptation of some type would lead him to a wager, and where, against extravagant odds, he would come into considerable cash—the purchase of a passage—but for Ray Scofield, a man who had decided to live a life free of divinities—including anything that might be written in the skies—for him it was just luck, it was a sudden advantage, a chance, an unsought, unearned opportunity.

Miriam learned of his expressed attitude toward the bet and its lavish payoff while Ray Scofield's disappearance was being investigated. The investigation itself was confused, for at first the authorities did not know exactly whom they were looking for: Austrian, Englishman, Jew. Nor did the wife appear to have a clear understanding of the sort of man her husband was. For instance, they learned from people at the betting parlor of Ray Scofield's success at the track, and in the course of their questions, just how he had taken it: not as a gift from God, not as the final arrival of Good Fortune, nor as a Matter of Course, but simply as an accident, similar to a sudden fall; but his wife would not accept that reaction, for she said her husband would have fallen to his knees and thanked God, after apologizing, first, for the sin in his wager. His suits and sleeves and collar might change, she claimed, but his heart would never alter.

She and the children had come home, if that's what you could call it, to find not even his customary shadow. Naturally they had worried and fretted for a time before going to the police. Something had befallen her husband, Rudi Skizzen—no, in her nervousness, she seemed unsure—something awful had happened to Yankel Fixel. And he worked where? In the leaflet house, she answered—no, the betting office, not so far. Yet so very far. All those bombs had missed them only to have this—whatever it was—happen, come out of nowhere, to make her Rudi a . . . what . . . ? a what . . . ? an *Opfer,* a victim . . . a runaway. She couldn't believe it. Do you believe it, she repeatedly asked Dvorah, forgetting that her daughter was supposed to be Deborah now. I'm glad he's gone, I hate him, his daughter said. You don't hate him. He changed my name. Maybe he's hurt somewhere. He took us from our home and changed our names, Dvorah went on relentlessly, repeating the sentence. You were too young really to remember. Graz? I remember. No one is too young to remember. And my name I remember. His horrid beard. He shaved, dear, he shaved. To leave us on a weekend, his daughter said. Miriam howled. Deborah howled. How . . . how is this possible? But there was no answer from the authorities until many months had passed, months during which Miriam had to fend off foster care for her kids, quit the laundry, try the church, and go on the dole. Then the authorities learned, while apprehending some counterfeiters, of Raymond Scofield's purchases: a passport, a ticket, a license to drive. Drive? Rudi rode a bike. Drive? That didn't matter, the authorities explained; it was a useful document. Miriam felt bereaved. Dvorah felt abandoned. Yussel appeared to feel nothing at all.

The young priest who heard her confession became solicitous. He dropped round. Unlike the Jews who had confronted Yankel, this priest had no face fuzz; you could see his smooth red cheeks and red lips, always moist as if they were sides of a stream. He had a properly soft voice, full of concern, and he tried to joke with the children, though it was clear, Miriam said, it was Miriam who interested him. Her round flat Slav face seemed huge where it perched like a lollipop above her now bone-thin body. Her dark hair was already flicked with gray. Miriam began to worry about what she wore because she could feel his eyes fixed on her in far from a fatherly way, and this attraction did her more good than baskets of fruit. She smiled for him while Dvorah glared.

It would be so romantic, Miriam thought, if her beauty pulled this priest from his church like a cork from a bottle. She longed to hear him say: I cannot help myself; I must have you; you have enslaved me; for you I give up Communion, I give up Confession, I give up Latin, I give up God, and so on, though she had no interest whatever in responding to such amorous advances beyond tittering and smiling and saying the equivalent of "pshaw" in her Austrian. Her devotion to the Deity did not prohibit a daydream flirtation with one of his representatives. In another age and class she would have rapped Father's knuckles with her fan and laughed like bubble-risen wine. Nor could she maintain this fantasy in front of the mirror in her mind. Maybe, she thought, like a farmer, he sees how I would look when properly fattened for the market. The image gave her hope: that one day she would be.

Already angry at the flight of her father, Dvorah was jealous and outraged and shamed by her mother's little play. Which she dimly understood was only a dance. It was as if, for a moment, with this woman, the priest was allowing himself another life . . . and not merely that he was, for a change, an unemasculated man but that he was actually a rowdy one, preying upon a poor abandoned refugee woman, as so many did, a Romeo without scruple or regard. He had a way of running a pale shiny-nailed hand up his black-sleeved arm—she told Joseph often of it in the after years—a gesture that told her he was wishing her stockings were just as dark and felt the same. Years and repetitions later, she knew that caress would feel like the path of a barky stick.

Finally, the priest managed to pry her story from her, so when she said she believed that her husband—what's the rascal's name now?—had probably been an *Opfer,* the victim of foul play, having been seen coming into money by a lot of lowlifes; or when she said she believed her husband had simply preceded them to the New World—the New World where they would begin again, each self as new as a store shoe—and that he would in a while send for his family to live decently in some hilly Austrian part of that far-off Yankel country, moreover in a sharply peaked cottage at the end of a rocky flower-dotted lane—Oh, we are almost there, she said—to a house with curtains in the summer, shutters in the winter, and an open gate; not an absconder, Miriam maintained, not a fugitive from their marriage, a runaway who had left her with two young children to seek his own good luck in America just because he'd won a wager on a horse. When she went on, her eyes closed and dreamy-faced, through the possibilities, the priest simply said, Yes, yes, I understand, but remember he left your country, as you say, suddenly, and he was just that abruptly no longer an Austrian, just that cruelly a Jew, a refugee, a Scofield who could enter Canada as easily as he could place a bet where he worked, and so, dear lady, he could leave you.

This was not endearing. The priest, however, while he wished to win her to his side, meant only—we must imagine—to the side of religion. You must return to the church, you must purge yourself of every taint of Jewishness, no matter how feigned; for it was sacrilegious to have behaved as your husband did; did she realize he had endangered their souls, the souls of her children as well as her own? I wouldn't wear a wig, Miriam said in her defense. I never really kept kosher. I didn't eat with noise. I didn't hide money under pillows. I had no family, no friends. My husband—I didn't walk behind. I didn't learn jokes or how to tell them. She remembered Yankel's favorite, though, which he had memorized for her use, and whose form he had carefully explained, failing to realize that it was never the women who told them. It seemed there were ladies having tea at a fine house. That was the setting, the situation, he said, ladies, tea, fine house. The hostess, a woman rather well off in the baking business, is passing and repassing a huge plate of butter cookies. That was the action, the send-off, passing and repassing the cookies, he insisted, the joke is now on its way. I already ate three, one of her visitors is supposed to say, sighing as she eyes the full fan of delicacies the cookies form on the plate being held out to her. That cocked the pistol, it was the setup, he explained. Excuse me, her hostess then says, you've had five, but take another, who's counting? That, Miriam instructed the priest in her turn, was the clincher, the blow, the snapper. She remembered, and her voice was full of satisfaction. The joke, he said, was clearly not Catholic.

The priest could hear how Miriam's heart remained faithfully beating in her husband's chest, and perhaps it was then that he decided to desist from his social attentions and help her as her confessor should, instead of watching her face in wonder as he might the moon. Miriam must join her husband in America, retie her family ties, and give the absconder one great big surprise. Because Raymond Scofield had obligations: he had mouths to feed, children to raise, and a wife to instruct. The trouble was, no one knew where he was, who he might be at the moment, or whether he was even alive.

Oh, how I wish we were ordinary, Dvorah wailed whenever she was given the opportunity. Couldn't we be common? just plain people? normal even? Only in Austria, her mother always answered in tones of such triumphant outrage that Dvorah shut up and went into a sulk so severe a little wailing would have been a comfort.

The magic formula that determined Miriam's frequent appeals to numerous authorities went this way: Miriam and the children needed to join her husband and their father, whom she retained in his role as a Jew for strategic reasons she saw no advantage to mention. Reuniting families was a holy and patriotic duty. So Miriam and the children, now some years later, set sail for the New World, perhaps not as their husband and father had, in flight from a contaminating present, but to secure a past that had seemed to Miriam to have been at peace. This world may be new, she told Debbie and Joey, but we shall remain as we were, as old as an Alp. Remember that.

3

The fear that the human race might not survive has been replaced by the fear that it will endure.

Joseph Skizzen caught himself looking at the sentence as if he were seeing his face in his shaving glass. Immediately, he wanted to rewrite it.

The fear that the human race might not endure has been succeeded by the fear that it will survive.

Now he saw that the balance of the first fear with the second was too even—what did one say? Steven—even steven—so he gingerly removed a small amount of meaning from the right pan. This move saved the first "that" at the expense of the second.

Skizzen swung his foot at the soda can but missed it.

The fear that the human race might not endure has been succeeded by the fear it will survive.

Was it fear, or was it merely worry; was it the sort of anxiety a sip of sherry and a bit of biscuit should allay? He liked the words "might" and "race" where they were, and "succeed" was sufficiently ironic to make him smile, though mildly, as he was at heart a modest man, though not in the realm called his mind.

How could he have missed? The can was in perfect position. A remedial kick struck the tin a bit high so that it clipped the top of the target box at the other end of the attic.

The first "fear" was a fear all right, but a fear measured by the depth of concern inside it and by its abiding presence, not one of surprise or sudden fright as at a snake or burglar in the night; whereas the second "fear" was a fear like that for death—the ominous color of a distant cloud. Nonsense, he shouted. Professor Skizzen spoke harshly to himself—to his "you"—as he was frequently forced to do, since his objectified "other" often required correction. You are thinking nonsense again! You are a dim head! A buffo boy! A mere spear bearer! He could shout quite safely. Even when practicing to be an Austrian whose small mistakes might be endearing—"spear" instead of "cup bearer," for instance. His secrets were safe. No one would hear him. He could kick the can like a kid on the street. Mother lived like a toad in the garden, far away and well beyond the house's walls, among bushes, behind the red wild bee balm, and was somewhat deaf to boot. So he shouted at himself, as if he were a bit deaf too. Well, he must be deaf; did he listen? Did he heed?

What he hated most was fetching the missed shots back to their launch site.

The comparison with death was incorrect—inadequate—inaccurate, because the fear in question was for life itself—life—human life was the threat: multitudinous, voracious, persistent, pitiless as a plague . . . of army ants . . . Japanese beetles . . . of locusts, the insect Joseph Skizzen thought we most resembled; yes, it spread itself out, life did, and assumed the shape of a swarm. We devoured one another, then the world, and we were many . . . many; we darkened even the day sky; our screams resembled stridulations. The professor could have howled like Mr. Hyde. There he was . . . there . . . seeing himself in his shaving glass. He took inadequate aim. He altered, yet **he** remained **he.** Austrian to a T. Mustached. Goateed.

One's concern that the human race might not endure has been succeeded by the fear it will survive.

"One"? A word that distanced responsibility. A cowardly word, "one." Why not another number? Why not the can in a corner pocket? "It" . . . "it" was the concern of not one but three monkeys, or was "it" that of "sixty-five"? "Five hundred thirty-two citizens of Oakland, California, said they were worried that their neighbors might survive the next fire." A cowardly word, "one," because it refused to choose: anybody, whoever, what's the diff? Okay, so perhaps write "our worry" instead. What did the pen—the page—the sentence think? Yes, the difference between "concern" and "worry," "worry" and "fear," "fear" and "apprehension," "anxiety" and "unease," must be respected—represented.

Professor Skizzen made his way slowly toward the north end of the attic where cans that missed their cardboard goal could be found. On the way back he would imagine he was a damp dog and shake his sentence free from his wet ruff. Then he would kick that damn thing through the wall.

If "one" was merely an elision whose omitted matter might be restored, would sense be thereby achieved? By substituting "Someone's concern that the human race . . ."? perhaps "Anyone's concern that the human race . . ."? or "No one's concern that the human race . . ."? Absurd. Absurd. You will never understand this language. Skizzen spoke aloud in his own space. You will never understand this language, even though it is your nearly native tongue.

The dent in the side of the can fit his shoe. He had nearly kicked one curve through its converse. There were two others, somewhere, under the slanting roof. Now and then their bruised aluminum would wink.

One's worry that the human race might not endure has been succeeded by the fear it will survive.

Not yet. "Worry" was the wrong word. Too busy. Too ordinary. Too trivial. White rabbits worry. White rabbits dither. White rabbits scurry. Moreover, "our" was the opposite of "one." "Our" was complicit and casually cozy. Who else has had this problem? This worry? Is it widespread enough to justify "our"? Possibly only Professor Joseph Skizzen owned up to it. The professor wasn't wide; was short, slim, trim, fit, firm of tummy; wore a small sharp beard upon his chin below a thin precise line; and was quite noticeably alone in his opinions.

"Concern" suggested a state maintained with some constancy in our consciousness like low heat under a pan. When we worry, our thoughts rush hither and yon and then thither again like Alice's rabbit. But when we are concerned, our thoughts sit quietly in a large chair and weigh the seat, configure the bottom of their bowl. Strictly speaking, though the designations are often misused, we can properly worry only about ourselves; language allows us, however, to have concerns for others. And he, Joseph Skizzen, as well as the rest of us alive right now, wouldn't be around for Armageddon when it came, in any case. So not to worry.

An important kick was coming up. Keep it low. The box lay on its side and yawned.

Nevertheless, it would be prudent to remain concerned. For, like death,

IT would come: Armageddon. There would be—without exaggeration—a series of catastrophes. As a consequence of the evil in man . . . —no mere virus, however virulent, was even a burnt match for our madness, our unconcern, our cruelty— . . . there would arise a race of champions, predators of humans: namely earthquakes, eruptions, tidal waves, tornados, typhoons, hurricanes, droughts—the magnificent seven. Floods, winds, fires, slides. The classical elements, only angry. Oceans would warm, the sky boil and burn, the ice cap melt, the seas rise. Rogue nations, like kids killing kids at their grammar school, would fire atomic—hydrogen—neutron bombs at one another. Smallpox would revive, or out of the African jungle would slide a virus no one understood. Though reptilian only in spirit, the disease would make us shed our skins like snakes and, naked to the nerves, we'd expire in a froth of red spit. Markets worldwide would crash as reckless cars on a speedway do, striking the wall and rebounding into one another, hurling pieces of themselves at the spectators in the stands. With money worthless—that last faith lost—the multitude would riot, race against race at first, God against God, the gots against the gimmes. Insects hardened by generations of chemicals would consume our food, weeds smother our fields, fire ants, killer bees sting us while we're fleeing into refuge water, where, thrashing, we would drown, our pride a sodden wafer. Pestilence. War. Famine. A cataclysm of one kind or another—coming—making millions of migrants. Wearing out the roads. Foraging in the fields. Looting the villages. Raping boys and women. There'd be no tent cities, no Red Cross lunches, hay drops. Deserts would appear as suddenly as patches of crusty skin. Only the sun would feel their itch. Floods would sweep suddenly over all those newly arid lands as if invited by the beach. Forest fires would burn, like those in coal mines, for years, uttering smoke, making soot of speech, blackening every tree leaf ahead of their actual charring. Volcanoes would erupt in series, and mountains melt as though made of rock candy till the cities beneath them were caught inside the lava flow where they would appear to later eyes, if there were any eyes after, like peanuts in brittle. May earthquakes jelly the earth, Professor Skizzen hotly whispered. Let glaciers advance like motorboats, he bellowed, threatening a book with his fist. These convulsions would be a sign the parasites had killed their host, evils having eaten all they could; we'd hear a groan that was the going of the Holy Ghost; we'd see the last of life pissed away like beer from a carouse; we'd feel a shudder move deeply through this universe of dirt, rock, water, ice, and air, because after its long illness the earth would have finally died, its engine out of oil, its sky of light, winds unable to catch a breath, oceans only acid; we'd be witnessing a world that's come to pieces bleeding searing steam from its many wounds; we'd hear it rattling its atoms around like dice in a cup before spilling randomly out through a split in the stratosphere, night and silence its place—well—not of rest—of disappearance. My wish be willed, he thought. Then this will be done, he whispered so no God could hear him. That justice may be served, he said to the four winds that raged in the corners of his attic.

His kick felt solid. The can bounced from the back of the box. That was a relief—as if he'd passed stool.

Well, we wouldn't hear anything, see anything, feel anything, of course, because we—who were we, now?—would have perished. As we went into the ground we'd pass former fellows, previous persons, being flung forth—the Catacombs coughing up their bones. There'd be billions of corpses and no one to count them. No one to photograph weeping mothers for the evening news. No mothers, no news, at last. Human life on automatic pilot. Reruns till every inch of film flames. No more microwaves. The air would soften, ease, grow gentle, when the human frequencies fell silent. A few birds would float above the mess and look for eyes to peck—eyes still fresh and moist from wild surmise and well-meant weeping.

Our concern that the human race might not endure has been succeeded by the fear it will survive.

My concern . . . it's my concern . . . alas . . . mine. My concern that mankind might not endure has been followed by the fear it will survive. Succeeded—succeeded—has been succeeded.

Professor Joseph Skizzen's concern that the human race might not endure has been succeeded by his fear that it will survive.

The sentence had begun forming—as if it were going to be significant—during breakfast on a mild May morning many years ago.

He could not remember the fruit or how it lay in the bowl of his spoon or how it tasted when it became mush in his mouth. As a music critic—a musicologist—as a philosopher of music—he was used to working with words; they held no special terrors for him; he thought of them simply as tools; they were not instruments like those in an orchestra, because he did not think of his books and essays as performances. His ideas, of course, needed them, but he didn't dress up his thoughts like toffs or tarts and parade them about on the avenues. He could not remember the bread or roll either or whether they had a plate to themselves. He could not remember the nature of the day.

The sentence had simply passed through his ears and lodged in his head like a random bullet from a drive-by gang. Sorry, meant to shoot the little girl standing with her doll on the front stoop. Meant to shoot Grandma in the porch swing. Meant to shoot the geraniums through their pot. There was another sentence in the barrel. Sorry, meant to shoot you with something harmless, such as: "green oranges are picked when barely yellow and dyed orange to reassure consumers"—certainly not anything disturbing: the fear that the human race, etcet.

"Unripe oranges"? "Scarcely yellow"?

And of course, a word like "dyed" was disturbing, even in a sentence about dissembling, about misleading. Nothing was safe anymore. You could hug caution and try to prevent it from being thrown to vicious winds, but tides would overwhelm its NO SWIMMING signs nevertheless, while earth opened to let the timorous attitude fall, alive and alert as caution is, to the central fire.

During the weeks following its appearance, the sentence had struggled to free itself from the entanglements of a professorial unconscious. Every morning before work, before beginning the routine of the day, the professor was compelled to mess with it. Like a cat kicking a sock stuffed with mintnip. It remained, after every assault—the sentence, the sock—somewhat shapeless. Yet maintained—the sentence, the sock, did—its former attraction. Or perhaps it was like sucking on a sick tooth. Though sucked, the tooth stayed sore. So kicking or licking it was an exercise he did routinely the way others jogged. Its words needed to be whelped because it was a serious sentence—not about companies colorizing fruit, not about academic worries, not about his dim—to him—and dubious past—yet a sentence that had to be made right somehow, properly completed, because it was never right when he read it, though what was wrong was never clear either.

His game of kick the can had come to be a coarser instance of a sock attack. The cans failed to rattle as noisily as they might have if kicked down a concrete street, but it was the best he could do under the present circumstances, and engaged another portion of his anatomy in a way that had to be healthy.

He hadn't seen the sentence in his mind's eye as though MENE, MENE had been written on one of thought's walls; he heard it, yet heard it all at once, as if at a glance, the way he would study himself in his shaving mirror: one bit of face in focus, where the razor aimed, the remainder in the realm of the vague . . . yet there—though vague—certainly there—a dim presence.

Since he couldn't be sure whether the sentence was a war wound or a tapeworm, he didn't know what to do. Maybe rewriting was the wrong tack. Maybe he needed to find a context for it instead. Maybe it had been translated from the Austrian and begged to be returned to the language it came from. "The idea that the people might not persevere" was perhaps a better beginning. Not "the people" just "people." The idea that we might lose the human race and come in last . . . the idea that our might was a Maginot, potent so long as unemployed—fearsome only of physique—as showy as a circus—no more serviceable than a costume—was . . . was unendur . . . insuff . . . and if . . . if fired like a battery of Berthas—our powers and our vainglory might explode in our—the shooter's—face—as if . . . if our shell had been sent through the calamitous curve of a bent barrel . . .

The sentence had slowly appeared, gradually shaped itself, and as it had, so had the compulsion to perfect it overcome him, filled and overflowed him as if he were a tub. Enough, he had cried, yet there the flood came, out of nowhere, rolling down stairs like a rapids.

The thought that mankind might not endure has been replaced by the fear it may survive.

"Supplanted." How about "supplanted"? The notion that mankind might not endure was after all a happy one, optimistic, hopeful, so it could hardly be described as worrisome or a cause for concern.

But it was not really a happy thought. Skizzen was saddened that one had to hope for humanity's demise, for the wipeout of every man woman and child. And their goddamn sidewalk shitting dogs. And their insatiable greed. And the misused intelligence—caviar on cake, invention for invention's sake. And their mountainous indifference. Horrendous cruelty. He was sorrowful. But we had done enough damage. Enough. We had done enough harm. Enough of us. Enough of this. Nevertheless, he was constantly compelled to recast the notion, to reconsider it, to suffer its shortcomings.

Moreover—now—his wrestle with the thought would be followed by a reverie on the catastrophes that could accomplish . . . could complete the idea, round it off: fire, flood, earthquake, howl of wind. Fog. A foul fog. A fog that knew no lift. Miasma for a million miles. A fog of farts from a billion bodies. Rancidities. Shit streams. Stack smoke. Cigarettes. Autocide. Sour breaths. Cook pots. Sweat glands suddenly unparalyzed. Rubbish rot. Microspill. Odors previously unidentified.

Puzzled by the onset of the sentence, Joseph Skizzen examined his memory and found that his recollection of its birth changed when he changed its wording. It appeared gradually but all at once—whole—like a ship or a plane approaching. Or it arrived in servings like courses at a dinner. When he read a score, he heard the music ahead of what he read. What would be, already was. Yes, he decided. It came into his consciousness like a familiar phrase of music.

There is no single sound for C major either. Mozart's . . . what? thirty-something symphony is hardly a single sound. Enter the enemy—the diminished fifth—as in *Der Freischütz.* "Here it is," Don Giovanni cries, shaking the hand of the Statue. Mephistopheles, as a woodwind, invokes the furies of fire: "*J'ai besoin de vous!*" Caspar calls for the Black Huntsman Samiel to appear, Alberich curses the ring. *L'homme.* The crack in creation. Listen to that: *l'homme. Diabolus in musica.* The Fall. The Flaw in the fig. *L'homme.*

The woeful hope that mankind might not endure has been succeeded by the miserable fear it may survive.

My. My woeful hope. Wan hope. Who else so hopes? *L'homme.* They love their lives. *L'homme.* Cling to existence however ruinous like the pin oak's leaves through winter. They try to thrive. To multiply. To make murder a method of management.

4

Miriam became convinced that her husband was dead only when his image in her head no longer intimidated her. It was, she said, his Jewish look, since he hadn't had it when he married her, or, at least, he hadn't taken it out of hiding then to sic on opposing opinions like a bulldog on an intruder. Yet, if only an act, what a reality! She would quiz the sky: Who was he? and Joseph, now in his wiseass teens, would reply, Who is anybody? which would mightily annoy his mother, for she felt, in her world, you knew for a lifetime, and a lifetime before that, because you could perceive in the grandparents, provided you knew them, who someone was, and how they would be when good or bad fortune came; who would shovel when it snowed or cough when it rained; who sharpened the scythe before they swung it; who, when burlap bagged the apples, drank the most cider; and who would be a column and a comfort when sickness overcame your life and lowered it into the grave. He's a steady fellow, folks said of steady fellowy sorts, as if there was nothing higher to be attained.

His Jewish look? Smelling the world, Joseph Skizzen could not do what his father had done to save them: become a Jew. The Jew had lost his oily ways, his oily skin, his oily nose, his oily eyes, and now looked just like everybody else. Jews drank like the Irish. The Jew was a Republican. He had abandoned the book and wore a rifle. Everybody was Israeli. Everybody had an uncle in the IRA or a nephew in the PLO or had arrived as cargo or had crossed a border in the dead of night. Equality had arrived. Nobody was better. We were all illegal. Nevertheless, enemies were atmosphere. Everybody claimed to have received, in his or her inherited past, a horrible hurt. This justified their resentment, though it was the resentful that had harmed them. *Opferheit.* Victimhood was commoner than any common humanity. Mutual suspicion and betrayal feuded men together. Exile was birth by another name.

The garden his eighty-year-old mother had made for him beckoned. There was a bench, a small clear pool bottomed by slate, shade so soft it seemed to surround him like cerements, iris as graceful as grace gets. Enjoy, he said to his conscience, take pleasure in the garden your mother has cultivated. Was it not Béla Bartók who heard birds deep in the woods, uncannily far, and smelled a horse in the exhaust of a motorcar? He watched the gently dancing points of the forget-me-nots: five itty-bitty blue petals that chose to surround a tiny yellow symbol for the sun. They skipped about the garden, their little blue dots like scattered seed. Out of bits and pieces, Skizzen could complete his mother's bent blue-denim form behind the irises now voluptuously blooming: deep violet, royal purple, a cool blue so pale the petals seemed made of puffs of air. Later in the year, the red wild bee balm would replace it with butterflies. A garden was a good thing, wasn't it? This garden was a good sweet place. Though his mother was ruthless with the weak. Nothing mimsy was tolerated, nothing was permitted to be out of place, nothing diseased or otherwise sick was allowed to live. Cleansing was continuous.

And when a bloom closed in upon itself, brown and wrinkled, its petals now like a body bag, his mother pinched it from its stem. She deadheaded it . . . listen to that . . . *L'homme.* Fearful word, now fearful phrase: dead head. Dead head. Dead head.

In the center of the garden a vine, glossy and vibrant and leafed like the sea, clung to the trunk of a great beech with such intimacy it seemed a skirt, meanwhile other tendrils streamed so prolifically out along the tops of the beech's upper branches—running every twig as though they were channels, doubling the greenery, putting a leaf inside a leaf—that the birds forsook the tree to nest inside the thick entwinement. Was this rampant plant a garland or a garrote? Surely the beech would die. And afterward, its lover would be—wedded to a corpse. What was the diff? It could climb brick.

After the Fixels arrived in New York, they were handed over to New Jersey until they could be relocated in a small town in Ohio. Miriam, at first more discombobulated than she had ever been, was reassured by the fact that nearby their college community there were Amish living a modest rural life. She began to work in a plastics plant with the word "rubber" in its misleading household name. The serene streets slowly brought her serenity again. And the people of the town were kind. Americans love to feel sorry for others and are happy to have someone worthy of their concern. Routines took over like overlooked weeds. Yussel and Dvorah were sent to school as Joseph and Deborah, a change that officials welcomed as a sign of good adjustment. In no time, they were no more Jewish than they had ever been. The boy, Joseph, began to imagine he was as Austrian as his father and, of course, his mother was as Austrian as anybody. Joseph had his father's apish gifts and an ear for accents. Soon his English was perfect, yet with a charming, reassuringly distant, Germanic shadow.

Gone, his father had seemed distressingly present, but after a time, during which Middle America distracted Joseph from his history and its wounds, Rudi Skizzen receded into harmless anecdote, and Joseph and his sister could grow apart as good kids should. Deborah disappeared into majorettehood, dating the better automobiles, and dancing through gyms in her socks. Her grades were ladylike Bs while his were gentlemanly Cs, averages adorned with pluses, most often as afterthoughts. Joseph was careful not to draw attention to himself, he made no effort to hold on to his German, and it, too, waned, leaving behind a few words to be treasured like curious shells. In what proved to be due course Deb married a nice-looking boy, nearly Catholic, who would almost enter Yale. The ceremony meant she would move a mile or two away, though it was still far enough never to be she who was seen again, even if, occasionally in town, a missighting would be made.

So Deborah made her escape by fashioning herself like someone on a magazine cover—American health, curls, and cleanliness—just as her father would have wished her to do. Joseph was sadly certain that she would feed her husband wieners and bear babies, but in the USA way. Her house would wear tricycles, aluminum awnings, and a big glass grin. Of her past there would be not a trace, but she had longed to be ordinary, and it looked like her husband would help her to achieve negligibility.

Joseph's aloof, slightly exotic air could have given him girls if he had not feared he might have to present a certain self to their inclinations, a self some of them might fancy, and tend not only to expect but to desire. He abbreviated his time in life, solely as a youth, to a boy he called Joey, a kid who hated sports but could ride a bicycle. Days, for him, went by like the windows of a jerky train. For how many months of his short life had he been poorly dressed, hungry, and generally uncomfortable, sometimes seriously sick, full of fear for the future, scrunched in a crowded railroad car, staring out of smudged windows at dim meadows, distant cows, poles in regimented lines like those on rulers; or how many hours had he passed standing in the aisles of buses under the elbows of adults or spent being borne about in a blanket, eyes on an unrecognized sky, helpless and in ignorance of every outcome?

Not to mention the heaving sea, the spray that affronted his face, and the creaking speech of the bunks and walls and covered pipes, which he recalled with the vividness of nightmare, although these memories were more continuous and complete than those he retained of London under the Blitz or of Britain during the bland baconless days of victory and reclamation. The only positive spaces were the spaces of the church where Miriam brought them for mass after Rudi ran off, memorable because they felt made of the music that filled them. Mostly, when he recalled parental faces, he saw anguished eyes and swollen cheeks, voices tired beyond terror—flat, dry, hoarse—bodies that could scarcely bear their clothes: these were the companions of his every moment, and their figures became faintly superimposed upon the interested eager jolly features of his teachers whose feigned enthusiasms were no more encouraging to him than the false hopes his mother had—over and over—held out to him, even when she wished he'd cry and carry on the way his sister did instead of sitting silently, as if his wish to be elsewhere, in his small case, were a success, and he was.

A sack of groceries would remind him of a bit of body he had encountered in the rubble when he was barely able to walk, a coated shape lying in a soft soilous heap he hadn't recognized of course but had held in his head for labeling later. Then the ghost of a bathtub he'd mistaken for a corpse, when his eye caught—beneath wallpaper tatters, wallboard shatter, and plaster dust—a gleaming porcelain rim, rounded like an arm, humanly smooth, bloodlessly pale. And something smelly he'd been asked to eat would push his present plate away as if it were a threat to his life.

Why, he would wonder, had his father thought this nightmare world of bees that buzzed before they bombed was better than Austria's woodsy hillside peace, especially when his mother would speak about the land they—at least she—had been taken from, with its quiet village, comfy cottage, its honest close-knit farming life. She painted cockcrow and sunset on a postcard and mailed it to their imaginations. She made them hear fresh milk spilling in the pail. Woodpiles grew orderly and large while they listened. Flowers crowded the mountain trails and deer posed in glades cut by streams whose serene demeanor was periodically shattered by leaps of trout that only lacked for lemon.

Later on, when the family was living in its small sterile London reclamation box, he saw on a walk his mother made him take (because, though walks were Austrian, they were also British), black and outrageously out of place in the middle of the street, an abandoned piano that he now knew was an upright, warped and weathered, whose scattered, broken keys he struck again when he began his lessons from Miss Lasswell, as if he were returning them to their tune and time and harmonic order.

His approach to playing was like that of someone trying to plug always fresh and seemingly countless leaks—his fingers were that full of desperation—so Miss Lasswell was soon out of patience with him. Easily, easily . . . softly, softly . . . , she would croon, her voice moving smoothly and quietly and slowly at first but soon running up the scale of her own impatience toward staccato and the shriek. She told Miriam, whose idea the lessons had been, that Joey was hurting her instrument, and she couldn't allow that, think of all the other children who had to learn upon it how to court and encourage the keys, although they were black and white now because they'd taken a beating.

Putting that piano back together, hauling it out of the street where it had fallen from a truck or otherwise been left to die, getting it over the curb, and carting it up a flight of stairs into a proper alcove in a splendid room became Joey's daydreamed crusade, and to his later lessons with Mr. Hirk (cheaper at least) he brought an intensity and a commitment that impressed even that morose man and caused him to move his arthritic fingers as finally Joseph's moved, up and down the scales, through tunes, in and out of motifs and their identifying phrases.

Nevertheless, Joey learned every note and stave in a wholly backward way. He heard a piece of music, then found by hit or miss, by hunt-and-peck, the combination that would reproduce it, forking about until he was able to bunch familiar combinations together almost automatically: in short, his fingers felt for the sounds he heard in his head, so that the score meant, at first, very little to him. Hum it and he would hit it was the motto of Joey's music making. His skills were suitable for a saloon. He was a honky-tonk kid. Yet they led to—they fostered—his subsequent career.

Joey's general schooling followed a similar pattern. He appeared to learn from the air rather than from any focused or ordered instruction. Algebra he nearly failed, chemistry as well, but he read like a pirate bent on prizes and plunder. He swallowed the contents of shopwindows; he kept up on the news, unnatural in an American youngster; and he browsed through mail-order catalogs like a cow in a meadow. So Joey was self-taught, but what self got taught, and what self did the teaching?

Mr. Hirk's hoarse instructions, the tunes he fairly howled, the beat he banged out with a book upon the piano seat: none of these meant music. Mr. Hirk had been found living in penury at the edge of town, his livelihood, as meager as it had been, taken from him by the stiffness in his fingers and the popularity of the guitar, which could apparently be played by sociopaths without any further training, its magnified twings and twangs emerging from an electrical outlet as if the little holes spoke for appliances of all kinds and for unoiled engines everywhere. Perhaps Miriam pursued the problem with more determination than she did most things because her husband had possessed some small skill with the fiddle, and as a mother she wanted to find in her son something of that talent, since she saw in Joey otherwise nothing of his father that she wished to see, only his ability to mimic and to mock, especially after she had to endure the fury and flounce of Joey's sister when he pretended to twirl her baton, pucker up to kiss her date, or slide about in a pair of socks to a tune she had never heard.

In any case, Miriam gossiped around until Mr. Hirk's odd name came up. To Joseph it had to seem to be a motherly whim that became a parent's punishment, because, quite apart from the lessons, which were by definition disagreeable, Mr. Hirk was a hideously misshapen man, bent and gnarly, with hands like two ill-fitting boots. He held a pencil by its unsharpened end and poked the keys with the eraser. The poking was so painful to Mr. Hirk it seemed that the sounds themselves were protests, and they were produced with rests between them marked by sighs and groans, not by signs or words of instruction: *tangk aah tongk ooh tingk oosh*. Perhaps Joey's ear-to-finger method was the only one with a chance to achieve results.

For all Joey saw, Mr. Hirk's house had just one square room whose several small windows were hidden by huge plants, a feature that Miriam found reassuring. Wide thick fleshy leaves intercepted what of the sun there was so that greenish shadows were the ghoulish consequence when the day's light was bright. These shadows came in shades of several kinds and seemed to fall with great reluctance as if lying down on things the way Mr. Hirk had to—awkwardly, slowly, and with groans. A goosenecked lamp with a low-watt bulb hung over the playing surface, always on, always craning its brassy cord in the same curve, causing the black keys to cast in turn a smallish almost dainty darkness of their own. Yussel Fixel saw torn wires and a violence-infested space into which he was being asked to submerge his fingers, so at first he poked them in and out at great speed.

A few pieces of furniture that Joseph Skizzen would later recognize as in the style of mission oak gloomed in those corners the piano didn't occupy, and his feet often scuffled with a rag rug. Dim walls held dimmer portraits up to failing eyes. Dust kept time, wafted as if on sound. Nothing was propitious. Yet when Joey lifted the lid of the piano bench as Mr. Hirk instructed him, he saw sheets of music whose character was heralded by the picture of a canoe on a moonlit lake or that of a lady in a dress with a preposterous behind, perhaps even hers, or a boy and a girl on a two-seated bike or, better, in a merry Oldsmobile. He practiced scales, of course, pursuant to the mastery of "Indian Love Call" or "Song of India" or "A Bicycle Built for Two."

Perhaps Joey began by protecting the broken keys from the light that played over the board itself; or maybe "Song of India" was easy to remember, as was "Goodbye to Naples," a tune in Italian Caruso sang when Mr. Hirk wound his Victrola. Joey would never understand how his pounding managed to make any music at all, nor would Mr. Hirk let on that his pupil had accomplished anything harmonious either, for he was always critical, although Joey's facility must have astonished him. He taught doubled over as if in pain from what Joey and the piano played, so to be censorious he need only point to his posture. You must woo the keys, he would growl, poking them with his pencil. Here is your voice. The music must sing through your fingers. The tunes he used to tempt Joey into practicing were simple, from another age, before bombs, Joey ignorantly thought, when women wore fluffily cute clothes and lived in rose arbors or kept birds that were blue; back when the world rhymed and strummed, tapped its feet and tickled the ivories.

Mr. Hirk saw that Joey sat forward on the bench when he began to play, and this pleased him. Joey's posture did not. You are not the tower of Pisa. Do not lean, do not lurch, do not slump, do not wiggle, Mr. Hirk would admonish. Only Pisa can prosper by tilting. Arms—arms at right angles—so—straight to the keys—see—back straight. Why must boys bend!

When you give another kid the finger—you know what I speak about—up-up-up yours, that sign? Mr. Hirk could not make the gesture. The thumb does not go up yours. The first finger does not go up yours. The middle finger—yes—because it does go up. It does. All alone it goes. So every note has a finger for it. Your hands do not reach the keys higgledy-piggledy, this way or that, but in the most efficient way to press down upon them—just right. The piano is a fancy gadget—hear that!—but you are not a gadget, and your fingers must be suitable, supple, suitable, strong yet tender, suitable, soft, as on a nipple, swift like a snake's strike. *Zzing!*

Joey had one kind of harmony with Mr. Hirk neither of them understood. When Mr. Hirk showed him a clawlike fist, Joey knew at once he was to splay his fingers. Mr. Hirk didn't think Joey's reach was wide or flexible enough. When he banged with a book, Joey softened his touch, and when Mr. Hirk was still, so still he clearly meant to be still, Joey sped. The piano was small and seemed old as its owner. Its tone was weak and hoarse, with a scratchy undercoat. Yet the sounds it made were Joey's sounds, and he adored them. They might have come from a record made before recordings had been invented.

"Daisy . . . Daisy . . . ," Joey would sing to his inner ear while his fingers felt for the equivalents. I am only pretending to play, he boasted, feeling that he was putting one over on his mom as well as Mr. Hirk. However, Mr. Hirk knew exactly what was going on, and to Joey's surprise he approved. Suppose you are playing a Beethoven sonata—as if that could ever be, Mr. Hirk said. What are you going to remember—the notes? No. The tune. In your head is the tune like a cold. Then your fingers follow. And you play the notes.

Many of Mr. Hirk's records, which sat in a dusty stack near the Victrola, had, to Joey's surprise, only one side. Yes, one side was smooth as pine. And they were heavy as plates. Empty plates. But if you got a record turning, a voice, like a faraway bird, high and light and leaping, somersaulting even, certainly atwitter, would come into the room. Amelita Galli-Curci, Mr. Hirk would say hoarsely yet in some awe, as she began. Joey had never heard the pureness of purity before. It was the soul, for sure, or the sound of angels, because weren't they birds? and didn't they dwell in a hidden sky? It was called "The Bell Song," the song she sang, though there was another aria a girl named Gilda was supposed to sing about someone whose very name had smitten her as by a stick—so suddenly—with the stunning blow of love. It was a song that would be overheard just as Joey was hearing it, yet that hearing would be followed, according to Mr. Hirk, by a consternation on the stage quite unlike the contentment that Joey felt during its blissful moments of performance.

The pedals, the pedals were a mystery. They were so far away from the keys, from the strings, from the place the music rose from; they were so hidden and other, that Joey fought them, tromped upon them, kicked them in their sides. Joey thought Mr. Hirk was cursing him at first, but he was saying, "Damp . . . damp," to no avail. Finally, he shouted, "Forget the pedals." "They wet the notes," he managed to explain. "Play to clear skies. Clear skies."

The tacky church Miriam took her children to had not a single spear of light, no rebounding shadows, no mystery, no majesty, no music of note. The congregation sang almost as badly as the choir, and cliché determined the selection of hymns. The services were in an inept Latin and the acolytes always a step late, as if they had fallen asleep. Catholics had not prospered here. The county and its seat was filled with Amish, odd Protestants, slow roads, bad organs, and poorer organists.

Mr. Hirk honeyed up to him during Joey's senior year. Joey would simply show up and play, mostly something he'd heard on the radio or a few things he'd begun by improvising, and then they would both sit in the cool gloom and listen to the Victrola that Joey had begun winding up because Mr. Hirk's fingers were presently incapable: Emma Calvé, Galli-Curci, the stentorious Caruso, and "Home Sweet Home" by Nellie Melba. Mr. Hirk no longer marked time by banging even a thin book. Now, when Joey left, with a gratitude that exceeded any he had ever felt, he would squeeze Mr. Hirk's upper arm (because he didn't dare put pressure on him anywhere else); Mr. Hirk would sigh hoarsely and watch Joey bike, it must have seemed nimbly, away, leaving Mr. Hirk alone in his room with his body's disability and his machine's recalcitrance until another Saturday came along. Joey always cranked the Victrola one more time before he left, so a few sides could be managed if Mr. Hirk could spindle a record—hard to do with his crabbed hands growing crabbier by the week. Joey rode off to an era of LPs, vinyl, and other speeds, but only Mr. Hirk had Olive Fremstad and her sound—Calvé's, Caruso's sound—sounds—hollow, odd, remote—that created a past from which ghosts could not only speak to admonish and astound, they could sing again almost as they once sang, sang as singing would never be heard sung again, songs and a singing from somewhere outside the earth where not an outstretched arm, not a single finger, could reach or beckon, request or threaten or connive.

If Joseph Skizzen later could imagine his mother, with whom he had lived so much of his life one would think he'd not want to add another sight or an additional thought of her to his consciousness; if he could clearly picture her in her culottes and gloves grubbing in her garden, literally extracting coiled white webworms from the soil and flipping them indifferently into a coffee can filled with flat cheap beer (only one moment of many he might remember), it was partly because, at the commencement of his piano lessons, he had begun envisioning Mr. Hirk, who had also unwittingly given him life, painfully bulked in a bulky chair or doubled up in a daybed he could no longer refold, waiting through the hours for Joey's bike to skid in the gravel before his door. It was a picture that prompted him not to ignore his pedals but to push hard, hurrying to arrive and kick his kickstand into place, to knock and enter Mr. Hirk's house all at once, to say "Hiyuh, Mr. Hirk, how goes it?" and slap his happy hand down on the piano bench before sitting there himself to play a new tune he'd heard that week on *Your Hit Parade,* a song already at number 7 although it was the first time for its appearance on the list. Mr. Hirk would pretend to hate the new stuff—trash and drivel and noise, he said, or treacle and slop and lies—but he would listen as if only his large ears were alive. Joey would then play the new hit from the week before, going back over his own list, making the slim recital last, turning it into his lesson, performing each of the songs on the sheets in the bench, and ending, as the order firmed itself, with "Danny Boy," as if he knew where it belonged, and without being the least embarrassed by its schmaltz, its treacle, or its prevarications.

5

It had to happen. One Saturday afternoon, searching for a football game, Joey tuned in the Metropolitan Opera's matinee during a moment when all its throats were rapturous. His mother stood in the doorway, somewhat dazed herself, because her intention had been to ask him to turn down the volume. The voices weren't of tin but of gold, and the orchestra was full, not a fiddle and a drum or a faint hinky-tink piano. Even Miriam sat and listened, too indifferent to her hands to fold them in her lap, until the evident sadness of events withdrew her. Neither had the slightest idea what was going on until between acts a commentator, with a voice melting over its vowels like dark chocolate, recited the plot as it was about to unfold. The tenor, it turned out, would be in a jail cell awaiting execution, and the act would open an hour before dawn at an artillery emplacement at the walls of a castle overlooking Rome. Rome! The audience will see the Vatican in the distance, the announcer says. Then, after an orchestral interlude, with the song of a shepherd boy barely audible in the distance, the tenor, told he has but an hour left to live, will be brought to the battlements where he will write loving last words to his opera singer while sitting at a wooden desk set to one side of the stage. He writes something splendid, Joey remembered, about the shine of the stars perfuming the world. Of course the tenor would sing the words in the moment that he wrote them. Here, in this magical realm, singing words were all there were.

Joey heard everything happen as it had been foretold. The tenor's voice soared despite its despair, and Joey felt his own throat ache. It was a moment in which sorrow became sublime and his own misfortunes were, momentarily, on someone else's mind.

Now when he had a lesson, he would ask Mr. Hirk his opinion of the singers of today, not all of whom Mr. Hirk loathed; indeed, there were a few he praised. Mr. Hirk was impatient with Joey because, after all their sessions, his improvising was not improving anything but his ability to mimic. Although Mr. Hirk formed his sentences with reasonable clarity, his words emerged as if they too were rheumatic, bent a bit, their heads turned toward the ground, their rears reluctant to arrive.

No . . . noth . . . nothing gained. You are copying the cat as if—that way—you could become one. Shame. You are hitting the keys a bit like my stick here, Mr. Hirk complained, when your fingers—your fingers, young shameful man—should sing; you should feel the song in their tips—on the ball where the ink stain blues it—like a tingle. Your technique—oh God—is terrible. You need to do Czernys . . . and . . . and I don't have any for you, not a page. I am a poor teacher. Naw. Nothing can be gained. I couldn't sing or whistle them. They are not for copy, the Czernys. They are for the fingers like lifting weights. Which you either do, or you don't do. Czernys. So you either get strong in the fingers or you remain weak . . . and if in the fingers, then in the head.

What Mr. Hirk hated most about Joey was his forearm. Do not move the forearm. Forget the forearm. From side to side from the wrist the fingers find their way, kneading the notes—your hands must be big slow spiders out for a walk.

Early on Mr. Hirk had grasped Joey's hands with his voice. Show me your nails! Show me! They're bitten! Look at them, poor babies. That is no way. Are you a beaver in a trap to be gnawing at yourself? Nails should never be long—short is wise—never so long they click on the keys, so they interfere with your stroke—no—but not bitten, a bad bad habit—they are not to be chewed like a straw. Nails are to be nurtured, nicened. Yes. Filed with your mother's file. Not long like a lady's but smooth, short, and smoothly rounded like the moon that is in them. That is the way. Remember. Short, round, smooth. Better if they're polished like flute keys. Hooh, he would conclude, exhausted.

Dressing Debbie was getting expensive, and Miriam felt that Joey's progress was being hampered by Mr. Hirk's physical impediments. To the point of pointlessness, she thought. Joey looked forward now to his miniconcerts, but he could not protest his mother's decision even if it was not adequately based or sincerely made. Joey was to inform Mr. Hirk on Saturday next that the present lesson was to be the final one. This, Joey had no desire to do. You hired him, you should fire him, he told his mother in the most aggrieved tone he could muster. It makes no sense for me to make a special trip just to do that, she answered in what would be her last reasonable voice. You send him his money by mail, Joey argued, why not end it the same way? That would be cold and unfeeling, she said sternly, that would be inconsiderate and impolite, even rude. Shame on you, she said. On me? Joey was unusual in his anger. Mr. Hirk is a sick old man! He has no income! He hasn't even one Czerny. He lives mostly in the dark waiting for me to come and play. I give him that relief. This was said with pride. Now you want to take his single pupil and his only pleasure away. Joey was embarrassed by his own heat. Such novel opposition was quite beyond Miriam's understanding. It made her furious. She blamed his poor upbringing on America. As someone who had been browbeaten, she could browbeat now with assurance, and she could be furious with Joey without worry because, though Joseph Skizzen was of the male sex, he was still a Joey. Ah, how you overcount yourself. How do you know what that man's pleasures are! Joey's stiff face told her that his certainties were unchanged. Then say nothing, just don't go again, you obstacle, she shouted. Whatever you do, I won't mail another fee. She ended the argument but not the issue by leaving the room in a huff that would have seemed more genuine if it hadn't had wheels.

Joey knew now that the singers on Mr. Hirk's old records were ghosts in truth, though he did not love them less for that. And Mr. Hirk had begun telling him of other singers, such as Marcella Sembrich, whom Joey had not heard, and how she had studied for years with an old piano teacher who discovered and developed her voice by taking her, willy-nilly, to the best teachers. Mr. Hirk was a bike tire turning in gravel—hard to understand—but Joey listened to his history of Marcella Sembrich as if she were a star of film, an actress of dangerous beauty. Indeed, Marcella Sembrich was her stage name, not her real name, Mr. Hirk told him. Her real name was Marcellina Kochanska—Kochanska—as a name Kochanska would not do—and she came from a part of Poland the Austrians owned. I know the place, Mr. Hirk said proudly. Lem. Berg. It runs in families like my arthritis does. The gift, I mean. I know a lot of similar histories. Her father—her father taught himself to play—from hell to hallelujah—half the instruments. So she knew notes by the time she said daddy. She was sitting up to the piano by four. Perched on a Bible. I know. It's as if I was there. And she was playing a violin her father made for her when she was six. Six! In ringlets. It's so. It's not even unusual. That same father—the father of her—taught his wife the violin. Yes. True. By seven . . . you just linger on the number, boy, linger on her age . . . by seven she was playing in the family string quartet with her brother, who was born before her, a cello's child. Then an old man who heard her, when the family minstrelized around the country to make ends meet, sponsored her for the Conservatory because he loved her as she should have been loved. In Lem. Berg. I know the building. I know the halls.

Joey had read of worms that glowed in the dark. Mr. Hirk was glowing. Like one of the plant's leaves, his face was glowing, and his voice cleaned itself up as if it were going to church.

When Marcella went to him—to Stengl, her teacher, sent by one lover to another—she was about your age—how Stengl must have adored her little fingers—with a waist that didn't require a corset. Though in later years . . . Mr. Hirk spoke of Marcella Sembrich as if she were an old friend. He spoke and he glowed. Yes, yes, Marcella stayed with him—with Stengl, stern as he was—studying—she stayed despite his sternness for eleven years. Joey heard the word "stayed" with a pang. Eleven years of piano. Mr. Hirk made a point of it. Not eleven years of voice, not five. No. Though she sang in some community choruses during that time and was thought to have a pretty soprano. Mr. Hirk always stood to talk, because scrunched up he was short of breath, but his voice was aimed at the floor. She married the old man, Stengl, eventually, after he'd kissed her fingers often, growing old in his role as her teacher, and after she, who had arrived as a bud, became a blossom. He had taken her to Italy to study singing, because he believed there was more to her "pretty" voice than prettiness, that inside her small light soprano there was something big and dark. Oh yes, he did hear a darkness. And that "big" voice was born there too, in sunny Italy, like a baby born to a giant. Then he swept her off to London without even telling her why. He had said to his young wife one day, We are going away to London. Why? She wanted to know of course. It was natural to want to know. You shall see, her husband said. It will be for the best. And Stengl figured out a way to get her heard there. Not just heard there . . . heard well. She sang a selection from *Lucia* with the Covent Garden Orchestra accompanying her. Imagine. The entire orchestra playing, she singing. Just imagine. You have heard of Covent Garden? On that legendary stage. She sang. There, where the great Patti had just rehearsed. She sang. Marcella Sembrich sang. Well, they rose, the violins first, to applaud her performance. They said she sang like a violin—and in fact she played that instrument, though not as well as the piano. After that the happy couple—wouldn't they have been a happy couple?—his wisdom and her fingers, her figure and her voice, his worship and his passion—traveled to Russia and Spain and America, too. Where she was an astonishment. In *Lucia.* At the Met. In *I Puritani,* in *La Sonnambula.* What vocal calligraphy! You know about the Met? You should have heard her in *The Magic Flute.* Such a queen—such dark power—with her voice—she invoked it. Like a setting sun calls forth the night. For a moment Mr. Hirk was proud of his age. A piano teacher had flown the soprano to these great heights: an old man was her wings, as well as her lover, and saw her soar.

Joey knew then that he would not be able to tell Mr. Hirk he was fired, that the lessons were over—"terminated," a word Miriam had learned at work to fear—now that Mr. Hirk was finally reaching out—only figuratively, of course—to his pupil, and opening his heart's attic to him, unwrapping his enthusiasms, and—young Joey recognized—confronting the death of his hopes, the ruins of his life. Mr. Hirk, after all, lived in a small dark leaf-lit room; he was no one who had ever played or sung before the public; he had probably never even taught another who might, then, have gone on to earn acclaim. And for a pittance, for pity, he was beating booktime to a boy who was only, at best, a mime, a faker who had never faked a measure of Chopin, and didn't even know what a Czerny was.

Mr. Hirk had managed to raise an admonitory finger. Marcella Sembrich, wisely counseled, he said sternly, had not strained her voice singing Wagner. Oh she was pure bel canto, pure Italian, he said with hoarse approval. Always, small Joey, she studied. Her whole career. To sing *Lucia,* to sing *Traviata.* To sing Verdi, Donizetti, Puccini. But you are playing at playing, not working at playing, you are only pleasing yourself, small Joey. Well, you must stop having fun and learn the fundamentals. Then you may be able to please someone else.

In these words small Joey heard he hadn't made Mr. Hirk happy. That's what he heard. Moreover, the name—Small Joey—was new, and not nice. These criticisms restiffened his resolve. He would hand Mr. Hirk his envelope, give him the small sum he was charging for the lessons, and say his services were no longer needed. He would do this with a dignity for which he was presently searching.

But Mr. Hirk, who had not heard what Joey was resolving, who had not felt the stiffening of anyone's will, went on without pause to another tale. This anecdote was about a true pianist. It might have been titled: "Ignace Jan Paderewski and the Spider." The story was wholly unfamiliar to Joey, who had decided not to listen. Like you, Paderewski was slow to become a student; like you he had bad teachers; like you he learned through his ears and had no technique, only instinctive fingers that went for the nearest note like kids after cake; yes, yes, like you he did not know how to work. Yet he became the greatest pianist of his time. Of his time . . . And more than that . . .

Joey let his features settle into the sullenness that Miriam found so insufferable, but Mr. Hirk's mind was in another country, an ocean and a sea away, where Joey was an eager auditor whatever his face let on. Mr. Hirk cleared his throat of phlegm that, fortunately, never materialized.

Paderewski was studying in Vienna with Leschetizky—a name you do not know, because I have taught you nothing—and he had taken a couple of tiny rooms near the villa of this greatest of piano teachers, the author of a method named for him that had helped to eminence some of the most famous pianists of that age. Young Paderewski, as I say, had no technique; he was like you in that, small Joey, though he was, I must also say, a master of the pedal, he pedaled better than you do perched upon your bike. He did not kick the pedal, or otherwise abuse it, he caressed it—"footsie," we say, you know—he played footsie with the pedal. Never did he chew upon himself neither. He was growed up! Anyway—are you listening? This is a lesson, which is what you are here for—so—one day, in his little candlelit room as dark as this one on account of the plants, Paderewski was practicing a piece by Chopin, an exercise in thirds. You do know thirds? While he was playing, a tiny spider dropped down from the ceiling to just one side of him, a bit above the deck of the piano, on a threadlike length of web. Do you know the word "gossamer"? The spider hung there listening to the Chopin. It was no more than a dot suspended in the air—a piece of punctuation. The spider hung there while Paderewski played. Hear him? How he played, that man!

You may smile, Mr. Hirk said, although Joey hadn't softened his sullenness by a twitch. Paderewski smiled himself. He was charmed. So . . . when the exercise in thirds had been completed, he went on, as was his habit, to another one in sixths. The spider immediately scampered, as it seemed, up his silver line to the ceiling. Observing this—you see it?—Paderewski returned to the exercise in thirds and began to repeat it. Lo, believe it and behold, eh? down like a fireman his pole the spider slid. All the way to the piano deck where he sat and once more listened. At the end of that exercise, which he had to repeat entirely because it so enchanted the spider, Paderewski went about his other business. How long must one entertain a tiny spider, no bigger than a period? Especially one who hasn't paid for its seat at the concert . . .

Joey did smile now, but he thought the story was at an end. Mr. Hirk stared vacantly into vacated space. Time in the tale . . . time in the tale was passing. That's why he stared. A stare that was to stand for elapsing hours. Then his head moved back to Joey. It was an animal's maneuver.

The next morning Paderewski returned to the piano and his practice. The thread hung there still, and down that thread came the spider again the moment the study in thirds commenced. Paderewski pursued the étude, and the spider continued to sit on the deck or hang just above it from the thread so long as the piece was played. This behavior went on, not for another day, or a few days, or a week, but for many weeks, Joey . . . many weeks . . . Faithfully the spider appeared, quietly it listened, its brilliant tiny eyes shining like diamonds, and just as often, just as promptly, it disappeared up its rope when the étude concluded, as if annoyed, even angry, Paderewski thought, leaving beneath it the detestable sound of sixths.

I once had a small mouse that kept me company, Mr. Hirk said, though he was only foraging for food and was never an enthralled audience for my playing. No enthrallment. Not for me. So . . . where was . . . ah . . . I am here . . . but Paderewski . . . Well, vacation time came for Paderewski. He didn't practice in that room again for a number of weeks, and when he returned in the fall, the spider was gone, as was the spider's thread, rolled up after him perhaps, when he went searching for a more melodious space.

What is the lesson? Is that your question, Joey? Joey had heard Mr. Hirk's story despite his intended deafness and would remember it too, against every wish, but he had no curiosity about its character and therefore no question about its content. It was just an amusing oddity—this story. Like the fables of Aesop, Mr. Hirk said, rather portentously, this trifling occurrence has a moral.

The major third, my young friend, Mr. Hirk continued, changing his tone, is that upon which all that is good and warm and wholesome and joyful in nature is built. Not for it the humble, the impoverished, the sacrificial, the stoical—no—it is the ground of the garden, it signifies the real right way, as Beethoven knew when he wrote the finale for his *Fifth Symphony.* Mr. Hirk leaned like a broken pole against the piano. Hold out your hand, Joey, hold it out, the gnawed right hand that plays—there—that hand is pagan, it is a human hand, it is for shaking and touching and grasping and caressing; it is not made to be a fist; it is not made for praying, for gestures of disdain, for tearing one's hair or holding one's head, for stabbing, for saluting; well, now, see my hand here? this crab? this wadded clutch of knotted fingers? it is the sacred hand, the scarred and crucified claw, the toil-destroyed hand, fit only to curse its God. It has given up every good thing. Having given up every good thing, no good thing comes near. Not, certainly, the major third, the pagan chord. The foundation of nature—which is vibration . . . Nature is nothing but vibration.

These hands—my uglies—my hands are a denial . . . they deny life. They deny you, Joey, all others' bodies; they deny me. They deny light; they keep caged the darkness clenched in their clench. They are my shame—these uglies—my pain—these uglies—my curse. It makes me sad—sorry—sad and sorry to see them. You understand? Sometimes I hide them inside of my shirt. Then I feel their heat hot on my belly.

Out of breath Mr. Hirk sat in silence for a few moments. When Monteverdi wished to say "joyful is my heart" he did so in the major third; when Handel refers to life's sweetest harmonies he does so in the major third; what is central to the "Ode to Joy" but the major third? in *La Traviata,* when they all lift their glasses and cry "Drink!" "*Libiamo!*" they do so to the major third; and what does Wagner use, at the opening of *The Ring,* to describe the sensuously amoral state of nature? he employs the major third; then just listen to that paean of praise in Stravinsky's *Symphony of Psalms* or the finale of Shostakovich's *Fifth,* and you will hear again the major third.

And the spider heard it, suspended there between floor and ceiling, felt it when the thin silver thread he hung from vibrated in sympathy with Chopin, with the étude's instructional thirds. Joey—look at the green-gray light in this room, at this secondhand light, the pallor of death . . . and what do you hear in my voice, or what would you hear if you were to hear my heart? you'd hear the minor sixth—the sixths that the spider fled from, the gold ring in *Rhinegold*—the source of so much contention—Leonora's bitter tears in *Fidelio,* sorrowful Don Quixote, yes, sixths serve anguish, longing, despair, so tell me why should the spider stay when the line he clings to trembles like a tear? Only *we* wallow in bitterness, only *we* choose gray-green lives and devote ourselves to worlds, like the shadow-lean leaves of those ghost plants littering the floor—leaves, worlds—which do not exist, the traces of a light that is no longer there.

Joey made as if to go, rising from the piano bench, when Mr. Hirk's nearby presence pushed him down. Mr. Hirk hung over Joey now, supported by the piano itself, bent because of his bones. If one day you learn to play, Joey, you must play, whatever the key or the intervals are, as if *for,* as if *in,* the major third, the notes of praise. Play C. Joey struck a key. There were several Cs, but Joey knew which was meant, a key that would sound a certain way. In filling our ear just now it was everywhere, Mr. Hirk said. Every. Where. Was it sitting beside that pot? No. Was it lying on the rug? Of course not. Everywhere? Ah, in the piano? No? Where it was made? Not this tone. Suppose someone shuts the door and then you, Joey, ride away on your bike. Where is the slam? eh? where is the small growl of the tire in my gravel? Why there it is—the growl—it's in the gravel where it was made; there is the slam, too, where the door shut on the jamb! Bam! Do D. Joey did D. Hear? The note is everywhere again. Not at the end of your finger. In its own space! That's where it is, filling us up with it, making a world of its own on its own. Just one note is enough. Do E. Joey E'd. Another filling, yet the same jar! Each note makes the same space and then floods it.

Joey thought he sensed relief in Mr. Hirk's voice, like someone wound up dangerously tight might feel once they began unwinding or the spring of a clock that was finally allowed to tell time.

Oh, a dunce might say, hey, it came from the piano. And the French horn's passage is from the middle of the rear of the orchestra, while the violins sing to the left of the conductor, violas and cellos moan on the right, the strings closing in on the winds from both sides of the fan. Like the door's slam, the dunce hears only the jamb where it was made. Because the bang, the gravel's *brrr,* means something. So he fastens them there like tied dogs. But if you insist on silence, enjoy a little shut-eye when you listen, so there's a bowl of darkness where your head was—then, in the music, where notes are made to appear through the commands of form, not by some tinkler on the triangle, Joey, not because they say something about their cause—then you can almost perceive—though squeeze-eyed—you can see what you hear, see the space, and see how one note is higher than another, farther away, or closer, closer than the heart. See, sir, the brightness of the trumpet among the constellations like a brighter star? Closer to whom, though, Joey? brighter than what? not to you or me, for we are no more than gravel or doors. Oh no. Brighter . . . closer . . . meaningful . . . to one another.

In this damn dark, Joey, when I get the phono cranked, I can follow the song exactly where it goes, and it, not Galli-Curci, it alone is real—is a rare wonder, not of this world—a wonder and a consolation.

Nor will you hear its like anywhere but in its own space. A sneeze in C? Hah. A laugh in E? A siren that runs the scale like a soprano? The notes of music live in music alone, Joey. They must be made, prepared with care. To give voice to feeling.

You will never learn anything about music that is more important than this. Mr. Hirk, with a groan, straightened somewhat. Then he used his groan for instruction. You hear it, my ache, emerge from my mouth. It has a location. Because it is in ordinary space. It is there, fastened to its cause. My grunt, I mean, not my pain. My pain is nowhere, but that's another matter. And my pain is a call like a child's for its mother. But when we listen to music we enter a singular space, Joey, a space not of this room or any road. This you must understand.

Sound them together, sound the chord, play CDE, Joey. Can you do it? Joey protested by doing it dramatically. Suppose I mix a little yellow and a little green together. What after all are my sick plants doing? Is chartreuse two colors or one? Joey naturally made no answer. One. One. One. One. The book beat on the piano seat. But in the chord I hear clearly C and D and E. They penetrate but do not disappear into one another. They are a trinity—a single sound in which I hear three. C is the Son. D is God the Father, the sacred root, and E is the Holy Ghost. Now, Joey, can you do this? play all at once a loud C, a soft D, and an ordinary E. Which Joey did, triumphantly. Again and again to demonstrate how easily. There! You can hear them! They are everywhere yet in different places! They are one, but they are three. If theology wrote music . . . Mr. Hirk's voice trailed away. At the heart of everything, in music's space, multiple vibrations . . .

Joey was relieved to get away. Mr. Hirk was somewhat embarrassing in addition to being ugly and poor and pitiful. Needy too. His hands were beginning to look like tree roots. But Joey rode away sad himself—a small sad-infested Joey—for he had not canceled the lessons; he had been allowed no suitable occasion or merciful excuse, moreover he had permitted shame and cowardice to dissuade him, and now he would have to mail, messageless as was his mother's habit, a few small bills in an envelope the way he understood a payoff would be made, so that next week, when the time arrived for his bike to skid in the gravel in front of Mr. Hirk's door, at the time when Joey would be expected to pop in and ask, How ya doin? there'd be nothing and no one, no bowl of silence ready to be filled with the latest tunes, only patient expectation, puzzlement, disappointment, hurt. Joey felt guilty and sorry and sad. He pedaled recklessly. He hoped his father had, at one time, felt something of the same shame.

6

The fear that the human race might not survive has been replaced by the fear that it will endure.

You cannot end an English sentence with a preposition. Skizzen had more than once read that. Or the world with "with"—leaving the whimper unwhimpered, for instance. Or with "on account of"—overpopulation, for example, unspecified. Or with "in"—omitting fire or flood or wind . . . a storm of hail each one the size of an eyeball. Can you imagine what it will die of? There will be many endings vying for the honor. And any agent of our end will have a radiant sense of ruin. Any agent of our end will dance where the score says rest.

In the garden the cornflowers watch my small mother, Skizzen thought, watch my small mother wash her small hands in the soft loamy soil of the beds. She has dug in compost over years, compost mixed with sand, with bark, with mulching leaves, a little manure, a bit of bone meal; and with a fork she has carefully circulated the soil, turning sand and leaves and rotted peelings under one another, down where the earthworms slowly pass everything through themselves and thereby imagine shit as a city. She handles the leaves and touches the blossoms. She knows how to do it. Her grasp is vigorous, never shy or uncertain. The plants respond. Eat well. Thrive. Go to nefarious seed.

Our concern that the human race might not endure has been succeeded by the fear it will survive.

Oh—Skizzen oh'd, in his sermons to, in his repetitions of, himself. Oh—the decomposition of man will stench the sky at first but how immeasurably it will manure the soil, how thoroughly it will improve the land with all those fine bones added, while plants cover and trees stand. For worms the climate will be tropical, they will grow longer than tunnels, and their four hearts beat for blocks. Lakes will deepen and be blue again. Clean sky will harbor happy winds. Mountainsides of aspens will be able to color and flutter without having their picture taken. Waterfalls will fall free of enterprising eyes. It will be grand.

Unless there is a universal flood and fish school in corner offices; unless there is an atomic wind and an image of our race is burned into the side of a glass cliff; unless glaciers creep down from the North almost as blue as green as winedark as the solidifying sea.

The thought that mankind might not endure has been replaced by the fear it may luck out.

End zone to end zone, Armageddon's final field was nearly laid out once before. It was half a cataclysm—a clysm—maybe. Preliminary bout. A third of the world sickened during the three years of the Black Plague: 1348—1349—1350. And the plague swung its scythe four times, its last swath reducing Europe to half what it had been the century before: in 1388—1389—1390. They believed the disease was Evil advancing like an army. They said it was Satan's century. *Diabolus in musica.* That was before Passchendaele. The population of the planet diminished by a fifth.

Those who suffered the plague and survived: they suggested to Joseph Skizzen the unpleasant likelihood that Man might squeak through even a loss at Armageddon, one death per second not fast enough, and outlive the zapping of the planet, duck a fleet of meteors, hunkerbunker through a real world war with cannons going grump to salute our last breath as if horror were a ceremony, emerge to sing of bombs bursting, endure the triggers of a trillion guns amorously squeezed until every nation's ammo was quite spent, and all the private stock was fired off at the life and livestock of a neighbor, so that in battle's final silence one could hear only the crash after crash of financial houses, countless vacuum cleaners, under their own orders, sucking up official lies, contracts screaming like lettuce shredded for a salad, outcries from the crucifixion of caring borne on the wind as if in an ode, the screech of every wheel as it becomes uninvented, brief protests from dimming tubes, destimulated wires; though the slowing of most functions would go on in silence, shit merded up in the street to be refried by aberrant microwaves, diseases coursing about and competing for victims, slowdowns coming to standstills without a sigh, until the heavy quiet of war's cease is broken by . . . by what? might we imagine boils bursting out of each surviving eye . . . the accumulated pus of perception? a burst like what? like trumpets blowing twenty centuries of pointless noise at an already deaf-eared world . . . with what sort of sound exactly? with a roar that rattles nails already driven in their boards, so . . . so that, as the sound comes through their windows, houses will heave and sag into themselves, as unfastened as flesh from a corset; yet out of every heap of rubble, smoking ruin, ditch of consanguineous corpses, could creep a survivor—*he* was such a survivor, Joseph Skizzen, faux doctor and musician—someone born of ruin as flies are from offal; that from a cave or collection of shattered trees there might emerge a creature who could thrive on a prolonged diet of phlegm soup and his own entrails even, and in spite of every imaginable catastrophe salvage at least a remnant of his race with the strength, the interest, the spunk, to fuck on, fuck on like Christian soldiers, stiff-pricked still, with some sperm left with the ability to engender, to fuck on, so what if with one leg or a limp, fuck on, or a severed tongue, fuck on, or a blind eye, fuck on, in order to multiply, first to spread and then to gather, to confer, to wonder why, to invent, to philosophize, accumulate, connive: to wonder, why this punishment? to wonder, why this pain? why did we—among the we's that were—survive? what was accomplished that couldn't have been realized otherwise? why were babies born to be so cruelly belabored back into the grave? who of our race betrayed our trust? what was the cause of our bad luck? what divine plan did this disaster further? why were grandfathers tortured by the deaths they were about to sigh for? why? . . . but weren't we special? we few, we leftovers, without a tree to climb, we must have been set aside, saved for a moment of magnificence! to be handed the trophy, awarded the prize; because the Good Book, we would—dumb and blind—still believe in, said a remnant would be saved; because the good, the great, the wellborn and internetted, the rich, the incandescent stars, will win through, that . . . that . . . that we believed, we knew, God will see to our good outcome, he will see, see to it, if he hasn't had a belly full, if the liar's, the liar's beard is not on fire like Santa Claus stuck in a chimney.

The thought that mankind might not endure has been replaced by the fear it may make it through another age of ice.

In spite of death and desolation, music, Professor Joseph Skizzen assured himself, would still be made. Toms would be tom'd, the earth beaten by bones born to a rhythm if not a rhyme, a ground swept by sweet dancing feet. There would be voices raised in song to celebrate heaven, to thank the gods for the radish about to be eaten, to pray for victory in tomorrow's war, or the reinvention of the motorcar. Someone would, like Simonides, remember where everyone was sitting when the roof of the world fell in, or how the stars were configured, and would be able to identify the dead, if anyone cared. With that feat on his résumé, Simonides could easily sell his memory method for a lot of cabbages, many messes of pottage, thirty carloads of silver. Because we would want everyone properly buried in their appropriately consecrated ground, sacred ground we would kill one another to acquire, to protect and fill with our grateful dead—each race decomposing, each would allege, with more dignity, more delight to those worms, more . . . more to the nth than the others.

We would bury our dead with more tender regard for their bits and pieces than we ever had shown a shin or a thigh while elbow or knee was alive.

Soon there would be family clans and prisons again. Beneath all ash, hate would still be warm enough to make tea. That's the state in which Professor Skizzen's mind would be when he left off worrying his sentence: imagining man's return, the triumph of the club and the broken knees of enemies, the harvesting of ferns, the refinement of war paint—each time taking a slightly different route to new triumphs and fresh renown. Upon our Second Coming, we would hate the earth and eat only air. We would live in ice like a little bit of lost light. We would grow fur and another nose. Fingernails, hard as horn, would curl like crampons. We would scuttle in and out of caves, live on insects, bats, and birds, and grow blue as a glacier. Perhaps we'd emerge in the shape of those ten-foot tropical worms, and like *Lumbricus terrestris* have many hundreds of species. It was so discouraging, but such thoughts had one plus: they drove him away from his obsession with words like "fear" and "concern" and "worry" and returned him to his profitable work—the study of the late piano pieces of Franz Liszt, a passion that his former colleagues found amusing, especially in an Austrian such as himself, who ought to disdain the French/Slav Musical Axis in favor of a hub that was purely German (little did they know where he'd already been!), and who had foolishly chosen a solo instrument to play when the entire Vienna Philharmonic could have been strumming and tootling his tunes.

Yes, in that very orchestra where his father might have played had he chosen to imagine himself a concert violinist instead of a fleeing Jew. His mother carried him to London like coffee in a thermos. To grow up in a ruin, amid the blitzed, the burned and broken, a foretaste of the soon-to-be forlorn and fallen world. Joseph preferred to think of his father's moves as resembling, when he left Vienna in the guise of a Jew, a profound departure from the tonic; and his father's sojourn in London, until he went to work in the betting parlor, a deft modulation back to the Aryan fold; but it was difficult to account for the abandonment of his family, his departure for America, and his subsequent disappearance, in some sort of sonata form. Changelings required impromptus, variations, bagatelles, divertimenti, to do justice to their nature. He, Joseph Skizzen, was a weathercock too.

Joseph Skizzen's surmise that mankind might not survive its own profligate and murderous nature has been supplanted by the suspicion that nonetheless it will.

The gothic house he and his mother shared had several attic rooms, and Joseph Skizzen had decided to devote one of them to the books and clippings that composed his other hobby: the Inhumanity Museum. He had painstakingly lettered a large white card with that name and fastened it to the door. It did not embarrass him to do this, since only he was ever audience to the announcement. Sometimes he changed the placard to an announcement that called it the Apocalypse Museum instead. The stairs to the third floor were too many and too steep for his mother now. Daily, he would escape his sentence in order to enter yesterday's clippings into the scrapbooks that constituted the continuing record:

Friday June 18, 1999

Sri Lanka. Municipal workers dug up more bones from a site believed to contain the bodies of hundreds of Tamils murdered by the military.

Poklek, Jugoslavia. 62 Kosovars are packed into a room into which a grenade is tossed.

Pristina, Jugoslavia. It is now estimated that 10,000 people were killed in the Serbian ethnic-cleansing pogram.*

*The reader is invited to substitute or add a similarly focused report whenever this point in the text is reached.

Now there was no one left in Kosovo to kill but gypsies.
Or

Tuesday April 16, 2001

Cotonou, Benin. The boat at the center of an international search for scores of child slaves believed to

> have been roaming the West African coast for more than two weeks arrived early this morning in this port.
>
> Next day
>
> Cotonou, Benin. Authorities boarded a ship suspected of carrying child slaves after it docked at Cotonou early today but found no sign of such children.
>
> Next day
>
> Cotonou, Benin. According to the manifest, there were only seven children aboard. UNICEF officials said thirty-one were placed in foster homes. The Men of the Earth charity had forty-three at their refuge. The ship's chief mate insisted that there were twenty-eight children onboard, all with their families.

Skizzen decided that his paste would have to wait on further reports, since the incident would not be a keeper unless some of the kids had been thrown overboard.

With great energy, and with a confident smile, he sent two cans into the cardboard. Such skill, he thought, was rarely seen.

Skizzen clipped a few local items, but his harvest was mostly taken from the *New York Times* and the weekly newsmagazines. He ignored most crime and ordinary malfeasance. Occasionally he would include a shooting on the subway or the theft of donor organs, but he felt that you had to discount things done on account of poverty or madness. Actually, human stupidity was his principal target. Stupidity was shifty. It often pretended to be smart. For instance, the other day, he had saved yet another article on the preservation of small vials of smallpox—on the off chance, just in case, for scientific use, with the understanding that no species should be intentionally lost. In the same spirit, he ruled out the petty suborning popular with politicians, but he carefully saved accounts of elections in which a blatant scoundrel was voted into office by a smug, lazy, or indifferent electorate. He scissored when he spotted superstitions singing like sirens or when he caught stupidity fleeing the scene of one of its debacles, stupidity that especially embodied willful blindness or was an instance of greed or one of the other deadly sins overcoming weak reason once again. Judgments could be dicey. Dust Bowl pictures were included because it was Skizzen's conclusion that human mistreatment of the soil, not Nature out of whimsical meanness and acting alone, had made the plains barren, wasted the cattle, and scoured the barns to their bare boards. Hoof and Mouth were the names of two instruments in his orchestra. Mad Cow a must. Anthrax had no alternative. AIDS, of course, was easy, ignorance and stupidity fed and spread it, but river blindness, say, was a close call, and he ultimately rejected some very moving photographs of scar-closed eyes.

On the walls of his attic area were everywhere pinned atrocity pictures, some of them classics: the weeping baby of Nanking or the wailing Vietnamese girl running naked amid other running wailing children on that fatal Route 1 near Trang Bang (even the name a mockery); numerous sepias of dead outlaws with their names on crude signs propped beneath their boots; clips from films that showed what struck the eyes of those who first entered the extermination camps—careless heaps of skins and bones, entirely tangled, exhibiting more knees and elbows than two-pair-to-a-death ought allow—amateurishly aimed shots of the sodden trench-dead as well as bodies hanging over barbed battlefield wire; the bound Vietcong officer, a pistol at the end of a long arm pointed at his head, a picture taken in the act of his execution by a so-called chief of police; then, to add class, the rape of the Sabine women, etchings of chimney sweeps, delicate watercolors of sad solitaries and painted whores; or, for the purposes of education, the consequences of car bombs, mob hits, informers with their genitals wadded in their mouths, traitors hung from lampposts—Mussolini among the many whose bodies were publicly displayed—as were niggers strung, as a lesson, from the limbs of trees; but most were images transient for readers who saw, now with only a slight shock, countless corpses from African famines, African wars, African epidemics, ditto dead from India, ditto China but adding bloats from floods; there were big-eyed potbellied starvelings, wasted victims of disease, fields full of dead Dinka tribesmen, machine-gunned refugees on roads, misguided monks who had set fire to themselves, ghoulishly smoking up a street; and there were lots of Japanese prints that seemed to celebrate rape, paintings and pictures that glorified war or sanctified lying priests, flattered pompous kings and smugly vicious dictators; still others that celebrated serial killers and tried to put a good face on fat ward politicians or merely reported on the Klansmen, dressed like hotel napkins; the Goya etchings depicting the *Disasters of War,* in poor reproductions to be sure, were all there, as well as Bosches xeroxed in color from an art book, a few stills from snuff films, violent propaganda posters, numerous Doré's, Grünewalds, a volume of images devoted entirely to the crucifixion, saints suffering on grills or from flights of arrows, details from *Guernica,* examples from Grosz, close-ups of nails penetrating palms, then boards, illustrations in volumes of the Marquis de Sade (one, particularly prized, of a vagina sewn up like a wound); lots of photographs of the dead on battlefields or in burial grounds from *Gardner's Photographic Sketchbook of the Civil War,* many of them tampered with and staged, which created an added interest; there were drawings of medieval implements of torture, each aspect and element precisely labeled, as well as photographs of instruments of persuasion—the iron maiden, thumbscrew, rack—from the collection kept in the Tower of London; paintings of autos-da-fé by the Spanish master, firing squads by Monet, cavalry charges and combatants at the barricades by Delacroix; the guillotine with several of its severed heads was there, as well as emasculations, circumcision ceremonies, buffalo hunts, seal cubs as they were being clubbed, executions of various kinds—by knife, by fire, by gas, by poison, by lethal injection, by trap drop, by jolt, by shot—Indians massacred, natives forced over cliffs, notable assassinations—but only if the victim wasn't deserving—scalp and shrunken-head collections—as well as wall after wall, not in Skizzen's room but those depicted out in the world, where rebel soldiers or Warsaw Jews were lined up to be gunned down and photographed after, during, and before by the documentary-minded; close-ups of scattered body parts, many of them less identifiable than steaks or chops, including abattoirs in operation, fine watercolors of slave ships under full sail, a clutch of Salgado gold-mine prints depicting humans toiling in holes more horrible than Dante had imagined (and then had imagined only for the deserving); children huddled in doorways, on grates, coal miners in blackface, breadlines and beaten boxers, women working in sweatshops or shrouded in worshipful crowds, torch-lit Nazi rallies or the faithful as they were being trampled on their way to Mecca, six volumes of tattoos; and the professor's prize, an original Koudelka picturing a tipped-over tortoise, dead on a muddy Turkish road, handsomely matted and framed and hung center stage.

With great energy, and with a confident smile, he sent two cans into the cardboard. Such skill, he thought, was seldom seen.

Mostly, though, from every place not already tacked or pasted, clippings were loosely pinned or taped so that they would have fluttered had there ever been a draft, as they did wave a little when Skizzen passed or delivered one of his kicks, dangling for quite a ways down the wall in overlapping layers sometimes, even stuck to flypaper Skizzen had cannily suspended from the ceiling; the whole crowd requiring him to duck if he didn't want his head and neck tickled; and giving to the room a cavey cachelike feeling, as if some creature, fond of collecting, lived there and only sallied forth like the jackdaw to find and fetch back bright things; or, in this case, cuttings from the tree of evil, for which purpose paper shears had been put in every room of the large house, every room including entry, bath, and laundry, because you never knew when you might come upon something, and Skizzen had learned not to put off the opportunity, or delay the acquisition, since he had, early on and before this present remedy, forgotten where he had seen a particular picture or news item and was sadly unable to locate it again. He vividly remembered, too, how he had lost an image on a handout by postponing its extraction when he should have scissored it out while he was still standing on the front stoop holding in his shocked hand a leaflet bearing a grotesque beard and a text attacking the Amish because they were receiving special privileges, which allowed them their own schools; when children, whose God-loving parents were faithful members of the Church of Christ's Angelic Messengers, were called truants when kept from class and made to study—by a sick and godforsaken society—demonically inspired views of the development of life.

Next door, though the room was doorless and open to all those who found their way there, was the library, three of its walls lined by crude plank-and-brick cases crammed with books bearing witness to the inhumanity of man; especially a complete set of the lives of the saints, the *Newgate Calendars*, several on the history of the church, the many-volumed *International Military Trials* in an ugly library binding (for sale at a very reasonable price by the Superintendent of Documents of the U.S. Government Printing Office), and several on the practice of slavery through the centuries translated from Arabic, lives of the Caesars, careers of the Medici, biographies of feminists, the fate of the gypsies, Armenians, or the American Indians, and, of course, tome after tome on holocausts and pogroms, exterminations and racial cleansings from then to now, where on one page he could feed on names like Major Dr. Huhnemoerder, Oberst von Reurmont, Gruppenfuehrer Nebe, OKW Chef Kgf, and General Grosch; however, the library did not merely hold works on barbaric rites and cruel customs or on spying, strikebreaking, lynching, pillaging, raping, but on counterfeiting, colluding, cheating, exploiting, blackmailing and extorting, absconding, suborning, skimming, embezzling, and other white-collar crimes as well: proof through news reports, through ideas, images, and action, of the wholly fallen and utterly depraved condition of our race—Slavs killing Slavs, Kurds killing Kurds—testimony that Joseph Skizzen augmented, on the few ritual occasions he allowed himself to observe, by his reciting aloud, while standing at what he deemed was the center of his collection, alternatively from a random page of some volume chosen similarly, or from a news bulletin pulled down blindly from whatever stalactite came to hand; although he did occasionally cheat in favor of *The Newgate Calendar,* from which he would read with relish accounts of crimes like that of Catherine Hayes, who contrived, by egging on several of her many paramours, to have her husband's head cut off, in the punishment by which the righteous were seen to be even more wicked than the criminal.

When the wretched woman had finished her devotions, an iron chain was put round her body, with which she was fixed to a stake near the gallows. On these occasions, when women were burnt for petty treason, it was customary to strangle them, by means of a rope passed round the neck, and pulled by the executioner, so that they were dead before the flames reached the body. But this woman was literally burnt alive; for the executioner letting go the rope sooner than usual, in consequence of the flames reaching his hands, the fire burnt fiercely round her, and the spectators beheld her pushing the faggots from her, while she rent the air with her cries and lamentations. Other faggots were instantly thrown on her; but she survived amidst the flames for a considerable

time, and her body was not perfectly reduced to ashes in less than three hours.

Joseph Skizzen put his whole heart into his voice, happy no one would hear him, satisfied that no one would ever see his collection either; for he was no Jonathan Edwards, although his tones were dark, round, ripe, and juicy as olives, because he had no interest in the redemption of the masses whose moral improvement was quite fruitless in any case. He did privately admit, and thus absolve himself of it, that Joseph Skizzen was a man who enjoyed the repeated proofs that his views were right.

The drug trade and all it entailed, including bribery and money laundering, bored him—Joseph Skizzen had to confess to that partiality and to the fact that the relative absence of this and similarly vulgar forms of criminal business, as well as many of the brutalities of ordinary life that rarely reached the papers, was a serious flaw in his collection and, presumably, in his character as well. But who would know or care? That was a comfort. His work had been protected from its critics.

None more severe than he, when he missed his target and the can rattled through its vulgar leap toward the dormer ceiling.

Movies that would pan a camera about a serial killer's poster-lined room (or a delinquent adolescent's sometimes), after the police had invaded it, in order to astonish the audience's eyes as police eyes presumably were, would cause Skizzen an unpleasant twinge on account of the situation's distant similarity, especially when the lens would dwell on newspaper clippings, lists with circled names, or photographs of Charles Manson, but he bore such surprises well and avoided them altogether when that was possible.

There were images that had nowhere to hang but in his head, images he remembered from books but of which he had no other copy; particularly one, from a strangely beautiful illuminated manuscript called *The Hours of Catherine of Cleves,* that depicted the martyrdom of Saint Erasmus. The presumptive saint lies on a raised plank, naked except for a loincloth. His abdomen has been opened and his intestines attached to a windlass erected above him. Thereupon, like a length of sausage or a length of rope, his innards are being wound by two figures, one male, one possibly female, each working hard to turn the spokes, their faces, however, averted from the scene. The saint does not appear to have wrists or hands. Eight turns have already been taken. The sky is empty except for a few clouds; the earth is empty except for two hills and some small yellow flowers. Around this painting, framed like a picture, is a delicate thin line made of curlicues and a field of tiny petals stalked by imaginary butterflies. At the bottom a small boy wearing a collar of thin sticks is riding a hobbyhorse.

His curiosity aroused by this calamitous vision, Skizzen sought more bio concerning Saint Erasmus. One source simply said that "although he existed, almost nothing is known about him." This sentence stayed with Skizzen as stubbornly as the piteous illumination. What a blessed condition Erasmus must have enjoyed! Although he existed, almost nothing was known of him. Although nothing was known of him, as a saint, he existed. He existed, yet he had lived such a saintly life there was nothing of him to be known. Still another authority was not as sanguine. It claimed that the cult of Erasmus spread with such success that twelve hundred years later the martyr was invoked as one of the Fourteen Holy Helpers, whoever they were, and had become patron saint of sailors as well as kids who had colic. What was known, during those hundreds of years, was not known of the saint but of some figure he had thrown about himself as you would a ghostly garment or a costume for the dance. Proudly, Professor Skizzen pasted Erasmus in his memory book. A.d. 300. He was sprayed with tar and set alight. He was jailed, rescued by an angel, disemboweled. On a day in a.d. He died for me.

So as time and life passed, Professor Joseph Skizzen took care of Miriam, with whom he still lived; he played his piano, once a nice one; he prepared his classes and dealt with his students, studied Liszt, obsessively rewrote his sentence—now in its seven hundredth version—or clipped affronts to reason, evidences of evil action or ill feeling, from books, papers, periodicals, and elsewhere, most of them to paste in albums organized in terms of Flaws, Crimes, and Consequences, though many of the more lurid were strung up like victims on lengths of flypaper, nothing but reports of riots on one, high treasons on another, political corruption, poaching, strip mining, or deforestation on still others, and in order not to play favorites, he decorated a specially selected string with unspeakable deeds done by Jews, among them—in honor of his would-be forgotten father—the abandonment of the family.

Professor Joseph Skizzen's concern that the human race might not endure has been succeeded by his fear that it will quite comfortably continue.

7

Rudi had not left his family in the lurch, Miriam told the children at first, frightened of the effect the truth would have upon them. It was Raymond Scofield who had done that. Rudi had, she insisted, gone to America, where he would find work and, in due course, a pleasant place to bring them. After the second year, this lie could no longer be lengthened. Who knew what foul thing had befallen him in that faraway barbaric country of cowboys? And when they sailed for the States, that was the story in charge: their dear father had been killed by wild beasts, outlaws, or Indians in New York or Canada. He had doubtless been buried on the lone prairie, because neither the immigration authorities nor any of the refugee organizations had any record of a Rudi Skizzen or a Yankel Fixel or a Raymond Scofield. But, by the children, this was no more believed than Santa Claus, though the pretense was for a while maintained. We should have gone to Halifax, Miriam said, that's where your father is. But Miriam and her children were now in the hands of the system, so they went to a tiny two-bus town in Ohio, where they lived in a very small house at the edge of whatever civilization there was; Miriam got a routine job making rubber dishpans; the kids rode hand-me-down bikes to a very small school; Miriam caught one of the buses to work where she made friends readily; and life in Woodbine, Ohio, was safe, calm, regular, and quiet. About her occupation, Miriam always said it was better than the laundry. She still smelled of something, but it was no longer soap. Debbie loved her school where she soon had plenty of chums and took up cheering the boys at their American sports. When Debbie jumped up and down her breasts bobbed beguilingly beneath her sweater, and that was the real reason for the acrobatics, Joey felt. He liked Debbie better younger when she was without them and their gentle wobble. Imagine being popular for such a reason or made happy because you stuck out.

Joey was not so pleased with himself or his place. He was uneasy with everybody but Mr. Hirk, who had also made him uncomfortable at first. Perhaps it was because Joey fancied himself an Austrian of aristocratic lineage. Or because he began a grade behind and never got over the shame, though the normalcy of it all was explained to him countless times—wartime risks, irregularity of life, uprootedness of family, loss of father, poverty, the rest of it. The fact remained that he had been put back and was regarded as a stupe on that account. What he didn't like was standing out, being noticed, for whatever reason. He felt endangered by attention. During the rest of his schoolboy days he settled for Cs and gradually found a spot in the back row.

From the back row he never asked a question or answered one, if he could help it. He never took chances, shuffled his feet, whispered or passed notes, or surreptitiously read an illicit book while it hid inside the assigned one. He dressed as plainly as possible, stayed awake in study hall, didn't join, date, suck up, or hang around. He was resolutely friendly but had no chums. He owned nothing so valuable he felt responsible for it.

With Mr. Hirk out of the picture, Joey had no piano to play and no place to practice; however, he remembered that there was an old upright in his former grade school gym, so he went there after classes had let out, walked boldly in—such was the laxity of that peaceful place and those peaceful times—and played honky-tonks with its sticky keys. The tunes echoed from the vast expanse of wooden floor as though it were a sounding board. He found he could reproduce the little marches his fifth grade had been made to parade to, so he began with those, and no one still left in the building minded; perhaps the janitor thought Joey was working on a project or preparing for a pageant . . . as, it would turn out, he was.

Joey would find that, in America, at least, if you turned out a tune when you played the piano, then you played the piano; the skill was given you as easily as a second cup; appearances were better than reality; and the sight of someone slightly inept was immensely reassuring to those woefully without ability. As had to happen, teachers remaining after hours for a meeting heard the racket and a few came to the gym door to investigate. Joey was playing the "Parade of the Wooden Soldiers," something they recognized, so they went away again without a question. However, the teacher, into whose hands and hoarse voice the children's instruction in music had fallen, sought Joey out and asked him to play a few times after school for ceremonies and such things. Joey said he would be happy to, on one occasion playing his own variations on "Three Blind Mice" to childish laughter and parental applause.

In this way Joey learned that music is an enemy of isolation. People gather for it as if it could not be heard without help; it certainly could not be enjoyed without all those whom it employed: the place, the performer, the piano, the passive rows of people in chairs, devoted to their own silence, all ears.

The music teacher—who often rented instruments for this or that child in her charge from a sheet-music and record store in town that had such a sideline—recommended Joey when she learned that a clerk-of-all-work was needed there, and so, after relatives and friends of the owners were found to be uninterested or unavailable, Joey was approached. Through such a turn of fortune, Joey found himself with a real piano to play on and in his mother's grateful good graces at the same time. He began working after school and on weekends, but when he graduated he was taken on full-time at the High Note, so named because it was on High Street, a street so named because it lay across the edge of a ridge and looked down on Main, though only by a little. Through two small bleary windows at the rear of the shop Joey could look out over a small valley toward the low hills on which Whittlebauer College was perched, since every college in Ohio, maybe every college ever built, had to have a hill and be said to be "on the hill" and therefore come to be called, not the college, but the Hill. In short, he could see from High to Hill, although he could not know then that it would be his life's ironic trajectory.

Who was it? ah yes, the father of Marcella Sembrich. That gift-giving father, Joey remembered, learned to play many of the instruments of the orchestra without any formal training. At the store Joey blew into everything that had a mouthpiece and soon was able to do party, wedding, or retirement tunes on a lot of them, which pleased Emil and Millicent Kazan, his employers, since he could thus provide customers with demonstrations. He handled the rental business and then sales of sheet music as well, an addition to his work that increased his musical knowledge, too, because Joey devoured the liner notes, and his score-reading markedly improved, though, of course, it was for catchy melodies that were not long on difficulty or merit.

His fellow clerk was a kid called Castle Cairfill. At first, Joey felt sorry for him. Apparently, all through Woodbine High, he had been called Airful or Careful or, with another kind of scornful irony, Sir Castle, not Caz as he had hoped, and Joey was by his plight reminded how happy he was to be a Skizzen (odd as the name was) and not a Yussel—Yussel Fixel, what a burden!—even though he was called Skizz, because Skizz wasn't so bad. But Airful was an asshole. He was Joey's first asshole, though a regiment would follow. Airful had a head of stiff red hair the color of brick that he wore unevenly short so it resembled the bristles of a military brush that has been through many enlistments. You saw a lot of that head because Castle was noticeably tall as well as thin and, apparently embarrassed by his height, went about as if under arrest and concealing his face from the press. The belt he wore—there seemed to be two that worked each week—had so much tongue, when cinched, it fell from his waist like a panting dog's. Caz's complexion was both pale and flushed—that is, it was splotchy—and the splotches appeared to pulse when Airful was himself hot about something, whereas when he was frightened or anxious, his skin grew whiter than a fish's belly, so he looked sickly, tubercular, Joey imagined, like a male Mimi.

The seamstress but not the singer. Singers, he'd learned, were plump as geese, even when the character they sang was poor, overworked, and ill. Ill, overworked, and poor was as Caz seemed, but there was nary a song to suit the pallor of his personality or the blood-pink splotches on it either, nor was Joey the fat guy hired to sing it for him. Castle's long fingers were good for forking through sheets of music or stacks of records; he was even rather nimble at it; and these same straw-thin fingers strummed the guitar and the banjo fairly well except that they played nothing on these instruments that interested Joey's ear now that his taste was turned toward finer kinds—the most sentimental of operatic arias, he would later realize. He had recently come across the tenor of tenors, Beniamino Gigli, and "Una Furtiva Lagrima" was, at the moment, the apex of all art.

Castle wanted but wasn't granted amplification because Mr. Emil forbade the sale of noise cannons, as he called them, since they were instrumental in making much of the music Mr. Emil hated (a hatred, fortunately for profits, the parents of his principal patrons shared); however, his store did stock records by metal, cotton and earcandy rock groups, both hard and soft, as well as country-western naselizers and Broadway belters, because, otherwise, Mr. and Mrs. Kazan would have had no customers. Semirural Ohio was no place for blues, rap, hip-hop, jazz, or rag. But in the High Note store you could mosey a long while on the nostalgia trail from Kay Kyser or Guy Lombardo to Wayne "the Waltz" King or go as far as Benny Goodman and the big bands.

Joey's education was advancing by octaves. He already sensed the importance of airs, which, just before he went to work, he put on as regularly as his shirt. With a smile of condescension, Caz watched Joey gobble up the classical music section, such as it was; but it wasn't long before he could see the entire floor coming under Joey's reign, because kids who'd known and teased Airfill at school didn't have to ask him where a certain album was now or even pay him for it but could deal with Joey, who was a sort of cipher, and ignore the Castle where Sir Skinny lived.

Joey sensed the social meanings inherent in each sort of music: the old folks' need for a lullaby lady, the frat boys' for a glamour-puss, or that of a lamenting wife for a lamenting wife, as well as the value to obnoxious youths of eardrum-bruising yowls. The world-weary were soothed by sighing strings and entranced by Hawaiian hammock music. In addition there was a general though unacknowledged affection for ironically romantic baby talk: *whose yr lit-till whozzis? whoze yr turtle dove?* Crooners were well named, making sounds like soft stools. The honky kids he knew loved ghetto music. They felt it suited their mood when, for instance, they couldn't have the car. Volume alone was medicine, a defense against the world, or a cry of protest. Trips down memory lane were exclusively for the old folks; young folks like to think they have nothing to remember, so they have little patience with hoedowns and disdain for turkeys in the straw, no matter how noisy and frantic the violins get. In every case, for every age, whether loud, soft, rough, or gentle, music was used to obscure reality. Even if rural Ohio didn't have much.

Nevertheless Joey forced himself to become familiar with this oddly assorted sonic material in order to better serve his clientele—as he wished his patrons would learn to be. Pop buyers preferred singers who couldn't sing and musicians who couldn't play because these performers were—as they rose out of sight in their idolaters' eyes—like pop people themselves, their incompetence was the common touch and made them seem more sincere. Folk music, for instance, had to seem simple, uncouth, and untutored, or it wasn't folk. Joey thought it might be a good tactic to hum in the neighborhood of the customer. He rather liked "Moonlight in Vermont," but he didn't remember if any words went with—who was it?—Glenn Miller's version. It was the words the fan wanted to hear, interpreted and heightened—the message, the story—thus allowing opinions to be expressed and verified while feelings were shared and legitimized. Whereas, for his favorite aria, Joey knew only that it was about a furtive tear, and that the tear was as foreign as its language. For him it was the music—the music in the voice—the voice—smooth, sweet, easy, athletic, soaring above this poor earth—its sounds said all that needed to be said—*un ah furr teev ah la gree ma.* They went where the world wanted to go: out . . . outside itself . . . out of the ugly and painful and tawdry and cheap, out of the reach of reality just like everyone else, even in disdain of tears, to the place of beauty, its serenity, and its certainties.

In short, beauty was protection against the ordinary way of being. And rural Ohio had a lot of ordinary.

By present taste, the more difficult and sophisticated instruments—the violin, the clarinet—were avoided in favor of anything you could hammer or strum—the piano, alas, the drums, the guitar—and wiggles replaced real rhythm. Pop stars played the microphone like masters because electronics could turn bad breath into big-time bucks. They knew what their listeners wanted—what they themselves loved and served—substitute feeling and the pointless energies of borrowed life.

Joey had to admit that like the others he had his head hid, but their heads were buried in the sand while his was immersed in the clouds.

In a rare moment of frankness, Joey had to ask Joseph whether *un ah furr teev ah la gree ma* didn't do the same thing with the same success as "Red Sails in the Sunset."

Joey harbored these thoughts only in a hidden cove, but he recognized very early the importance of snobbery as a support for principles. Snobs never sold out their class. However, that unlikely loyalty may have been because their class was all they had. Steady on. Hold course, he'd learned to say from a seafaring novel. Had he wished to, and there were moments when he wished to, hear what other kids heard and share their certainties, it would have been denied him, for he was as odd as an oyster. Later, Joey would exhibit, as if for a textbook, the progression to the higher stations of appreciation: he'd begin by extolling Puccini and Tchaikovsky and pouring scorn on Ponchielli while admitting that the London recording of *La Gioconda,* with Zinka Milanov, was a splendid one; after that he'd advance to middle Verdi and *The Ring,* bringing with him only *Turandot* as a kind of mangled hostage, in the company of *Gianni Schicchi,* of course; then he'd continue on to Mozart, preferring *The Magic Flute,* annexing late Verdi, and adding Berlioz, with rare daring, on account of *Les Troyens*: meanwhile Joey would have been shifting his interest from opera altogether, especially anything that was popular in Italy, in order to embrace the chamber music genre and particularly those composers with the genius to predate Bach and Handel (some of whose immense oeuvres it was still permitted to admire), especially Palestrina, Purcell, and Monteverdi; but these enthusiasms would be swept away by the inevitable but notorious Schoenberg phase, which would naturally include the fanatical Anton von Webern and Alban Berg orthodoxy; the entire progression would culminate in Joey's ultimate sidestep to the Bartók Quartets and the *Transcendental Études* along with some Bach unaccompanied partitas and certain of Beethoven's late opus numbers, almost the only music left worth listening to, unless it was some pieces by Aleksandr Skryabin (especially when so spelled).

The snob in motion is hard to head off. But the seventh sense the snob attains is most dearly prized: that of a superior taste. And the smug possession of taste is far more infuriating to the wide world (which is, of course, lamentably without it) than any offensive lyrics or annoying noise.

The fact was that the true snob, even if he wielded his taste like a stick, cared about the quality he kept waxed in his garage and did know at least enough to make an effective show of superiority, which, for the most part, was all that was needed.

In the academic world where snobbery was native, it earned you enemies and promotions in equal measure. Being an Austrian émigré didn't hurt at all either. Joey wondered whether if his name were Amilcare like Ponchielli's, he would fare better and have more friends. But were friends worth the risk?

You really like that stuff? Caz's crooked smile pretended to honest interest without success. In *this* role—Joey would reply, negligently waving the cardboard sleeve of the store's only *Tosca* arias—well, in *this* role I prefer Giuseppe Di Stefano. In Joey's case, ignorance encouraged certainty. According to Caz, if Joey liked opera, Joey was a fairy, and that would account for his curious lack of interest in girls, although no one could have had less success in this area of life than Caz himself. He responded to Joey's withering scorn with sullen malice.

Joey took to addressing him, when he had to, as Mr. Castle Cairfill—Mr. Castle Cairfill, could you come over here a moment please and assist this young man who wants something in grunge—concluding his request with a smirk that Joey, on his way to becoming Joseph, would later edit out. Caz, during maliciously spent after hours, would put Benjamin Britten in the Brahms box and distribute Debussy randomly among the Strausses, or he would hide the store's single Massenet altogether. Not that anyone ever asked for Massenet.

Joey's fondness for Giuseppe Di Stefano would later fade, indeed disappear, when he learned that there was an Argentine soccer player of that name. For "Moonlight in Vermont," which he couldn't remember, he substituted the signature bars of " 'A' Train."

These were small skirmishes both parties tried to keep from Mr. Kazan, who brought his beard around every morning at ten when the store opened, if he remembered the key; otherwise Joey would have to go to the drugstore next door and phone Mr. Kazan's wife to ask her to fetch it, please, as Mr. Kazan had forgotten again. Caz and Joey would wait with Mr. Kazan in front of the door as if they were customers eager to get in, though Mr. Kazan never held a sale or marked anything down, not even demos (though he insisted they be clearly labeled as such), so there was no point in looking eager. A reasonable price is a reasonable price, and if the price is right there is no reason to change it. Otherwise, he'd say, anything that's fair is fair forever. As a consequence there were a great many old records in brand-new condition that remained at the price of their issue years ago; and in the back of the shop there were bins of 78s and 45s no one wanted or could play—speeds limited to the poor and lonely, Joey guessed, thinking of Mr. Hirk's even more antiquated equipment.

In his knotty dark beard, Mr. Kazan's wet red lips lay most invitingly. Joey, almost from primeval instinct, was partial to them. Mr. Kazan spoke in a gentle voice and often smiled without cause, lengthening his lips and softening their glint. However, he appeared to be a very nervous man, lingering near the office at the back of the store but only after peering up and down the street through the window in front. He only approached customers after he had watched them browse in the bins for a bit. By noon, though, he'd be gone for the day, unless some special business, such as inventory, required his presence. He sometimes seemed happy the goods he had once ordered were still there in case and box, on shelf and counter. Mr. Emil's absence in the afternoon meant that either Caz or Joey would turn the worn-out lock and set the antique alarm before they left at five, except on Saturday when Mrs. Kazan, pleasantly dowdy and mildly overweight, would appear to pace the floor till nine.

The Kazans were a pair of decently agreeable shopkeepers who had apparently more interest in keeping a shop than in the items it sold. Nor did it seem to concern them that Joey often stayed for hours after five to practice on the piano from scores in their stock, or to play the few operatic records the store had—of course only albums that wore a demo sticker—unfortunately *La Gioconda* and *Parsifal* were among them. To Joey's private "Why these?" there was no answer. A great deal depended on what the salesmen were flogging, of course, and the samples they were prepared to offer, as well as the specials in catalogs and other mailings. The Kazans clearly couldn't keep up with pop culture and depended on promos to stay abreast, or on the advice of their principal clerk, Mr. Castle Cairfill, whom Joey felt they trusted only because of his name—Careful—which was a switch, his name normally giving Castle nothing but trouble.

Mr. Emil was unaccountably close with money, and Joey supposed that was the reason, though there was an old phone fastened to the wall, they had no operative service. Imagine trying to run a business, that far back in the habits of the old days, in these lazy technological times. Like driving a car without a horn. But Mr. Emil said only bad news came through the receiver; that's why it was black, why it gave off an odor of death, and why only gossip got spoken through the cone. But suppose, Joey said, you had a fire—only for instance, mind—or one of us fell ill, and you wanted to call for assistance? Mr. Emil's beard would wag. Nit, he would say, nit. You see them sometimes? eh? they all wear boots, those Cossacks. Caz reminded Mr. Emil that Mr. Emil had a phone at home, which was a good thing because they needed it to call about the key when the key was forgotten—as it, a lot, was. On account dear Missus Kazan wants one, Mr. Emil said, wiping his mouth. So we have one. Consequences come like bad news through those threatening wires. We know you can call—understand?—consequent we are careless about the key. He shook his head more emphatically. If you have to walk eight streets, you make yourself careful and keep to your character and don't forget the key. Without a phone at home I'd be a better man.

Joey would often stay till the light failed. While he played he'd whisper "We were sailing along on Moonlight Bay" or "Moonlight becomes you, it goes with your hair." Oldies weren't pop anymore. They were just easier to play. Into the slender stock of scores had somehow slipped a copy of an instructional book called *Theory and Technic for the Young Beginner.* It taught you to play by numbering the keys, and Joey found this little book so wonderfully helpful he took it home but quickly brought it back so the book could be propped where the music stood. He sat and dreamed. Streetlights would come on, and Joey would go faintly gooey, feel slightly soft inside. Sometimes he'd slip on the "Moonlight Sonata" in a performance by Claudio Arrau, which was the only one they had, although the album notes had warned him that Beethoven hated the popular sentimental description of the *adagio sostenuto*—the latter word one Joey had adored long before he knew what it meant or how something *sostenuto* sounded: in this case, a dreamy drifting calm before the storm. Despite Beethoven's disapproval, the streetlamps made moonlight when they came on. The stand-up cutout of a strumming Johnny Cash would become a silhouette against the shop's front window, and then Joey would slip out the back and walk home, haunted by grave meditations on beauty, futility, and change; though with winter coming, since he didn't want to turn on the store lights, his practice time would shrink—it might entirely disappear.

As it threatened to anyway, because Castle Cairfill, catching the drift of things, had also begun to stay after hours, in his case on the pretext of dusting records, ordering racks, or redisplaying the Beatles, happy in the knowledge that his presence would make Joey too uncomfortable to play. Is this on your own time, Joey would ask. And Cairfill would reply, The same time as yours, running a rag over Dolly Parton and looking an album of Dusty Springfield right in the eye. He had heard Joey humming—it was an unconscious habit—so he hummed rather loudly though awkwardly in order to get on Joey's nerves, which now felt as if jangled by the interminable ringing of the phone they didn't have. Because it was not simply his humming but Castle's habit of hanging around to overhear what was being said when Joey was helping a customer that annoyed; as well as his tendency to lurk near the door to intercept patrons the moment they came in and thus carry them off; or his loud forceful suggestions of this or that recording or label or artist—his choices seemed random—a tactic at which he aggressively persisted although the customer had already presented him with the phrase "just looking" like a card on a tray, or the curt word "no" had been testily uttered—by itself, never enough—or even after a definitive request for "Alexander's Ragtime Band" had been made by someone flustered and in a hurry.

It became a contest to outwait each other by finding some excuse to stay late, each on the side of the shop he had chosen as his territory and each lingering into the edge of the evening, eyeing his enemy uneasily across the display tables, until, as was increasingly the case, Joey, his plans undone by darkness, would abruptly disappear through the rear door, suffering Castle's triumphant snort like an arrow in his back.

8

One morning, when Joey and Castle entered the shop with Mr. Emil, they found it slightly ransacked, some money and a few records taken. Perhaps they are satisfied, perhaps they will not be back, Mr. Emil said. Should we take an inventory to find out what was stolen, Joey asked. No, it is of no matter, never mind about it, hooligans in uniforms no doubt, a notice, a warning, Mr. Emil said, we're lightly off if this is what it comes to. But now he visited the rear window as often as he did the front one and seemed to lurk in corners or behind displays as if the marauders were going to return even during broad day. His lips looked chapped, no longer wet and rosy, his eyes wandered, and he had a habit of thrusting the splayed fingers of his left hand out of sight into his beard, which looked bigger than before because it was so unkempt. Joey began to realize that most of the things that were missing, except for a guitar that could not be found, came from the classical boxes, the "Moonlight Sonata" for one. There were no signs of forced entry, the policeman reported, but the back door was unlocked. The authorities seemed at a loss. There was very little crime of any kind in the town. Mr. Emil did not seem able to digest this information. He heard it as if he hadn't heard, his wife said.

Another morning Millicent accompanied him to the shop and, carrying the key ready in her hand instead of having to have it sent for, opened the door. She stayed with Mr. Kazan till they left together at noon, sometimes tenderly holding the hand that was not playing bird in the bush with his beard, the pair of them getting in the way because they tended to block aisles, wander aimlessly, and otherwise seem unresponsive. Castle, on his best behavior since the robbery, no longer stayed, as it were, after school or played pranks. He did look flushed now, as if he had just finished running hard a great way, and his splotches were bright with—maybe—bad blood beating beneath them. Perhaps, Joey thought, he has tuberculosis and he is a Violetta or a Mimi man after all.

It had to happen that one morning Castle was not in position at the door when Mr. and Mrs. Kazan arrived to open it. Poor Cassie is ill, Millicent said. He phoned to say. She drew back the door, and her husband plunged into the store as if eager for a swim. With a gesture that lightly touched him, Millicent held Joey back a moment. We aren't angry that you left the shop unlocked, she told him with a warm small smile. Everyone forgets, Mr. Emil most. Nothing matters that is missing. Do not put it deep into your heart. She followed her husband, disappearing into the store whose lights had not yet been switched on. It was the turn of Joey's cheeks to burn. He stood stock-still and stiff in the morning chill—dumbfounded, ashamed, helpless, enraged.

It was the same morning, serving a customer who needed a new needle, that Joey discovered a box holding half-a-dozen diamond points was missing. He felt as guilty as if he had just then slipped them in his pocket. After the sale, there was only one remaining in the entire shop. Should he tell Mr. Emil that he needed to reorder right away; should he tell Mr. Emil that some of the points had been stolen; should he assure Mr. Emil that it wasn't he who had left the shop unlocked; should he head off any suggestion that it might have been Joey who had actually swiped the stuff that had been swiped; should he?

He would tell Mr. Emil he needed to reorder right away. Yes. That's what he would do. He would tell Mr. Emil he needed to reorder right away. Mr. Kazan, sir, Joey said, suspiciously respectful, when I sold a needle just now I noticed that we need to order more, for we are nearly out of stock. Mr. Emil stared at Joey in astonishment. How can you say, he said. How is it that you can? You *oyss-voorf!* This word, which to Joey was just a noise, was nevertheless received by him as a terrible indictment. He had been denounced.

Millicent hurried to his wounded side. Please, Joey—Mr. Kazan, you must understand, is not himself since the roundup—since the invasion of the store. He is variously a nervous man. She took Joey's silence to signify skepticism. Oh, you couldn't know, for years, at night, at home, you see, we stay we eat we sleep with all the lights on, all the lights, all the time. Poor man! He stands sometimes wrapped in the window curtains. Poor man! He believes darkness can come in the middle of daytime like a moving van. So. Do not be dismayed. Please. At last Joey responded with a nod and hurried to a fictional task, in imitation of his tormentor. To dust a cardboard Dolly Parton.

Massenet hadn't been misfiled. Massenet was missing.

Several Chopins. Of course. The Dinu Lipatti waltzes. Such wonders.

The disk had been an economy repressing, but Joey could not yet afford it, cheap as it was.

By closing time Joey could no longer remember the sounds that had signaled his condemnation. The shame had left his face, his chest, and settled in his stomach. To be falsely accused was bad enough, but to know he had no recourse and would forever bear the stigma of such a petty pointless cruel crime, that was unendurable; and Joey sank into a tippy ladder-backed chair Mr. Kazan kept at the rear of the main room so he could sit and survey the shop against what he called lifters—a shop now so dark only shadows could be seen in the light from the street—and there in his boss's chair, his head at his knees, Joey wondered whether, addressing Mr. Emil, he had said, "When I stole a needle just now," which might account for the ensuing conniption. In any case, Joey had begun a life of dodging disaster.

He rocked the chair a bit forward to the right, a bit backward to the left, and a bit forward to the right again, in a rhythm that imitated the opening of the missing sonata, although at first he was unaware of the connection, rocking only as the grieving do, back and forth, as if their grief were a crying baby: *dum   doh dee dum   doh dee dum   doh dee dum*. Then above it, as he rocked, he heard the treble. First, the heartbeat of the quiet world, steady, indifferent, calm, and then the higher incry of consciousness—Joey's—fluttering, hovering, over it. He sat up then, stood up then, and went to the piano where he played the three-note base just as slowly as it was given—again and again—just as it was given. The initial *dum* became the final not the first note of the triplet, while in the treble another triplet was performing as though without a net.

Next he worked on deepening the thrum as Beethoven darkened it—there was pedal—damn—there was pedal—but he couldn't get the treble to go where he wanted it to go. That first *dum* was in a sense never the first *dum* again. Rather it was an end, so the music repeated, not its departure, but its return, again and again—*doh dee dum*—as if a series of numbers that began 1 23 became 1 231 231 231 . . . eventually 312 312 312 . . . then 1 23 once more. It was all so simply managed yet not with the same sort of simplicity that governed "Indian Love Call" or "You're a Grand Old Flag." And while working, Joey lost the music's mood, felt it leave him, because his perch in such a beautiful space was so precarious.

The line of consciousness that the treble drew . . . he couldn't continue to make it his.

Joey realized that he was sitting at his fourth piano. His first was the now dimly remembered wreck sitting in a London street; plaster dust had silted between both blacks and whites and was so completely and so tightly packed there that each key was highlighted and none of them moved. The second was Mr. Hirk's beloved relic with its bench filled with tattered scores; the third the dime-store castoff in the grade school gym; and the fourth the decently tuned instrument he had just fingered, betraying Beethoven in a manufactured moonlight.

Joey struck the three notes and let them resonate in the room. The street through the window was fading from view because High Street in the early fall began twilight early. Just three notes and all the dimensions, most of the elements, some of the dynamics, the shadings, of the musical world were there. Of course he knew where these three notes belonged in the rest of the piece, yet, after all, they were an announcement. At the opening of the sonata, these tones were what there was, and nothing else was . . . nothing else was; though soon, Joey heard, they were gone . . . instead of being there, they were gone . . . immediately . . . in an instant they were gone; and nothing else could have been in the place they made but them . . . those three . . . just them; they were the entire past; and if they came again, they came at a different time, took up a different part of musical space; and if they appeared at another time and space, they were like an actor in another role, a cherry melting in a pie and not atop a sundae, a person in another country.

When the light flew in, the wire racks were the first to glint. Some shiny covers that had been left exposed, or the glass in a case, would vaguely shimmer. Tomorrow, there'd be a replay. The same cellophane packet, counter corner, polished knob would ping as it had pinged night after night before. Nothing could be more fragile or unlikely than the arrangement they composed. A spot upon the floor, the bell above the antique phone, a pin sticking from an announcement board, would have unexpected presence. Somehow it stood for, and sounded, his sadness—this constellation of stars.

It is I, Joey thought, who should become a castle. It is I who should be careful. It is Caz who should be called Skizz.

Joey tossed the few things he kept at work in a handled paper sack:

umbrella, comb, fistful of small change for the pay phone, handkerchief (on this occasion found to have been already soiled and consequently wadded in a drawer), lip balm his mother had insisted on, nail clippers, the stained cracked coffee mug he had rescued from the store trash and scrubbed into continued use because it had a bold black clef on it, several plastic packets of catsup but only one of mustard—he was careful to erase every mark he'd made; he'd have collected his breathing, too, if that had been possible—and a whalebone toothpick for when he'd eaten enough meat to leave some in his teeth, plus a matchbook from the Rodeo Roadhouse, a bar out of town he hadn't been to (as if he'd been to any), but treasured for daydream reasons; and by these meticulous attentions removed and disposed of all traces of himself before he locked the door and left, listening to his footsteps in the alley and feeling that everything he had on his person was stolen; though he did wish, while regretting the loss of "Moonlight," he had the Lipatti beneath his shirt.

Miriam was distraught, weeping on Joey's account and furious with him, because the police had come to the house—were there in fact waiting when she got home from work—stern and full of questions about her son. With a list that appeared to be long if not complete they went poking about the house, peering in Joey's closet with a flash, and even rummaging in his room, although with considerable caution. Miriam was in ignorance of her rights and fairly terrified by authority, so she fell back from the door as if pushed when they showed her who they were, told her why they were there, and explained to her what they desired.

How many? Joey finally had to shout. How many . . . ? how many? Well, two, it turned out, in what looked like a pickup truck. Uniformed? Uniformed? Well, one had a star on his coat lapel.

The pair were particularly surprised that the family had no TV and no record player, but took no notice of the little radio. They did inquire about instruments, however. Autoharp? Guitar? Miriam was confused beyond redemption. As the men prowled the house without flushing any game, she quit keening and began to pay attention to what was going on, resolving to come to Joey's defense; and when they left without results, she was positively triumphant. The police went away without apology, and this reinfuriated her. By the time Joey had walked home, having stayed late yet another evening in his manufactured moonlight, her anger had become formal, more hurtful, righteous. Belatedly, Miriam realized that this official visitation meant Joey's job. Now she knew whom to blame, and she did so, nearly spitting, reverting to Austrian. Joey heard his damnation in her words the way he had heard it in Mr. Kazan's, though he understood nothing in that case, as he did little of his present accusation—at least at first, for Nita went on and on, knotting her skirt and bringing it to her nose, repeating—though she would have been revolted at the word—her kvetch.

Nita had been borne away from her birthplace—her sweet green hillside farm—exposed to bombing, fire, the charity of strangers, and left like an orphan amid enemy ruins. Her name and nature had been taken from her, too, and after that she was further betrayed, left with children to feed and house and scold, with nowhere to go but America, cut off forever from her homeland by the sea, and subsequently by miles of dinky forests and wimpy mountains. Then just as it seemed they might be at peace in this no-account nowhere town, with Deborah happy and married and fitting in like you wouldn't believe, and just when a few friends had been made, and a little money was coming in, he, her son, Joseph Skizzen, had brought the police to their little home—he—Joseph Skizzen, so soon like his father, a petty thief, a stealer, a gambler, a liar, an ungrateful no-account moony wretch—had heaped their house high and hidden it beneath disgrace, so, she, Miriam, would have no more friends, could count the trials of her life as having accomplished less than nothing, and now would be compelled to subtract this cruel boy's wage from what little they had to live on, and face winter without hope or happiness or funds, hence to live on ingratitude as well as she could, since that was all there seemed to be an abundance of. She spoke as an outraged victim to a judge, not facing her son, rather addressing the world or some god who had been brought in to preside at the catastrophe. Joey could only stand there: mute, helpless, enraged on his own behalf, ashamed, a destitute.

In the months that followed, Joey was able to convince his mother that he was not a rascal; moreover, the family's disgrace was nowhere rumored, let alone known. Caz disappeared like a case of hives. Life went on, in its quiet way, as before. Better yet, Joseph had been accepted as a student by a small Christian college nearby with the proviso that he serve as organist, which, while it did not add any income, gave him a mouse hole to live in and a redemptive occupation. It was better than bagging groceries, Nita agreed, or repairing roller skates or selling noise to adolescents. Joseph pretended to be reforming and toning the instrument while he was learning to play it, and now had a piano at his disposal as well. The choir claimed him as an alto, so he sang from his seat, in the middle of the music. Miriam could not believe their good fortune, though unknown to her, on his application, Joseph had rather upgraded his scholarly performance and his musical skills. The Augsburg Community College liked the name Skizzen and somehow understood it to be Lutheran. He'd catch a ride home now and then with a student who commuted from town, so Miriam didn't feel as lonely as she expected to be; although she had hoped for his good riddance often enough to be surprised that she dreaded it.

For the first time in his life, Joseph began to read like a rodent. He chewed his way through the school's few books on music, ate his way into history and almost out again, and was groped by Professor Ludens in the organ loft. The professor's hand, he felt, was no nicer than his own.

On Sunday, over his shabby ordinary clothing, Joseph Skizzen donned a gown. Under the gown he grew to be a man; he seemed renewed; he was transported to another realm—that of the imagination. His hands emerged from his gown's dark sleeves and with rare purpose touched the organ from whose pipes vast sounds emerged like the voice—to be sure—of a local god, but not confined thereby to that modest space—no—capable of calming chaos. The chapel was small and undistinguished, as was the campus as a whole, as were the students—their brains inactive yet otherwise unharmed beneath the mulch of superstition that lay thickly over them—as was the staff: inept without exception, inadequately trained, incapable of advancement anywhere else in the world, all of them like swollen sacks leaking envy and malice, yet convinced of their dedication, their wisdom, the hone of their skills as well as their vigorous application, while sharing a sanctity they extravagantly admired.

Joseph Skizzen's soul (which he had been assured by the community he very likely had) was fed, for the first time, with words, so that his mind grew, weedlike, in a dozen different directions. Whatever fell in front of his eye he read, read with both wonder and acceptance, ingesting a great deal of nonsense along with what was wise and sending it into a system not immediately able to discern any difference. The book disappeared from his hands and he was in Savonarola's Florence or Conrad's Central America or Gibbon's Rome. He failed Faulkner, he flunked Carlyle, he rejected Joyce, and at Hopkins simply blinked, but Tennyson he could tolerate, and Shelley appealed to an ideal he could admire so long as it remained romantically vague—which it did. Thomas Wolfe triumphed over him the way a masterful man, he thought, took a woman, an attitude his lack of experience allowed him to entertain because it included the novel's jousts with the Jewess Mrs. Jack, as well as his dim remembrance of his father's shrouded grunts in a bombed-around bed. He would further confess, as if he had a confessor, that steamy scenes simply embarrassed him. Writers must have to write them, they appeared with such regularity, and Joey felt sorry for the sordid obligations of the profession.

Paragraphs imprinted themselves as if he were in fact the first blank tablet manufactured by the human race. *You Can't Go Home Again* was a title to turn his head, and he sailed toward book 5, "Exile and Discovery," like Columbus, his mouth watering from the dream of wealth, his eyes likewise moist at the thought of fame, only to be slowed by chapter 31: "The Promise of America." Which he knew beforehand was the chance at an unnoticed life. Joseph so far forgot himself as to corner schoolmates, his finger at the ready where the honored passage was, in order to read aloud in their direction with such heat and vehemence they were at first held in ear range by surprise and trepidation before annoyance released them. Just listen to this! Isn't this it? Really, isn't it? Just listen!

> The Chinese hate the Japanese, the Japanese the Russians, the Russians also hate the Japanese, and the hordes of India the English. The Germans hate the French, the French hate the Germans, and then look wildly around to find other nations to help them hate the Germans, but find they hate almost everyone as much as they hate Germans; they can't find enough to hate outside of France, and so divide themselves

> into thirty-seven different cliques and hate each other bitterly from Calais to Menton—

In Joseph's enthusiasm—Wolfe's words had struck such a chord, he could have been hearing an opera sung for the second time—it didn't occur to him that his auditors didn't care about the feelings of the French for the Japanese or the Germans, or the hordes of India for the English, especially since, in early 'Nam time, this rant seemed oddly out of place; or that "Calais" might as well have been a cheer they could expect to hear at a football game—Cal-ay! Cal-ay!—or that none of it had any significance for them since they deeply and dearly believed what Jesus had taught—to love—only to love—just to love—or that they had been victims of Skizzy's hectoring habit ten times too many already—so it was despite their drifting eyes that he pressed on, perhaps a bit more noisily than was normal.

> —the Leftists hate Rightists, the Centrists hate Leftists, the Royalists hate Socialists, the Socialists hate Communists, the Communists hate Capitalists, and all unite in hatred of one another.

Sometimes Joseph would slow himself up and remember to say, This was published in 1934, this . . . ! Think of it! . . . '34! Hey—

> In Russia, the Stalinites hate Trotskyites, the Trotskyites hate Stalinites, and both hate Republicans and Democrats. Everywhere the Communists (so they say) hate their cousin fascists, and the fascists hate the Jews.

Though his quotes were pearls, his auditors were the swine the occasion called for, and they were indifferent to anything they decided they couldn't eat. Why do you read such stuff, Athletic Sweater pretended to wonder. He's a ruffian . . . a ranter, this Wolf. What was that about Stalin, the Giant Beanpole wondered, suspicious. There are writers more agreeable, Miss Pleat Skirt smirked. She knew she and her friends were better dressed. I hate him, whoever he is, Fat Blouse said, stumbling into the text. Stinking baloney, decided Mr. Yellow Corduroy. Keep it in your sandwich. To every gesture of disrespect Joseph would say: There's more. With you, Skizzy—they'd generally share a giggle before turning their backs and walking away, only to toss a shout over their collective shoulder—with you, Skizzy, there's always more.

You never left high school, Joseph would volley after them. In retreat from the truth! All of you! Book-bag babies! But then he would realize—it would stop his shouts—that he was making a scene, becoming a character, and, as a minor nuisance, entangling himself in their lives.

Often Joseph just wanted to hear the words in their first form, their real guise—hear them said aloud, promulgated—and he didn't need listeners, just as years later he would prefer the absence of an audience when he recited scripture in the company of the clippings that sanctified—muralized—his church.

In the center of that future room, amid strips of bad news like shags of animal hair—dangles ready to applaud a bellow—cans to kick like points after touchdowns—Joseph Skizzen would call out Wolfe's words in the triumphant tones of "I told you so."

> And so it goes—around, around, around the tortured circumference of this aching globe—around, around, and back again, and up and down, with stitch and counterstitch until this whole earth and all the people in it are caught up in one gigantic web of hatred, greed, tyranny, injustice, war, theft, murder, lying, treachery, hunger, suffering, and devilish error!

Around and around the tortured circumference of this aching earth . . . the shrinking circumference of this tortured planet . . . Devilish error? What's been done is done and no mistake! Round and round the mulberry bush the monkey chased the weasel. The human race thinks it runs for fun when *pop bam boom bang guny gun gun*—horn hid and tail tucked—Satan shoots his meal—monkey brains and veal.

But these thoughts would come later, when he'd heard more music, had been immersed in other books, and his sentence had seized him. Right now his future self was no bigger than a chrysalis, his goatee-to-be barely tickled, its womb rarely giggled. Wanna see? your baby—future you is kicking! No! I don't want to see the bughouse bounce!

He lived at the church in the janitor's room and did janitorial work to earn his keep, in addition to sustaining the organ in tone and tune. He felt his room, though small and bare and gloomy, was a mighty fortress, and there, surrounded by walls of damp stone, he would preach his gospel though it went unheard: around, around, around the tortured circumference of this aching world . . .

Despite Joseph's new enthusiasm for the word, he was no better a student in the classroom than he had formerly been. It was true that his teachers were pathetic and his fellow students pitiful, nor had his dislike of the limelight lessened, but he was led away from education by learning. In his memory Mr. Hirk had already become a magnificent teacher—his one and only—quirky as the great tutors had to be—and since Joseph was determined to be self-schooled, to learn from books as he imagined Lincoln had, and possess a mind free of received opinion, what he needed to gain from any academic enterprise was its cachet, which could be obtained from Augsburg Community College with an ease that would put a pan of grease to shame.

The school's library was woeful. Though well stocked with hymnals, apologetics, hagiographies, testimonials, old atlases, and sermons, most of its worn and shaken volumes were in such sad shape they would qualify as cast-offs from charity book sales. Still, to someone who felt underfed, they were feast enough. There was even a ragged spine-loose volume of Bach scores. Joseph loved the long shiny table set in the middle of the stacks where he could sit in an appreciated silence and outstrip the table's surface in its devotion to reflection.

In a library who knows what book the eye may fall upon and curiosity withdraw. Among such was the sixth volume of *History of Dogma* by Adolf von Harnack. Augsburg had three of an apparent set of seven: two tattered, one unaccountably mint. Nita might know something of the sixth's subject, Joseph guessed, since it spoke in passing of a pope named Innocent III who was accomplished in the sponsorship of crusades, having initiated one against the Moors in Spain, another to obliterate a group called the Albigenses, and finally a grand one, as if they'd been arranged in a series like Adolf von Harnack's volumes, designated as the Fourth. But it was this pope's establishment of the doctrine of transubstantiation that caught Joseph's attention, since, for him, the word was full of mystery and promised much.

Names that seemed redolent with the romance of antiquity, of distant times and climes, fastened themselves to Joseph's mind. They stood for nearly hidden lives, for quarrels worthy of Tweedledum and Tweedledee, such as was the one between a monk of Corbey called Paschasius, who believed that bread could be converted into Christ (what a wonder!), and another member of that abbey who thought that the connection was purely spiritual.

One work he especially treasured was *The Paderewski Memoirs.* He was a happy reader until the book's conclusion neared; then the master went on and on about the importance of the pedal, passages that left Joseph discontented with his idol and dissatisfied with himself. It seemed that, even as a boy, Paderewski had displayed an instinct for pedaling. Well, Joseph thought, so did I.

In this way, though, he discovered that there was something unsafe about books. You began one; you were suitably entranced; the style, the subject, the arrangement—the noble sentiments, the brilliant thoughts, the charming creatures therein portrayed, such exciting situations: each seemed so satisfying that the eye could scarcely wait for the page to turn. It was, he remembered, how his fingers felt when they were playing well and music was majestically flowing from them as if by magic. But then the Paderewski passage would occur: a gesture that stooped, a boast that offended, an idea that was as grotesque as a two-headed calf, a sentiment that steamed like rotting flesh, like a childhood ramble in the ruins that suddenly betrayed you with a sight not meant for living eyes. You'd turn like the globe did in a day. You'd learn that men were murdered over the meaning of a wafer.

From a student who had to leave school suddenly because of the alleged illness of his father, Joseph purchased a record player so technically adept it had three speeds—33, 45, and 78 rpm. Consequently, the remainder of his discretionary funds, small enough as nearly not to matter, was set aside for records he didn't dare try to obtain from the High Note and would therefore have to do without, for there was no other shop in miles; but by cutting back on treats and by not buying any books and by mending a pair of his own pants, Joseph was able to mail-order several: the Chopin waltzes played by Dinu Lipatti, *Great Opera Singers of the Golden Age,* and some outrageously discounted pieces for two pianos by Erik Satie, a composer entirely unknown to him, and to everyone, he assumed.

Joey needed to replace the needle of his "gramophone," which was worn sore by the previous owner's pop rock; and he could have pressed into service one of the diamond points he had been accused of stealing had he actually done the deed. For his mother the entire affair had been reduced to an episode, now only occasionally remembered, but for Joseph the injustice he had suffered had become a chronic ailment like migraine, and he would lie on his bed sometimes compacting, as though his hands held snow, an explosive bunch of curses to catapult at Castle Cairfill till the castle's walls came tumbling down, the castle's keep was breeched, and Cairfill's limbs and organs were put to the sword; although he knew in his heart that his curses were popgun and pasteboard, that "May your nose drip forever" would not send a shiver through grass let alone a wall of stone. As for Kazan, he imagined the terrors that kept the storekeeper's lights lit at night had multiplied like germs so that even on a noonday street Mr. Emil would now need torchbearers every few feet to put the *bogeymensch* to flight.

9

When Skizzen first became aware of it, he laughed, for he had miss-spelled "spell." Well, not exactly. The additional *l* was a typo. "Spelll." It was a machine-mad e rror, but the extra *l* could be easily deleted. That was one of the great virtues of this new invention. If words magically appeared on the screen (he was often unaware he was typing his fingers flew so fast, so briefly did they need to light upon the keys), they could be sent away just as readily. Not like a note that would leave of its own accord yet could not be erased and could not be said to have disappeared. He had been saying that a spell had been put upon mankind. Writing, not saying. He had been writing that a spell had been put upon our race. As if Circe had changed us into swine so that our little noses were wrinkled by concealed snouts, and inside those of us who possessed a male member a hog's reproductive implement curled—a pig's . . . sexual implement—a memoir of the moment of enchantment. Anyway, we did not see how foolish, how absurd, how wicked we were being. That was the gist.

Joseph had pursued a request for some books that he had asked the library to acquire as far as the library entrance, where a smilling young man had greeted him with this suitcase fulll of magic. We ordered some of these computers, he said with some excitement, and they just came. Want to play? The Music Department had been threatened with digitization, but their three-person claim on modernity was weak. So Professor Skizzen dutifullly sat at one end of a long library table and began pecking away: It is as if a spelll had been put upon mankind. How quickly the spelll enveloped the screen. We oinked and thought it singing, he wrote. The young man approached bearing his grin like a tidbit on a salver, so Skizzen hit DELETE and saw nothing more, neither his practice sentence nor the grin. Go on, the young man said, take it for a spin. Our new system will make it easy for us to keep records, he boasted. The bursar is out of his mind with delight. We rolled in the mud and believed we were bathing, Skizzen wrote, with his best hunt-and-peck. He knew Grin was grinning again, over his shoulder. Let the piker peek, Skizzen thought, I shall complete my edifying lines about the spelll that been put upon mankind. "We fought one another and afterward celebrated the carnage" soon materialized. With writing, he said aloud, the writing inscribes the letters, letters build the words, and, subsequently, the thought arrives—handmade like kneaded bread. With typewriting, you get letters by hammering them into existence. Or out, with *x*'s, if you don't like them. With this sweet machine here, you issue a requisition. Well, now, I hadn't thought about it that way, the Grinner said. With pen and ink, before we write, we think, because we hate the sight of corrections. With the computer we write first and think later, corrections are so easy to perform. I like the delete key best; it has a good appearance, Skizzen said, typing furiously. "We ate our farrow and supposed it was a splendidly healthy, indeed toothsome, way to dine." Joseph determined to leave something behind as an animal might to signal its presence, so he keyed: "We eagerly awaited our own slaughter, as though we were receiving an award." Now he spoke it as he played it. "Our haunch would hang in the smokehouse to season, and those of us who remained to feel would feel, like parvenus, that we had Arrived." I'm glad you got these, he said to the Grin, though the young man didn't seem to have any more grins to spend. I wonder how many unordered books these cost me. He slid his words the length of the long table where they disappeared over its edge into delete. Then Skizzen took his goatee away where it would be better appreciated.

Professor Joseph Skizzen had been apprehensive about the survival of the human race but now he was worried that it might, in fact, endure.

For the moment, there didn't appear to be such a place. He knew these machines swallowed data, and that vaguely threatened him. No formal charges had been made, so Skizzen's written defense was not yet needed, nor would it be very useful in his case to refer with such obsessive constancy to the evils that men do, when it was only his paltry transgressions that were at issue. Could Skizzen persuade his prosecutors to admit that his malfeasances were entirely precautionary—lies white as alabaster, or at least chalk—committed in order to prevent his own contamination and having, otherwise, no hope of profit. They were crimes only in his enemies' criminalized eyes. Because he had lived apart from the system even when inside the system, it appeared that he had made the genuine less to be esteemed than the fraudulent; that his counterfeit bill would buy more than their good one. Well, that admission they would not make; it ate at their pride; it proved they were as fundamentally stupid as they superficially seemed to be; it made a mockery of their allegedly superior educational enterprise.

Any misgiving one might have had about the continuance of the human species has been replaced by serious concerns that it might muddle through after all.

So he was not one of them; he had not, as the common saying was, paid his dues; worse, he had surpassed them too easily. He, the least likely to succeed, the laziest boy in the class—the least eager, the least attentive—had solved the great conundrum, the most mysterious equation, the sphinx's riddle; and they were angry, the way Cinderella's sisters or Grimm's evil brothers were, when the simpleton showed up with the solution. They were reluctant, but they had promoted him. It was grudging, yet applause was applause. They had accepted his advice; let themselves be led by an apparition.

Skizzen had to admit that his case would continue to worsen as the number and complexity of his fictions became known, and the machine would make record keeping simpler: he was not quite his alleged age; he did not know those he said he knew, only their secretaries, only by mail; he did not prefer the foods, the wines, the books, the music—even the music—he pretended to prefer; the habits he had were not his own; he frowned at what made him inwardly smile; he had taught his outer self to strut and curse while his private self cringed; his history was a forgery; his intentions could not be read; and when he said: I can play the organ, he meant: One day I will. In short, everything about Skizzen was askew.

His head was full of his own defense. In spite of himself, he rehearsed his forthcoming trial; he bore witness to his own worth; he thrust and parried, proudly protested, lamented and pleaded. Should he use this argument, try that twist, make this move, or exploit that? It was all, of course, done in the hopeless effort to blame his beliefs on the ghost of his father, to excuse his deceptions on account of lofty aims, and to explain his sure and calamitous demotion to his mom.

Analogies occurred to him that happily drew the mantle of malfeasance over others. For instance—if Mr. Mallory, the mountaineer (Joseph thought he might argue), had not belonged to the right clubs; if Mr. Mallory had not been schooled by pros; if Mr. Mallory had not made many preparatory climbs, defeating the most arduous Alpine peaks many times; if Mr. Mallory had instead used the wrong gear, unsportsmanlike aids, an ill-chosen route, and had made his ascent at the worst time of year; if Mr. Mallory had selected an inept partner in place of the redoubtable Andrew Irvine; if Mr. George Herbert Leigh Mallory had had fewer names; if Mr. Mallory had simply walked up one afternoon on his own despite the icefalls and blizzards that beset him: could the envious, quite in the face of these facts, deny that Mr. Mallory was at least a Climber deserving of a middle C, especially at the moment he stood in triumph on top of Everest where his heart would surely be heard when it howled at heaven, though, if truth be told, he was not one of the finer sort, a member of the best set. Would he still be unworthy of the honor due his feat if he were not one of the finer sort then, a member of the best set? should he not be warmed with admiration upon his descent despite not being one of the finer sort, a member of the best set? and his frosted face thawed by remedial ceremonies, although they'd have to be performed for someone not yet, not ever, one of the finer sort, a member of the best set? because he had achieved the peak; he had put his small flag in the obdurate ice; he had bested the best; and it would be only for him to say that his ascent had been a stroll in the park, that he had been grossly favored by fortune, and deserved none of his fame.

Of course Joseph Skizzen had not done anything comparable; he had merely obtained a post and eventually a professorship in this insignificant college called Whittlebauer by the dubious means of slightly squinked credentials. Notwithstanding his somewhat inaccurate résumé, he had done his job so decently he was widely admired and asked to piano at commencements, and on patriotic or religious occasions to tickle the ivories; he was also beseeched to speak at various women's clubs, as well as now and then to offer some uplift to the Lions or cause Rotary to revolve; moreover, as a scholar he was held in the highest regard, for it was rumored that his several articles in important journals of music might be collected and published as a book, putting him high on the local hill of achievement from which there were naturally many who would be happy to watch him tumble, or even discreetly offer to push a bit if he seemed promisingly close to an edge.

Mallory died, they'd say, so we don't know and cannot judge of his success.

Well, after achieving the peak, he climbed the skies.

And he is now the Man in the Moon, are we to suppose? Skizzen heard them reply . . . heard them reply . . . heard an echo among the mountains.

How happy the faculty and their dean had been when he had come to Whittlebauer as a young Turk, bringing to their small puddle, if not a large frog (such as Joseph Skizzen could have been had he puffed himself), then at least someone with news of the musical world (for instance, of Arnold Schoenberg, whose daffy ideas were all the rage). These notions might be tipsy-turvy to Skizzen's two new colleagues, Morton Rinse and Clarence Carfagno, but even they had to be happy at the school's hiring a young man already proficient in six instruments, learned in musical history, an Austrian actually, and with enviable experience in the classroom as well as someone with solid publishing promise.

There are few faculties, especially those of any college with a religious affiliation or one located in some dime-sized Toonerville, that honestly desire to hire staff whose degrees are more esteemed than their own or whose skills are likely to be more proficient than theirs or whose reputations may cast any kind of shadow, even though their protestations while serving on the search committee will conceal (without success) their fears and their intentions. In solemn session, behind fiercely cherished closed doors, they will find faults—with any candidate who is forced on their attention—cracks so minute only the eyes of a smidge could see them; they will be unsure of the lady's suitability (she will be too young or too old, too homely or too pretty—she'll be married in a minute, knocked up within a week, and borne off by her husband to hostess tea parties in Shaker Heights); or they'll be smugly undecided about where the new fellow will be in his work twenty years hence (is there any honest future in Willa Cather studies?); they will wave the flag OVERQUALIFIED like a military banner, be convinced the spouse will hate the school, his neighbors, and the town, and that both will gallop to greener pastures before a year is out, citing several precedents such as Professor Devise and his titillating daughter; they will be disturbed by what seems to be an absence of the proper faith in Mr. Brightboy's background and be instead rather high on Mr. Dimbulb, whose dossier is superlative and whose letters, especially the one from Professor Dormouse, incline their fog to drift in the pip-squeak's direction.

In private they will wonder why anyone with Mr. Brightboy's highfalutin Ivy degree would want to live in Meager, Pennsylvania, a.k.a. Woodbine, Ohio, or why such a hotshot is even bothering with them, or why she is or he isn't married. Minority people are certainly a priority, but how will this guy, black as a burnt match, his wife, and three kids make out in a farm-fed white-bread town? They do tend to marry young, don't they? After which the men abandon the family and disappear.

At Whittlebauer, for the above reasons, the president had taken over hiring. Even the janitors and the secretaries. The librarian, the bursar, and the registrar. The groundskeeper. The nurse. President Palfrey, former head of history at Hiram State Junior College, who had held a degree from Yale like a sandwich board in front of him for so long his nickname was "the End of New Haven Is at Hand," actually wanted to attract the best people possible, assuming they weren't remotely near his former field of competence; but he was hampered by the fact that the college gave minimal benefits and minuscule salaries; took notice of attendance at church; prohibited alcohol not only to its students but forbade it to faculty living within a fifty-mile radius; regarded smoking, card playing, and nonconjugal intercourse as subversive character flaws; certainly was not, as its president put it, "a dell for the frolic of fairies"; and could offer only such cultural excitement as the community of Whittlebauer provided, which was the county fair that yearly featured harness racing, hog calling, bake-offs, sheepherding, pie, jam, and livestock judging, bottle knocking, and the ring toss, as well as pony rides during the whole second week of October.

One-half of the student body—perhaps one might call it the upper half—was too devout to be taught; their minds were safe behind a moat of tradition; and the other half had been compelled to come to Whittlebauer by parents, usually alums, who wished to protect their children from the temptations of the world or, at worst, were trusting the college to reform, rewash, and restore these wayward children to their parents in a condition as swaddle soft and blameless as they were when babes. Of the holy half, the upper quarter disdained the delinquents and held themselves aloof, while the lower quarter was energized by missionary zeal and sought to save the sinners from themselves. When it came to the bottom of this body, a quarter of the forlorn were morose and otherwise indifferent, serving time like convicts made of solid sullen stuff, but there was a coven of Satanists—in effect—who loved nothing more than the seduction of the innocent and the soiling of the pure, through patty-cake and pot, mostly, not certainly by means of unsettling research, offbeat scholarship, or heretical thought. In short: the hoity-toity, the condescending, the morose, and the mischievous made up the student body.

This division, Joseph would eventually discover, was universal among men: the snooty upper crust, the missionaries in the middle, the downtrodden, and the criminals. There remained only people like himself—floaters, like those dots before the eye—much in the minority, who could be found, momentarily, anywhere, who seemed to signify a problem but who could not be pinned down and were eventually ignored.

The aforesaid president of the school was a jowl-shaking enthusiast and mother's boy whose specialty was the cultivation of a secularized piety more sugary than any breakfast bun. His name was Howard Palfrey, and he forgave everyone everything, moist-eyed and caring, his voice afalter with feeling—mostly that of awe for the blessed of God or, conversely, pity for the piss-poor—and projecting, especially through his vowels, if not much sense, at least sincerity. The ditherers adored him; the sanctimonious wanted to wash his feet; but Palfrey was too modest and too cautious to allow it, consequently the fawners were permitted to fawn a few at a time and always head high, with cheek pecks, because Palfrey's handshake was infrequent, woeful, and wet. A bachelor, he exuded need; he called for care: the inept shambly neatness of his clothing begged for a presser for his pants crease, a starcher for his shirt collar, a knotter for his tie's bows, and for his sock holes, frayed cuffs, and sweater ravelings, he wanted a knitter whose needles were calming, quick, and restorative.

Howard Palfrey loved sinners, he loved their pitiful state; he sorrowed for them; he was sensitive, supportive, and sweet. Except when sin showed up in his students, who were to be steadfastly righteous or please him by leaving with all dispatch for the Ivy League's devilish teachings and fleshy corruptions, an option he liked to believe was real from janitor to provost, not excluding himself, who could have been head of Harvard had he not chosen his present humbler and purer service. Businessmen, who privately thought him a fruit, saw what a success he was at drawing to his side widows still sanctified by their grief—women who, as he wept for their loss, he knew had wills he might rewrite and would, after a wait neither too long nor too arduous, be pleased, for the school's sake, to execute.

He cast a spelll upon them, rattled their old bones, gave them leave to practice the safest sort of sex, the imaginary: Palfrey as the secret seducer in senility's lascivious dreams. Joseph had laughed to see his additional *l,* for it was just right—Howard cast a spelll.

But he had never entranced Professor Skizzen, not even after promoting Skizzen to the chairmanship of a music department no larger or more distinguished than a trio of cacophonists. There was Morton Rinse, who played numerous wind instruments indifferently well—piccolo, fife, flute, and clarinet—Clarence Carfagno, who was the string man but did not pluck—neither harp nor harpsichord—and Joseph Skizzen, thought to be at his best with band music transcribed for a keyboard, who played the national anthem, the Grand March from *Aida,* and the school's alma mater at various academic functions, as well as, in secret, with affecting hesitation, some of Liszt's Mozart and Bellini transcriptions.

Morton Rinse had impressed Skizzen with his wit and way with words during the first weeks of Joseph's howdydos. Morton offered the following judgment of the skills of Clarence Carfagno as a musician: Clare has three quarts of vinegar in his basement, so he calls himself a wine merchant. Of the cantankerous schooner-shaped librarian, Hazel Hazlet, Morton observed that her very face was a breach of the peace. If not the most politic of things to say to a newcomer about some of those to whom he has newly come, Skizzen thought them shrewd as far as he could tell, and cattily put. Rinse had a reassuringly jaundiced view of the world—he wore, he said, liver-colored glasses. Actually, he wore worsteds and wide ties and showed far too much cuff.

Morton was as thin as his flute and seemed shiny, as though he had had his chin and cheekbones polished. Not only did he have a characterization for every colleague, he believed data were trumps and delivered obscure information as if he were betraying secrets, not quite in a holy whisper but in a slightly lowered voice, *entre nous.* The best time to visit Haigerloch is at Whitsun when the lilacs are in flower. He would then put on an expectant look as if awaiting confirmation or enlargement. Naturally Rinse could recite the names of all the antique instruments. To Joseph's considerable surprise and subsequent consternation, he knew who had established the two-hand-and-foot "sock" style on the hi-hat cymbal. He also appeared to be a specialist on the size, age, and quality of German organs and organ lofts and assumed that, since Joseph had played that instrument at his school, he would be eager to know details an ant might overlook if, as it always turned out, he wasn't familiar with them already. My God, Skizzen thought, am I to pass my life among this lot?

Most of the rest of it, yes . . . most of the rest was the right answer. Nor, at this time, did Joseph know that Morton Rinse professed to be an amateur magician. The high point of his party performance was to play the violin with his tie. My God, Joseph would say to Miriam, am I to pass my life among this lot?

Yet it was true that when he had first arrived and had begun to settle in, his colleagues had been kind and friendly; he had listened to a little history on the width of railroad ties from his newfound friend Professor Rinse, who also knew what kind of clinkers bedded best and where they came from. Moreover, Professor Carfagno—who, with Rinse, had to endure a great deal of name play and consequently brought forward the figure of Castle Cairfill out of the haze of history to which he had been insufficiently consigned—Professor Carfagno seemed most attentive to Joseph, almost, it might have been fair to say, hanging on Joseph's every word, and naturally this was flattering to a new recruit who saw everyone as a likely top sergeant, especially since he was fearful of being found out. They will know immediately, he felt. They will see the way I walk, and know. They will listen to me answer even an idle question, and know. They will trip me up without trying, licensed (as they all are) from tony schools far away; and his musical colleagues will be phenomenal prodigies, play rings around him, sight-read, have scores by the score shelved in their heads; and they will know. Instantly.

Actually it took them four decades. In the meantime, Clarence Carfagno died. A few others moved on. A number retired. The bleak sentence appeared. It became a yearly habit for a dozen datura to bloom and fill the south porch with their languishing flutes and heavy scent. The yew hedge grew. Nita disappeared behind her shrubbery.

Of course when a wit is witty at another's expense, you must wonder when the wit will be at yours. After rinse came wring. And the devotions of Carfagno were those of a cultural toady, me-too, and mimic. If Skizzen indiscreetly professed a fondness for Berlioz, Clare boned up on bios, suggested recordings released that morning or those that were impressively out of press, would suddenly observe that "Au Cimetière" was really written for a tenor; and if you admired an article on "The Pines of Rome," as unlikely as that might seem, he would be around next day with his annotations. Skizzen had hardly defined himself in terms of his own preferences before Carfagno had made these choices his—except that Clare's announcement of them was a lot louder. So Skizzen said he loved Delius and watched his tormentor consume the Englishman's drizzly confections instead of preempting one of Skizzen's real passions.

During former times, when he and Miriam regularly had dinner together, he would bring up his disappointments, but she was never helpful, only forceful, chewing while she still had a mouthful of advice.

Professor Joseph Skizzen had a number of worries, chief of which was the fear that the human race might yet survive, a concern that had supplanted his previous wish that they might perish well past toenails, hair, and bones.

You have to listen harder than the jokes, Joey, his mother would admonish, and look where they pop from, and hear what the joker says when he jokes, not what the joke says when it's said. You are so smart it makes them shiver in their skeletons when they see your smartness dressed for a party. So don't tremble to them. They get brittle in their brains and fend you off with obscure facts and lapdog loyalty and such. Was it the width of the Thames at the Tower that the silly man wanted to show off about? Think how it must feel for them to have to study up a book just to tap-dance past your mastery of music one more time. You are a Schoenbuggy man, and who knows he but you?

That's why Skizzen had chosen Uncle Arnold in the first place. To be his trophy wife. In a faculty such as the one Skizzen was likely to find at Whittlebauer, Schoenberg's fearful name would be known, but not his music, the techniques of his teaching, or the import of his ideas. However, there were other reasons: not only was Skizzen now an Austrian, his life's loyalties, if musically inverted, matched the strategies Joey's father had set for his son, inasmuch as Schoenberg was a chameleon who had been born a Jew yet brought up a Catholic in a Vienna crowded with folks devoted to their beads. At eighteen, out of typical teenage rebelliousness, Skizzen supposed, Schoenberg turned himself into a Protestant, not the best way of leveling the path of one's life, but splendid as a punch-in-the-eye for Mom and Pop and the smug burger-coffeehouse bunch—if they cared. Many years later, when Hitler came to power and Schoenberg was dismissed from his post in Berlin, he reclaimed the Jew the Nazis knew he was and fled to the United States—to teach in LA alongside other exiles—Adorno, Brecht, and Mann—and live in a yarded white stucco mini-manor in Brentwood with a small house for his setter built behind it and an Irish dog inside.

Joey felt his father felt—in the thirties waiting for catastrophe—the way Vienna felt to its artists and writers in the century's early years, waiting for catastrophe, too—loathing the city as Karl Kraus did and fearing war, or bored with the *Zeit*'s complacent *Geist* as Georg Heym was, who wanted the greasy peace to end and welcomed strife and chaos that would clean the sewers and give swift passage to the shit of life. Sharing Karl Kraus's apprehensions gave his father's cheap violining a little class and his motives, so mysterious, some respect. Nita said his father said he smelled the carnage coming. Musil smelled it. And I smell it now, Joey told his mother. Ach, it's my manure, she laughed, showing him her hands.

A man, Miriam said, should change his coat, if he must, only to do the world's business, not for his family or for his friends to whom he is fastened by feeling. That is not so easy to do, Joseph answered, because she was actually asking a question. Hard or not, that's what Rudi ought to have done. Ought, Joey exclaimed. Ought? You, too, don't forget, Mother, were supposed to be as converted as Rudi was—Joey laughed because he needed the practice—you were supposed to be a newly pregnant Jewish mother. But I was the same, Miriam insisted, the same, the same, all Rudi did was change my name—and even then only my name when it was written, not when I heard it spoken to me, not when I thought about myself, not when I remembered my life or his once or twice tenderness to me concerning which I say no more, no more, no more, because, though I now stand silent, I stand on my own path, amid my own rocks and grass, my tears do not spill from a false face, and I do not get my flushed forehead from a paint box but from kneeling on the ground.

At first Professor Skizzen thought the world would not put up with our monkeyshines for another hundred years and would throw mankind aside as a mistake the way it had so many other species, a rejection we no doubt deserved; but now he feared for the world—a world that was alone in the universe as far as he knew—the only earth—which he cared for more than he cared for himself.

10

Augsburg Community College was not a community college. It received no support from either state or city. Its misleading name came from a settlement called the Augsburg Community, a Utopian farm founded in 1822 by some heretical Lutherans most of whom ran away like unhappy slaves within the founding year, leaving two buildings and a few inadequately fenced fields. Utopia had not lasted long enough to fail or allow its tenants time to grow at least an imposing pumpkin. Two families remained behind, hoeing a plot, scavenging berries, and feeling more like squatters than founders. Much is made, in the history of the school, of the early struggles and the eventual success of these sweaty settlers. God smiled upon them, and they built a stone barn. God smiled again, and up went a spire. The two farms became four, ten families turned into a town, and the town, before everything fell down, became a college—the town square the college quad, the stone barn a dorm. There were more reassuring miracles here than Jesus had performed, not excluding Lazarus or the baking of loaves and the seining of fishes.

For a brief spell it served as a finishing school for milkmaids and put the name AUGSBURG ACADEMY on stationery it could scarcely afford. On warm days girls, aspiring to be ladies, in flowing white garments, could be seen dotting the lawns with sketch pads and easels. Local youths liked to imagine the academy was a huge whorehouse where every attending girl was free, easy, and scrumptious. To support this myth, they made up others, relating stories of fleshy revels that everyone enjoyed though no one bothered to believe. The faculty comprised old men whose privates were presumed to be long past erection and maiden aunts whose charges had died and left them unemployed. The academy's sole published catalog began, "In a quiet sylvan environment" and bragged that in its precincts even the offspring of deer were safe. All that remained, now, of those daisy days were a few signs, one in a parking lot, another, directional, toward a stream that had dried up, and a third, partly hidden by shrubs, that read, confusingly, AUGSBURG COMMUNITY ACADEMY. After a short time the finishing school returned to Lutheran arms and virtue's camp where no one gave its coeds the compliment of slander.

Augsburg Community College did not pay its students for their chores. If you clerked in the bookstore, mowed the lawn, or washed the dinner trays, you might get a break on your board bill or free books in exchange, a slight reduction in your tuition, a cut in your room rent, or, more likely, a waiver of student fees. Joey hoped to get out of phys ed, but he couldn't cut a deal. We've given you a room, that should be quite enough, he was rather severely told. He didn't know America that well, and at first accepted the system as standard, only to find out later how unusual it was to have half the student body on work-study, which included painting, sweeping, and tuck-pointing. An answer to the question, What's your major? might be Latin and lawn care. Augsburg, Joey decided, was either a very progressive artsy-craftsy school or a license-plate prison.

So he never had any money to speak of and was living, in consequence, a good Lutheran life. His innocence forbade him to notice how often the poorer pupils augmented (only they called it Augsburging) their income by doing favors for those better off, another clever way Augsburg had of readying its students for the world. Some stole exams; some altered records; some sold sections of themselves for sex; some swiped candy from the commissary. Joey thought he was being original, acting like a criminal, when he slipped a few small packages of flower seeds from the groundskeeper's shed; easy enough to do, the door was often open, and guarding a few ageratum packets was no one's urgency.

Joey didn't know which to feel worse about—his empty pockets or his criminal pursuit—but he needed a token gift for his mother's birthday, and he was confident a few small packages of seed would not be missed. Untutored pilferator that he was, he did not consider that the seeds could be out of spritz and as old as Nita's memories. His gift was meager, his mother forgave him that (there were exactly half-a-dozen common annuals, all edgers); it was also a surprise to her habits, since she had shown no interest in either their dismal yard or absent garden; but she understood her son's circumstances and did appreciate the gesture the way the cliché said she should, so she let only her eyebrows rise when she undid the thin green string and pressed flat its flimsy wrapping. The seeds went in a dresser drawer where, if they were lifeless, they grew even more inanimate.

Among the flaws in Joey's character, which, at this age, he was quick to reveal, was his adolescent's demand for praise and reassurance before doing anything more meritorious than exist. Everyone he knew was as stupid as a brick, and he pitied his plight: that he had to pretend to be another brick packed in a stack stuck among them.

Joey practiced keening on the organ—faithfully, which meant religiously—and tried to carry away a few things from his classes; but his teachers were largely wizened one-note relics from the bottom of the barrel, bent by holy poses into zeros. He believed that the world despised them whenever it thought about thinking of them at all; they despised one another; mostly they despised themselves. They were noticed because they were so unremarkable, and this Joey took note of: do not fall so low as to be treadable, because people tend to watch where they step, curse when they stumble, and tromp upon supines and other grovelers. Never fail, merely pass. Slip by. Don't miss the class photo but, if short, find a place in the middle of the back row. However, he did learn from the texts each course required—even the shabby ones, used ones, out-of-date ones, boring ones, schoolbookish, double-columned ones with dictionary-sized archival photos spotted about like illustrations of things no longer made and for uses no longer remembered—he learned not to highlight every other line or deface margins with doodles or smart remarks, dog-ear pages or enlist a paper clip or rubber band to do the work of a ribbon, because these practices reduced the books' resale value. And you would never have any further use for *Amo Amas Amat,* the Latin first reader, or *A Concise History of Lutheran Thought,* required for all students, or *Biology for Believers,* a junior elective. Copies circled endlessly like stratospheric trash.

Madame Mieux's laughter preceded her like a warning siren. She taught French in a loud raucous voice that went with that language as smoothly as wool with silk, though her gutturals were okay and her *r*'s rolled like dice. Madame Mieux had breasts, and breasts bothered Joey. He preferred them hidden under clothes that billowed. Madame Mieux used makeup, and that was disapproved of; she wore tight skirts, and that was frowned on; she hennaed her hair in a style she said was à la française, and that was widely thought vulgar; she collected bracelets on her wrists, and that was deemed tasteless; she hobbled about on open-toed high heels that made her look ridiculous; she put her hand on your arm when she spoke, her eyes widened as if to swallow your ears; and her accent was so fraudulent as to mock your meager understanding of *la patrie* and *la parole.*

She appeared to take a fancy to Joey, who had initially enrolled in *enfant* French in order to avoid Latin for at least another semester. He was told that Latin would help his English, but it was Latin that was dead. German was the other tongue that the academy was prepared to make you wag with some proficiency, but when, during his application interview, he saw that knowledge of German was, in his case, assumed, he kept contentedly quiet and let them believe what he had only let on. It was a technique he would perfect. So to graduate he had to have French. Madame Mieux was a spilling handful, however, and he began to have doubts that he would make it. At first Joey appreciated her apparently genuine vulgarity in such a crowd of stodges. As it proved, she was a deceiver, too. She came from some coarse place in New York City; she was an old maid and not an old madame; her hair wasn't hennaed, she wore a red wig; and she yelled in her classes and stood close to talk because she was hard of hearing. Every student of hers eventually discovered these things—it was what they learned.

However, in addition, Joey acquired this: among Madame Mieux's affectations was a love of French music, and indeed she could do a good imitation of Edith Piaf growling the verses of "La Vie en Rose." One day, on a portable player that Mr. Hirk would have listened to without complaint, she played for the class a song by Hector Berlioz. Listen to the diction, she admonished them. The song was called "Absence" and was sung by Eleanor Stebber, of whom Joey had dimly heard. Now he understood what was meant by "the long line." He was transfixed. Here was a purity, a beauty, of which he knew too little to dream.

The rows of impassive faces alongside him—listening to the diction, he supposed—made him realize how lucky he was that he could hear what was being sung and how unlucky he was that he could neither sing nor write nor critique but simply be moved by this poignant work whose words he understood only through the sound of the song itself, having let his attention to the diction slip. It was his solace, his secret delight, his cherished difference, and because his expression was probably as wooden as the others', his response was as hidden as a bee in a blossom. Yet Madame Mieux had caught something. Her quest for a protégé had sharpened her faculties. She had seen light like the shadow of a cloud cross his face. It was no doubt on account of the diction.

When the song was over, she said to the class: This lady was born in Wheeling, West Virginia. If she can speak French, so can you. Wheeling, West Virginia, Joey thought, running the words back and forth between his ears, what a paradisal place the name must designate. A number of years had to be disposed of before Joey discovered that the divine singer was Eleanor Steber, pronounced "Steeber," not the Stebber of Madame Mieux's mangling. Marcella Sembrich, Eleanor Steber: worth a caress.

Madame Mieux scribbled a note to Joey on one of his examination papers. It was a vapid vocabulary and conjugation test that she had decided to award a C even though a minus should have been added—her note said. Your classroom demeanor shows promise, she wrote, beginning to pencil her observation in French, a gesture that she then thought better of and crossed out. Joey knew what "demeanor" meant. It meant she had designs. Had she, in class, been more properly dressed, this thought would not have crossed his mind, for he was not vain about his person or interested in hers. She asked Joey to fetch books from the library for her. Delivering them to her office, he was requested to fill a vase with water from the bubbler in the hall to refresh a few flowers she was rearranging. At receipt of them she grabbed him and delivered a peck to each cheek. She saw how red her busses left him, and this encouraged her. See you in class, she said to his retreating back in a tone she usually reserved for speaking to her cat. An angora, it lay its swollen body down to sleep in a basket that Madame Mieux parked on the windowsill in her office. There it could look out without opening its eyes.

Sundays he would sometimes hitch a ride into town to see his mother. They'd have dinner together and chat. Miriam would tend to fall into reminiscence if Joey did not keep his hold firmly on their present life. Madame Mieux was useful for that. As Madame was presented to her, Miriam could only be amused, and she asked detailed questions about the teacher's dress, questions that sharpened Joey's eye for such things. Miriam concluded that Madame Mieux favored autumnal colors—rust, plum, ocher, tan, mauve—because they complimented her henna dye job. Miriam, whose hair had been jet as a Jew, and blond when English, insisted that, though it was true that Europeans, the French in sad particular, used henna as if it were soap, nothing whatever went with it but the dance hall.

And Miriam wanted to know what the flowers were, and was the vase nice? However, Joey had not done his homework. He had paid no attention, disappointing still one more expectation. Well, it's better to have your teacher sweet on you than you sweet on your teacher. Maybe you can get a B out of her. Joey wondered—not aloud—what it would take to reach an A. Nor did he say he didn't want a B, because that would relight an old argument. His mother did not understand her son's preference for mediocrity. At first she thought he must be basically a plodder and was pretending to be aiming at what he couldn't miss. It's smart to want to be dumb if dumb is all you can do, she said, but where was his ambition? where was his pride? how did he feel when Debbie brought home Bs? and was so bubbly inside when he was so sober? because she did dates and all the things that teensters were supposed to do—examined herself in all the mirrors, felt wounded by the wind, would sulk in her room if the phone that rang wasn't ringing for her, loved the drumstrum music kids liked at her age . . . while Joey's lugubrious preferences were for distant English horns or Saturday orgies at the opera . . . at least a little *Fledermaus,* Miriam thought, a bit of *Gypsy Baron,* would be a relief.

Madame Mieux was hard to pin down, and Joey appreciated that. Her name wasn't her name, her hair wasn't her hair, her cat was on loan, her house was a rent, the flowers in her little vase would die, not to be replaced, and her knowledge of French was suspicious. The difficulty? she was now defined by these deceptions. Her love of music appeared to be genuine, although Joey gradually realized that all the composers she was possibly pretending to admire were French: Berlioz foremostly, Erik Satie had surprised Joey by turning up, Debussy and Rameau, Gabriel Fauré. Fauré? Then he made a mistake. He was young and new at the game that, on this occasion, was his Hide and her Seek. He made a mistake. He told Madame Mieux that he had begun reading Berlioz whom he understood had quite a reputation as a writer. On the alleged basis of that encouragement, he was invited to Madame Mieux's house to listen to music. There would be a sofa and sweets, he suspected, but a better Victrola than Mr. Hirk had. She promised him Berlioz—a trombone concerto. What could that be? He made a mistake. He accepted her invitation. And on the appointed night, he went.

Joey rang the bell and was startled to hear her laughter enlarging as she approached the door. She seemed ever so short and was dressed in a fulsome robe. Her head wore mist like a mountain. The smoke smelled sweet. In order to get in—Come in, she'd commanded—he had to squeeze by a deep loopy sleeve and avoid the red end of her cigarette. Smoking was frowned upon at Augsburg. It was spring, so she didn't have to take his coat. He saw a rose-colored room. There were pillows everywhere. Piles of pillows that glistened or glittered. Little pillows. Large fat smothery pillows. Paunchy pillows. Pillows with hortatory mottoes. Joey swallowed his own laugh—one of apprehension. He thought maybe a nearby pile was heaped upon one of those currently popular beanbag chairs, but it was pillows, all pillows. None of them, as far as he could see, were bed pillows, but they did feel as much at home as they would in a boudoir. There were pillows with tassels; there were scalloped pillows; there were embroidered pillows; there were patchwork pillows. There were round, rectangular, three-pointed, long, flat, cubular pillows. He followed a path to the center of the room and slowly turned to see where he might go next. Make yourself comfy, he couldn't believe she said. The lid from a large tin lay on the floor in the middle of a barren moment. It bore a drink and received ash as if there would be anything left of Madame Mieux's roach but the afterglow. Where, Joey wondered. Anywhere, she said, and flung herself down in front of him as far as her brief length would. In a mirror Joey saw her burnt head floating above a sea of cloth.

On the walk where he had fled Joey tried to draw air from the stars, his ribs closing on his lungs like the doors of a cage. He realized already that he was not embarrassed or repulsed, he was terrified, and that terror was not the appropriate response: amusement maybe, disdain perhaps, a sense of superiority or a feeling of pity: any one of these might have saved the situation. Instead, he had humiliated himself, fleeing from Madame Mieux's pillow party. But it was iniquity's den. And she was the den's mother.

11

Mother . . . (a formal address for a serious subject) . . . Mother, perhaps my father was a 'fraidycat.

He was brave enough to risk England.

He was just fleeing from the Nazis.

Your father was a good Austrian; he had nothing to fear from the Nazis.

Then he had no reason to skelter away to England.

If you do something without good reason, Joey, does that make you feig?

I guess it's what you run from without a good reason. My father said he was avoiding evil by shunning the wicked—always a good reason.

No, Joey, sometimes you have to confront crooks with their crookedness.

It didn't do, did it? to confront Nazis.

Nazis? no . . . but your father only claimed—aloud and at length—he claimed that the fruit of fascism would poison its tree and that the roots of such a tree would contaminate the earth and that the evilized earth would seep through our boots and travel up our legs and—well—damage our desires, curdle our blood, and beat out our brains, but saying so doesn't print it in the paper; he just said that: said it—said it—louder didn't improven the noise—he couldn't know he was right at least as far as the roots—their poison—went; how could anyone know such a thing, how could anyone even guess? he invented it—the danger like the lightbulb—even if it would become—okay—sort of true eventually on account of Austria's bad luck in living nearby Germans; he pretended to see dark clouds, and if it rained like he said it would, if it came down as it did sometimes at home in strings, even if the ground drowned, it wouldn't change the fact that he imagined clouds before there were real ones.

Maybe my father had foresight; didn't he say so?

Say so—*sie sagen*—say so—is say so, so? no, Joey, his foresight was a boast like the butt of a nanny.

Mother, maybe getting out of a bad place isn't such a bad idea and can't be called cowardly—careful at worst, prudent perhaps.

He didn't take me out of a bad place, Joey, he took me out of my homeland and lovehouse and marched me off to war; we went where the bombs would be; where we—I include you—would see people burned—skin and bones, worst of all, hair, like celluloid, nails; where only cats had the sense and slither to be safe.

I want to think my father ran away from more than blame, Mother; that he tried to do no harm when harm was a universal habit.

He harmed you, didn't he? We lived on water for weeks, maybe you were too young to remember—just as well—and slept in the same clothes the livelong day, day in and day out, as if they covered us like bark; and he hurt your sister, holding her so hard when we sat in—what in hebe do they say?—the Tube, adding our stink to the stink of the sewer, to the smell of other smellers; and the bricks shook from the bombs, and the lights dimmed from the bombs, and people screamed or fainted, fearing to die in the middle of their complaints as if their complaints were dinner.

But Father thought, I imagine, that London would be a safe and civilized place, that England would be accommodating and out of the reach of brutes; he couldn't know that bombs would follow and fall upon you.

Where was his foresight then, Joey, where was all of that moral wisdom he was full of when it was really needed for his family? Didn't he know—he was just a fiddle-playing fellow—didn't he know that trouble follows and falls upon Jews, that as soon as he pinned that silly hat to his hair the cooties were collecting? Jews are the wind that lets evil in; Jews have brought damn bad luck from the beginning because they crucified Jesus, not a chance for them after that.

Mother, you and Father weren't Jews for very long.

Rudi was denounced, that's why we weren't Jews for very long.

But he never planned to stay Jewish, to . . .

He wanted me to wear a wig, to call myself Miriam . . .

You still do—call yourself Miriam.

The USA, too, they preferred us as Jews; they wanted no Austrians in their country; they processed us the way I box up rubber dishpans.

It isn't so bad here, is it? decent enough?

My hometown town was a town; there were mountains, a river, good bread; these towns are chicken coops; these towns are slower than ooze; they have no inner character.

You mean no binding beliefs, Mother, don't you?

No binding beliefs, that's right.

Just like parochial Catholicism, Mother, like anti-Semitism, Mother—they bind more than sheaves.

Joey, you are American and have no convictions.

I was almost arrested.

But not convicted.

I was blamed. A blame not unremembered, Mother. Anyway, Joey said, it's the binding I can't bear—the joining, the brotherly embrace—because if one anti-Semite is a curiosity, three in a room are a zoo, and any more than that are a plague.

Joey, what do you see in Jews they shouldn't be singled out?

Not any more than in anybody.

Still, she said, someone should be singled out.

Then let it be your Jesus. He wanted to be singled out.

Ach, you have gone so far to the bad in your beliefs . . .

In my disbeliefs, dear, little and light like puffballs from the cotton trees.

Dandelions, you mean, Miriam said with satisfaction, and they're weeds.

So, Mother, why do you think he left us?

For none of the usual reasons.

You mean he didn't leave us for a woman?

Not for a woman, not for a life of crime, not for freedom from his duties.

You're sure?

He wasn't a man's man or a ladies' man; he was a soft sweet steady man; we held hands; he didn't walk fast; a lot of the time he smelled of ink, not bad; but then he changed, became an actor on the stage; we weren't who we'd been to him, or he to us either, because he became afraid, and we were safe in the theater, maybe, he thought, because the audience was going to play out the tragedy, not the actors; anyway, we were better off being somebody else—imagine, Joey—being somebody else.

Maybe, Mother, it was money.

Gelt? why?

I mean, maybe he was ready to go off a lot of times, just as he left your land for England it seemed all of a sudden, but maybe, the way he thought about it, it had been in his mind for months or years, he just hadn't known what to do till he found out how the Jews were leaving, and maybe he took us with him because at first when the wanderlust overwhelmed him he didn't know it was so private a feeling, so personal a journey; he didn't know that taking us made his hope impossible to realize like trying to fashion a fresh look to surprise a mirror while still wearing the same old hat and coat; so naturally when he ran away to England he took us with him only to find out after he'd been there awhile that it was the family all along he was running from, not Jew haters, not Germans, but the hat, the scarf, the dog, the coat, the sound of some voices—you know—always there, the same voices saying the same things in his ear, maybe, and then money all of a sudden came along, fit in his pocket like a bar of candy, so he could completely and entirely go, do what he'd always wanted to do, leave his self behind like a footprint in the snow . . . where they have real snow . . . in Austria.

Miriam sat with her arms over her eyes, the worse to see the world, the better to see the past.

Your father didn't leave you, Joey, or your sister either; he left me, left me and my soap smell, just because he was unhappy with himself, sleeping, eating with a disinfector, working at a stupid lowlife job with lowlifes coming and going in and out of his own lowlife life, nothing to go to work for, nothing to brag about to the boys, nothing to come home to but a sterilized room in a cinder-block building near a neighborhood where he'd be snubbed every day he was seen, a no-account squalorman himself because he worked in a betting parlor, and lowlife, too, because of me, a laundry lady, the lowest of life, washing dirt off the dirty drawers of dirty people, tired in our legs and in our hearts, when he knew, Joey, what he'd done, how he'd pulled us up out of our own earth so that now we had nowhere to grow, nowhere to flourish, losing our looks, our youth, our energies, our dreams, for nothing, in order to live in other people's catastrophes as if they were summer camps for the city poor.

Guilt is very Jewish, Mother.

Die Schuld . . . no . . . not me . . . now Jews do nasty naughty things and are as black with *Schuld* as a stove with soot and still go on burning with their business as if they had no more breast to beat. The guilt goes up the flue. *Schuld* bore your father down, Joey, I could see his knees in a bend like an old bow that can't return to straight, nor did I help him with his load because I added to it every day, I complained whenever I saw him, back turned or not, dressed or not, asleep or not, I said I am not a Jew, Rudi, I want to go back to Graz, the war is over, there's no reason to remain here, in this country where people ski down the slopes of their noses, in this ruin of a city, in this mountainless town where every window's broken and they boil only big roots.

How could Father disappear so . . . like a smoked cigar?

Your father didn't smoke, Joey, he was a good man in his habits, he didn't overdrink either, or pinch bottoms.

He gambled.

Oh, that was a shock, when they told me, because he never bet even on a fight among roosters.

Well, he bet on the ponies one time, Mother—and won—it must have felt as though he'd been touched by the gods.

He never said a word, he never showed me a happy face, all that time while he must have been waiting for his forgers to forge a passport for him, steal a vehicle permit, make a birth avowal—whatever it was, his money, his winnings—what do they say?—burning a hole in his socks, he never let on to anybody that he'd bet or, having bet, that he'd won, or having won that he was going to leave us like we were not people but a place, like Graz, an embarrassment to him—old ways, old folks, old days—those of us he'd said he loved and held tight in a dark Tube—a cellar that shook as if it were solid but not solid enough—a piece of us broke off like shaken brick—he wasn't solid enough—he divided himself from his family and sailed away as if we were the shore and he a so-long ship.

We can't be sure of that, though, Mother.

I should have known, I should have known, because Rudi changed; he, who was soft like a patch of moss, grew hard and harsh as bark; he'd glare at me full of rage all up in his face; not that he ever hit me, but where a smile once went the boils of a pot were; and there was anger also in his throat, his eyes; his eyes never brimmed anymore or went wide to take things in; his silence scared me into silence, too; I couldn't say a clear word.

He changed before he won his bet, you mean, not after?

Rudi thought of himself as a prophet, not as a modest decent printer with a wife who let him do what he wanted with her, to be happy in her arms, and calm after, snoring as softly as a purr.

Father just disappeared, Mother, that's all anyone knows: he was here, he was there, then he was nowhere at all.

They told me—the police did—that he was seen collecting his bet, so we know he had some money on him; then they told me—those detective men—that one of the crooks—those counterfeiters of Canadians the police had taken in—admitted selling Rudi a passport as well as a black-market steamship ticket, and another officer later told the father—

Him?

· about a license, Joey, the father guessed it was, that Rudi had also wanted.

He?

· the holy father, yes, he liked my round face, I think.
· So Rudi had the money, the passport, and the ticket . . . ?
· *Das Gelt—der Passkarte—der Zettel* . . . he had them while he was living with us still and sometimes kissing me on the mouth.

Of course, Mother, the police didn't pursue the matter very energetically, did they?

If there was ever a false-paper man, Rudi was it, or rather Fixel was, the slyboots he became, so of course officialdom did little, after all who were we? unwanted emigrants, driven from our land our living and our loves by **E**vil, **E**vil that couldn't have a capital large enough in father's old print box to stand for it and consequently had to be let in and cared for like a stray font, but then . . . because we were Jews, that is, Persecuted People, and so on, and were bedraggled, misspoken, confused . . . because we were Jews and therefore the subject of jokes and other forms of embarrassed amusement . . .

You were too young, Joey, to ever wonder how much or how little Joseph Skizzen was Yussel Fixel, but it was a lot harder for Trudi Skizzen to become the Dvorah of that name; your sister suffered, I can tell you, having to answer to Deborah Scofield, too, before she came to rest on Debbie Skizzen.

III

Now that she's married to Roger, Mother, she has his name, so she's had to change again.

That's the way it should be, Joey, as it was long ago set down; the one time a woman gained was when she gained a name, just as you will give a girl yours and lighten her load in life, because I know, I have been a girl born Rouse, a wife who was Skizzen, then a widow called Fixel, and I know it is easier, it is better altogether, to be married and settled and fruitful and safe, as the Lord's will is spelled out by the church. Because a girl, Joey, is searching for her real name; the name she is born with is only her maiden name, a name for someone so far unrealized; and I, stupid unfortunate that I am, I thought I had found in Rudi my real name, the name I would lose my flower under, the name I would enable him to pass on through you and you through another—and so and on—it would be proof he was here on this earth and had done God's good bidding; that was my duty and my hope, that the Skizzens would fill out, fatten, and come to be people that would be noticed, that pride could be taken in . . .

When Father took his name away from you, it was like being divorced, wasn't it, Mother? I mean, you were no longer a Skizzen.

Yes . . . yes . . . and I never married Herr Fixel, who was he? had I said vows to him? hung on his words, cooked his food, swept his house, had I? no, I had a stranger in my arms, shaming me in front of my husband.

And you weren't a Rouse either, Mother, because you were no longer a maiden.

Oh, Joey . . . you are making me sadder by the minute.

Debbie married a Boulder.

Shut up, smartie.

Father went to Canada, you think?

He went to hell.

He might have meant to send for us after a bit.

Oh yes, a letter all smoky like ham would arrive to say please join me in the flames; oh sure, many times he told me how he'd won some money, how he'd got a ticket and a passport, and how he'd send for us as soon as he got to Halifax or as soon as he'd found a job or as soon as he'd made a million and had a mansion with a long yard and a dozen dogs; oh sure, I should dream it, of the many times he told me, many times till I got a sore ear from hearing how he'd won some money, how he'd got a ticket, how he had a passport, sure, if he'd done these things he'd certainly tell his wife of them, tell her and tell her till her ear withered at the root, I sure should dream it; so he can't have got to Halifax, can he? he can't have found a job, can he? he can't have made a million, can he? and since he didn't really consult me about calling myself sappy names, wearing a wig, and traipsing to London with nothing but a belly swelling for my luggage, why should he start now by asking me how to spend his winnings—I should dream it—for an instance, to rent an apartment with windows, with a bath, with a pair or three of beds, please, with a stove—that would be nice—with a picture of a town in Austria on one wall? or how about a family rate on train tickets home? sure, I should, I should dream it.

Maybe he didn't want to argue with you, Mother; he knew you'd be upset if he left you with us in London to fend for yourself, and he knew he had only one chance and one ticket . . .

Joey . . . rails ran across France then, rails ran through the mountain passes and through tunnels into and out of the mountains, rails ran along the Mur, through forests of fir trees, because the war was over, the sirens had hoarse throats, all the bombs they'd dropped on one another had gone plode, and so we could have traveled home together, because there were no more warplanes, no more lights fingering the sky, no more Nazis; it was, we used to say when we slunk from our underground huddle, the large lot of us, and looked to see if our rubble was still standing, we used to say that the sirens said—the sirens said, All clear.

12

Although Joey's management of the organ was improving by pipes and bellows, and he had overcome his aversion to the swelling pedal, things were not going well for student Skizzen. He was not performing so badly in the classroom as to be threatened with failure, or acting so mischievously otherwise as to be in danger of expulsion, but—as he dimly feared—he was about to fall from a high pile of pillows. Madame Mieux had let it out that her softpuff collection—whose existence she had kept secret—well, somewhat secret—and whose value she lovingly inflated—had been defiled—that was her word—defiled by a person or persons unknown, though that person—to which persons unknown immediately shrank—would have had to have been a male and was probably a student, most likely a pupil—that was her word—in one of her classes—one for beginners, she let on to an intimate, supposing she had any.

Whispers were the favored mode of this story's transportation, and it was thus innuendoed that some small number of pillows collected by Madame Mieux had been . . . well . . . semenized; thereby desecrating not only those most immediately affected but, in her heart—through her affection for them—the whole lot. There were in the world, she knew, bad boys; but had she harmed any of them? possibly by giving one of them an unacceptable grade? nor did it appear that the soiled cotton silk or satin could be safely or even somewhat successfully dry-cleaned on account of the intimate relation of cover to stuffing prohibiting their dismantlement without considerable damage. Semen stains, some said, were indelible. Certainly irrevocable. And evidence in court. Though Madame Mieux denied it, there were worries that she had been assaulted, even raped, that an assignation had gotten—this part was accompanied by giggles—out of hand, when it was the story itself that was now in a runaway mode: how had the pillows been abused? had she not recognized their attacker? were there reasons why these three or five, pink or violet or puce or candy brown, dinky, medium, or grandiose puffins had been chosen for contamination rather than dozens of others? did a fetishist inhabit the college like the bats they had in the attic of Assembly Hall? or was anyone who collected pillows to be considered similarly afflicted, so that the crime may have been one of passion, pitting a male pillow fetishist against his swansdown-fixated counterpart? was there perhaps a scene stitched, printed, or embroidered on one of them that enticed an attack?

All because of Hector Berlioz and his trombone thing? He should never have gone into the lady's lair, but, after all, he hadn't committed any sort of crime, and he had, readily enough, reversed even his innocent course; he had not, for example, thrown himself onto a heap nearby her recumbent form—he could no longer utter or even think Madame's name—although she had, by her own sprawl, suggested it: Make yourself comfy, hadn't they been the words she'd used? and hadn't the Madame been inhaling weed? the odor in the room wasn't incense, it was what he'd been told was the smell of pot when he'd smelled it on another occasion. She had on her face a large loopy grin and over her arms loopy sleeves and around her torso a loopy wrap, the actual wrap of it a bit loose. So Joey had, quite properly, bolted, hardly inhaling the entire time. There were washes of silk and satin foaming up against the walls. He'd nearly tripped making his way out. Had he fallen he'd have drowned and/or suffocated.

Had he fallen anyway? There were some who wondered about that. Joey began to receive stares, and he felt he might be the subject of unseemly gossip. Perhaps it was his guilty conscience—a condition that exasperated him further because he believed he had done nothing wrong but bolt like a scaredy. He searched his heart for hidden longings and found none. An inventory of his daydreams came up empty. A minor social gaffe should count for nothing, no more than dandruff on the shoulder of a dark suit, and the momentary embarrassment he had suffered should suffice for punishment.

He was, however, haunted by the concerto he hadn't heard. Poking about in a few books turned up nothing by the name "concerto" and nothing that might resemble something written for a band instrument whose social status in the world of instruments stood only a few notes above the saxophone. Had he been conned by Madame, lured into her pillow parlor on altogether false pretenses? In class (classes he now prepared for with sweaty desperation) she was as coolly indifferent as he was, carrying on with the other students in her usual loud and quirky manner, while he continued to ignore his classmates entirely, perhaps maintaining a distance that was more carefully policed, and an atmosphere more densely anxious, than usual.

What he had done, of course, was embarrass Madame M, and Joey was not wholly convinced that she had it coming; perhaps she had been an innocent, too, extending her hospitality to a student, willing to take some of her private time to expand his musical world, only to be rebuffed by his childish flight, and rudely, too, without so much as a lame excuse. Certainly he could not put a word to what he feared was about to happen when he weighed himself upon a pile of pillows beside her, had he done so; nor could he confide the affair to his mother, who might have a description in two languages readily at hand and a willingness to redden his ears with her recital. If his skills in most things were rudimentary, and his knowledge of facts and theories spotty, his acquaintance with such a sordid world was indirect, dim, and skimpy. He had no lengthy register of quirks, for instance, to which he might turn, a catalog of eccentricities in which he might find Joseph Skizzen's reluctance to reveal himself listed alongside men who wore corsets under their suits or women who rolled down mountains of pillows . . . while smoking . . . the forbidden weed. With a groan he curtailed his imagination lest he begin to see Madame's breasts blend into the pile.

Suppose she had said: The pillows are more fun if you're naked.

His first thought had been that Madame had made this foul business up and was, out of revenge, whispering it in Francophile corners; however, it was possible that someone else had actually done the dirty deed, and it was Joey's own ineptness that was making him self-conscious and ashamed. Joey was perhaps not the only student she had lured into her delinquent rooms where she had, after some Debussy, made who knew what sort of indecent proposals, or perhaps the stains on the cushions were the consequence of one such invitation being actually taken up. He drew the curtain on any enactment of that possibility.

Suppose she had said: These pillows have an interesting history.

It came to Joey with the force of a revelation and remained as a conviction: this poor Skizzen had to have an education. Joey needed to become Joseph. In self-defense. This was not something Augsburg Community College was prepared to accomplish or encourage. His classmates did not stimulate him: their interests remained coarsely commercial, socially commonplace, and daintily divine. Every gesture they made in his direction turned out to signify a seeyuhlater. Joey was asked if he played bridge, and when he replied that he preferred chess (though his knowledge of either game was minuscule), he was invited to join the chess club. The very idea of belonging to a club made Joey nervous, and, since he could not in any case play, he told the club president that he'd given the game up because he realized he cared for it too much, a confession that got him tagged as an ascetic and admired for a life that was perceived to be austere instead of simply empty.

The faculty had some dogged enthusiasms, but they were really not well informed; how could they be when the administration's expectations were as low as their own, and they worked for salaries that an organ-grinder's monkey would refuse. The Salvation Army had a better stock of books; he could not afford to buy even the texts Augsburg's instructors assigned anyway; and there was no library worthy of the name in the dinkyville where he and his mother lived. Nevertheless, he could not continue careening from author to author, book to book, subject to subject, and period to period, especially—what was most confusing—bouncing from work to work and composer to composer like a golf ball in a parking lot. He had recently dragged himself through *These Twain* and *A Laodicean* without realizing that Arnold Bennett was minor and Mr. Hardy's *A Laodicean* obscure. When at last he had puzzled out the meaning of this awkward title, a project that had taken far more time and effort than it should, its significance seemed clear enough; however, it was the length of the line of relations involved that surprised and admonished him: a wealthy city in ancient Asia Minor named for the wife of the second of thirteen kings, Laodicea was chastised in Revelation (which he made a note to read) for its lack of commitment to Christianity, the city's name appropriate to the charge because the water in its aqueduct, unlike the hot springs that fed nearby Hierapolis, was lukewarm or tepid; hence Hardy's use of it to describe his heroine's inability to choose between a modern man of good sense and a suitor who represented the romance of the past—condo or castle were the alternatives. In the end, she accepts the former while still wishing the latter were the former. Joey felt the novel did not live up to its author's massive reputation; however, he was also impressed by the vast areas of ignorance that were not likely to be rumored, Joey was still so young, nevertheless gaps that were not likely to be removed or even reduced. Saint Paul had apparently written a letter to the Laodiceans, although now the letter was lost, and in a.d. 60 an earthquake had shaken the city, but not its pride, for it had refused Roman help in rebuilding. Was this sketchy bit of information relevant to the events of the novel, because the question of whether a castle should be rebuilt or replaced was central to it? Joey had played the piece, but he had not heard all the notes.

Because it was a school presumably built to teach and to observe the tenets of the Lutheran branch of Protestantism, Augsburg Community

College was a quiet, placid, unassuming snare for the unwary; a snare for the unwary because its Lutherans did not believe they were merely a branch with its bark but the roots of true belief itself, the trunk the twigs the leaves as well—the earth that held the tree, the water its roots drank, the sun that fed its leaves, the air that trembled them; it was a snare for the unwary because it was more than a cause, it was the corrective of the cause, the righting of a course gone awry, a cleanser for a soul that had soiled itself, a savior of the Savior; it was a snare for the unwary because it was a church that opposed the power of the church, a clergy that resisted the powers of the clergy, a group that dissolved groups into holier members; it was a snare to snare the wary as well as the innocent, to entrap both informed and tenured dupes and naïve unprepared waifs and bumbling chumps like Joey, because they might believe that fellow Lutherans were as one—united—in their love of God and that the church and its clergy would find it quite impossible to be tyrannical, vengeful, obsessed, nitpicky, and absurd, when in fact there was no one Lutherans hated more than Luther, other Lutherans, and themselves, who once had been unwary, who had since been duped, and now were snared.

Members of the Catholic church in town, into which his mother now and then wandered, were accustomed to the sounds made by their ill-tempered organ and to the complaints of their bad-tempered organist; however, when Mr. Tippet fell ill they wondered of Miriam whether her son, Joseph, so well named, might be available to play at a few of their services. They recognized that he had schoolboy duties at Augsburg, but perhaps, for the short while they envisioned Mr. Tippet to be incapacitated, her son could squeeze in some hymns for them. They would be grateful for Joseph's help and could pay him with gratitude and a sum just short of insulting.

Joey was happy for this excuse to visit his mother, whose cooking had improved remarkably since he had started attending Augsburg. On Sunday evening she would serve him *gedünstetes Kraut* to which she would add grated apple and *Würstelbraten,* each slice shot through with rounds of sausage, a dish she liked because it extended the service of the beef. Then they would talk about old times if Joey was unable to steer her away, about the food she fancied from her childhood, such as *Steirisches Schöpsernes,* a mutton stew served by her mom with horseradish and plenty of potatoes, but now and then there would be events at school he could introduce to their conversation, and lately some chaff concerning the row of white ageratum that had suddenly appeared in a line along their front walk. Miriam had chiseled out a furrow with a screwdriver, thrown in some of her birthday seeds, and to the amaze of her eyes saw plants pop into view.

This surprise, he told her, reminded him of one he'd just had with a Thomas Hardy novel that he had read with some pleasure to be sure but not without suffering a number of disappointments along the way. However, certain facts about its composition had come to light with a similar bright suddenness: namely that Hardy was ill in bed—in a town called Tooting—wonderful name—no, no, it was Upper Tooting—he was ill in bed with a urinary infection—he was sometimes almost delirious—he was ill in bed in Upper Tooting dictating the first draft to his wife—well, Hardy was actually lying on an inclined plane with his head lower than his pelvis the whole time—the whole time was almost six months—compelled to complete the book despite his pain because he felt bound to honor the date for its publication in *Atlantic Monthly*—a magazine, did Miriam know? called *Atlantic* because it came out simultaneously in New York and London. Naturally, the novel would have its ups and downs. It was remarkable it had gotten written at all—well, dictated, then revised. Moreover, he had learned that Henry James—was Miriam familiar?—had also dictated some of his last works to a typist—his novels were serialized, too—though James wasn't in anything like the same pain, just getting on and disappointed by the world . . .

Miriam did not see any connection between Joey's tussle with Thomas Hardy and the delight given her by ageratum popping up in a nice regimental line along their walk—or her walk now—who would have guessed? She was even a little tiffy about it. The packets had turned up in a drawer just as her need to plant their seeds somewhere had accidentally appeared. She was a bit ashamed of so whimsical an impulse and remembered her implement with good humor—a screwdriver, who would have guessed?—yet here they were—these little button-shaped flowers—as if stolen from a nosegay. One plant, which hardly interrupted the run of white, was—well—purple, she guessed, a black sheep.

Joey found it quite amazing that a man should lie on a board for weeks, even months, making up a novel in his head; it wasn't like music, which always signaled the next step to take and stuck to your memory as naturally as taffy to the teeth. Miriam had just shoved the dirt back over the seeds with the side of her foot and then stepped on the place to tamp it down. Joey thought that maybe he'd read *Far from the Madding Crowd* next—didn't Hardy choose strange titles?—and such descriptive names, too, so appropriate as to be odd—quaint to a fault—he'd looked into this novel about the crowd, leafing about a little, and seen Mr. Oak mentioned, Farmers Boldwood and Poorgrass, Bathsheba in front of Everdene. Could you take Boldwood and Poorgrass seriously? Miriam had been very encouraged by her success with the trim; it was more fun than she'd expected, and she planned to put in more—at other edges—since Joey had given her only seeds from short plants.

The kraut was red as a red wine, with a soft broad leftover taste. Joey could understand how it had become a comfort, not only taking his mother back to her farmhouse childhood but also soothing her tongue from a run of bad words and steering her thoughts from complaints. If Mr. Tippet cultivated his condition perhaps Joey could earn enough to buy some Berlioz, or maybe a hoe for his mother if she was going to dig in the yard. He did worry a little that they might want him to play difficult pieces that he had no previous knowledge of, but Joey remembered the tawdry services he had attended and believed the priest would just say "play" the way he said "dominoes." Luxury lace is next, Miriam said. What's that? What it says on the package. White, too. She looked, shook the packet—Alyssum, she said. Do you ever see pinks? Did she know he had pilfered them, Joey wondered, beginning to blush—I'll . . . I'll poke around.

Joey wheezed his way through several Sundays of early mass and shook off effusive compliments; meanwhile, at the other pole of performance, he managed to snitch some dianthus from a potting tray where there was a loose pile of seed packets still, and dwarf marigolds, too. Rakes, hoes, spades leaned against the shed wall tempting him into significant dishonesty, but he refused to surrender another inch of his already abbreviated virtue. The trips to and from school were a nuisance, but various parishioners did drive duty for him, full of curiosity about Augsburg and its quiet ways. Joey made up a life that was regular and serene yet far more interesting than the one he knew, since this college's life seemed to have no real qualities at all, and his only anecdote was one he dare not tell on himself. He stayed at his mother's over Saturday nights now in order to make early mass and be driven back to Augsburg for elevenses. More than once his chauffeurs observed with amusement how late Protestants slept in.

The grass in the Augsburg quad, the college catalog said, was the same grass that had spread its welcome across the colony's common in its first days; and the main hall, of limestone and granite, had stood nearly two hundred years of student food and student chit and student chat and student sing-alongs at lunch on Sunday when visitors were frequent; moreover the light that fell through the chapel's glass to stipple the floors and pews had fallen every day in the same way since the glass had been installed with evangelical ceremony and in exultant sunshine; so that when you walked beneath its principal line of stately, though now infected, elms, you heard in the moving leaves the hum of history, indeed history was where you were headed, for at the heart of the school, in the center of its campus, a large door, said to have been rescued from an abandoned Catholic church, had been stuck in a hunk of concrete that represented stone, and upon its crackled panels had been pinioned a symbolic copy of Luther's Ninety-Five Theses in the shape of windblown bronze leaves.

Mr. Tippet had warned of his recovery and incipient return, so Joey's month of work was nearly over when Joey was notified that the rector of Augsburg Community College was anxious to see him. Joey was scarcely aware there was a rector or any sort of pooh-bah higher than the dean or the chaplain who tended to preside over the school's Sunday services. As a student he was in good standing, though not quake resistant, and he felt his organ playing, admittedly pissy at first, was now at least adequate to the four square tunes he was expected to perform. Surely, rumors about Madame's defiled pillows could not have reached the rector's distant ears, however large they might be. So Joey was at a loss.

He went without evident anxiety up a staircase protected by mahogany rails. A door on the first landing displayed a plaque below its frosted window that read DR. GUNTER LUTHARDT, RECTOR, splayed out in old German type. The name and title were gilded, but much of the gilt was worn, as though Dr. Luthardt had been in his position longer than paint; indeed he might have been there since the building was built for all Joey knew, and this time Joey's considerable ignorance about everything near and far dismayed him, and he felt a flicker of resolve. Dr. Luthardt had black hair and a deep dark suit, and he was sitting in a high-backed dark chair in front of a window heavily draped, so his very white face glowed like a malignant moon. This effect was doubtless aimed at. His eyes were small and his lips were as thin as the edges of a letter slot. Through this slit his voice emerged like a blade from a block; its speech seemed to glint, although you couldn't see teeth; it hadn't a hint of accent despite the rector's formidable look and Dutchie name.

Mr. Joseph Skizzen—Dr. Luthardt appeared to be looking at a piece of paper held just above the top of the desk—it has been reported to me that in a session of Lutheran Studies during your first semester here, you said that—ah—you wrote that—from what you'd read Martin Luther seemed awfully eager to get God on his side, and that's why our namesake decided to become a monk . . . as a bribe—as you put it—to bribe God with his good behavior.

Gee. I don't remember.

By becoming a monk in a monastery—it was reported to me—a monastery supported by a church that Luther later decided *wasn't worth much,* and no place to go or be if you wanted to *get right with God*—

I just thought . . .

Since the church—what else is written here?—*wasn't right with God either*—

Well, I guess I meant . . .

So his choice of monastery—hence his choice of church—to honor with his piety was *the choice of the Devil's* as it turned out—

Dr. Luthardt's voice came at him like something swung, and a corner of Joey cringed—*and a sign he was a sinner not a saint.* What do you say to this, young sir, that has been reported to me?

I don't . . . he was more Catholic than most before he became a Lutheran. He was scared . . . his horse was frightened by a bolt of lightning, so he promised to behave . . . to be a monk . . . but the monks weren't going to heaven just for beating their chests . . . Joey received the rector's look like a slap to his face. I don't remember what I said, he said.

You knew well enough then, didn't you?

We are all sinners, sir, aren't we?

Some of us sin more than others; some sins are small as rice, and some are more sizable; some sins are momentary as a sneeze, some are lifelong; some sins are made worse by their situations and surroundings, but others shrivel and become limp; some sins are normal and occur in the course of things, while some sins are aberrant, outlandish, and perverse; yet God can grant grace to the worst of us, forgive sins both grand and grisly; but for those who wallow in the wickedness of sexual desire, or sin outside the true church, there can be no salvation.

I suppose so, sir.

Suppose so . . . ?

Suppose no salva—

Martin Luther was clothed in the grace of God; and when God chose him to become a monk he did so—you know very well and should have thought very long about it—in order that Luther should eventually learn the extent of the moral diseases that infected the Catholic church, and consequently be motivated to make his great protestation, for what do you think would have come of us had he not left the law and its secular license for the cell and its sacred walls?

Sort of a spy, then?

Of course not. He was aware of the maxim: Know your enemy.

And for those who don't sin outside the church . . .

What?

But only sin in it?

Who?

Can there be salvation for them?

I just said, young sir, that God is grace, only God is grace, only God can purify, only God can steer us aright. Your mind is a mess, Mr. Skizzen. To be outside our church is itself a sin.

Oh.

The very worst kind.

Oh.

For nothing we have done are we saved. God extends his grace—as I said—in a way most mysterious, for reasons incomprehensible—extends it—

To Lutherans who have sinned.

God helps them stay straight. Upright. I just said. Their faith is a sign they shall be redeemed.

Keeping the faith must be hardest of all.

Failing the faith is the one sin. Actually, God keeps the faith for us. As I said. We are weak. We are woeful. Yet he sees in us a solid vessel for true belief.

But only some shall be saved?

Some.

Some. A few?

A few.

A remnant?

"Remnant," sir, is a Jewish word.

Like "the chosen"?

"Chosen" is another of theirs—yes—an arrogation, a word full of false pride, indicative of the devil. We, sir, are elected.

Dr. Luthardt sounded neither weak nor woeful but triumphant, a solid vessel indeed. He sounded saved. The paper slid across the desk unimpeded.

Another matter, Mr. Skizzen, remains.

Sir?

I understand you play the organ for us.

Yes, sir.

The rector pointed himself directly at Joey, though he was busily silent, as though adjusting his aim. For a terrible moment Joey thought he was about to say: And you have played your organ at Madame Mieux's and come off on her colored silks and cottons.

But now you play for Saint Agatha's?

Their organist—Mr. Tippet—is ill.

You play.

But he is nearly well again.

Lutherans do not blend; we do not meld; we do not weave, Mr. Skizzen, you should know that. It is one of the sins—did I mention?—to mix our worship with sewer water.

I didn't—weave—whatever you meant.

We do not dilute.

I did not water down on purpose. I just played some hymns. Hymns they asked for. I could get you the numbers.

Your mind is a mess, young man. Our denomination frowns on any ecumenical or interfaithless activity. That means we do not pray with others; we do not sing with others; we do not in any sense or in any aspect jointly perform or share our service with others. The word for your failure is "syncretism"—something you should have learned about by now and a very serious thing. You must reconsider your employment and cease your playing at once.

Mr. Tippet is returning.

All religions are not created equal. All but ours are sordid.

God must have a reason for permitting other religions, mustn't he?

God's reasons are quite beyond our ken. But hell will be filled.

Catholics are Christians, aren't they?

Just barely. They maintain idolatrous ways. They worship images of Mary. Had you played for Mormons, for instance, Mr. Skizzen, you would have participated in heathenry and might have been expelled from the church. You must stop this ignorant mingling at once. And beg for forgiveness. Hope for forgiveness. Long for forgiveness.

Mr. Tippet is returning. He is over whatever it was.

And never accede to their blandishments again. How they blandish, those Romans. Luther wanted our sense of the sacred to serve us in the work of the world, while they—their priests—are one with the world, as-one-as one-into-one is one; they are a wholly worldly order—they want the work of the world to determine their sense of the sacred. Imagine.

I didn't know.

Their priests smoke.

13

A ridge of pressure, the result of many questions, controlled the climate of Joey's consciousness, and he felt his thoughts go dark and slumberous like a layer of low cloud. For several weeks his mind moved—*larghissimo*—like the slowest sections of symphonies. How often would an answer be repeated by the cello and like a rising woodwind exit as a query? He did not believe that Professor Ludens would have turned him in; he would not have remembered anything Joey said because he never really listened to anybody and interrupted every response that lasted more than a minute; but if it hadn't been Ludens it had to have been a kid in the class—yet who? No one had seemed particularly devout or even interested in Luther, his concerns, or his causes. Most of them probably came from Lutheran households and were thoroughly tired of pious precepts by this time, though they wouldn't have shrugged them off. Dogmas, tenets, creeds: they doubtless meant dates in church basements to them, hours of solemn Sunday services, and scheduled interruptions of life—little more. So who?

Then what about the oddly long delay in tattling? Had that denunciatory paper sat in a basket awaiting the rector's eye? or had news of Joey's heretical organ recitals drawn a description of his muddled classroom comments from a sleeping file? Did the spy only recently report Joey's behavior, which would be strange because the class on Luther had been a first-semester course, and Joey was well past that now; it was a period of his life so out of his own sight already, he couldn't remember saying any of the things he was reputed to have said; he had no clear understanding of what they meant or what the issues were. It was silly beyond billy. The rector was the chief absurdity. Where had he come from? Who had seen him on the campus or even in the church? Like a circuit rider did he go from little Lutheran school to little Lutheran school and at each school briefly rector: sniffing for sin, calling kids on the carpet, reviewing accounts and recalculating the take, staring the faculty into a renewed submission?

It occurred to Joey that during the years they lived in London, whispers of this sort might have started to surround his father, since it was certainly true that he had entered England under false pretenses, that he was really an Austrian, not at all a Jew, and might have been a spy. After all, there was no protection from gossip, from calumny. The most innocent act could create suspicion. Just a fortnight ago, Joey had walked into English class only to see, taped to the blackboard, his last pop quiz, and on it, in red, the signs "100%!" Miss Gyer rewarded the righteous with such announcements, but Joey never expected to be one of them; it must have been a bit of luck that got him to such an uncustomary percentage; the altitude made him breathe more quickly. But guys smiled or winked at him, and Joey had to assume they felt he had somehow cheated his way to perfection. They did not honor good grades—on the contrary—but they prized chicanery, and any successful dodge, so long as it did not threaten the curve, and Miss Gyer had no curves. She was a tall women made entirely of posture. The *y* in her name was her best feature.

Perhaps his father began to feel beset. No matter what he did, it was misinterpreted. Gossip about him was spreading like a puddle of printer's ink. If he innocently wins some money—what happens?—a chain made from the hiss of whispers begins to join one hundred ears, and he is said to be buying documents or going out with whores or plotting against the Jews some further harm. How would his wife know if such tales were true or even being bruited about, having had nothing whispered in her own ear? Joey felt compelled by precedent to believe that in some minds he was a foul defiler, in others a cheat, in still others a heretic, whereas he saw himself as merely a petty thief of seeds.

Joey felt he could not help it. He began taking notes on the behavior of his fellow students in order to determine who the moles were who might be sending regular reports to the rector, not just about him but about anyone who spoke out of turn or recklessly, anyone who showed resistance or skepticism or disdain, anyone who could have weaseled his way into Madame's pillow parlor to do a dirty, anyone who might have borne, as if on the air all the way from town, a reprise of the ho-hum hymn tunes he wheezed from the organ of Saint Agatha's, a church that Joey was now finding out was Augsburg's religious enemy. The transmittal of this musical information had to be the most mysterious snoop of them all.

His mother—was she the leak?—was she the dripping tap? First, to a friend of hers at work. Drip. That friend, then, to a friend who happens to char at Augsburg or whose child is also a student at Augs. Drip. There must be a path of transit. Mother (with pride) to Friend: My son Joey is now the organist at Saint Agatha; then that Friend (idly) to Son or Daughter: Isn't Joey Skizzen the organist at Augsburg? I hear he's playing at Saint Agatha as well; next, that same Son or Daughter (without malice) to Pastor Ludens: I understand Saint Agatha is enjoying Joey Skizzen as much as we are; Pastor Ludens, finally (motive unascribed), to Rector Luthardt: drip ditto to downfall.

The Eighth Commandment

Thou shalt not bear false witness against thy neighbor.

What does this mean?

We should fear and love God that we may not deceitfully belie, betray, slander, nor defame our neighbor, but defend him, speak well of him, and put the best construction on everything.

Clarice Rumble: she wasn't uptight, not nearly stiff or stern or dogmatic enough. That was it: he should look for an arrogant, no-nonsense stickler. Chris Knox had a lean look, but it was from playing tennis. Becky Wilhelm was a pudding, puddings were often resentful and malicious, but she was too stupid to understand how to spell "theology." Who . . . ?

Hey, this is only Joey, who sits in the back of the room with his mouth shut mostly, you are picking on . . .

. . . maybe the guy with the green teeth and glasses, the double dork whose pencilitis drove everybody crazy: *tap tap* here, *tip tip* there, cleaning his nails with the sharpened end, chewing the eraser, rolling its yellow length between his palms as if he were an Indian making fire with a pointed stick. If not him, then . . . ?

It's true, I make fun of other people, but only in my head, to keep my spirits up . . .

. . . maybe Jackson Leroy. One of Joey's stereotypes about Negroes was that they didn't stoop, fink, snitch, or tattle. Or was it Leroy Jackson?

Seek and ye shall find, but only in my mind . . . suppose the tattletale was me . . .

Ah . . . Maurice. Maurice. Shorter than Joey. Nearsighted. Like Joey—little-nosed. Eyes that, when you looked at him, shifted into low. Picked his dinky. Seemed constantly uncomfortable. Sat in last rows. Near me. Maurice . . . something. A distinct possibility. Probably preferred Wagner to Berlioz. But he acted like a little sneak, not like an arrogant toe-the-marker.

Clarice Rumble. Joey's trouble was, Joey slowly realized, Joey's trouble was that he was too busy dodging people to see them except as obstacles.

He caught glimpses the way some people caught fireflies. When he recollected them their image relit for a moment. Clara. Clara Rumble. She wore pins: little pins celebrating Olympic sports, her father's membership in the American Legion and the FOE, a yellow ribbon commemorating . . . who knew? reminding her of whom? When Joey, feigning admiration, or at least interest, asked her what loss the little ribbon stood for, she said she didn't know, it was just part of her collection, except that right now it was for her dog . . . well, had been for her dog, who had wandered off, but, only the other day, had wandered home again. You don't need to wear it, then, Joey said, sporting his own smile of sympathy a bit unnecessarily.

They don't let me wear jewelry, said she.

The last months of Joey's stay at Augsburg were ordinary and awful. Despite his fearful expectations, nothing happened. He heard and learned diddly, as if his fingers were always idle at the piano. The plans he had made, and was making, seemed unnecessary now that the campus had become rumorless and routine as drill. Two years at Augs were too many, although the availabilty of a piano and an organ had been a plus. Still, all he had discovered in that time was that he needed to master what might best protect him; he needed to have learning to hide behind; he needed to know a great many different things to shield his soul from Paul and Pauline Pry; particularly he needed to be conversant with various eras in history, periods of literature, and schools of music, because those subjects seemed to be within his grasp; and he had found out he was not going to fish anything basically beneficial from Augs's comfortable little pool of banality and superstition. In fact, the place wasn't even as restrictive and intractable as it should have been . . . in order to be genuine. As for achieving a reasonable level of religious fanaticism, neither students nor faculty were even fans of God; they just tuned in when a good game was on. They were too smug to be defensive or suspicious. The librarian cut dirty passages out of Chaucer with a razor and kept Rabelais, Baudelaire, and Lawrence locked up. That was the extent of it.

Oh yes . . . there was the rector and his network of spies . . .

But if Paul Pry were to open him like a tin, what sort of selves packed so closely would he see? The tin would be empty, not even oily, it would have a tinny sheen, and light would fly from it as a fly flies from disappointment—that was what he'd see. Not a single self or sardine.

Well . . . not exactly. There *had* been an unprotected period . . . Joey had had quite a checkered past, a quite romantic former life in fact: an escape over many borders hidden in a womb, survival of the Blitz, ocean voyage, slow trains, bad buses . . . charity . . . dinky gifts . . . humiliation . . . ah . . . piano lessons. A tiptoe through the tulips. With Mom. During that time, he'd simply been who he was. Hadn't he been? Hadn't he been a habit hard to break?

Becky Wilhelm was a whiz at checkers. She was studying how to be unattractive, so she went to a lot of socials where she played checkers with old men when no one else would, not even other old men. In that way the skill surfaced. She was mistress of the multiple jump, she told Joey proudly. Hey. Wow. He said. Nevertheless, she was a whiz. That she was a whiz was a surprise. Joey beat his soul up about that. Could he call his playing the playing of a whiz? Skizz izz not a whiz, he imagined he heard Chris Knox scoff. Knox had gone out for track—a hurdler, he claimed to be—but twisted his knee at a meet and had to give it up. It took him so long to rehab he lost his tennis stroke. At Augs, this was a serious loss, because a long time ago someone had decided that tennis was to be the college sport. They recruited tennis players who were all tall blond slim kids from Florida and California who looked good in shorts and their tanned cancer-inclining skin. God was a tennis pro, at least that was the suggestion of one Sunday sermon titled, he remembered, "Thirty Love." Many mornings the *thonk* of tennis balls could be heard even in the quad, and the high mesh fences around the courts could be seen shining in the sun even some way off. Joey found the sport an anomaly at Augs until he learned that community colleges all over the country, most named honestly enough for their communities, were infamous for supplying prospective standouts in various sports with the decent scholastic records they didn't have coming out of high school, so that after a couple of years they could enter the colleges and universities that had recruited them in the first place. Augsburg, through the coincidence of its name, became a feeder—as the word was. So Knox might be—might have been—a whiz, Joey didn't know . . . didn't want to know . . . and therefore Joey would continue to live in the dark and see folks as flickers of phosphorescence—alluring, amusing, whizzes—but briefly.

When you're young, time is a puzzle, like interlocking nails. You wonder what you ought to be doing or what the future holds or how things that don't seem to have worked out will work out; and in such a mood, even when you are focused on the future because you are yet to get laid, to bloom, to beget, to find your way, to win a tournament, you nevertheless don't detail far-off somedays in your head; you don't feel your future as you feel a thigh . . . because the present is too intense, too sunny, brief as a sneeze, too higgledy-piggledy, too complete, too total a drag already, whereas there is simply so much future, the future is flat as the sea three miles from your eye while the beach you are sitting on is aboil with sunshine and nakedness. The future is constantly killing off the present by becoming it. The future is too—thank God—vague to deal with. The future may not arrive. Yet that is all you value, all you hope for: fine future things; so you think, I'm not here at present; I'm just a movie made of slow-motion dreams; haven't I always been, then and now? wondering about *when:* when the dust will settle and the sky clear, *when* I will hear cheers and I'm handed my trophy.

Joey imagined that if old—when he would be old, if he could be old, because in his dream he was always dressed the way he was dressed when he dreamed—he'd wonder what his death would be: when it would arrive, how it would do him in, what he would be wearing: during the early hours of the morning? while sporting his only suit? lost in the ruins of the city? would he die from bawling through tired eyes? go like a bathtub blown through a once-fine view from an upper floor? fall from a break of a board? because death is nothing but detail—a little cough that causes your ribs pain—a siren that stirs you to sit up on your deathbed and regurgitate a ricocheting nail.

So much time lost in thought . . .

Maurice was Joey's equal in suspicion. He realized at once that Joey's sudden interest was a ploy, and he wasn't particularly pleased to be in someone's self-help program. Even standing stock-still, Maurice sidled—sidled in a circle—as if searching for the center of the sky. Did Maurice remember, for example, the assignment for Friday? Indeed, it would turn out, he did, but for another class. Was Maurice living in the dorm or did he commute? He didn't live in the dorm, but he did sleep there sometimes. If you were waiting for the worm to turn, Maurice would keep you waiting until you walked off arm in arm with your impatience, whereupon, leaves eaten, the twig to which his freshly finished cocoon was fastened would sway a little in the wind. Joey completed his scrutiny of Maurice with grudging admiration, yet he didn't mind he'd been outwitted—he didn't care. Maurice's motives were much like his own—not to be caught, not to be known, not to be disclosed.

Joey asked himself whether he hadn't cared for Mr. Hirk and found out that although he was grateful to Mr. Hirk, he was only connected to his ailing teacher through music, and that what he really cared for were some mythical singers with magical names and the thin long-ago sounds Joey could, with voice or fingers, never revolve so well around, though they were the center about which he turned, because he did so at a different speed.

Madame Mieux—there! he'd invoked her—name, naughty thoughts, and all—now he'd brought the weird one into view—what were you up to when you asked me over to listen to a piece by Berlioz you knew he'd never written? why didn't you pick up your pillows, they make a sorry scene, quite tasteless and unsettling? and to come to the door in a drug-induced daze to greet a young and simple pupil? in billowy belongings that didn't seem quite fastened on you? Seeing you in school standing in front of us in your tight hips and tall shoes; hearing you shout French as if you were on an unreliable telephone . . . well, Madame, seeing you, hearing you, did not entice any of us to touch or smell or taste Mieux, too; no, did not tempt us to come closer than we had to, loll on one of your souvenir pillows, our noses full of pot smoke, and—who knows? after music, after chocolates—to be done to.

On gray days, when the light was soft and the grass was greener than seemed possible, Joey would often see Professor Pastor Ludens crossing the quad in his customary black suit, stiff-legged, too, like a crow, a bit pompous, bearing two dark books, each held against his chest into which they disappeared—a Bible and the hymnal, Joey guessed. He appeared especially often on autumn evenings when the sun was low and hid behind the treetops as well as in the clouds, possessing so little strength it could not lend the pastor a shadow to precede him on the path to the chapel from whose loft windows Joey would observe him approaching so that, suitably warned, he might slip swiftly from the choir himself, as if his practice were concluded, to sit in his basement room sheltered by the sort of careful silence that signified he wasn't there even when he was.

After a canny edit of the details, Joey told Miriam about his interview with Rector Luthardt. She was ready to hit the rector with her purse. How could that man and his renegade church possibly object to Joey's playing for Saint Agatha? Joey had found a word for Luthardt's complaint—miscegenation—and Miriam embraced it. It was better, both thought, than "syncretism," which sounded barbarous. In her eyes, nothing could have justified Joey's suggestion that he leave Augs more readily than his account of the moon-faced rector's remonstrances and the suspicion that spying had to be their cause; however, if he were to decamp (as he subjunctively put it to her, though he had made up his mind already), he would need to find work, since her income scarcely kept her afloat; she didn't need his weight in the boat. In the settlement's infrequent newspaper, the *Woodbine Twines* (a name of uncustomary originality unsupported by its content), Joey read that a librarian was wanted in Urichstown, a community squatting nearby that was slightly larger than Woodbine and had a distant view of the river. Posting the opening in the *Woodbine Times* (he was disappointed to learn he'd misread its name) was a little like nailing a note to a tree to advertise your lost dog. There was a Greyhound, and he boarded it for what was an annoyingly slow ride, since it seemed to stop like a school bus at every mailbox along the way. When the windows began to move, Joey remembered without nostalgia his long railroad journeys and the sense he had of falling through farther and farther patches of foreign country. It was late spring, and fields and forests were a wet raw green. Tree leaves had reached their fullness for the first time, and Ohio's low easy hills lulled the eye. The road made slow undulating music all the way to the river.

Just off the customary courthouse square, which told Joseph that Urichstown was a county seat, he found a small tidy stone library funded by the bobbin boy Andrew Carnegie, bless his generous Scot's heart. At a large semicircular desk sat a woman wearing a huge head of gray hair that the wooden triangle lying there said was the hair of Marjorie Bruss. She raised her head from her reading, and her hair flew as though quail had suddenly taken flight from a hidden nest.

You're not from around here.

No, ma'am. I'm from Woodbine.

We beat you in basketball.

I wasn't aware.

That's a good sign.

Gee. How did you know I'm here about the job?

You don't have a card. No one comes in here without a card.

How did you know I don't have a card?

I know the face of everyone who has one, and the hand that holds it out to me. Except for the too-olds and too-ills who can no longer climb the steps.

Well, whom do I see about it?

Indefinite reference.

The job.

You see me. You said "whom." "Whom" is also a good sign. Miss Bruss paused. It was apparent she was questioning herself. We did put an ad in Woodbine's fish wrap. She caught his look . . . read it . . . revised her remark . . . Its newspaper.

I went to Augsburg Academy. I live in Woodbine.

That's a long commute.

I live with my mother, but if I had this job I'd come over here to room.

The way you do at Augsburg?

Yes, ma'am. I played the organ at the school, but now I'm through.

What was your major? For the first time, Miss Bruss picked up a pencil. Her fingers were unmodified.

Um . . . Music. Um . . . English.

Music. Good.

The piano is my real instrument.

Are you . . . ? I hear something.

I'm Austrian. My father was. My mother is. She brought me over ahead of the Nazis.

What's your name?

Joseph Skizzen.

Two *z*'s? She wrote.

Yes, ma'am.

You graduate this spring?

Um.

This job doesn't pay much. What do you want it for?

My present job doesn't pay much either. The college covers my board and room.

You're on a scholarship?

Um . . . Same as.

Can you catalog, check out, check in, reshelve?

I can learn. I can count. I know the alphabet. They don't cover cataloging at Augsburg.

Are you a Lutheran? Religious?

I can be if I have to.

Ms. Bruss laughed like a contralto, though her speaking voice wasn't notably dark.

What do you want it for—this job?

I can't live off my mother anymore. She can't afford me. And I want to go further on in school, but I didn't feel . . . well, frankly, I didn't feel I was learning enough at Augsburg.

Augs. She laughed again. Ugh. She thrust the pencil—point first—into her hair. "Further" is good. Delicate distinction. But you're too young. You don't look twenty.

I'm nineteen.

Through Augs by nineteen?

I accelerated.

What do you go by?

Jo—Joseph.

Below her hair, Marjorie Bruss had a rosy round face, quick laugh, and happy wrinkles like lashes about the eyes—beneath her hair, no neck and lost ears. I have to tell you.

Ma'am?

No one wants it.

Don't you get to read?

For days. Maybe that's a reason no one wants it. But the pay is poorer than bad cheese. The only applicants I've had are eighty. They are trying to earn the price of their plot. They will bore me till I lie in one. I need someone who can carry armloads.

I have two forearms.

You're quick. But a tabula rasa.

I will ask you lots of questions. What's a rasa?

You're a blank page.

I'm a clean sheet.

Okay, Joseph. She gave Joey a piece of paper with a dollar figure on it. Accept this and you've got the job.

14

First, he walked around the town. It was located in a valley that had one obviously open end because you could follow the accelerating water of the creek, as well as the main drag that paralleled it, in order to see now and then at some distance the broad blue Ohio into which the fast stream poured, earning for itself the name Quick Creek, though the natives said Quick Crick, since the stream was often like a line of ink and also because they couldn't help themselves. The many elms that once shaded most roads were ill, but not all of them had been taken down. Squeezed as it was between hills, Urichstown was only a few streets thick, and cross streets were short, stopping at the crick or giving out like a winded runner some small way up a slope. Apart from a square of judicial buildings that had been set to one side as if by a picky eater, the main points of public meeting were the three brief bridges that spanned the Quick, and kept the two halves of the town together. They were said to be "brief" because they had no great distance to span and because spring floods often rushed roiling water through the town to wash one or more of the crossings away. These floods were consequently measured by the spans they engulfed—"one bridge," "two bridge," or "three bridge," as sometimes proved to be the case. Only when the Ohio was so full it forced itself up its tributaries, and the rapid water from the hills ran into the river like a truck into a train, was the flood actually fierce enough to endanger homes or public buildings.

Joseph sat on a bench at the bus stop whiling away the half hour he had until the posted time of its arrival, and then the fifteen minutes more that would pass before its actual appearance. The weather was perfect. Sun ran over his calves and flooded his feet. There weren't many people about, and those he could see kept to their missions and paid him no mind. Traffic was subdued. He thought how differently he felt about this change in his circumstances. For many such moves he had been but a burden with a runny nose, a loud sore throat, and a pair of frightened eyes, someone who inconveniently remained the same armload of duties wherever his mother and sister bore him. However, since then he had begun to strike out on his own. After all, hadn't he half chosen Mr.

Hirk, sought out the High Note, and taken all the ceremonial opportunities that came his way to play "Beautiful Ohio," even if he did so with a notable lack of enthusiasm? As for Augs—he hadn't enjoyed it very much. He'd rarely been stirred the way he had been when playing Mr. Hirk a new tune or even receiving the polite applause of mothers or finding a record worth a turn. Instead, he had become confused. Augs was education? However, the tidy little library with its rosy round-faced librarian appeared so welcoming, and the look of the books gave him heart they seemed so available, as did the quiet of the reading rooms with their promise of repose (a purposeful quiet in which one might sit as if in a pause between movements), that Joseph was encouraged to approach his future with a confidence and an enthusiasm he had rarely known. He wasn't fleeing from, he was running toward, and what he hoped to learn would be free and unassigned, known only to himself; so that, consequently, to the world Joseph would remain undefined—a vague reference.

For the first few miles the only other passenger was a vast woman with spiky hair carrying a teddy bear. Joseph preferred to think that she had boarded the bus at the last minute in order to save him the embarrassment of being the lone ticket, but she chose to sit in the aisle seat next to him and his window because "We'uns the onlies here, might as well chat to spare the hollows." Joseph wondered whether she hadn't been inflated like a float toy by someone fearful of the water. The enormous lady was a comfortable talker and as redolent of goodwill as she was of cologne. He stared at his own glass-imprisoned face—wan, transparent, and stuffed with trees, grass, and bushes—while her chat went on, rarely addressed to him, mostly headed for the ear of the bear. We needs the warmth of this weather, she said. I don't know where you bin, but I bin here, and we needs the warmth of this weather. It's misery—and I am witness to it—when—even here—at the bottom of April—clothes freeze on the line. Joseph felt obliged to nod. Like they'd of died—that stiff. And Billy Bear's blankit here—frosted like windy glass. Her hair as stiff as 'cicles, too, Joseph thought. It must be rather wonderful to assume that the world would receive with interest whatever came into your head. As Joseph was considering the distance between himself and this crazy creature, in order to marvel at it, he remembered that it had always been his job to hang the wash, pinning even Debbie's panties, bras, and blouses to the line that hung behind the house, carefully stretching the sleeves out with clothespins at the cuffs so she wouldn't complain of wrinkles; and at that moment he shared this overlarge lady's hatred of hanging damp trousers up with freezing fingers. Billy Bear likes to travel, see sumthin of the whorl, so sumtimes I jus git a tickit and come on for him to injoy the trip. Nice day for it, Joseph offered. Oh gawd yes but not today, today aint for him, we bin to town on bizness an now we're goin back to LouElla. Lowell was a village the size of an intersection. Joseph was grateful for the information, because Lowell was the next stop; even now from the crest of a hill he could see where the train tracks turned toward its station. So you live in Lowell, he felt himself safe enough to venture. Sum of the time. Sum of the time I live in Whichstown. Sum of the time I live in Gale. Sum of the time it seem I live on dis bus. Her flesh shook, the heavy flesh of her arms shook when she laughed. That's a bit unusual, isn't it? to live so many different places—I suppose not all at once—but so near one another. Oh you guessed it, dear—all at once, shure. But Billy Bear live in only LouElla. Hey, we is home, honey. And she heaved herself up from her seat and waddled toward the driver as the bus brakes sighed and they entered Lowell. Bydeebyby, she tossed to him over Billy Bear's shoulder. He saw that, though the hair on top of her head was drawn up in teepee-shaped points, it fell like a flap over her neck in back. In a moment, Joseph became the sole passenger on the bus again, but now he was cuddling a mystery against his chest the way Miss Spiky-hair carried her bear.

As far as Joseph could see, Lowell consisted of a wooden warehouse, very weathered, whose southerly lean lacked conviction, a gas station with a porch roof shading the pumps, a store of some kind hidden behind rusted signs, and a junkyard cum car lot that sprawled alongside the road as if everything it contained had been tossed there by someone passing. Joseph couldn't decide what was more emphatic: lot, junk, or car. A worn sign threatened that not far from the highway a trailer park lurked.

The bus boarded a pair of passengers from Lowell and added one or two every three to five miles until it was about a fourth full by nightfall, when it reached Woodbine. Joseph followed the failing light with a pleasure that caught him by surprise. The bus is returning me to Woodbine, but I am starting afresh in Urichstown. I'm out of the reach of Madame Mieux. I'm out of the grasp of Rector Luthardt. And beyond Ponsonby's reach. No. Ponsonby was in a book. On his left the hills were as dark as those on his right were bright. Shadows fattened or shrank as the bus turned, showing no signs of indecision. Now and then a window would come alive: disclose the entrance to a low, otherwise lost road, feature a fruit stand not yet in business, or a gate with its mailbox like a sentry—each vision as romantic as his ignorance could make them. He would learn of the world now—even if from books—the way he'd learned to play: by ear, by hunt-and-peck, by instinct, by guess and by gosh—by means of his inner talent. The bus lights blew down High Street sweeping obscurities from gutters, walks, benches, and façades. Joseph stepped off a block from the Point and whistled his way home, rehearsing the piano opening of a Brahms quartet, the first one in G major, with Rubenstein and the Guarneri, pretending to be the piano as it tiptoes down a short flight of stairs into the strings.

After Joseph had been shown around the library, Marjorie Bruss handed him several employment forms to fill out. For tax purposes he would need a social security number, which Joseph realized he didn't have because he wasn't in fact a citizen. As a refugee his mother had been given something she called an alien labor letter along with other dispensations, but Joseph, though born in London, was still an Austrian to the bureaucracy, a fact that filled him with delight but was now a real difficulty. It occurred to him that in all likelihood not a single penny he had ever been paid for selling records or playing music had been reported to the government. You could study and become a citizen, and then apply for a number by which you would be forever known; or, for a simple work permit, you could allow yourself to be caught in the inky coils of a distant and indifferent bureaucratic squid. Joseph had Miriam's distrust of officials, and, though his English was as American as the next guy's, and his invented numbers had been accepted by everyone throughout his schooling, he had absorbed from Miriam the uncertainty of one who wasn't native. Nor did he wish to ride the bus with the frequency boasted of by Miss Spike, whom he might also meet going to and fro from Whichstown, Gale, and LouElla with her bear. These demands meant he'd have to purchase a car, however cheaply, learn to drive it, and get a license upon which, he feared, the social security number he didn't have would need to be prominently posted.

Joey immediately reported his good news to Miriam, who disapproved of his salary, questioned the distance, and worried about where he'd live—in a tent, on a dime, at the edge of the earth. After a few more congratulations of this kind, Joey described his quandary: on the forms he had been given there were blanks aplenty for a social security number. Your mother is a resident alien, a mother from the moon, she said.

But you must have one?

Yes, yes, now, yes, it took years, yes, I have one, but you don't, you are an unregistered resident alien.

And what is Debbie, then? Is she numberless, too?

Your sister doesn't have to work. She doesn't have to drive. She married well, a man who nearly went to Yale.

That's how it's done? to live numberless you need to marry?

It's true, you do lose your real name.

You can hide behind your husband's credit, I suppose. Live in his house.

Bear his kids. Slice his beef. But you can't drive his car.

She has her own chauffeur. She gets to sit in the back, wave to the crowd.

If she's so well off now why doesn't she come around sometimes? She could help you with a few things.

Wither her husband went, she goes, Miriam said in her quotational voice. He's busy planting potatoes. She can't drive. So she drops a line, sends a card.

She went into another county, not another country.

Deborah has her proper social number . . . somehow . . . I'm sure.

With this ID I thee wed, said Joseph in a copycat voice that managed to be harsh.

She'll be by . . . I'm sure.

Joseph called around and was told to pick up some more forms at the post office.

An applicant for an original social security number card must submit documentary evidence of age, United States citizenship or alien status, and true identity.

Evidence of age could be supplied by a birth certificate, a religious or hospital record, or a passport. He returned to the office of Miriam Skizzen with a request for his birth certificate. Who do you think I am, she said, bristling at what Joey thought was a routine request. Who do you think I am? a clerk of the city? a recorder of deeds? This is not the house of courts. Days went by during which Joey kept a prudent silence but an intimidating presence. From a shoe box, wrapped in rubber bands that the postman had once slipped around bundles of mail, she withdrew an official-looking paper—not a birth certificate but a hospital record of the arrival at a London lying-in of one Yussel Fixel, infant, to Yankel and Miriam Fixel, weight six pounds five ounces, baby blue eyes, trace of brown hair, print of foot. Oooh, look at that, so small!

Liberal feelings, a desire to help the unfortunate, led to sloppy record keeping and sorry observation of the law, with the present confusion its unhappy result. If he submitted this certificate as proof of who he was ("who" is good, he heard Ms. Bruss say), he'd be Yussel Fixel forever—butt of jokes, object of scorn and derision, laughingstock. Yussel. Yussel. Yussel. Mother of God, Miriam exclaimed, I am a Mother Fixel. Undo this calamity, Joey, do undo it please, undo it, she said, unaware of any oddness in her words. He stared, as if thoughtful, at the unbanded box and the wormy rolls of elastic. It can't be undone, he told her, but it can be ignored.

Just then a bit of grammar bit him: "as proof of whom" or "who he was"? What would Ms. Bruss say? Stay with "who he was." That had been a close call. It would not do to be caught in an un-Americanism. And be found out.

An applicant for an original social security number card must submit documentary evidence of . . . true identity.

Ignoring statements and citations was a skill both Fixels had perfected. They would quite forget this shitty piece of paper: fold it as it had been folded, slip it back into its box, lid it, and snap rubber bands about its cardboard bulk, six to each end, find a remote spot to lodge it, stiffen their backs before decisively turning them, pinch each nose, squinch each eye, zip up lips, shutter minds. The carton with its new elasticated cover would be shelved in a closet behind hats, gloves, and mufflers, so that soon—thus wooled, furred, and felted—it would cease to exist. However, the fix Joey found himself in would not hide itself away as simply. He would need a new "true identity." Further research, which Joey sullenly undertook, suggested that the salary Miriam had ridiculed was probably so small he would not have to file a tax return, or the library to admit the presence of his person to any authority. Joey could catalog and shelve as if he had rung the doorbell and asked to rake the lawn of its leaves. Moreover, driver's licenses were regularly used to cash checks or to prove your age if you wished admission to a dance hall, bar, or club, and they did not have to have your sosec number on them. However, if your license number wasn't your sosec number, wouldn't that be suspicious? But at a glance, who would know? He had to manage a license somehow. To have an identity in this country you had to be considered capable of driving a car. Otherwise you had to have a husband who did. And if you opened an account at a bank, you would soon receive, in the mail, an application for a credit card. Your identity would then be as secure as a dime in a dollar.

There are several pluses to being poor, Joey assured his mother: you can remain unknown to the government who will have no concern for your existence, nor will you ever have to contribute to its wars or its plunder of the planet. Since you are powerless, blame for most of the world's ills must lie like an iron crown on other heads. His identity, Joseph Skizzen slowly realized, was wholly his affair. Further, the best security for that secret self was the creation of a faux one, a substitute, a peephole pay-for-view person. Did we not have two hands so that one of them could wipe our ass while the other remained unsullied and ready to be clasped? That was what his father had attempted, Joseph now felt certain. Why hadn't he—when he had been a simple Joey—taken advantage of the driving lessons his high school had provided? But how could he have guessed so simple a secret? He did feel excused. So . . . establish credit. How? Go into debt. Get a loan. Buy a car. Learn to drive. Pass a test. Receive a license: with a face on it that says, Hi! I am the guy I say I am, see my smile? read my date of birth? my weight? my height? in my head, brown eyes are brown, make no mistake, I am that guy—there—under the laminate.

Students had vacated the dorms. Now only athletes—or so they said they were—choristers, bookstore clerks, and cafeteria servers were clearing out their lockers, returning their gowns, counting stock one final time before leaving the Augsburg campus for the summer; and Joseph

Skizzen was foremost among them, since he had, in a manner of speaking, lived in the church for two years and even had a cache of candy near the organ that it wouldn't look well to leave half eaten and thereby lead Pastor Ludens on a chase through indecent dreams. It was Chris Knox whom Joseph approached about the momentary loan of Chris's driver's license. Because Chris the K (for "King") was taking his spoiled serve to another school. Because Chris the K had been deposed. Because said Chris was waiting by a pile of bags for his parents to pick him up. And consequently, he appeared handy. Joseph was as honest as he dared to be.

Hey, Chris, I'm glad to see you because I need a favor.

Yeah? You are? You do? How come?

I've got a chance at a job for the summer, but it's at a bar—you know, cleaning up—and you've got to be twenty-one to work there, so I need to raise my age a little.

You? Yeah? So? There's no exercise for that.

Yes, there is. It's called living longer. But I can't live longer if I don't have a job.

I can't help. We live in Indiana.

A short drive home for you then.

My dad's not hiring. I don't have a job either. If he was hiring maybe I would have a shot.

Well, you've got a driver's license, haven't you?

My dad does the driving when we're together in the car, but we're not together a lot.

Well, see . . . I need one to imitate—a license—to be a model for the one I'm going to make—the one that says I'm twenty-one. If I could borrow yours just for a minute—to copy, you know—there's a machine in the rectory.

Oh, hey, I couldn't do that. My dad won't give you a job either.

I don't want to actually use yours. I only want the form to follow. I'd white you out, put in my own name, and paste my photo over yours—where yours is—was. Your identity wouldn't do me any good, would it?

I don't want to be whited out. You want a job in a bar? You don't have a license? You can't work around alcohol, you're underage.

My mom won't let me drive. She's afraid. Of collisions.

I don't think so. That's funny, though. Mine aren't . . . my dad isn't . . . afraid of collisions. My quick reflexes, I suppose. On the court.

Insurance is expensive.

Is that right? My dad says he doesn't make enough. He sells it. He's got no job even for me, even sweeping up.

Come on—it's nothing—and it would only take a sec.

I don't think I can. Anyway, my parents will be here any minute. My dad is prompt. The bird in the clock doesn't beat him. I'm standing here—I'm early—because I don't dare be late. He's strict, but he was never in the military.

A minute is all it'll take. I'll run like a rabbit both ways and be back before your parents know it, before you can load the car when it comes. Besides, you owe me. Come on. I know what you did, and I haven't said a word. I need the license for just a minute. That's all.

Owe you . . . ? Did what? Say . . . how . . . what do you mean owe . . . ?

You know . . . that time . . . when you . . . when you . . . you know . . .

Chris Knox had an ear that turned red then like a stoplight. He fumbled for his wallet, let Joseph, who was instantly off and running, whisk the card from his fingers. He hollered but did not pursue. Joseph, with panting hands, made a number of copies, both front and back, and returned in time to see Chris's ride arrive—a large black car that contained specimens of wealth and possibly glory.

Thanks a lot. I took only a minute like I said. Joseph waved sheets on which the copies appeared to be large blots. These will be a big help.

I don't want you to meet my parents, okay? Chris shoved his license in a trouser pocket as if even its plastic were ashamed of what he had allowed it to do.

Don't forget where you've put that.

I don't—

Okay. I won't. Many thanks, though. I'm gone.

Joseph walked rapidly away through the gate with his copies, his own ears red now. He gave a wave that featured paper flutter and thanked the Lord for the craven nature God had given us, as well as that primordial sense of guilt that makes patsies of us all, including those with reflexes and a good serve.

15

You're doing what your father did, you know that?

You said he bought his.

You paid nothing for this? It came that cheap?

I don't know how I can use these copies anyway. The rectory didn't have a decent copier. See how DRIVER OHIO LICENSE is printed in blue on a white band that seems to scroll across the top?

Mein Gott, you've sold your soul!

Then there's a kind of sepia background, I remember from Chris's—the seal of the state in a web of globelike lines, faint, yes, to imitate a watermark—

Worse . . . your body . . . !

And another little red stamp by the photograph where the director of revenue has signed his name in something like the same ink . . . see . . . so many things to get right . . . the photo has a bright blue background . . . so many facets, none of which I can reproduce without a genuine license in front of me. Even then . . .

Don't get yourself in more trouble, Joey. Give it up. Just buy a cheap car on credit and drive careful. If you don't have a permit—well—won't you be careful then? you'll be careful; you'll take every curve as if you were drawing it.

Drawing was what Joseph tried. The back of the permit was a snap; it held codes concerning driving restrictions (*C* for daylight, *F* for forty-five miles per hour) that the copier reproduced quite well. He'd shrunk a picture of himself taken in a photo booth at the five-and-dime. It would do. But the sepia tone and the director's signature, the faint thin global lines . . . these were impossible to realize. Onto some heavy paper, cut from a candy box, he pasted the faked back and front of the license, applied the snapshot with watercolored blue around it—not too bad—then inked in the appropriate typewritten data where he'd whited out King Knox—M | 507 | 135 | HAZ—a process that had required him to reproduce the altered permit yet again. I've rubbed you out, Chris K, he said, during his only moment of satisfaction since his own shame had eaten him, red and raw. At least His Majesty had granted Joey's request—rewarding his guess that the guy had some sort of embarrassing prank—at least an episode—hidden in his history. Despite Knox's athletic swagger, despite that bunch of big bags . . . dark car, vast trunk . . . there was a tiny Achilles in the heel of him. Finally Joseph placed his counterfeit license facedown on a sheet of self-adhesive laminating plastic—it was sold in a four-by-five-inch-card size as if the manufacturers expected its illegal use—bought also at the five-and-dime; then on the back of the license he pressed another piece of the plastic, sealing the crime whose edges he then carefully cut around, releasing the completed permit to lie to the careless eye at least with some chance of success.

How is it? Is it good?

I don't know how it's supposed to look. How can I be a judge? But it looks bad, Joey, what you're doing. It's bad. Bad. Better to get caught without papers than to get caught with a forged set. American cops aren't bobbies, Joey: they are beery; they beat people; they are short and fat, not like tall polite bobbies; they are bound with belts they loosen in secret to black and blue their prisoners; unlike bobbies, guns hang from their hips, they shoot to kill, and their killings are common; they lay the bodies in front of saloons on tilted boards to frighten people, cars, and horses. I've seen photos of it. They wire tags to dead toes.

In his own wallet, itself almost a makeshift item, and unusually fat with funds he had borrowed from his mother, Joseph nevertheless felt comforted to have slid the card. Indeed, it made him feel as if he knew how to drive; after all, he had a permit with his picture on it and the seal of the state. Having not yet been dishonest about anything, Joseph boldly wrote, Have no ss num on the employment forms he'd been given and reboarded the bus to Urichstown in order to deliver the papers in person, secure his situation, hunt for a room, and prepare to assume his duties. Could he interrupt his journey by getting out in Lowell and continue it by catching the next bus, he asked the Afro-headed driver. Sure, I'll just punch a hole alongside "Lowell," but remember to hang on to the ticket. The Afros have hair they feel they have to do something about, Joseph thought, taking his position on the left side of the aisle, by his count halfway back to the back of the bus. He was remembering Miss Spiky, but only with amusement. She wouldn't be coming from Woodbine. Still, it would be prudent to doze.

He remembered then to be curious about why he thought of this immense and immensely shapeless lady as Miss Spiky, as if her hair outweighed the rest of her. Did others think of him in terms of some body part? nose or thumb? as Mr. Featureless, he hoped.

The bus stopped at an oil drum that had been painted bright yellow. This was Lowell. Joseph had remembered rows of possibly wrecked cars lined up alongside the highway, but maybe they were merely very used because they had, he thought, signs in their windshields that might have been prices. He was right both ways because a few yards back of this rank was a junkyard, crammed with looted bodies, stacks of tires, and rusty parts. Sitting in cinders were bumpers of chrome and a scattering of wheel covers. Joseph saw many soggy cardboard boxes in which wipers, window rollers, and door handles had been collected. They could still give off a smart shine in the sunlight. Up front, nose to the road, was an off-orange vehicle with an iridescent side-view mirror whose price—fifty dollars—seemed written on its window in soap. He noticed with some satisfaction that all its tires were full as hogs and went to ask anyone if the car still ran.

A battered Airstream trailer that sat now on cinder blocks served for an office, and there, literally darkening the doorway, was Miss Spiky, abloom in an amazing flower-within-flower dress—that is, a cream-colored cotton shift covered with large lavender petals into which roses had been thrown as if by a lady angrily disposing of her former beau's bouquet. Heehee, if my name aint Ant Hellan, what do I see? she sort of sang, fortune smiles. You couldnt get ennuf of me. So it seems, Joseph said, trying not to stammer, because he was suddenly embarrassed. You work here? I own this junk, evry jink uv evry jonk. Really? My husban willed it to me, evry peece uv evry peece. Well, gee, I thought you moved about more. I was willed one uv these here in LouElla—which you see cuze you are standin in it—an one in Gale, an one in Whichstown, which is where I thought you was.

Three? gee. No wonder you have to bus about. That's a lot.

It all comes to this. Miss Spiky waved her right arm grandly. We take what we have, we make cars outta it, and then when we run the cars hard all around till theres no more desire in the wheels to roll, then we junk em, whole mines uv ore, wells uv oil, tanks uv gas, plushes for the floors, plastics leather for the seats, glass in the windas, rubburr for the mats, it all ends up here, thats why theres so many yards of lizzie iron in this cuntry, on account uv cars.

She moved from the doorway toward him as smoothly as the shadow of a passing cloud. Joseph thought you could play ringtoss with the stiff spires she had made of her hair. Later he would learn that her hairdo was called a mullet. Nevertheless, for him, her name remained Miss Spiky.

Where is you cummin from, sonny?

Well, up to now I've lived in Woodbine, but I have a new job in Urichtown.

Whichstown, you know it is.

Which—?

Whiches is what it was named for, crowds and covens of them one time. They still flies through the trees in the night, but they is in dreams and does no harm.

I didn't know Uhrichsville—sorry, town—had such a lively history.

History aint lively, my pinyun. History is dead as the nex chicken I eat. Whatshoe want?

Miss Spiky had ripe fat red lips and a smile that stretched across her face from one cheekside to the other. It was an honest smile and went with her wide white eyes and her large active hands that seemed to be conducting her emotions. Young man? He was being respectfully prodded. Ah . . . I was wondering if that car over there was for sale? Joseph heard her say "man," not "mahn." He had always been sensitive to such differences.

You see a sum writ on the winnshield?

Yes, ma'am, I did.

What was that sum that was writ on the winnshield there?

Fifty dollars.

Okay. Thats what the car will cost you. In munny. In chokin and stallin and buckin and in genneral disappointmens itll cost a lot more. That's a Rambler there, that one for fifty.

I was thinking about it. Does it run?

It has plates, four tires, an a battry. For fifty its a good buy.

But does it run all right.

Them tires turn pretty good given enny encouragement. But I dont give out garentees.

In the window of the Airstream, looking out at him with one good eye, was Billy Bear. Hello there, Billy Bear, Joseph said with a cordiality he actually felt.

Its got a quarter gas. If you got a foot for it you kin squeeze a lotta miles outta the ole wreck. Thats a car, tho, wasnt worth much new.

Are you trying to discourage me? Fifty is about all I can afford.

I figgur you dont know doob about em, do you? She was smellably close, and Joseph recalled the cologne. Billy Bear wouldnt buy it, tell you that. He knows moren you, kid—my my—you dont know doob. Her splayed hands measured an amount of air no more than a crack's worth. Though her skin was dark, her palms were very pale. In London, when he saw his first such person he thought they had been painted; then he thought they were diseased; finally, he figured they were smoked like some of the buildings that bombs had charred.

I've never owned a car, that's true. Actually, I've rarely ridden in one.

If I sells you this Rambler for thirty-five you got to promise never to come back here to complain. You kin come back—welcome enny time—but not to complain. You kin come back sos the car kin die here, shur—but not to complain. Youre strange, you know, kid your age as ignorant as you about—of all the whurl's ring-a-ding things—about cars. She then engulfed him. Cotton cloth roses were flattened on his face. You led a deeprived life, I guess, she said, her mouth just above his ear. A hug closes the deal.

Joseph groaned for air on account of the cologne, not on account of the squeeze.

You got your hug, now I want my thirty-five, then you get keys.

Much obliged. Joseph counted out thirty-five as the blood receded from his face. The bills had been wadded. They wouldn't keep still.

Fortunately the car was facing the road. She pushed his knee to shove his foot down on the clutch, put the key in for him and turned it, forced the shift into low, and shouted go! Joseph drove with a lurch onto the road where he stayed peacefully in that gear his whole wobbly way to Urichstown, where the engine stalled in the fenced lot of a fast food.

Joseph had been scared, therefore nervous as a fly, the entire drive, but drive it he had, with no background in vehicles beyond bikes, so when he stood before Miss Bruss and Miss Bruss's desk, he stood as one proud, as one who had returned from a dangerous mission.

Are you practicing to be a butler?

No, ma'am. He held out the requested papers. All filled out. Except for a social security number that I don't have. I doubt I'll need one for a while.

Are you complaining about the pay?

No, ma'am. But I figure there's not enough to bother the government about.

We don't want to bother the government.

No, ma'am.

Sit down if you're done practicing posture. You will have a few things to sign. Then you'll be mine.

That's good, I guess.

If you don't turn out deaf dumb and blind.

Her hair still hung about her head like a cloud around the moon. And she continued to be terse with him, but it was not a dismissive terseness; it felt like well-meaning banter. She was amused. Maybe he should consider a career in gaucherie. Madame Mieux had already suggested that.

When do you want me to start?

Library hours are nine to ten. Settle on the eight you want. Have you a place to live?

No, ma'am. I was about to look. Maybe you have some suggest—

I have a room for rent if you want to take a look at it. It isn't fur. You wouldn't need a car.

I do have a . . . a sort of car . . . but—

You'd have a little fridge and a hot plate. I don't encourage a lot of cooking. No pets. No girls. No cigarettes.

I don't smoke.

That's a good sign. I loathe smoker's smoke, but that's not why. I don't want my house burned down.

The room is in your home?

"Home" is a nice word. I had an attached garage redone. And redone. Redone by an electrician who was deaf, a carpenter who was dumb, and a painter who was blind. You could park your car in what's left over of the drive.

That would be handy.

I rent it cheap because I like to have somebody near.

I should say. On account of crime.

Criminals are too smart to live in Urichstown. We raise them, but they move away.

Don't they come back for Christmas?

It's nearly lunch. I'll show you then. You haven't met Miss Moss.

No, ma'am.

Well, now's the time. She extended her arm, a finger, and a nail. Don't neglect to sign.

A car. A job. New town. A room all his own. Oh boy. He signed.

16

Joseph Skizzen was running out of room. The floor was bumpy with books and magazines, the ceiling rustled as though leaved, the walls were lined with chronicles and records in anonymous colored covers, and in the past year there had been a huge influx of ecological disaster stuff but no place to store let alone display it. Perhaps, from other parts of the house, he could steal more space for his archives. Miriam had the basement devoted to her grow lamps, potting benches, seed starts, and tool storage, as well as occupying half of the second floor in whose several rooms she slept a little, clipped catalogs, made bulb orders, and kept accounts. They shared the kitchen and its appliances, each eating the little they ate at carefully different times. Joseph's music books, records, and scores were obsequiously hidden in closets, but he had placed his piano in the middle of the dining room where the table had once stood (it was at the moment imprisoned in the basement and forced to bear bags of fertilizer, potting soil, kelp meal, and various biofungicides, as well as boxes containing the long wait of wintering geraniums). She had plants perched in every window and on every sunny table; there were puddles where pots had leaked or she'd overwatered; and in addition to the ubiquitous presence of his scissors and her little jars of paste for labels, you could find trowels, gloves, and clippers absentmindedly disposed on the seats of chairs, in drawers and cases, or misplaced among a pleasant scatter of dead leaves.

One's concern for our species, namely that it may not survive, has been overwhelmed by a terrifying conviction, specifically that it will endure.

Joseph Skizzen had neither concern nor conviction himself. He was confident that the matter would not be settled in his lifetime, indeed, could not be settled, because even after many millennia, during which the human race—we might imagine—had suffered its own persecutions to a point beyond sustaining, it still might have rebuilt all its war-gutted cities the way Prometheus had magically repaired his liver overnight so that ingeniously improved bombers could exercise their skills with renewed rains of destruction; and no one had any assurance that the building and the bombing would go on or that, ultimately weakened, the ruins would remain during ensuing centuries to smolder or that, good sense at last prevailing, towers would be topped out for the last time, only water and winds to worry their rosy and untroubled future.

At this moment, a childishly named African tribe was massacring another (he had the freshly scissored clipping in hand); but Professor Skizzen had not read, nor did he ever expect to read, about exercises of goodwill and displays of generosity—of how one mellifluously monickered forest nation, for instance, learning of a drought that was decimating its neighbor, had rallied round with ferns and water bottles to rescue and return the sad tribe's present desolation to its customary languid life of meadow, coppice, and stream course. Instead, men, women, children were attacked as you might an infestation of rats and slain as if there were a bounty on each bone.

At this moment (the mail had brought more papers) there were coal-mine fires burning out of control all over the world—China was adot with them, the map looked infested with red mites—noxious fumes and pillars of pollution were besmirching the air in the same way that Pittsburgh (as he'd read) smoked up an entire valley during the big steel days, coating the lungs of the inhabitants with soot, or the way the four-stack steamboats lined the Mississippi River levees belching smoke so black and in quantities so heavy you needed a light to read at noon.

At this moment, an arsonist was setting fire to several thousand acres of California's brush and dry grass, as if, this time, the cretin hoped to surpass Wisconsin's Peshtigo logging fire of October 8, 1871. The railroads, as well as farmers and loggers, had cut away acres upon acres of forest, leaving, like the worst guest, the slash from their harvest in drying piles for sparks from the steam engine's steel wheels to ignite them. Skizzen clapped his hands with delight when he learned that during Peshtigo's initial night Chicago's wooden buildings had also burned. Thousands of people living in the tinderbox structures of upper Michigan and Wisconsin were charred beyond naming. God has rarely been so just.

Professor Joseph Skizzen's initial concern was for the survival of the human race, but after a careful examination of the record he was compelled to reverse the direction of his worry, which was now that the race might indeed survive and by that survival sentence to extinction every other living species, cause most of the mineral elements to disappear, many mountains as well, both ice caps to liquidize, and deteem each of the seven seas.

From the majestic summit of a mountain, a pair of good eyes might see only streams and vales and groves of trees, fair distances and charming towns, losing sight of mining scars, litter, and slummy lanes; but reason, as Goethe wisely noted, will observe only madness and disease when it surveys the world from such a vantage. Similarly a city, seen from above, could be a gay urban scape of red-tiled roofs or a depressing collection of filthy chimneys. However, Skizzen was not so much surprised by human selfishness and greed (one-half of reason's judgment) as by human stupidity, because the desires that men displayed, either alone, at social clubs, in political parties, or as communities, leagues, and nations, were fundamentally so measly and uninteresting, and the methods employed to achieve them so borrowed, makeshift, and inadequate, that what was eventually obtained was a shambles, leaving their suitors dissatisfied, angry, and searching for more satisfactory targets.

For a long time, he had regarded himself—if not the sole proprietor of these estimations—to be fairly divided from his fellow man as freethinkers always are, and perhaps quietly but thoroughly detested by them the way someone whose teeth are mired in caramel hates being asked a chewy question. Moreover, preachers of all kinds have always been eager to proclaim the importance to God of every Jack, Jill, and stage-door Johnny whose pitiful belongings they were about to ransack and pilfer. God, they say, sets the value of the poorest insignificant wretch beyond the worth of any natural element (oil), object (house), or entity (bank). The wretch weighs not only as much in God's scale as a cloud of gnats, or perhaps a field of flowers, but grander than a mountain lake or fruitful valley, more than a symphony of psalms or a philosopher's system of ideas; because a single human being is of infinite worth; he is filled with soul like a bowl with soup and must not be demoralized or damaged or denied his needs, whatever the cost to lakeside or coastline, forest, ionosphere, rainbow, or geyser; not a hair of the head or of the chinny chin chin should be harmed, since even nail clippings, phlegm, and footprints have magical powers; so glorious is man, so beyond mere price, whatever his cost, so amazing his muscles and other achievements, that he surpasses the worm who makes silk, the beaver who builds dams, and the bird who flies miles and miles on its own over empty seas.

Was there ever a more laughable hypocrisy? when daily men with women, women with children, children with dolls, dolls with dresses, are attacked as you might an infestation of rats and slain as if there were a bounty on each bone.

Should humans die or survive, disappear or endure? his indecision rattled like a die in a cup; but at the moment it tended to tilt toward the latter.

Skizzen pondered man's real place, based on his actual experience of him, and concluded that the human race was like a gang of small-time goons parading a big-time attitude through a midtime town.

From the only attic window he hadn't pasted over with posters advertising bullfights, Skizzen could see the garden, now in its utmost refulgence—borders and beds abloom and buzzing—his mother's small back bent over a tea rose, one hand holding a small brush and painting the bush's leaves with canola to admonish aphids, Joseph supposed, to ward off hoppers, intimidate rollers and sawflies. Her footsteps, darker where the dew had been stepped on, marked the morning grass and showed how she'd come from the path to bedside. She wore her wide hat now in shade and shadow. It went on when she went out like every article of clothing the work required: her gloves, her plurally pocketed apron, her white absorbent wiping scarf—each leaf was dried before the oil was offered—her woolly red blouse and her knickers like Japanese gardening pants, padded at the knees with inserts of sponge and lashed about her waist with elastic.

The garden had come to her rescue, there was no doubt of that. As soon as Skizzen's salary was able to support them both, he had insisted that his mother quit her rubber-works job and retire into enjoyment. She might read, relax, cook recipes she remembered from the old country, putter about, visit friends; but with an alacrity he hadn't expected, Miriam had allowed her interest in gardening, which had gradually grown to a full-fledged hobby, to consume and define her. The seasons were like semesters: full of plans and preparations, periods of supervision, training, continuing care, sometimes painful evaluations, and other duties aimed at aiding her plants to realize their true potential—to "strut their stuff," a phrase Miriam picked up at work, for some reason liked, and now overused. Thus regularity reentered her life, though it was now one of her choosing, in partnership of course with the climate, as fickle and ruthless as she would become herself. She was also fond of quoting the passage from Ecclesiastes about there being a time and a season for everything, until—trite for centuries before it came to her—its banality wore on Joseph's nerves.

He felt a little mental unpleasantness like the pang of an errant tooth. A distasteful memory had been recovered from its attic storage: of a time when "strut their stuff" was "strut her stuff" and was said of Debbie, the vain and zealous cheerleader. She should be allowed to strut her stuff if she wants, all the girls do—and she sure has the stuff to strut with, Miriam would add with a kind of pride and a show of salacious satisfaction Joey loathed. He had been so angry when Miriam had spent their precious money on that silly uniform—pleated skirt and letter sweater, one Debbie whirled and the other she joggled—that he had refused to go to the games and watch her make an exhibition of herself, although he had not offered that as a reason but had declared, rather, his indifference to football amounting to dislike. Actually, Joseph had a hatred of sports, based on his inadequacy, that he disguised as apathy.

In any case, he complained of having to witness her performance every day when she practiced leaping and twisting in the backyard, the skirt rising around her higher thighs as if blown from below so that her hair flew up and down about her shoulders and her neck, Woodbine's red *W* undulating as though it were sewn on rapid water. If you don't like it, don't look, he was told, as if that were possible.

Of course, it was their large Victorian house with its wide porches and ample back and side yards that made his mother's new vocation possible, because she had cultivated the patch of ground their first house sat on about as far as root and branch would take her: lining the short front walk with Joey's first gift of seeds, then placing beds in customary fashion like a moat around the building before digging up every inch of the front and back except for a few narrow paths paved by thin wobbly boards and marked at metered intervals by geraniums in sunken coffee cans. She was a drillmaster in those days, and her flowers knew they should fall into straight lines and salute as she passed.

For a time, the size of plants defeated her; they began so daintily as bulbs or rhizomes or seeds sunk out of sight in the anonymous earth that she felt they would all have the same adulthood, but they ended flopping on the ground like alyssum or raising their flags like iris and looking silly standing all alone waiting for the marigolds to arrive. Daisies shaded asters and asters denied violas their share of the light. Glads were a major defeat. She stuck them around like sentries, and those that bloomed stood at funereal attention in nearly barren patches of moss roses that hadn't made it or in thickets of ragged robin that unfortunately had. They were also all orange. After Miriam had scraped them from her palette, Joey told her that, like Easter lilies, glads were largely florist flowers and sent by the living to the dead.

There was nothing shy or particularly nice about violets, Miriam—and Joey, through her—learned. At first admired, they invaded what little lawn was left, and every other area that offered an opening . . . well . . . like immigrants, pushing out established plants and covering the earth with an impermeable carpet of dainty-looking but devilish little flowers whose rootlets, in their eager exercise of total war, throttled worms in their runnels. These darlings, when poisons failed, she had to dig up inch by inch, ripping apart the dirt in a search for bits of root as if she were after patches of seasonal drifters. Over the years she had forgotten about her own alien history, even her present status, and had begun to resent the Mexhex, as she called them, because they worked for potty and were taking positions at her place of work.

The vine phase lasted a long time. Miriam tacked up wire mesh to the outside of the house where clematis began to climb as soon as the opportunity offered, as well as Blaze and White Dawn among roses, each competing for space among morning glories, honeysuckle, and moon vines. About plants, she cared only that they grew; that they grew in her care was a marvel; they made her feel worthy; a dull house and idle earth were now supporting blue, purple, white, and red bursts in a show called helter-skelter. At the vine-*heit* of the season (Miriam's accidental pun), the cottage began to be submerged, and people drove by perhaps to laugh but maybe also to admire the sheer amount of bloom Miriam's untutored efforts had amassed, nor could you ignore the smart rows of marigolds, zinnias, petunias, and pinks now drawn over the formerly unkempt little property; they made a definite and lasting impression.

As Joey became Joseph, his approval of his mother's "put-a-plant" procedures weakened. He remembered how he had envied, at Christmas, those houses that sported a wreath, Santa's face, or an electric candle in every window; but now he thought that you didn't need to use something just because you had it, nor did he believe that dormer windows would threaten to shatter without a familiar seasonal icon pressed against their panes. Add-ons were also unnecessary. Every holiday, at least one new decoration—a lamb to feed upon the snow-covered front yard—would be purchased for display or a crèche built that would be embarrassingly incomplete without three wise men and one camel, adding to the expense of the season, or perhaps a glowing guide star at the top of a pole would be deemed essential as well as straw for strewing and carols piped through a cow; and then—if not on the lawn—on the ice-slick roof, Saint Nick with a fat sack would be peering down the chimney, his precariously overfilled sleigh about to be pulled into space by all those deer; inevitably lights would be flung over nearby bushes, or they would outline doorways, loop along eaves, climb appropriate trees, till every wall and corner was agleam with holiday gimcrackery got up or laid out with considerable effort and at appreciable cost, not to demonstrate religious zeal or seasonal joy but rather to advertise the householders' vulgar predilections for excess.

Of a silent holy night the choristers sang, shivering and cherry-cheeked, on doorstep after doorstep down the street, spreading goodwill, gay on account of the birth of Christ, and in their songs promoters of peace; yet, in spite of that, enemies were everywhere, hatching their plots, spreading their poison like a plague; consequently they had to be attacked as you might an infestation of rats and slain like African enemies as if there were a bounty on each bone.

Miriam (whose educational level was low, and who rarely read much of anything because she preferred her childhood tongue and because her adopted language was largely verbal and so heavily accented it was hard to connect what she said with a printed version) did not this time allow these impediments to deter her from feasting on seed and tree catalogs, garden magazines, and glossy foldout ads that came like bluebirds unbidden in the mail. Loose snow might be blowing down their empty cold gray street and onto bushes bundled up in their own twigs, but Miriam had no eye, no nose, for winter's dullness, because full in her face a glorious peony would be bursting or a field of daisies blooming yellower than butter or a vase full of tulips, vase-shaped themselves, held in her hands near her nearsighted eyes to direct their gaze and thus her vision, not to the past, where her memories usually possessed her, nor to the cold gray day outside, but to the sunny future only pages away when just these daisies would cover her head with sheep-shaped cloud and vivid sky.

When young and full of fellow feeling, Professor Joseph Skizzen had been tormented by the thought that the human race (which he naïvely believed was made up of great composers, a few harmlessly lecherous painters, maybe a mathematician or a scientist, a salon of writers, all aiming at higher things however they otherwise carried on) . . . that such an ennobled species might not prosper, indeed, might not survive in any serious way—symphonies sinking like torpedoed ships, murals spray-canned out of sight, statues toppled, books burned, plays updated by posturing directors; but now, older, wiser—more jaundiced, it's true—he worried that it might (now that he saw that the human world was packed with politicians who could not even spell "scruple"; now that he saw that it was crammed with commercial types who adored

only American money; now that he saw how it had been overrun by religious stupefiers, mountebanks, charlatans, obfuscators, and other dedicated misleaders, as well as corrupt professionals of all kinds—ten o'clock scholars, malpracticing doctors, bribed judges, sleepy deans, callous munitions makers and their pompous generals, pedophilic priests, but probably not pet lovers, not arborists, not gardeners—but Puritans, squeezers, and other assholes, ladies bountiful, ladies easy, shoppers diligent, lobbyists greedy, Eagle Scouts, racist cops, loan sharks, backbiters, gun runners, spies, Judases, philistines, vulgarians, dumbbells, dolts, boobs, louts, jerks, jocks, creeps, yokels, cretins, simps, pipsqueaks—not a mensch among them—nebbechs, scolds, schlemiels, schnorrers, schnooks, schmucks, schlumps, dummkopfs, potato heads, klutzes, not to omit pushers, bigots, born-again Bible bangers, users, conmen, ass kissers, Casanovas, pimps, thieves and their sort, rapists and their kind, murderers and their ilk—the pugnacious, the miserly, the envious, the litigatious, the avaricious, the gluttonous, the lubricious, the jealous, the profligate, the gossipacious, the indifferent, the bored), well, now that he saw it had been so infested, he worried that the race might . . . might what? . . . the whole lot might sail on through floods of their own blood like a proud ship and parade out of the new Noah's ark in the required pairs—for breeding, one of each sex—sportscasters, programmers, promoters, polluters, stockbrokers, bankers, body builders, busty models, show hosts, stamp and coin collectors, crooners, glamour girls, addicts, gamblers, shirkers, solicitors, opportunists, insatiable developers, arrogant agents, fudging accountants, yellow journalists, ambulance chasers and shysters of every sleazy pursuit, CEOs at the head of a whole column of white-collar crooks, psychiatrists, osteopaths, snake oilers, hucksters, fawners, fans of funerals, fortune-tellers and other prognosticators, road warriors, chieftains, Klansmen, Shriners, men and women of any cloth and any holy order—at every step moister of cunt and stiffer of cock than any cock or cunt before them, even back when the world was new, now saved and saved with spunk enough to couple and restock the pop . . . the pop . . . the goddamn population.

Even a small order from a single catalog would bring dozens more to your door, since seed and plant companies appeared to trade mailing lists like stamps, and these glossy thick pamphlets and magazines were, in January, the lights of Miriam's life. Every ripe tomato drew her gaze as though she were famished, despite her decision, taken almost automatically, to stick to flowers because of the squirrels. As a result of all this reading Miriam became knowledgeable about neck rot in onions and the use of apple maggot flytraps as well as the importance for vegetables of sulfur and manganese in the soil. She did not seem deterred by the sameness natural to repeated discussions of fire blight or thrips or the super-scented language used to describe the new flowers for the year, their familiar innovations and awards, reliability of germination, rapid growth, huge blooms, resistance to pests. Last year's moonglow marigold may have been whiter than white, but this year's version was even more so. Soon Miriam knew there were nematodes that would defend iris rhizomes from borers, insect barriers that have had excellent results when used against the flea beetle, and she would learn of a new variety of cucumber that bites its beetles back, even the spotted ones that spread bacterial wilt.

The garden was a place of battle. It was not only where campaigns against insects, disease, drought, wilt, and scald were hourly and repeatedly carried on but also an arena where flower was pitted against flower for water, food, and sun. Peace was largely an illusion, and health, prosperity, security, were as momentary as the cover of a cloud. But Miriam warmed to it, read about it over and over, so that her English, though in an odd corner of its world, greatly improved, and her interests—for instance, in soil makeup, drainage, hybrids, chemicals, birds, bees, butterflies, moles, slugs, and worms—widened and intensified. She knew that mealybugs were covered with a white powdery wax; she learned how to control pathogens such as, for instance, gray mold, bacterial leaf blight, downy mildew, scab, and pin rot; she could diagnose like a physician, prescribe like a pharmacist, and treat like a nurse; she knew in centimeters to what depth bulbs should be planted, what loved shade and muck and what sun and loam, how to improve the stickiest clay or give sand a sense of community.

She showed him an industrious ingenuity and meticulousness he had no idea resided in her. For instance, bulbs of various sizes and species were supposed to be dug in at different, and very specific, depths—too deep and their shoots would fall short, too shallow and they wouldn't last long in unfriendly weather—so she cut a number of dowels to the right lengths, then lettered, along the wood that was to stand aboveground like the warning flag for a gas line, the name of the variety she was going to plant, put a red line around each to indicate how deeply the planting should be, and inserted them into the hole being dug, to the depth marked, before following that with the bulb itself, now safely lodged in the right place. Miriam then resettled the earth and, with a cry of "There!" stomped upon it with a booted foot. She labeled peat-moss pots with tongue depressors, taller plants with lathes of suitable widths on which she clearly printed the appropriate names in black ink, easier to do than the dowels—though carefully, as a bow to her background, in the antique German style.

Joseph was impressed with her devotion but even more with its effects. Miriam began to reflect confidence in all her actions, because the world had been shrunk to the size of her garden, while the principles and problems of gardening became universal: the mantis wore the colors of its immediate locale, it knew how to wait, it seized its prey with a grace of movement equal to its surety and calmly ate its mate. Did so in Illinois as well as Ohio. There were deities in her realm, and Miriam was one. There were kingdoms, and she had hers.

The canola had to be applied in thin coats, and one day Joseph stood behind his mother in amazement while her small paintbrush flicked about its bush like an anxious insect applying the oil. She stood up with the ease of someone who kneels with regularity. Her color was good; she squinched, but her gaze was confident and direct; her weight was in her knees; she munched on certain leaves because they told her much; she drove her hands into the earth as though they had grown there; and she put more things up to her nose than a pup would, laughing with delight and recognition instead of wagging a tail.

Joseph Skizzen saw his mother's life begin to flower as her plants bloomed, while his—which had drawn for so long a similarly upward line—was climbing around his obsessive sentence like a predatory vine thereby—since the two pursuits were so obviously connected—adding daily to his inhumanity collection. But there was nothing to be admired in the results of his revising, snipping, and arranging: if he were writing in ink he would have made a blot; if he were molding clay, it would resemble a turd; if he were playing notes, cacophony would be heard; if he were working with string, he would have made a knot. Standing in the midst of his damning collection, his former pride in it would arrive as a belch.

Short of breath though thin as a scissor blade, Skizzen puffed up the attic stairs. Because he ate so irregularly he was always weary. Once his mother had welcomed him to her table, but now only certain holidays were celebrated with feasts. Miriam seemed to think that, like the cottage, this was her house and that he was the kid who wouldn't leave home but hung around Mom like a hungry pet. Instead of contriving to cook for himself, Joey had learned to unwrap. Occasionally, Miriam would call his attention to a leftover, but his mother often simply passed through the house at dinnertime with an apple in her mouth and snacked while studying a catalog covered with satisfied bees.

Meanwhile, Skizzen's eyes had become dim reading books built of footnotes. His muscles were wasted, he was so sedentary, the stairs his sole exertion since he had given up most of his piano practice. His knowledge was still spotty but intense. He had no patience, no forbearance, no sympathies. His mirror mocked him, and he mocked his mirror. The dirt he dug in was as infertile as news—in fact, it was news.

Nevertheless what Joseph Skizzen regretted most was that he would die before the decision to end Creation had been made, before the disease of human life had mortaled even earth, and all the ores and salts and oils had been removed, fertility driven from the land, the juice of every fruit drunk, waters pumped and gulped and pissed, carcasses consumed; indeed, well before the last movie had cost more than the last buck so that debt was the best bet; before every particle and property of matter had disappeared into a knickknack, a floral garment, or ceramic mug and there was nothing but uncycled trash and even dumps were being dumped; because he would like to have looked out on it a little like God on the first day and observed the mess we had made of ourselves, and seen spread out over infinity a single placid sea of shit. He would have liked to be there at the end to find accounts rendered and justice done. There was supposed to be a Last Judgment, wasn't there? Of course, he would not survive to see such. He would not be recalled to life, either, to enjoy the late show. Only Miriam's daffodils would enjoy that. Even if his cheeks were powdered by a peony and he was made immortal, he wouldn't see it, because there wouldn't be any—any end—to have an end you would have had to have some shape in time. However, there was no beginning. No end. No middle. No knowing where you were. Meanwhile, waiting for the end, he just turned and turned in one spot like the point of a top till the slowing top began to waver, threatened to flop, whereupon a new asininity would strengthen his circuits and, though he stayed teetery, would keep him going.

Among professional students of the earth there has been a growing concern about the many threats to the continued existence of the human race, but among scholars whose field of expertise is man himself, the worry now is that human beings are becoming even hardier and will never go away.

17

The library brought Joey Skizzen happiness. It is true he had no instrument available to him now or place to play, though he exercised his fingers daily and caught every radio concert he could. Moreover he had learned to sing a scale built from each of the twelve tones, observing the pattern: whole whole half, whole whole whole half, humming to himself as he worked in the stacks like one of the seven dwarfs. On a piece of paper where he had inscribed a circle he put *C* where noon would be if this were the face of a clock; then he would write around the dial the sharps from one to seven and after that the flats counterclockwise from eleven back to five, just as Newman's book on playing had taught him to do, by counting off perfect fifths. So his music was not utterly neglected.

Moreover, he read, rather systematically, every book on the subject in the Urichstown library, even the two on the guitar. To be sure, this was a modest number, but it was nevertheless many more than he had ever seen in one place before—shelves of opera synopses, opera gossip, singers' and conductors' bios and reminiscences (Caruso to Toscanini—alas, only the popular people), a little history, even some stage stuff. Ballet was less generously endowed: ballet plots, ballet dancers and their aching legs, their love-crossed lives, impresarios—bullies—as well as dancers (Nijinsky, Diaghilev and Balanchine, Gelsey Kirkland)—a little history, even less criticism, one Sert, which was really a surprise. Had the collection been tall enough to have a head, it could have been called top-heavy with performers (Beecham), rather than composers (Bloch), though the latters' lives were spottily represented: Schubert not Schumann, Verdi not Bellini, Beethoven not Bruckner, Bach not Webern. As in all libraries, however, there were volumes whose presence was inexplicable. Though musicology was represented by *Young People's Introductions to the Orchestra* and *Old People's Appreciations of the Classics,* there was Schenker present—Schenker, of all people, Schenker, about whom Joseph hadn't a notion when he first thumbed through the pages of *Harmony,* so his astonishment was entirely retrospective. There was Schenker and Schoenberg, there was *Style and Idea.* So if, by some standards, the collection didn't amount to much, by Joey's it was enough.

It almost painfully pleased his eye to run along the rows of titles, teasing his imagination with what really was a gesture, because it and longing were twins, and longing could not help itself, it had to experience the interiors of these volumes, again not as printed words upon a page but as words read, as heard, as realized, as conceived; and this building was so cozy, trim, and tidy, it was easy for Joey to feel the books were his; the small close halls made of shelves, the little reading room with its library table and its stately chairs were spaces in his new home where windows—casement windows—opened onto a side yard with great trees and forsythia yellower than a bonnet. He would indulge his fingers, letting them slide along the ends of books, as his eyes had, touching the titles, as if imbibing paper, cloth, and leather, feeling width, and with width, length, and with that, weight, and with weight, importance and ambition—a series of associations that did not always lead him astray.

Through his garage windows he could see his car. "His car"—it was a phrase he could not call customary. The car itself still scared him. Like being a grown-up with a tank full of obligations. Fortunately, he had little use for his vehicle. As it had sat, before its sale, it sat now. He knew it sat, and while it sat, it rusted. Already a ruin, it grew older out of enervation. Joseph had begun to assess the Rambler's ailments, which were many, various, and apparently serious, but why should that surprise him, what did he expect for thirty-five dollars? Miss Spiky would probably have paid him just to drive it off the lot. The plastic upholstery had split. Only every other dial on the dashboard registered. The overhead light would glow occasionally, although there seemed to be no reason for it. The speedometer sounded as if it were grinding gravel. Yet this Rambler had driven him to Urichstown, and it had driven him back to Woodbine, too, though this time in another gear—he still wasn't sure which—carrying him by the car yard in Lowell from which he had rescued its carcass and sent it into action to enjoy a last run of life if not a new one. Joseph had blown the Rambler's horn (it *awk*'d) as he and his auto passed Miss Spiky's place, out of thanks and in triumph, but he did not suppose she had heard him greet her or, if she had, cared to give notice. Anyway, he could not have seen her had her trailer been on fire because he wisely kept his eyes on the road, tense as most new drivers, even more ignorant, fearful of every curve ahead, of overtaking or oncoming cars—trucks were worst—trying to avoid clutch lurch and calculating how to steer and how to stop.

One wall of his room had been a retractable door with a row of square windows across it. This was infirmly fastened across the driveway, the end of which now served as his floor, by strips of felt and plenty of stickum. Shag rugs made from plastic rags had been used to cover ancient oil and grease spots. They tepidly warmed his toes, though it wasn't winter yet. He anticipated the cold creeping like an animal into the concrete and crawling under the door toward his bed to warm itself. Fortunately there was no odor of gasoline. The place smelled as if it had been taken fresh from its box, nevertheless it looked the way things long unused seem—new yet forlornly out of style. Two walls, rear and side, backed into the house, but the fourth wall had a standard window covered by bathroom curtains so you couldn't see the neighbors—or they, presumably, you. At the back of the garage, a door led into the house where a bathroom offered its mirror, a tumbler for a toothbrush, a towel hook, and a saucer that held soap. The badly stained john had a yellowed enamel handle that looked tired and familiar; the porcelain sink was spider-webbed with cracks; and crowded into a corner, a glassine shower, the size of its stream, had been amateurishly squeezed. Everything about his bed was brief, but its brevity left room for a desk served by a goose-necked study lamp and a stiff straight chair. He thought of Mr. Hirk's. The lamp's brown metal shade was schoolboy standard. Thank God it wasn't green. He also had a squat stuffed flower-covered chair with fat arms and a bulbous back that bent his knees but made him sit straight. There was a cardboard closet and a plywood dresser available for his things. On the wall was last year's calendar featuring a different library for every month. February, where it fell open, was distinguished by an archival photo of the Newberry Library in Chicago, sitting appropriately across from a park of snow.

Ms. Bruss's modest house perched on its hillside like a bird, so through his row of windows he could not only watch the drive roll briefly down the hill to the cross street but see the Quick and one of its bridges in the valley. It was not a long walk to the library; however, the return was a stiff one, and Joseph already envisioned hill snow and sidewalk ice making every step precarious. With the drive steep, and the car unreliable, Ms. Bruss provided bricks to place behind its rear wheels and prevent its return to the scrap yard.

Miriam was not impressed with Joseph's Rambler. You are like the simpleton who is sent to sell a cow and comes back with a few seeds.

But they grew upward toward heaven and a hoard of gold. Besides that's what you like most of all—seeds.

Weed the comparison, she said with some annoyance, you know what I mean. My fifty went for this ugly old thing?

No. Only thirty-five.

Oh God, the good bills—the twenty, ten, and five, I bet, not any of the ones.

It's just paper money, Mother, it doesn't matter.

Doesn't? ones are only ones like pennies are only pennies. Remember the penny pot? None of them was money till they were exchanged for a bill. You know how to destroy five dollars? Buy five hundred pennies with it. Less than worthless, then, just a bother. Heavy as Hades.

Put a penny in the ground, your hydrangeas will thank you.

Pennies? pooh. They're made of aluminum and brown paint, not iron.

I guess.

Joseph described his library, said nice things about his new boss, and, in general, blessed the town.

Woman at work told me the place—what's it called? I'm forgetting.

Urichstown.

Ugly. Ugly name. Urichsburg. Anyway, she said the place was cursed.

Cursed?

Some women were accused of being witches there one time. Ages ago, of course. The witches put a curse upon the place. It floods regular. As the Nile, she said. To wash away the stain.

I hope your room's high up.

Joseph described his digs to his mother, but discreetly, without any damaging details. He repeatedly mentioned the rent and how reasonable he thought it was. A garage, Miriam said dubiously, a garage isn't reasonable: a garage is going to be drafty, the floor will be cold, on a hill the wind will be shrill and biting, the windows—you can count on it—will fill with frost—they will—it will be cold, ears to tootsies cold, so be careful to keep plenty of blankets about, and if there's no charge for utilities, plug in an electric blanket, have a little heater, don't freeze.

Joseph agreed to every suggestion while trying to forestall criticism. What's this "digs," she wanted to know. It's not a basement. You've rented a garage. He explained that it was a word he'd come upon in an English novel. This is America, Lord save us. You are living in a garage. Like a car. You are living like a car in a garage. With your friend the rust-colored car living like a homeless one on the hard cold pavement.

I'll be fine, Mother, and it's such a brief walk to work.

Watch out about that Miss Brush—

Bruss.

It's too convenient for her, too tidy entirely, giving the space away after she's fixed it up, invested some of the little money she must make at that library—look at what you're getting—they pay in book paste, those people—in fines and petty change, dime a day for overdue. So be punctual. They'll expect that.

Joseph did not speak to his mother about Miss Moss, whom he finally met in the stacks one afternoon about a week after he started in his job, though he and Ms. Bruss had gone hunting for her a time or two so that he could be properly introduced. She was indeed—as Ms. Bruss had said after they'd missed her yet another time—a wraith. She drifts. And when she drifts all that needs to be there is a draft, a whiff, a puff of air—or so it seems, she said, a certain determination in her voice. I've been startled a hundred times. She drifts. Miss Moss reshelved, dusted, and repaired books. She had an office in the basement furnished with a book vise and adhesive. Breathe easy around her, Ms. Bruss advised, an unguarded sneeze could blow her into a corner. Loud voices will extinguish her like a match.

The library had a basement and above it two floors. The first contained a reading room which opened to the left as you entered, a central stairway greeted you, next to which Marjorie Bruss had her desk installed, and to the right a labyrinth of beautiful oak cases, many laid against the walls where there weren't windows or radiators, while the rest were arranged in military rows throughout the central space. These stacks were open to the public who might wander through them as they chose, though the only places one might sit and peruse a volume were the window seats, invitingly covered with soft plum pads. The public might ascend the handsome middle staircase, also of oak, to a balcony surround, behind which were further shelves and a lonely meeting space that contained several tables, an inadequate number of ladder-backed chairs, a portrait of Andrew Carnegie, and a silver coffee urn that was never used because, Joseph was told, the spigot leaked. He made a silent note to fix that.

The basement was restricted. Kept there were books that were so rarely wanted they had to be called for, or were so valuable they could not be checked out but were required to be read in the reading room where—now—Joseph delivered them. Books that needed repairs sat on a trolley, and near the trolley, which never seemed to trolley much, was a room full of volumes, donated by the heirs of the recently deceased, waiting to be checked, selected, or cast aside for sale at the library's yearly benefit and gala. Joseph was immediately tempted to remove a few, but he decided it wouldn't be prudent.

Miss Moss was in gossamer when he first heard, turned, and saw her in the space behind him, pale as a shadow and similarly bluish, light and frilly, insubstantial. When he tried to describe Miss Moss's dress to Miriam she guessed it was of voile, which told Joseph nothing. Her short hair was silver, her complexion a pale airborne shade of bruise, as if her veins had become pools, or perhaps spills, beneath her skin. She did indeed whisper in response when he introduced himself. I'm Joseph Skizzen. I'm new here. Thank you, Miss Moss seemed to bob.

I'm pleased to meet you finally, he said. You're the new . . . boy. Yes, ma'am. For the gar . . . age, is it so? Yes, ma'am, I'm to help check out and catalog and—. Not Ree . . . shelve, she asked with a tremor. Oh no. Not to dust? Yes, ma'am, I do dust. Oh no you must not dust till you've been trained. I hope you don't Ree . . . pair? I don't know how to do that, but I'd love to learn . . . to watch you work sometime . . . to restore an injured volume . . . to nurse to health a broken spine . . . oh . . . it would be a pleasure. A rivulet of wrinkles moved across her face and disappeared. When I . . . Ree . . . pair my door is closed, she said so softly he wasn't certain what he'd heard. Then, as if a wide cloth were furling around a stick, she turned and fluttered away.

Miss Bruss said that if ever she saw blue moss growing on a tree, it would be Miss Moss clinging to the bark of it. Joseph said she seemed a shadow. A shadow that has dark thoughts about its source, Miss Bruss replied, she is full of suspicion—apprehension and suspicion. But a harmless old thing. She haunts, I think, because she is haunted. I certainly don't know by what. Joseph did not say so, but he decided Miss Moss was an incredibly romantic figure and that it was splendidly appropriate to have her floating about in the dark lanes and corners of the library.

There was a backlog of little things to do as well as a lot to learn during the first weeks of Joseph's employment. Marjorie Bruss's library did not catalog according to any well-known scheme like the Dewey Decimal System or the Library of Congress. We don't have that many books, and we pretty well know our card carriers' habits and preferences. When Joey didn't smile she had to explain what a card carrier was. His ignorance she put down to innocence, and it did not seem to annoy her. After they are assigned an entry number, new arrivals are racked along the walls of the North Room, labeled on the their plastic jackets NA. No one ever removes our Klean Kovers, she said as if expecting the question. Washable. His blank look forced her to add, With a wet sponge. Ms. Bruss let that sink in. After six weeks they are cataloged, allowed to relax and take their jackets off (she smiled and Joseph smiled, too, only a breath behind), and those that have been checked out most often are sent to the South Stacks where they are shelved alphabetically by author under the subject matter to which we assign them: ARTS or OUTDOORS or SELF-HELP, you see? Do the library's patrons understand the system? Most do. We post the categories. So after a while they get the hang. Anyway, we know how it works, and that's what matters. Expensive, oversized, and rare books are placed upstairs and don't go down or out. The rest are sent to the dungeon. To Miss Moss, Joseph said, smiling his own smile this time. No. She only reshelves down there. She doesn't assign places down there. She doesn't understand the system we have . . . down there. Joseph nodded, but he didn't understand the system either, never would, really, here, there, or anywhere. FENCING was a category, for example, but he had noticed there were no books in it. Stolen, that's why. By that skinny pilferer, Joey privately imagined. We'll refill one day. Even FENCING. Ms. Bruss shook more steel-gray glint through her hair. Stolen by a rotten little red haired crop-headed squish who came here and started giving fencing lessons—imagine, in Whichstown—I should have called our cop when I saw him coming. Ms. Bruss says Whichstown, too, Joey marveled. Stole the whole category though the listing wasn't large. No, you needn't be on the lookout for him. He apparently punctured one of the little ladies under his tutelage and was run out of the county by her enraged papa. Marjorie's smile was slight but sly, a signal. No one to my knowledge knows if she liked her lessons or not or whether she learned to thrust and parry. Ah . . . but her father wasn't foiled, Joseph managed. Marjorie lit up. Good, that's good. You may do yet.

Marjorie Bruss presented a trim figure in her white blouse, navy slacks and jacket, and her halo of hair. Joseph liked her rosy complexion, her warm yet brisk manner, her play with words. Her speech was clipped but low, her face round as a dial, her smile consequently wide, and her lips had many expressive positions. She wore shoes with very soft soles and moved about quickly but with almost as much discretion as Miss Moss managed. She saw Joseph's ballpoint and took it from his shirt pocket where it was clipped. No pens in the library. Pens are poison. We permit only pencils with soft leads and dull points so any marks they make can be easily erased. Everybody . . . ?

the rule?

. . . is for everybody.

We can't frisk our customers—I wouldn't want to put my hands on some—but in the reading room or anywhere—if you see someone taking notes with a pen, you must caution them. Highli—? Indeed. Highlighters—highlighters are evil, they must be immediately confiscated and their users given a talking-to, even if they are marking up their own books or some harmless paper copies. Oh . . . Marjorie raised her hands to heaven. How I hate highlighters—you don't use them, do you? Joseph wagged his head. Good, she said, good sign. The dog-ear people do it, stupid students do it, and they will grow dog-ears in due time. You don't do dogs, do you, Joseph? We never could afford a pet, Joseph said. Good sign. Good sign. Dogs are bad for books. Don't ever do dogs. They chew. Cats are bad, too. They claw. They love to rub their chins on the corners of covers, leave sneezers of fur. Rub their chins and grin at you. Before they fade from view, Joseph said. Oh, you are a darling, I kiss the nearby air, Marjorie exclaimed.

But it would not be for the last time. The neighboring air got many a smooch. Marjorie's approval made Joey happy. He was a success.

Do not lean with heavy hands or rest your elbows on a book, even closed, even at apparent peace. You know why, I suppose?

Ah—

It compresses the covers against the spine and may crack the adhesive.

Oh.

Do not use a book as a writing board. Points can make indentations, especially—you'd be surprised—on jackets, many of which are waxy, slick, easily marked, for example, with a fingernail. And never put your notepaper on an open book, even to write a word—a dozen crimes in one action there.

I wouldn't do that. Open books are so uneven.

Never mark in a book not your own, but even then, unless you think you're Aristotle, never make a marginal note or a clever remark you will surely regret, and always assume the author is smarter than you are—have you written a book on his subject? . . . well?—so put down your differences on a piece of paper made for the purpose, or keep the quarrel quietly in your head where it will bother only you and never fluster another, not even your future self who will have forgotten the dispute, you can be sure, and will not wish to be reminded.

Yes, ma'am.

Marjorie. Not Miss, Mizz, or Ma'am. Marjorie.

Marjorie. It was a nice name, he thought, well syllabled.

Don't put your palms down on illustrations, reproductions, any page at all, really, because even the most fastidious sweat—men sweat the most, women have more discipline over their bodies—did you know that? except for their hands, their hands are public advertisements, they encounter a porcupine, a precipice, a proposal, and their palms get runny; oh yes, and in the old days, when men kissed a milady's hand, it was the top of it they put their lips to, not the palm, you never know where the palm has been or what it's been wrapped around. Well. Where was . . . Ah . . . Be wary. Inks may smear. Pigments flake. Thumb oils may seep into the paper, leave prints, and sweat attracts insects, did you know? also there may be a fungus in the neighborhood. Sweat is a magnet.

Gee, I didn't know that.

Joseph. That is your last "gee." Never even feel—"gee." You are a grown-up.

Okay . . . "Okay" is also out? Gee . . . Okay.

Marjorie laughed like a wind chime. Good man, she said. Good man.

18

Joseph had brought some new books to the basement for shelving. Miss Moss materialized beside him. Ah . . . Miss Moss, how are you?

Every day is the same, she whispered, as if she were sharing a secret.

Well, I suppose they are, down here.

No. The basement leaks a little when it rains.

Isn't that bad for the books?

It would be if the books knew where the leaks were.

I . . . Joseph felt himself in the middle of an admission of misunderstanding when it occurred to him that if the paper should sense and seek out nearby dampness, then—if it could—Miss Moss's point of view might . . .

You are shelving these?

Yes, that's right.

Because I Ree-shelve. I make all Ree-adjustments. I dust them first—she flourished a rag—and then I wipe them all over.

That's capital. It was another expression he'd encountered in an English novel.

Miss Moss tried (he thought) to fix him with a look, but she had uneven eyes. Of what?

I meant they'd be well wiped then.

Of course, I would not wipe otherwise, she said softly but firmly while moving off. She always lowered her voice as a sign she was about to leave you. It was like slowly closing a door.

These are first-timers—for down here, I mean—new to the stacks. He had begun to explain, but she was gone. It was perhaps the bare inadequate bulbs that created her insubstantiality. In which case, he was less material, too.

You must not, Marjorie had advised him, pack the books too tightly together on the shelf. They must slide out easily. Dyes will rub off or surfaces scrape. A browser is bound to pull them out by tugging on the headcap—actually, they'll do it anyway, their index finger shoots out and hooks the poor thing backward, weakening or even breaking the cap, tips the book out topsy-turvy, how would you like that? It's just the way you'll fall down trying to get uphill when ice covers our walkways. Some tend to hook the book by the tailcap, which is thereby determined to tear. Worse, women who wear their nails long, who have nothing to do but file and paint (Marjorie's were short, neatly scissored, and smartly filed, but Joseph sensed the gleam from a coat of clear polish), love to claw books forth by clutching their sides and in the process puncture the cloth—you see?—where it rolls in at the hinge. It is loose, soft, and unprotected there. Such dismaying creatures.

I quite understand.

Read, Joseph, read. But don't use the words you read in front of a casual public; the words you read and the way they are written are rarely meant to be spoken out loud in ordinary life the way one says "Hi" or "How are you?" with careless or indifferent intent. You may say, "It was quite large." That's all right.

Quite.

Good. You are a good Joseph today. You shall earn a cookie. Now then, where . . . ? was? Oh. Books must not be shelved so loosely they lean lazily to one side; that will cause them to become separated from their backbones and abrade their tail edges. Look here—she held up a volume by its covers and he could see how its pages hung down like fish on a string. So, remember to hold them as you hold your honey, not too loosely and not too tightly.

I haven't got a honey.

You've got a mother maybe. Joseph learned that Marjorie puffed her cheeks while thinking ahead. She did that now. Then: Don't—I'm sure you won't—pick up a book by just one board, and be sure to carry heavy folios with both hands. By the way, you might think that turning pages is easy and obvious and needn't be learned—a cinch to master, you might think—but people regularly tear wide pages by pulling too fiercely and too sharply down on them. I can tell because the tears will come about a fourth of the way along the top from the spine. Thick books have deep creases, consequently the book is rarely fully open. So when holding a book, especially when turning the pages, do not put your thumb in the gutter. Marjorie demonstrated. The page rolled awkwardly over even her small thumb.

Hands are important here, Joseph ventured.

Ah, yes, good. Your hands will get dusty in this world of ours, and you'll need to wash them often. Not just for the books' sake. You'll suffer paper cuts. Infection sites. A nuisance but a peril of the job. You've probably seen the notices I've put up in the bathrooms, yes? Dust jackets weren't idly named. We do risk the jackets for the first few weeks, when the books are NAs, because even protected they'll nick or fade a little, but then, after the volumes come back here to the open stacks, we store the jackets in basement boxes as if they were winter wear. Miss Moss . . . if she chooses . . . Miss Moss can show you where. Have you encountered Miss Moss?

Yes I have. We—

We allow pencils, but watch out for readers, usually women, who use the eraser to capture corners and roll pages over or, worse, who lick their fingers. Admonish them. Be gentle. But admonishment is necessary.

Ah—

I know the jokes. Do I have my hair in a bun? With a pencil thrust through it? But we have to admonish; we have to shush. We have few funds and can't replace books readily, so we must be particular. And we haven't the space to keep duplicates. We've got to sell them off, you know. Send them on their way. Patrons are always giving us duplicates. Miss Moss is in charge of the poor things, as well as the old folks and the orphans. Sometimes I think she is a faint late duplicate herself.

Joseph laughed in a way that showed his admiration for Marjorie's turn of phrase without making his mirth seem malicious about Miss Moss. He was learning, and Marjorie sent him a look that said "Well done."

Marjorie had told him to choose his eight hours from the library's day, but Joseph had hesitated because he wanted to pick what would be, for her, the most suitable times. She liked to arrive and leave late—working from ten to six usually—so he said he'd do nine to twelve and five to ten. Although Marjorie only nodded and made a note to install him at the early and late "stamp-out desk," as Marjorie called it, she appeared hugely gratified, particularly since she didn't like to make Miss Moss work after dark. In winter Marjorie worried about her steadiness in the streets. However, worry is the most she could do because Miss Moss wasn't a woman who was easily helped.

You dust each book when you put it back, Joseph asked Miss Moss, having thought of nothing better to say.

Yes, I indeed do. I do. Which is to tell you twice.

I—I guess you did.

I wipe them with this rag that Major doesn't like. She wants me to use the vac.

Noisy. Awkward to carry about, I suppose.

Because the rag just rubs it in, she says—pushes the dust down between pages. The dust is as fine as polish paper down here. It will work its way into the least crack or crevice. But I wipe it in anyway. The top ends get gray, as do we all. Including the Major. Why shouldn't they show their age?

Well, yes, you are certainly right about that.

You don't really think so. I'm sure you side with the Major.

Well, I—I really haven't sides.

We all have sides. I am at least hexagonal.

Well . . . that many?

Those who go to the well too often, often fall in.

Ah, yes, well warned.

Major wants me to fasten cheesecloth over the nose of the hose and then push the attachment in.

Really? Why? That seems extreme.

The Major is extreme. If any fragments of paper, cloth, or leather fly off when I'm hosing, they will be caught in the net of the cheese. Of course they'd be minute and of no worth even if they were pasted back where they bee-long.

Well, that is clever.

Ver-ee clever. Miss Moss held her swatch aloft. I am clever, tooo.

Joseph now noticed how streaked her cloth was. Miss Moss had turned her back. Her dust rag lolled over her thin shoulder like a small towel. Marjorie'd have us wear white gloves if she wouldn't have to wash them. Miss Moss managed to dial her voice up for that remark.

As far as the library goes, I guess, she thinks all books are fine ones.

Joseph thought Miss Moss hissed. She certainly sailed out of sight. Her world must be flat because she disappeared all at once rather than a bit at a time.

During the week, the busiest times at the desk occurred shortly after the schools let their pupils out. Many stopped by on their way home, high school kids mostly, though occasionally lower grades showed up with mothers in tow. Weekends could get heavy. Then only the front desk was manned. Sunday Joseph was free and took his obligatory drive to Woodbine. Miriam was always glad to see him, though she complained constantly of this or that—this or that condition, repair, or logistical problem for which Joey would have found a solution if he wasn't living far away in the country of the witches. He had gotten the Rambler to back down Marjorie's steep drive safely a few times—he just held the wheel steady, disengaged the clutch, and rode the brake—though always with great trepidation, particularly while essaying the turn of the car's rear into the road. Fortunately, there was little traffic. There, after sitting a bit to regain control of his breath, Joseph would start the motor. The Bumbler (he had given it the same name he had given its driver) made lots of funny noises, but they seemed to signal nothing that impeded his progress, so he learned to ignore them. Driving without a license was the least of his crimes. Driving without knowledge was probably foremost, though the car itself was threat enough. He did swerve unaccountably a number of times, and the gears were still inclined to clash, but he was beginning to enjoy the machine's passage through the country—with himself at the helm. The automobile enslaved and set free at the same time. This realization, appropriate to so many things, would become a constant in the character of Joseph Skizzen while he was a professor of music at Whittlebauer College. You think choosing the chromatic scale set the composer free? he would ask his class as acidly as he could. It made a slave of him!

In her own domain, Miss Moss could be as particular as Marjorie was meticulous. Perhaps that was the plan. In one hand Joseph had brought a new arrival, which had a slightly shaken lower spine, down to Miss Moss's workroom to receive a modest injection of paste, while in the other—Marjorie did not approve of towering stacks from which, when carried, volumes slid off to disaster—he held an old worn Bullfinch whose cover had come off entirely. These he placed on the trolley that stood outside her door and knocked. A knock, down there, was a real noise. He waited and was about to knock again when the door opened. Joseph did not understand that she was the Star and that this was—if not her dressing room—Her Office. Consequently a certain delay in response was necessary. He was, nevertheless, as deferential to her as to a dancer. Miss Moss, I just wanted you to know I've left these books—he waved in their direction—for repair. She actually seemed to be smiling until she saw the trolley.

Oh my, she said, as if in deep distress. I'm going to have to show you how to load a book truck. Don't balance books on the heads of other books, as you've done here. They aren't practicing to improve their posture. And if you row them like this, with their fore-edges down, see how the entire content hangs from the spine? These days so many books are glued instead of sewn, and it is particularly hard on them to do what bats do. On the other hand if you put them spine down on the truck, the back gets roughened up. The corners of the boards are also exposed, and these points are the most easily bumped and dented. That will happen to them soon enough. You can't know yet what people inflict on the poor things.

Marjorie has told me some—

It's Marjorie? but it's Miss Moss?

Well—

I don't doubt. I don't doubt that she's told you. I don't doubt it.

During this instruction, many of Miss Moss's mannerisms disappeared, and she seemed neither nervous, skittish, nor shy. Nor did she break her words to elongate their vowels. Had she learned her cautions from Marjorie, or had Marjorie learned them from her? A certain malevolent glow suffused her features so that she grew younger and her complexion less blue whenever she spoke about her present position, its obligations, its trials, and its powers. A book, you would think, is not a pocket, a purse, or a wastebasket, but people dispose of their sniffle-filled Kleenex between unexposed pages, their toothpicks, too, dirty where they've gripped them while cleaning their teeth—such in-decency—matchbooks with things written on the underside of the flap, usually numbers, of telephones, I suppose; or they leave paper clips and big flat mother-of-pearl buttons—imagine—curls of hair and all sorts of receipts as well as other slips of paper they've used to mark the spot where they stopped; and they file correspondence between leaves as if a book were a slide drawer—do they do that to their own books?—or they tuck snapshots, postcards, unused stamps, into them, now and then a pressed bloom—they stain, I've seen leaf shadows—one- to five- to ten-dollar bills, you'd never guess, yes, rubber bands, a shoelace, candy and gum wrappers—even their chewed gum that I have to pry out with a putty knife—people—people—I dee-clare—and newspaper clippings, often the author's reviews, that are among the worst intruders because in time they'll sulfur the pages where they've been compressed the way people who fall asleep on the grass of a summer morning leave their prints for the use of sorcerers like me to make our magic.

I've seen those cardboard-colored shadows.

Don't overload the truck. Her arm, as if it were all cloth, waved over the row of waiting books. When the Ree-shelvers arrive—those that have been out in uncaring public hands—I hold each volume up by its boards and shake it, yes, just as if I were tipping a purse in a hunt for keys—and let the cellophane flutter forth, the strips of foil, all their nasty personal stuff rain down. It is not easy on the books, but their bodies are purged, and they will all be better for it. She gave Joseph an impish look. I talk to them. I do. When I Ree-pair a book I tell it what the operation en-tails and how it won't hurt. They need to be shown some concern. She paused as if in obedience to a script, as if she'd confessed these things before. They need talking to not just reading from. She paused again. They need con-sool-ation.

With such instructors it didn't take Joseph long to learn the ropes, and he soon found, as he thought he would, that he had time on his hands. His dedication and energy enabled him to dispose of tasks as they appeared, and even when he looked for work by asking what he should do next, it was often accomplished more effectively than either patrons or staff expected. Through nearly all the hours he found free in his otherwise broken day, he read. Difficult books—those that would compel him to take notes—he checked out on his own card and took back to the garage for concentrated study. This pass—a prized document—had his photo on it and, in hollow red letters, said STAFF. He was rather proud of his place in Carnegie's palace, even as a mere factotum. When he showed the card to Miriam, it was in such a spirit. Maybe, when the police pull you over, you can flash that in front of them, she said. It was made of stiff pasteboard that he protected with a layer of lamination, and then, at Marjorie's request, he glorified her card, as well as that of Miss Moss. Without afterthought, he also did the janitor's, who had been given one as a courtesy, though he had never used it until the lamination gave it class. Now this simple workman took home volumes on hunting, American history, and firearms.

Joseph had looked it up, and so he wondered: How had "factotum" come to mean an oversize capital letter?

Occasionally, when at loose ends, Joseph would carry a chair to the main desk where, in a library empty of everybody but Portho, Marjorie sat reading a magazine; and then, in the privacy only a public place can grant, they would chat. Beneath that whoofy hair she had a receptive ear, and she delivered her opinions, or gave her advice, without any sound of impatience or disapproval in her voice—as if she were thinking with him and not thinking for him. She showed her interest with countless questions, and it was in answering these that Joseph remained cautious, because he feared that his life was too barren and boring as it had been lived and needed a few felicitations to sustain her attention; nevertheless, his additions were minor embroideries, never substantial, except for his father whose character he filled out in the most positive fashion, and whose absence was attributed to an untimely death beneath an apartment beam in bomb-burned London.

Marjorie particularly liked to hear about Joseph's experiences at the Augsburg Community. She seemed to have a malicious interest in the place. In response to her questions, he found himself recalling more about his studies and his fellow students than he thought he remembered. He could flesh out his accounts as he could not with his mother, for Miriam's probing often made him uncomfortable and drove him into places where he could not shine, whereas Marjorie's allowed him to enlarge the part he played in his own history until he could be seen to behave sometimes, with his humility assumed, like a boy wonder. Joseph made her laugh, and her laugh was meltingly musical. What better proof of sincere appreciation was there? He could not turn a phrase as rapidly as she could—hers were spun—but quickly enough so that some of his responses might pass for repartee, a word he had grown to understand and its referent appreciate. "Factotum" meant more than a handyman in uniform. It was a printer's capital letter. Why?

For Marjorie, in these moments, Joseph played his past, stretching late shadows across the quad, giving Pastor Landau both a lisp and a limp to go with the book he clutched, while emphasizing the pastor's sly moist eyes. He enlivened his cast of characters in that fashion, changing names to protect them as he broadened their behavior—Madame Mieux made more acceptable as Frau Bertha Haus, until, having been invited to Frau Bertha's apartment to listen to Richard Tauber records, he flung himself most comically among the pillows, poufs he did not need to multiply, only his panic to reduce and his subsequent suspicions to abridge, in an account that would also mollify his feelings of inadequacy. In short, Joseph made himself the butt of many a mischance without depicting himself as an ass. He steered his stories away from the far too lurid by giving Madame Mieux, a.k.a. Frau Bertha, a dirndl in which to greet him for her performance among the pillows—a dirndl and a stein of beer, a stein which she miraculously did not spill while sinking into swansdown's arms. Marjorie laughed so hard at this her cheeks and neck grew red.

They gabbled away with such pleasure they quite forgot Portho was in his customary spot near the radiator in the reading room; forgot him until he appeared with fisted beard to demand some quiet for his thoughts, a complaint which outraged Marjorie because Portho was as near to a bum as the town knew, with scraggly locks beneath a red baseball cap that now said only BEER, a beard he raked with uncut nails, and clad in poorly pulled up dirty pants, torn layers of shirt and sweater, and a fuzzy scarf he'd picked up somewhere that hung down his back like more hair; but her anger was also out of guilt, Joseph believed, since they had been rather loud when Marjorie's amusement at an anecdote became, this time, more than merely rippling. Yet he was a person whose unseemly presence Marjorie had decided to tolerate, even though he came in only to get out of the weather, to warm or cool himself, while pretending to read magazines like *Boys' Life* and the *Outdoor Companion,* even though sound asleep sitting up. Joseph had even seen her put a candy bar on the table beside him while he snoozed, and his heart melted, as the candy's center might have, had it been placed on the cover of the steam coils.

Marjorie and Joseph also discussed music and books. Schenker, Joseph kept to himself. He didn't know enough to discuss him in any case. But he was quite taken with the ideas of scale-step and voice-leading, which he understood as constituting the *x* and *y* axes of musical space. Tonal color, he thought, ought to serve as the third. However, he knew he hadn't grasped what the introduction called "Rameau's great error" concerning the figured bass. It would become clear, he hoped, in time, or as the pages turned. There were personages, like Joseph Fux (or Rameau, for that matter) who had not previously been in his landscape, and whose acquaintance he had to make. For the first time, Joseph's greed for knowledge might be satisfied. The many books that were at his arm's length made him giddy, anxious, hasty as a glutton who fears competition from a multitude of other mouths.

Time, too, became real, and its paradoxes fascinating. He had in hand, for instance, a book of Ruskin's originally issued in the 1850s; meanwhile Shaw and Shakespeare sat close by, with volumes about them from every ensuing decade. Yet all of these works were here in the sight of his eye, so that he—Joseph Skizzen—might read Shaw before Shakespeare, Piñero before Sophocles, the little or the late before the long ago and very great; because, for him, the past, which he surely recognized and honored as historical, was as real right now as it once had been; the past was present in an altered form, of course, but Ruskin's words on Ruskin's page were the same as the day Ruskin wrote them, as was his dislike of geometric form, expressed by him with such conviction. In these fulminations, Euclid's tidy squares, his pretty rounds and triangles, were set against the exfoliate nature and shape of plants, animals, and even men, as if the two realms were enemies—the abstract versus the organic for the title in fifteen rounds. This bout was as present to Joseph's mind as it might have been to one of Ruskin's immediate readers. The past is present on the page, he told Marjorie. This library is like the Savior, the whole dead world has risen and stands here as on the Last Day. Marjorie's smile was chaperoned by a pair of moist eyes.

Sometimes the library would grow unaccountably busy, and these "new found friends" were forced to break off their conversation to take up routine duties. The pair virtuously suppressed their resentment of this, though it was strong. Joseph would smile across the room at Marjorie as he passed her desk with some requested books, and both recognized that these periods, when they had to be apart, made them appreciate their conversations all the more.

Now and then, when he returned to his garage, he'd find a plate of cookies had been put beside his bed.

Marjorie recommended to Joseph the novels of Dorothy Richardson, none of which the library held, but volumes she owned if he wished to borrow them. Joseph was agreeably grateful, and their conversations continued over weeks and into months, Joseph regaling her with anecdotes, not only those dealing with his own past, but many taken from the lives of his new masters: authors and artists and composers he was reading about in various biographies. What remained amazing for him was the simple availability of everything: that he could reach out and pull from a shelf as he passed a mind—a mind—not merely a source of information as in an almanac, but someone's actual thinking, someone's real imagining, their honest feeling. Were Joseph to climb to a hilltop, innocent of any intent, and suddenly face a vast ocean about which the world was unaware, would his amazement be equal to that of Cortez? Joseph wondered whether any historical stranger's reflection and responsiveness were as nearby or as far away as his quirky selection determined; and whether there might be in any random volume pages that would hold his attention, almost painfully, as if his head were in the mask of iron, or possibly in a vise as the torture books recounted, where his gaze was fastened on a poker heated hot, or on iron pliers held in a gloved hand. With that sort of horror, that kind of delight, he read—he conceived—he envisioned a large lake . . . an island . . . a bastion rising through the mist . . . the slender wake from a boatload of plumed men . . .

19

When Professor Joseph Skizzen walked into his first class at Whitlebauer College—seventeen students had signed up for Trends in Modern Music, and they were all there—his chest could scarcely hold his heart, and he heard its throb as if each beat were being made by menacing native feet for a jungle movie. Your job, he said to himself, is to make them choke on their own snores. He had been an indifferent student himself. The memory was before him like a billboard. Only Mr. Hirk had made his blood come alive in his heart. Others of his teachers had pretended to a passion for Martin Luther or for French or for the early American novel, but they hadn't any enthusiasm really; they hadn't any feeling for anything; they just declaimed and paced or intoned and shuffled or mumbled or droned; and they believed they entertained properly by pouring tepid water into tiny cups. As a young newcomer to the faculty he was last in line for perks and had been given an 8:00 a.m. schedule to prove his unimportance. Early morning—what a moment for music. So Joseph assumed his students had sleepwalked from their dorms and zombied into back-row seats where they sat like the seats sat. He vowed. He vowed he would unsettle their sleep at least, but before him was the memory of his own bad attitude, now multiplied seventeen times, yet made odd by being featured in strange faces.

Professor Skizzen . . . of course he was not a professor yet, but what did they know . . . ? Professor Skizzen—trying to stride—went straight to the piano that sat athwart a front corner of the classroom directly opposite the door. This arrangement permitted him to walk directly to it, looking neither to right nor left, then slide smoothly upon the piano seat and sit with definition the way the piano seat sat, his hand poised without further preamble to play twenty seconds of "The Minute Waltz" (Joseph thought they might recognize that). This is classic, he said, turning slightly around. And this—he touched the few quiet widely separated notes of Bartók's 1926 sonata—is modern.

A moment later he stood with burning face before the class, his feet, legs, and waist sheltered by his desk, in traditional schoolmasterly position, hoping they would think he was naturally rosy; and with the furniture's protection he tried to greet the class, to introduce himself and their subject, to get the course going, to commence his first lecture, aware the while that he had blundered badly right from the beginning, for Joseph had meant to play the Minuet in G—that was the classic—*la dee dah dee dah dee dah dee dah, la dee dah, lah dee dah,* perhaps they would get the joke, if they had seen the right movie—next the Chopin was to follow as . . . well . . . the classic romantic—and then, only then, were those lonely notes of Bartók's to be struck.

Because he had been hired as a specialist in contemporary music, Joseph thought it prudent to find out what his subject took in—from whom to whom was the principal question, since, although the course was called "contemporary," its composers were obliged to be dead. He had been told to teach two sections of an introduction to music as well, one later in the day, the other on Tuesday, Thursday, Saturday mornings, likewise held before reveille's own notes had died away. His head felt like a fine apple, as crisp as the autumn air as he crossed the quad. In addition, he was to instruct half-a-dozen kids in piano, times that might nibble at the edges of his evenings. Joseph already dreaded the winter; he had felt the wind sweep across the hilltop, and he knew that, throughout the fall, it would rain the entire distance from his mother's house to the office; the office he shared with someone he hadn't seen, though they had briefly met, but whose papers covered the only desk, whose books filled the solitary bookcase, whose photo holding a fish crookedly graced the wall, and whose lumber jacket hung on the single hook like another trophy. There were, however, two chairs, the second, Joseph supposed, for a suppliant, as well as an empty corner where the petitioner might stand.

The students' faces were expectantly directed but uniformly empty. Joseph would discover that throughout the semester the surfaces of these faces would shift mechanically: they would show curiosity yet remain blank, look puzzled though blank, annoyed but blank, and bored and blank. They had probably enrolled because the course was rumored to be easy. Well, it would not be a breeze where he blew. They would like nothing more than an ear-long year of Ralph Vaughan Williams. Well, Schoenberg, Berg, and Webern would not be easy. Milhaud would not be easy (he had died just in time to become relevant), though they might have coasted through Debussy and Ravel if Debussy and Ravel had remained contemporary; there were, of course, Holst the programmatic, Delius the soporific, and Elgar the Edward to delight their tastes—Elgar was the Kipling of English music, he'd heard—however, the course could not include Aram Khachaturian, who was hanging on to life, nor Aaron Copland, the American mountaineer and jingoist. Oh yes, Messiaen—the Composer's Claudel, as he was understood to have been, although Milhaud had given sail to a bark called *Christopher Columbus*—this radical composer of conservative thoughts would not be easy either. His name had too many vowels.

How might Herr Fraudulent Prof survive his second class? These were not merely strange names he was threatening his poor pupils with; they represented his areas of ignorance, too: a vast bleak plain empty of all experience. He could not spell a signature, not to say sing a note, from one of their compositions. He could not crowd them all into the last weeks of the semester and then hope not to get there. Though he had experienced that strategy.

Two students dropped during the first week. Another after the first quiz. Latitudes of this kind were recent. Whittlebauer College had been traumatized during the Vietnam protests of the sixties despite the fact that not a voice had been raised or a placard waved on its campus during society's confusing hostilities. Its students were the children of Presbyterians, and although the doctrines of the UP were a definite improvement over the frightened sectarianism of Augsburg Community College, the school administration always acted to serve its church and keep its charges in line. After all, the servants of the Word were elected by the laity—in this case those who paid the bills—so its organization was more democratic than most. Nevertheless, a decayed Calvinism lay just under the school's fluster like a concealed corpse beneath the floor.

Joseph realized that religion went for a liberal education like an assassin for the jugular. If it weren't for righteous families, with their revered authoritarian ways, and schools like Whittlebauer that kept kids penned within the faith until they graduated, the sect would sicken if not die. However, on account of a declining enrollment, an increasing dropout rate, and the horrid headlines in the newspapers concerning the pot-smoking, free-loving hippies, those violent Students for Democratic Action, Gangs of Gay Bikers, or marauding Black Panthers, uncivil as the banks they robbed and fires they set, as well as the erosions of the war on everybody's patience, the college relaxed its requirement of regular attendance at church, allowed a student council to be elected, actually to convene, and even permitted it to rule in carefully circumscribed and unimportant circumstances. Three African Americans were captured in an admission's raid, while an Asian, without solicitation, enrolled. Diversity had been achieved. There were more dances than there had been, though the campus remained dry, and academic standards were so relaxed as to seem asleep. So students could drop a course at any time during the first three weeks. By the end of taste-and-decide time, Joseph had retained ten, one of them a boy . . . two others maybe were almost men.

How to proceed? His course had no prerequisite. Rock and rollers would naturally want to know what was happening in their world, but neither their minds nor their world were musical, a fact they would not understand, and one that would rile them. It would be like trying to instruct his sister. And, just as it was for his sister, their reality would be filled by a local future—nothing else: the next game, the next party, the next dance, the next dress, the next date, the next hot song, the next new movies, even the next exam. Finally . . . happy graduation day . . . money well spent, folks. Then there would be the wedding to think of, the couple's income to worry about, consequently the next raise, therefore the first house, a kid, soon kids, until their lives would no longer recognize anything novel and have run out of expectations like a keg that foams air; their present tense would slowly turn toward the very past they had once so carefully packed like a hope chest with their youthful future: the old games and their dead great players, the once-upon-a-time BYO parties, dances they had danced, gowns they had worn, the golden oldies, grade school friends, high school chums, and college buddies, first loves, wild drives, frat drunks, make-outs that were now adulteries.

Where to begin? how could he cut into a continuum and honestly say, "From this point on all that was cotton is now silk"? While he had been, as his CV supportively said, a librarian, initially reading at random and with intemperate glee, Joseph had begun to pursue subjects beyond the beauties they publically offered. He was dissatisfied with any account of things that assumed some fresh art or new sound had been spontaneously born and didn't know or need to acknowledge its parents. He had come to feel, with an ease he almost recognized, that events and their inhabitants had a source from which they'd sprung; and he needed to know how they had become the way they presently were; where their actual causes lay; why turns had been taken and choices made; the true parents of things set at odds, split and gone; so he was now at a loss because he had no beginning he could offer to his students. Even illness had its onset. Yet the modern movement in all the arts, as far as he could see, was partly defined by its hatred of history, by the intemperate rejection of a nineteenth century that had deified history's explanatory power, its moody course, its laws, its chosen heroes. What did you do when received opinion went so categorically against your own? Back down like the weenie you were? Or remain faithful to your ignorance, curled like a cat in its chair? Or one day, like the mysterious stranger in Western movies, get gone.

In Joseph's own mind, music, like Orpheus, looked back, then looked back again, just as every composer wrote with ancestral harmonies in his head; so the contemporary period that was his subject could only be comprehended if the changes brought about by the invention of musical notation were clearly recognized, even though that revolution was centuries ago; and only if the consequences of Music's First Freedom—won in its dim beginnings—were understood: namely when the dominance of voice and dance was replaced by the rule of the instrument in both composition and performance; for that was when pure music came with pain and exhilaration into being. After all, he would explain, contemporary electronic music was stagnant because it hadn't discovered how to represent on nicely ruled paper what it was doing. He had read that symbolic logic had been in the same fix, whatever symbolic logic was.

Joseph could accept the overthrow of the voice without a qualm because it was a benevolent coup. He would make his students understand that a music freed from song, like a son who has sailed away a seaman and returned at the head of a fleet, will give back to that most human of all instruments such songs as had hitherto been inaudible: there would be mournful lieder beyond number, bloody operas galore, even majestic masses from devout atheists. Oh, Miss Ankle Jingle, who sits in the first row and widens her thighs to disconcert her teacher, the long line of *Les Nuit d'Été* will run ardently up your spine; ah,

Mr. Moonfaced Boy with the smile you've had painted on your head to disconcert your teacher, Heitor Villa-Lobos's sublime hum will cause your ears to flower; hey there, Mr. Notebook whose cover opens and closes with the measured rhythm of a feeding butterfly so as to disconcert the teacher, the melancholy beauty of *Das Lied von der Erde* will make your eyes water with relief, and *Vier letzte Lieder,* a summa without a sum, close them on a heavy sigh.

The entire class will be happy to realize that the music they fill arenas to hear now—the wail, the stomp, the pounded drum, the rhythmic clap, the frantic strum—could be fit company for an ending, as it was in the beginning, even of the world.

Joseph realized, as he faced his task, that he had no mentors to whom he might turn, for he had never taken a course in music much less one allegedly this up-to-date. How others might have taught it—managed this material, ordered its presentation, emphasized Varèse rather than Antheil—was a mystery. What did he know about his teachers anyway? only that he had been greeted by one in a provocative dress amid pillows and the smell of pot. Or was it in a dirndl with a stein of beer? His own history was learning to be hazy.

In the short time since he'd left Augsburg, the Whittlebauer semester had been shortened by a bad barber. A week of reading had been installed just before exams, during which time louts, like the one Joseph had been, might chase the tale of an entire semester and—worn out by all-nighters and cramming—recite it while asleep. Finals swallowed another opportunity. Add the three hourly exams that usually dotted the semester and one more week was gone. Good heavens—he had but thirteen left in which to expose his unfitness. Panic followed him like a jackal waiting for a show of weakness—a slowing limp in his Anton Webern or an out-of-breath Alban Berg.

Students tend to slink to the rear of a classroom and will advance toward the front only when threatened, but the Boy took a first-row seat on the first day, looked at Joseph as if listening to him, not vacant-faced as most were, not nervous like the impassive young woman whose left leg nevertheless wagged rhythmically, jingling her ankle bracelet, and certainly not wearily like the girl who bore to class a backpack bigger than a camel's hump, or morosely as the guy who was staring down at the closed covers of a notebook embossed with the school's insignia as if he had been asked to memorize the medallion. How about the sallow fellow who Joseph feared might bite through the temples of his eyeglasses and made his teacher anxious with the expectation? By the time he had become, in truth, Professor Skizzen, he had learned not to look at his students directly. Rather he allowed his gaze to pass swiftly over the tops of their heads, unless, of course, the heavens fell, and someone asked him a question. Then he would fix the presumptuous fellow (as the fellow usually was) with an attention so intense the student often stammered. However, Skizzen also knew how important it was to treat every query with polite and devoted concern, to let his look rise eventually, as if it were seeking a solution in the skies. This upward gaze was not entirely for show, since his answers were often made up and he might well have found them there—immersed in cloud.

My name is Joseph Skizzen. I have written my office hours on the board. He looked at the board. I should say I've printed. He smiled into a silence wholly empty of affect. I mean I've lettered my name there where you see it. I encourage you to come to me about any relevant concerns. If you can't speak to me after class, make an appointment. He stood in a puddle of silence as though he had wet his pants. Oh my, that was an additional worry. By now everybody should have a copy of the syllabus. There is one at just those seats I want you to occupy. Up front. I shall wait while you resettle yourselves . . . The game is called "musical chairs." In . . . He had made another big mistake. They were not used to this. It also defeated the democracy of the classroom.

[Pause whilst everyone repositions.]

During this semester we shall be following the course of contemporary music, by which I mean those composers who flourished from, roughly, the turn of the century to this one's belly-button, which, if you haven't forgotten, is halfway.

Someone tittered. Good. Who? it wasn't the youngster with the pageboy haircut; it wasn't the medallion examiner; and ankle bracelet hadn't missed a jink. He had committed a stupid bit of high school humor. It was a measure of his nervousness.

He suddenly recalled a ramshackle London classroom where everyone sat in all kinds of chairs the teacher had collected, each with a name pasted on it. Why had he not remembered this experience earlier, when he was contemplating the installation of a similar kindergarten regimen?

Those who like to christen schools of literature, art, and music often overlook differences in order to hang their chosen clothes in the same closet, but we shall pay particular attention to them. To differences, I mean. Not only do many streams feed our river, it, in turn, forks as often as you do at dinner. From the Boy a smile—beatific. Joseph was so lacking in confidence by this time, small gratuities were gratefully received.

Where had the clothes and the closet come from? Joseph thought he had worried about every eventuality, but lecturing had dangers he had not anticipated. You might fail for words or lose the thread or express yourself poorly. Now he knew that you might also run on, revealing yourself not your subject as you rambled. Because, when a house had been found for Miriam and Deborah, he had wanted his clothes to hang in the same closet as his sister's and had a tantrum when his wish was laughingly denied.

He proceeded to explain the mechanics of the course and hand out a sheet on which texts and assignments, as well as points of examination, were listed. Then he realized that he had already placed one on each chair's swollen arm. To signify where he wanted them to sit. So he waved his extras as if at a gnat. Of particular concern were the pieces he expected the students to listen (even attend) to. These were listed beneath each reading and were starred: essential, three, suggested, two, additional, one. By asterisks. Find them? . . . the asterisks? His tongue was as furry as a sheep is . . . furry. Okay.

Occasionally, a particular recording was insisted upon, though he could not guarantee its availability. Did they find that information? Also asterisked . . . Okay. His hands were trembling, so he placed them on the lectern from which his own copy of the assignment sheet was . . . flackering to the floor near the ankle bracelet. Thus irretrievable.

He saw it. He tried not to see it. He moved. He tried not to move. Never clear your throat at any time that can be given significance. Miss Jangle knew what to do. She crossed her legs.

When Joseph had the second interview for his present position, he had shocked the committee by insisting that a satisfactory selection of contemporary compositions should be available for individual student or classroom listening. The committee didn't know the state the record library was in (nor did he), but they assured him funds would be forthcoming to remedy gaps as he discovered them. Once on the scene, Joseph saw more holes than cheese, so he made his requests, along with those promises politely remembered. Money was no more forthcoming than the committee, which failed to take the problem up, forgot its former assurances, and neglected to reply when opportuned. Nevertheless, its members had been impressed in spite of themselves by his demands and even more by his forceful follow-ups (rare in this atmosphere), so his little bit of youthful arrogance had helped his case to begin with, and his diligence brought to his otherwise out-of-joint nose a whiff of esteem.

Thank God this rinky-dink college behaved like a high school: classes were ended through the din of a buzzer, books were gathered up by eager arms in the single unified deed of the day, and bottoms began to rise before ears could rid themselves of the bell. So Joseph never had to hunt for an ending. Still he would always want to add a word . . . just a word . . . only one. But the annoyance that crossed those faces as their rumps reluctantly returned to zero convinced him of the unwisdom of any additions, and he learned to snap his jaw shut like a parsimonious purse. Let them wonder what that word would have been. Though they wouldn't. Wonder. Ever. When the room was empty of them, he picked up the errant assignment sheet. One corner had a gray shoeprint on it.

20

The First Baptist Church had an upright in its basement that Joseph might be allowed to use if he would play for a few social occasions. This opportunity had come about through Marjorie's intervention, but how his benefactress had managed it he did not know, because the congregation was mostly black as was the minister. The basement walls were cinder block painted a kind of cream, and the floor was covered with shiny haphazardly dented linoleum. One wall gave way to a window-like opening through which the rudiments of a kitchen could be seen. There were paper-covered trestle tables and folding chairs sitting about in creative confusion. None was friendly to his sounds. Joseph tried to avoid busy times, but occasionally he'd be practicing when the sound of a rehearsal or a service would sink down the stairs. Then he would cease his own feeble plunks to listen to dozens of deep voices singing something he couldn't make out except that it was wildly rhythmic and sounded ecstatic. He'd hear clapping, too, and, good heavens, "amens" made as though they meant something. Ultimately a contralto would break through the sunshine like wanted rain. Her voice, and the interfering floor and ceiling pipes, reminded him of Mr. Hirk's pitiful Victrola and its statically clouded recordings.

Finally, during one such interruption, Joseph sidled quietly up the basement stairs until, from its landing, he heard a single voice singing in dark supple hues:

One more valiant soul right here,
One more valiant soul,
One more valiant soul right here,
To help me bear this cross.

Then ten or twelve voices joined for the chorus:

O hail, Mary, hail!
Hail, Mary, hail!
Hail, Mary, hail!
To help me bear this cross.

Joseph strained to catch complexities. He'd never heard what he presumed was gospel before. The music could make a sewing circle out of a howling mob. He could hear it knitting the singers together the way a hallelujah did. Soon the chanting and the clapping and the singing stopped. Joseph interpreted footsteps and murmured talk as an approach, so he retreated to his piano and pretended his fingers were busy.

Indeed, in a moment, a large red figure rocked her bulk down the steps and emerged from the darkness of the hall. To Joseph's astonishment it was Miss Spiky who threw up her arms to see him at the piano, actually striking keys with his fingers as he had hurried to do. You, boy? Glory. What you doin here, Mr. Rambler? You realize we kin hear you down here? I can hear you, too, Joseph said before he realized that he was the guest. I'm sorry. I try to keep out of the way. You weren't in no way. We could hear you, but we dint mind cause we sing loud. You do, Joseph said, and nicely, too. And nicely, too, yes, Miss Spiky agreed. You play better than you drive? A bit. Anyway down here you dont endanger folks. Joseph ruefully touched a key. What you were singing sounded Catholic, he said. What did? Hail . . . you know . . . the Hail Marys. Thas Catholic? Miss Spiky's great red storefront shook its signs. Well, we aint particlar. A hymn to him—Adam man—is a hymn to him, and thas what we're about. Adam man? Joseph wondered, who's that? Sumbuddy dont know the score, Miss Spiky said with a laugh. There is religion, Joseph thought, and then there is religion.

Who was the contralto? She has a wonderful voice.

I sure am sprized to see you.

Ditto. Ah . . . me too. I work at the library. I catalog books. And oversee purchases. So . . . Marjorie Bruss—she's the head of the library—persuaded your church to let me practice on this piano since I . . . since my piano is home in Woodbine where my mother is.

Howd she do that? I couldn't beat on the back of our munny-pinchin pastor enuf he buy his truck from me.

I don't know how she did it. I didn't know she knew any . . .

For free?

For . . . well, if I play a little for . . . some ceremonies.

Chile stuff. You'll look suity. The little giggles'll be in white, too. For confirmation an ring-aroun-the-rosy.

You live here, too?

I church here. My husband leff me these three-town lots. He was used up, and in pieces, too, by the end. My voice was always mine.

So that was you? you singing? I mean, the solo part?

Miss Spiky opened a very wide mouth. I know moon-rise, I know star-rise,

Lay dis body down.

Oh, that's—

I walk in de moonlight, I walk in de starlight
To lay dis body down.
I'll walk in de graveyard, I'll walk through the graveyard,
To lay dis body down.

Gee—There was no stopping her. She sang with a full throat and without embarrassment. Gee—he'd said gee.

I'll lie in de grave and stretch out my arms;
Lay dis body down.
I go to de judgment in de evening of de day,
When I lay dis body down;
And my soul and your soul will meet in de day
When I lay dis body down.

Joseph dared to applaud. Miss Spiky's voice rocketed about the basement so rapidly and with such a roar it ran over its own echoes.

You can clap, but you can't applaud. Only the Lord is worthy of that, an he dont need it. He knows he's good. I beleeve, in the beginin, he sang; he didnt say those first letters, he sang; he sang, Glory glory let there be light.

All that Joseph could manage was: I like the car.

I tole you it'd run all right. So youre a music man not just a Rambler man?

I'm pretty much self-taught . . . except for a spell when I studied with Professor Hirk. Maybe you've heard of him?

About such, I dont hear much, Miss Spiky said, rolling her shoulders.

And how is Billy Bear? Back in Lowell? Still?

Worn out. Worn out from workin charms. Takes his stuffin, pinch by pinch. To do the burn. He is thinnin to match his grinnin.

There's religion and then there's religion, Joseph said, where only he could hear. He realized, just as it was now with his mother, that he should not try to extend this conversation by asking, for instance, how business went on. Their talk, even such as it was, would take turns he couldn't steer through. I don't remember a smile amid that fur, Joseph said.

He wasnt smilin. I dont think. That day. Sleepy maybe like a baby. You were goin home from Whichstown?

To Woodbine . . . yes.

But it's Whichstown now?

Yes . . . for now. I'm—

In a voice, like herself the size of three divas, she burst into a chorus of "Go Down Moses" as her back began to face him. She stopped abruptly. Spect I'll see you again then.

Expect so.

Mind the traffic.

Love your voice.

Its what it needs to be. Its loud.

Joseph very much wanted to tell Marjorie about his encounter. He very much wanted to tell Miriam, too. But he didn't think it wise to try to imitate Miss Spiky's voice; there were characters in the tale, like Billy Bear, he couldn't explain; background would need filling in; and he'd sound condescending, however he went about it. And when Miss Spiky disappeared up the stairs she was singing the way people do when they're happy. That Jordan was a wet river.

Joseph had spent more time than he had ever thought he would in church basements. The library's basement, in contrast, was lonely dark crowded silent, with floors of cement, racks of steel, and windows of brick, but he was adding up hours in it, too. He was saying to Miss Moss how strange it was that there were people whom you encountered at the edges of your life that you just sort of oozed around, as though they were crumbs on a kitchen counter and you were a little spill. Miss Moss was looking intently at him as if he had given her a crumb's role when they both jumped at a scream that came from above like a burst pipe. Marjorie, Joseph exclaimed, already trying to bound up the narrow stairs and stumbling so badly he whacked a knee. He hardly felt it happening, though he knew he would suffer later when the joint was swollen and purple as an onion. Despite his awkward fall Joseph reached Marjorie's desk rather quickly and from there saw her in the reading room being threatened it seemed by Portho who was yelling now loud as a train conductor while gesturing wildly, yet looking somewhat dazed to Joseph as he ran toward them, and his outcries increasingly mechanical. It was he, he would learn, who had screamed. Marjorie was holding her breath and her chest with both hands. Her hair was aloft as if it were momentarily on a cat's back. She was shrinking against a table with otherwise no good place to go. Portho was yowling more than anything when Joseph came up huffing and said, What's this?

I've asked—I've asked this man to leave.

From Portho a grimace as tortured as a shout. My goodness! Joseph said, a little late with his question: Did he just begin to yell like this?

Portho yelled again, but it was the size of a cough.

We can't have extemporaneous noise like this, sir, not in the library. Readers will be disturbed.

Aint nah peeple, Joseph made out.

Just get this man out of here, Joseph, just get him out. The first thing is out. Out for you, mister, you miserable man! You ungrateful piece of waste!

Unhand this woman at once, you varlet, Joseph half shouted himself.

Gonne donne nonne hands on her.

You shall have to go, varlet sir, at once. Joseph endeavored to push between the two combatants, though without enthusiasm. Portho at that moment seemed vile, composed of filth and froth and frightening behavior. Had it not been Marjorie in this encounter (or maybe his mother or maybe maybe Miss Moss) he might not have had the will. But he did not touch Portho, he was afraid to do that. He slid like a thin book between them.

Don't touch him, he'll scream again. I shook him awake, Marjorie said, still out of breath. That's what set him off. He was snoring so.

Ah, you see, sir, sleep is normally silent, Joseph said in a far-from-resolute voice. If you are going to sleep noisily you'll have to do it outside. Outside, sir. I believe it's a nice day. Joseph would try later to forget how fatuous he was being (had been), but the effort would never succeed. The moment became a permanent embarrassment, a scar on life's skin.

Portho was now still, arms limp, mouth slack. It was Marjorie who was growing shrill. Out, she was repeating. With an elongated *O*. Portho was passive. He was now an empty bottle in an empty sack. Joseph merely gestured like a waiter, and Portho shuffled away from

Marjorie toward the door, allowing Marjorie to lower her voice, though the *O* remained sizable and replete with huff. Aint nah peeple. Bother nah, Portho managed. But he went. To Joseph's immense relief, he went meekly out the door, pushing through it himself, and stepping slowly down the front steps in his absurd huge tennis shoes like a figure in a silent movie. Marjorie still leaned back against the rim of the library table as if she were being pushed, her face pale but with a hint of yellow in it like a page from an old book.

You are my hero, she said after Joseph reached her side. Joseph held her then the way Miriam had sometimes held him. His own blood began to return from wherever it had hidden. He thought he was embracing her, but when he relaxed his grip, he realized that Marjorie was enfolding him, cheek to chest, her hair, redolent, no doubt from overheated temples, yet fragrant in a light way like stationery that's been stored with a sachet, muffling, veiling his face.

Joseph sneezed. So they had to part. Sorry, he said, sneezing again. Tickle . . .

Bless, Marjorie said, even more briefly than spelled.

Ah . . .

Allergic. You're allergic to me.

No . . . ah . . . no . . . He sneezed. Your hair . . . my nose . . . tickled.

Well, back to your basement or wherever you were, she said. Our little excitement is concluded. He won't be back, I'm sure. Thank you for your help.

Oh no. I did nothing. You had matters in hand. He—

Screamed. It wasn't I who screamed like that, I can tell you. I shook him a mite. Put a hand I need to wash, oh dear yes, on an arm—his arm—and shook him just a little, he was snoring so, I never heard the like. And he screamed like a bird in the night. He—

Inspired, Joseph took her in his arms again. Poor dear, he said, moving his head out of the way of her hair, which wasn't easy. He felt her soften. My hero, my young hero, she said.

They stood together until they both became aware that Miss Moss was nearby. You screamed. I heard a scream, Joseph and I heard it. Joseph, you left me like an antelope from a lion. A scream like that—in a library—quite curdles the blood.

I did not scream.

I heard one.

It was Portho, Joseph said. His knee was beginning to hurt.

It was a woman's scream.

Yes, but Portho made it. Marjorie hardly raised her voice. Joseph's knee was throbbing like a thrummed bass.

Miss Moss was sure she had heard the Major playing Lady Macbeth. What need we fear who knows it, when none can call our power to account? she said in a firm theatrical tone, as if in character.

Joseph was nonplussed. His knee was speaking to him in Dutch. That was how his mother described her aches and pains: her joints were jabbering in Dutch, a tooth was yelling in Dutch, her stomach was mumbling in Dutch. Marjorie had clearly reentered her cool mood, a mood that hadn't been far away. Joseph was as silent as anyone who knows they are socially inept, but he felt gratitude when Miss Moss receded. Marjorie walked briskly by to reach her desk, where she was immediately busy, stirring her affairs; these were apparently steaming like a pot. Joseph looked around at table, chair, and radiator in case something required a tidy; however, all was as much in order as ever. He tried to pull a pant leg past his knee but couldn't, and the cloth when it rubbed over the spot where he'd had it knocked was excruciating. Despite the pain he limped from the library without a word of triumph, need, or farewell, except that he could still hear Marjorie through the open entry. She had recovered her aplomb but now was losing it again. Var let, she managed between fresh hilarities. Var-let, oh my, oh me, un-hand, oh no, un-un-han . . . ha ha!

Joey climbed the hill to his car, complaining to the slope as he strived to conquer it. He cursed his keys before he rolled the Rambler to the street—they never fit the first time—and weaved his way to Woodbine. Miriam would be shocked at what he'd done to himself, but also curious and solicitous. While he drove he rehearsed his story, divided nicely into edifying anecdotes: prestos with adagios after them, bright panels companioned by pastels more suitable on pajamas.

21

For a fake, this is an utter flop, Miss Moss said with a smile that suggested she would be happy to help Joseph improve the quality of his counterfeit—at the least raise its grade from an F to a gentleman's C. Because this, she said, holding the offending document by the tweezering tips of her nails, is the license of a loser.

The Bumbler and its presumptuous driver had suffered some near misses over the weekend when Skizzen had driven it to Woodbine in what had become his routine line of duty. He had nearly rear-ended an Amish wagon while cresting a hill, and the scare had opened him like a tin. Later, Joseph had taken a turn too fast and found himself riding the berm. It prepared him to confess his crimes and face jail. Luckily, the expulsion of Portho, a shabby instrument of Satan, from their run-down Eden, as Miss Moss, in inflated tones, preferred to describe the encounter, had apparently made "the dweller in the cellar" more approachable, though Joseph thought Portho's departure was scarcely sun enough to soften her. Whatever her reasons, Miss Moss had evidently decided to let Joseph admire how her deft fingers flew when she made some basic book repairs; and it was during these demonstrations that he had complained of the car's erratic behavior and mentioned his fear of being pulled over by the state police, whose eye for the flimsy fob-off driver's license he carried (and a "permission" they would surely demand he produce) might be sharper than any of the more casual cops from town. Miss Moss had asked to see the offending document whose clumsiness richly amused her. It was a state that Joseph had rarely seen. However, here, in her workroom, she no longer seemed to be a skittish spinster; rather she resembled a competent craftsman, diagnosing difficulties, choosing treatments, dabbing on glues with confident swipes, or even sewing up spinal wounds with surprising dexterity, applying healing oils, and squeezing books in padded vises as though they were patients instead, needing traction.

Although Urichstown's little library had only the most rudimentary equipment, Miss Moss seemed familiar with the miracles performed in places of wealth and regard—institutions that consequently had fancy restoration and preservation departments. She singled out the Library of Congress where she had seen sulfurous compounds harmlessly leached from brittle papers, and tears mended that seemed beyond a surgeon's skills. If Joseph's little secret had slipped out, so had the information that Miss Moss had once been the head of their modest library and had, during her tenure, made more than one visit to the Folger as well as to the Library of Congress. On one most memorable visit to the capital, she had been honored by a tour of its magical laboratories. As she spoke, she held the plasticized card high in the air at the end of a wavering arm. I understand the passport people use a kind of blue light that brightens the ink on a genuine document and forces any falsified design to disappear. Joseph didn't dare ask about the historic upheaval that had plucked her from the front desk and sent her to this small basement room with its odd inadequate lamps, few tools, and scarred workbench; nevertheless it was a hideaway, and out of all beck and most calls. Although Miss Moss still resented the Major as well as her own continued subservience to an upstart, she had happily adjusted to "debasement," a condition for which she had several other similar names. I hang about here like a bat in a cave, she said, making a boast of her banishment. I am the Keller Madchen. You are like a bottle of fine wine, Joseph suggested. Dusty from lying a-round, Miss Moss amended, but he could see that she was pleased.

We shall have to start fresh and see if we can re-place this dimestore dickydoo with one worth at least a quarter. For Miss Moss, repeatedly ridiculing Joseph's so far single foray into forgery was a convoluted form of acceptance, even affection. She produced a camera from a cardboard box otherwise so full of gray rags the Polaroid could not at first be located, although Miss Moss's dithering search for it was like a performance put on to tease a child whose birthday present momentarily cannot be found: Is it here? no? where could it be? In order to position him against the one white wall that was unobstructed by steel shelves, Miss Moss was forced to shove Joseph's shoulders into squareness. Then, from a compact slipped from her purse like a tip to be discreetly offered, she patted powder on one of his shining cheeks—There now, that's better—before she suddenly flashed him full in the face.

He who has lived and thought can never . . . look on mankind without dis-dain, Miss Moss said firmly, as if speaking about the photo she'd just taken.

I don't drive anymore—since the twenty days—but we can still use my license as a model. In fact, she said after a moment of apparently efficient thought, we may be able to do more. We can update and alter mine to achieve yours. Joseph protested that by no means could he allow . . . there was no circumstance that might possibly permit . . . but Miss Moss was not to be deterred by wholehearted protests, not to mention Joseph's halfhearted ones, and in a thrice her card was firmly positioned beneath a large rectangular magnifying glass whose surface she repeatedly sprayed with cleanser because each wipe of the cloth seemed to soak up the ammonia while otherwise smearing the lens. A curse upon all this in-competent equipment, she said, as if she were alone.

After a few minutes of swift adjustments that did not acknowledge his existence, Joseph was allowed to reenter Miss Moss's world, where she became an enthusiastic instructor in inks and alterations. Here, this is a slow zone, I mustn't hurry, but I've been hasty, she said aloud, yet again as though alone. Against the outside wall, where bottle-glass windows let in a grime-gray light, stood a photo stand made of card table, drafting board, and ingeniously twisted coat-hanger wire. Two rather long-legged flashlights were suspended over the board and a covering piece of poorly wiped heavy glass that had been dented or chipped as if it had suffered the fall of at least one of them. The license was moved to this makeshift mechanism where another fusty old camera had been hung from a clamp affixed to a pole, its barrel nose-down through the hanger's hook. The entire arrangement appeared perilous.

Every Christmas someone asks me to copy a page they've picked, or an illustration they fancy, so I just keep this camera in its place. I think they paste the photos in special homemade greetings. Anyway, they want them for holidays . . . nearly always . . . you can imagine . . . and for valentines. My services don't come free. Film is not cheap, you know, and people don't usually want to wait until I've finished a roll. Could be months. On your behalf I shall demand a day off for good deeds, Joseph promised. Miss Moss felt obliged to giggle.

I know a valentine. I am sure you do, Joseph said, uncertain of what he meant. I'm sure you've received many, he blundered on, with lace and flowers and little hearts. Miss Moss held up a flour-white hand. The valentine I know wasn't meant to be a valentine. The poet didn't mean it to be a valentine; he never meant it to be in such service, yet I call it a valentine. "Why should this flower delay so long to show its tremulous plumes?" Good question, don't you think? Asked of the chrysanthemums, all the late bloomers, but you know, chrysants don't have plumes. Plumes grow on hats. A palm remained raised in greeting or surrender. "Now is the time of plaintive robin-song," she sort of sang, and very softly and slowly, too, as if remembering the lines as she went along, "when flowers are in their tombs." Actually, I've been alone my whole life, she said then in a normal tone. That "bloom" rhymes with "tomb" is very fortunate for the poet, wouldn't you say? "It . . . the flower . . . must have felt that fervid call although it took no heed"—well, I didn't need a dower did I? great saving there. I went from womb to tomb . . . hee-hee . . . no stops in between. Alone in my stone tomb my whole life. I speak every day—and sometimes night—with the dead. There is a wonderful rhyme coming up. "Took no heed," yes, "waking but now, when leaves like corpses fall, and saps all retrocede." Don't you love that? I know a valentine when I read it. When the world ends the word will write on . . . wordulating. Yes, I know a valentine, heart of yours, heart of mine. On this project I can see we shall achieve some savings, too. A fine sentiment, Joseph said, thinking she was finished, but she shushed him with a look. "Too late its beauty, lonely thing, the season's shine is spent." Oh dear, Joseph thought, oh dear. "The seed its harvest, or the lute its tones," she hummed, but rather loudly, and then conducted with a forefinger the line to its conclusion, "tones ravishment, or ravishment is sweet if human souls did never kiss and greet." That kind of repetition has a name, but I've forgotten what it is, Miss Moss went on in a different register. The valentine is in the kiss and greet part. Oh, dear, I think I'm in another poem. Have you ever been lost like that? "Nothing remains for it but shivering in tempests turbulent." An arrow through the heart is a perfect emblem . . . well . . . for everything . . . She was still and silent then as if appreciating a memory and remained so until her raised finger fell.

The plastic that will subsequently be our friend is presently our enemy. Miss Moss kept her thumb over the spaces that stated her age and weight. Your eyes are—open, open'um up, dear—brown would you say? well, mine are hazel it says here, so we'll leave HAZ alone, hazel can be anything, and no one cares about eyes, they never check. The photo won't show but a whistle of what color they are anyway. You can open a checking account now. Establish some credit, don't they say? we must all die in debt. Height has to go up to what? 508 from 506? that's easy, but see—she ran a nail across the card—this coating won't let us get at your vitals . . . so . . . we'll alter . . . you know . . . mine. We'll duplicate it and remake the copy. So you needn't protest. My card will stay clean of any crime, okay? You are such a silly . . . Sweet, yes . . . But a bit silly . . . I don't write checks myself, never have. I like to pay in person. Then I know. I know a valentine. Miss Moss studied the situation. "Swell to a green pulp" is a coarse expression, don't you agree? "Pulp" is a poor word, Joseph, just remember. Weight? you have a weight there? Not much more than mine. You don't amount to much, dear, do you? Oh, dear. "Green pulp" is from that other poem, the one I got lost in. Miss Moss's head shook from side to side in a regret that was as slow as a lover's good-bye. I know I don't amount. Did once. Around here. But not after the twenty days.

Joseph made a sound that could have meant anything.

Got to squeeze your innocent face into that lower corner . . . tape over my signature with something the color of dirty dairy cream . . . to give you a nice blank space to sign. She tapped her index finger on the spot: Name and address are the difficult deal. Numbers, did you ever notice? if not, notice now. They lend themselves to defacements: the 1 to a 7, the 7 to a 9, the 9 to an 8 or a 3, whichever, or a 6 to an 8, alterations as easy as a sleeve's. *I*'s into *T*'s, or *O*'s into *A*'s aren't hard, like adding lobes to ears, but letters, on the whole, aren't agreeable. We'll remove and re-do them, pretend we can type. She gestured toward an ancient Underwood portable that stood in melancholy disuse upon a small metal stand in a corner facing the door.

While Miss Moss pondered the problems that attended these criminal proceedings, Joseph looked about, now with renewed interest. Everything seemed borrowed, nothing new. He felt a bit borrowed himself. On the edge of a very scarred old library table two vises—one small, one huge—were tightly clamped. They appeared to have been there a long time because the jaws bore patches of bare metal and there were dark dents where their present grips had bitten the wood. Between glue and paste pots, brushes, threads, and needles, pools of remaining varnish still glistened. He saw several weights retired from their grocery scale days, erasers sitting among grains of gum, a dry stamp pad, pens, inks, fat rubber bands, scissors in several sizes, a tweezers, too, as well as place-mark ribbons, rolls of Scotch and masking tape, a few scrappy endpaper pieces, and a teakettle clearly meant only for steam.

Miss Moss gently edged Joseph aside to remove two developer trays. She positioned his license next to hers on a sheet of bright white paper that nevertheless looked much used. Finding himself a chair length farther along, he counted a couple of clothespins that had been concealed by miscellaneous tubes and tins. At the table's end, a number of Miss Moss's ubiquitous rags had collected round a rather large roll of butcher's paper. There a slightly nicked magnifying glass lay buried near a pair of once-white cloth gloves. At her request he rescued it from beneath a coil of navy-blue velvet ropes full of what he guessed, as he hefted them, were grains of rice. Or beans. Perhaps beans. I always know where everything is, she said as if reading disapproval like a headline from his impassive face. Those are pythons. You know, snakes. So soft. So Mus-cular. They keep your book gently open. Dis-tribute their weight. Joseph read the label of a tube of stuff meant for cleaning suede shoes.

His expression had meant to mask the bewilderment of ignorance, but he was also immensely reassured by what he took to be the residues of creativity: the way pots pans and dirtied spoons signified a whirl of mixing and a busy chef's surety of measurement and touch. Miss Moss just needed someone to control and calm the fuss she made over the way Joey cleaned up after her. His mind traveled over lines noted down from recent books: all these happenstance arrangements needed a brisk dose of ship's shape, bit of spiff and polish, weight upon the waters. Nevertheless, he had to admit, the place was spooky. At one corner of the ceiling a small cloud of cobweb had gathered. There was little natural light and what there was looked weary, as though it had traveled a great distance only to die on a cluttered bench.

I do miss riding the bus though, Joseph ventured.

Snake, please. Miss Moss held out a small white palm. I need a weight. Oil upon the waters—that's it, he thought. Joseph handed her a length of velvet rope. He saw that each end was tied up in a knot by violet thread.

You see some interesting people on the bus.

Meet any? Miss Moss bent intently over her work.

One.

The air felt cool as a cave's, their voices artificially resonant.

Who?

A teddy bear.

Ever have a toy you were frightened of?

Nooo . . . Never had many toys.

I was given a bulldog once with a black eye and big teeth. Scared me so. I was supposed to hug him. He was stuffed like a club. Hard as a ham-mer. I buried him in the backyard, I was so scared. These villainous magi wanted me to take bowwow to bed. I screamed, I was so scared. So I buried it in the backyard with a shovel I had for sand. But that bowlegged dog with a pirate's eye still haunts me. To and in-cluding this day. Even this day. Even down here. Eventually we moved away from the house with its grave. We left that backyard in our wake, but the toothy bulldog followed me. He's al-ways—good, that should do it—a-round, barking loudly though you can never hear him. "He who has felt such fear is haunted forever . . . by days that will not come again," she suddenly half hollered. I bet the teddy bear was better company.

His mother—a great wide woman—was.

Mothers. I never liked mothers much, you know that? None of my mothers were . . . well—it's done, and now you are a person to the world—very motherly. Take a card.

Joseph decided silence was the better speech.

I left your weight the same as mine. See. I don't need weight now that I never drive. Because the cop that stops you always looks in the driver's window where you're sitting in your shame and guilt, and he can't tell, not even if God were to ask him, how much you're heavied. Of course . . . if he orders you to get out . . . the truth may get out, too.

Gratitude made Joseph brim over with that truth. It led him to overlook the misperceptions he had already encouraged: that he was Austrian, that he was a more accomplished musician than he really was, that he had graduated from Augs and done rather well there, when he had done rather poorly and dropped out. Or that he had friends like Chris the King of the tennis courts who would offer him their driver's license to copy.

Joey rather liked buses, Joseph said. He had ridden on double-deckers in London during the Blitz. They bounced about quite a bit because of the shell—no—bomb holes . . . craters. Yes, he had endured the bombing.

Hid in basements, sought refuge in sewers, often in the Underground, where people held one another when the earth shook. Yes, he had been frightened by near misses and had seen people blown to pieces before his very eyes. And a piano, too, every key flung up in the air to fall like rainless music. He didn't remember bus rides in Vienna, though—too young. But he could still recall vast parks. Vienna Woods—yes. Both cars and carriages. Vendors purveying ices and little cakes. "Purveying" was a new word Joseph was pleased to take for a walk. The sea voyage to America was worse than the Blitz because roaring storms bedeviled him and his mother the entire trip, the ship taking on water, whitecaps above the masts like angry spitting clouds.

Details filled in behind his recollections the way leaves blow into a hedge. Although Miss Moss led Joseph out of her office and returned him to his routines, he realized that he was welcome to rap at her door when down in her domain. He was also allowed to use her typewriter to compose a few letters of reference and a CV faithful to its form if faithless in everything else. She taught him a few tricks with inks. And how to steam off stamps and safely remove other sorts of seals.

Miss Moss admonished Joseph not to speak to the Major about his visit. He was to remain particularly mum about the ID and that she had showed him how to ink, Polaroid, or steam. Have you received the green glare of Major's eyes? Joseph hadn't. He rather thought her eyes . . . green in the import of them . . . I mean, green the way a fire burns. While Quasimodo plies his bells, Quasimama sweeps her keep, she said, adding mystery to mystery.

Joey's new driver's license already felt legitimate where it hid as it should in the wallet he had stuck in his hip pocket. Feeling it there made him calmer when he drove, if not more competent, and as the car rose over the low hills he saw endless possibilities in every barn and silo, as he had in his recent journey through his own past, since every memory was made of many elements, each of which had or could be given a diverting history. He felt front porches fill with people he could then pretend to know. Smaller roads kept crossing or leaving the highway, and he could travel over any one of them simply by turning his wheel to drive down the lane of the damaged piano or visit the day when his dad had disappeared (for public consumption, Joseph would call him "dad"), the bobbies arriving at their door as though Dad were dead or in dreadful trouble; or he could stop to admire the greeting-card view of his first Christmas in America or even revisit Debbie's wedding in the backyard of the groom's potato patch. For that miserable affair he could collect clichés and stereotypes like the stamps he had only today learned to lift from envelopes.

The Skizzen family had been driven to a small severe church for a ceremony that was simple and soon over, distressing Miriam, who of course was upset to be the sole Catholic in the crowd and often taken to be Jewish in the bargain. It was also clear that her daughter was the only member of this refugee family the groom's was inclined to adopt. Deborah wore a dress her mother had made for her and was given away by her brother, who was consequently compelled to be civil. She looked pretty in the way brides must, beaming like an ad and smooth as a counterpane. Afterward the congregation drove out into the country where, in a farmyard, the bride and groom recapitulated kisses.

After a decent interval the dismal couple departed for their prepackaged life with only one JUST MARRIED sign on their car and no tin cans to rattle at their rears. In a few days they would return to the family property where the groom's inheritance was being prematurely forked over like one of their hills of potatoes. Joseph determined to think of his new in-laws as small-town bovines who mooed when you pulled their tails and then blew smoke from their noses. As cartoons he could endure the folks they really were, people calm in their convictions, as secure about the direction of their life as a train about the destination of its track, and this serenity unsettled Joey, who admitted in dark moments to being envious as well as scornful of it, because the regularities of his own life had been so routinely interrupted and because it depended on an indifference to the wider world that was tended as carefully as one of their spud-filled fields.

But, if ignorance brings bliss, as he had recently learned, it is still smart to be satisfied. When he complained to Miriam about the complacency of his about-to-be in-laws, she told him he wouldn't have liked Austrians then, because they knew to a napkin how life should go on, what was right and what was wrong—be honest, work hard, trust God—everybody knew these things, they knew them, but they often didn't do them because honesty meant you couldn't steal and cheat and get ahead of others by using damnable devices. Hard work was hard, that's why it was called hard, so few people wanted to do it, though they knew they should, they knew to trust God, too, which was the most difficult, since it meant accepting the troubles that made up much of life, accepting them and getting on, even when you were uprooted, bombed, and abandoned.

As *she* had been, she was once more prepared to tell him.

During Joseph's many pensive moments in the library, he had an opportunity to reflect upon his own unearned sense of superiority. He began to realize that his friends would see him as they saw a Christmas package, decorated to entice but wrapped to conceal. By giving himself youthful myths and minor mystifications, he had donned, in effect, a powdered wig and a false nose and thereby could actually remain far away in his actual unoperatic life, doing nothing they might imagine, feeling nothing they could share, still pure as plain blue sky. Unsmudged by the smoke from a single chimney.

For as nice as Miss Moss had been to him, helpful and generous with her time, she was nevertheless a ghost with gloves and her own fake skin, wrinkled as though it had gone years without pressing, her animosities running about in her like disturbed ants. Joey now regretted changing Madame Mieux into a German. She had lost a lot in the move, and he was reconsidering the point of her presence. Good heavens, he had forgotten her new name as a Frau. Hilda something. That wouldn't do.

Some of his stories seemed to suit the self that Joseph was fashioning right from the beginning. He remembered the plotlines, the highlights, the deft amusing touches without any difficulty, but other features slipped away in the very moment they were being introduced. As his trees bore fruit he decided he should not let the flesh fatten too far from the core. "Swell to a green pulp," wasn't that Miss Moss's expression? When he had listed his age on his new license, he had added five years, no more, which would give him a little time in Graz or Vienna, the latter a larger presence, a more resounding destination, a better birthplace. Consequently, that flight to London, like the other Joseph's to Egypt, could be made more graphically perilous and prolonged.

Unfortunately, he also remembered the indistinct document, now carefully hidden away in a closet, that registered his birth in London, and upon which one of his palms was printed, or—no—it was a tiny foot. A footprint. No one need know about it. That path was safely covered. On the other hand, if he wanted to follow some official format when he made out a new one and became born again (as the students at Augs used to say when they had managed to memorize a particularly salient Lutheran fact), he had better dig it out and take another look. His mother would try to monitor everything, and she would not be pleased to think he was altering the date of his birth. Well, this fresher forgery was a problem that, because of the card Miss Moss had made for him, could afford to wait for an opportune time.

22

The expectation that the human race might be destroyed by its disappointed Gods as a punishment for mean and murderous madness of the sort that Professor Joseph Skizzen's Inhumanity Museum documents daily has been superseded by the horrifying possibility that the species may be rewarded for its follies instead, with citations for crime, awards for cruelty, and medals for madness.

During the same week that Professor Joseph Skizzen was preparing his final lectures on Arnold Schoenberg's *Moses und Aaron,* the newspapers were carrying reports concerning a celebrated Israeli rabbi who had, at last, solved the greatest theological question presented to the faithful by the Holocaust—namely, why? and six million times why? why? why? . . . why?

There will be no Judgment Day until we undertake to celebrate it. There was a why for Jews, of course: what had their people done to breach the Covenant so utterly and so reprehensively as to deserve annihilation? There was also a why to trouble Christians unless they could forget that German Catholics and German Lutherans had murdered all those German Jews; unless they could somehow reconcile God's bloodlust with their own thirst by viewing the Almighty's malevolence as carte blanche to give heretics and Christ killers what they surely deserved—a punishment long in coming and therefore most acceptable. There should be a similar why put to the followers of Islam about Allah, the One and Only God, because to single out Jews to exterminate, as he obviously had, particularly Polish and German ones among countless equally deserving Spanish, Russian, or American specimens, not to mention oodles of additional infidels of all sorts, is . . . well . . . odd . . . Was Allah merely miming the Christian God Almighty, already an epic anti-Semite? The consequences were especially unexpected because the remnants wound up unwanted on the doorstep of the Palestinians—not, one would think, a result in Allah's plans. No one has seemed similarly concerned that Joseph Stalin murdered many more millions than Adolf Hitler (Professor Skizzen had ample documentation stuck to flypaper in the south dormers). He had finally decided that the reason for this (apart from left-wing reluctance and unremitting Jewish propaganda) was the absence of an organized state campaign against a specific racial target. In any case, what were all these deities—G-d, Jehovah, and Allah—allegedly up to while their minions were slaying even one soul not to say massacring so many? because they were all responsible, weren't they (those Gods, that is, that existed)? since their power and their wisdom were such decided particularities of their nature like our height and brain size; they were the culprits, surely, weren't they? these Notables of the Sky? if not for turning on the gas directly, at least for closing their ears to the hiss, turning their backs to the passing trains, washing their hands lest they be stained, taking a snooze through repeated beatings . . . yes, every one of those Gods . . . silent bystanders to innumerable shooting parties held till the bodies of the dead lay in heaps like potatoes, and all that human consciousness, all that awareness—in each victim the very candle of the Lord, it was always said, the very Light asked for at creation—was snuffed . . . ah yes . . . snuffed . . . snuffed . . . — so that's what the smoke was.

But Professor Skizzen had noticed that God was always excused. Any and every God. For any and every thing. A tornado might trash a trailer park and the poor wretches who survived would thank him for sparing them, as well as preserving a children's plate and one photo of the family grinning at the Falls as if they'd pushed the water over by themselves.

Perhaps the Gods alternated fucking off. "I won't interfere with the destruction of the temple, if you won't prevent the crucifixion of the Savior." The pagans, the Christians, and the Muslims had taken turns burning the Library of Alexandria, but it was a moment of rare cooperation. Most of the time the celestial bodies were at one another's figurative throats. The thought of burning drove Joseph to his attic where there was nothing but paper, sticky strings of clippings, rows of books, piles of magazines, stacks of newsprint, rolls of placards and posters, so he was always frightened by any word that implied ignition. The fact that burning had occurred to him was significant. Set those mountains of painful testimony ablaze, shred the evidence, erase the stories: of the young woman who was raped by her judges in punishment for the adultery of her brother, for instance. Out of what dark corner of the human mind . . . ? or is it all dark, even in the light? or do our murderous desires lie hidden in the closet of the entry? under the runner unrolled down the hall? or disguised as that spot under the dining table where the rug is stained? By whom are we ruled if not by our nature? Remove all signs of those murderers who now make movies of themselves going through their grisly motions; and there will remain the badgering of sweet maids by their horny masters or the drowning of babies in their baths. It is impossible to conceal all the evidence. Yet how easily we forget who we really are. Because it should give us the creeps. His father's plight had been desperate indeed, for where could one go, really, to stay clean—worse, who could one be to be tolerable?

Many have wondered whether man would survive the catastrophes to come; one alone worried that some just might.

Joseph Skizzen decided that given the constraints of the rabbi's beliefs his reasoning was ingenious if not otherwise acceptable. Clearly, God had to be absolved. It was not he but Hitler who had to be horrible. Theodicy had excused many of the sufferings of the Jews by insisting that Yahweh was using the enemies of the Chosen as a rod to punish them for irresolution and waywardness. So that part of the explanation was ready-made. Then the rabbi simply borrowed a strategy devised by the wisdom of the East so he could conveniently claim that these persecuted, executed Jews had been previously alive and had died once before. They had been recalled to life by God in order that they might be punished—on account of sins committed in former times—in the hell our world would become for the occasion. It was to be, not the Last, but an Intermediate, Judgment. No doubt the ordeals of the countless slain would be cautionary and contribute to the perfection of the world, an aim of every righteous Jew.

The rabbi was sternly urged to reconsider his suggestion, and, to Joseph Skizzen's disappointment, he rapidly did so, though with what recalcitrance was not reported. Surely the Holocaust victims did not deserve their fate. This was an objection most effectively aimed. That the rabbi's solution required a resurrection in the midlife of the world was not an issue for the papers and was not reported, though it might have been raised. Surely theologically prepped reporters would have said that these Jews had been transmigrated, cleverly inserted into unsuspecting wombs by many an innocent but impetuous penis. After all, rotten karma had already humiliated, maimed, impoverished, killed the populations of the world many times by the ring of the bell towers. Professor Skizzen certainly approved of the idea that birth was our first punishment, and that there would most certainly be others. Camp guards who had lost their lives to old age were even now being readied for victimization on future killing grounds.

When Joseph Skizzen's scissors had saved these hypotheses for his museum, they almost immediately encountered other, less theoretical, more painfully real catastrophes: in the Union of South Africa, Sri Lanka, Serbia, and the Sudan, in Afghanistan, Algeria, Ethiopia, Pakistan, Palestine, in Rwanda, Colombia, and the Congo, the criminal consequence of tribal animosities of every kind and degree of virulence, in India, Egypt, Iraq, Iran, in Bosnia, Croatia, Turkey, Lebanon, Bangladesh, Timor, in whatever they were presently calling Burma or Siam, in Somalia, Fiji, Chechnya, Ireland, Algeria, and Zaire . . . which, Joseph knew, was only to begin strife's roll call, and without the solace of an ending.

With all our ironies under lock and key, Joseph thought, might we not find a way to praise this rabbinical folly; indeed, we could return to Erasmus himself and read how "man's mind is much more taken with appearances than with reality. This can be easily and surely tested by going to church." But Erasmus does not let the philosophers off either.

They "are reverenced for their beards and the fur on their gowns. They announce that they alone are wise, and that the rest of men are only passing shadows. Their folly is a pleasant one. They frame countless worlds, and measure the sun, moon, stars, and spheres as with thumb and line. They unhesitatingly explain the causes of lightning, winds, eclipses, and other inexplicable things. One would think that they had access to the secrets of nature, who is the maker of all things, or that they had just come from a council of the gods. Actually, nature laughs uproariously at them all the time." Yet it is not easy to find a funny bone in a charnel house. In the country of the mind there are calamities, not of the same kind, but equally worthy of our distress. The slaughter of reason is as regular as that of cows at an abattoir. This extraordinary human gift—the ability to think—is rarely used to recommend a calm and caring life, or even to find a just harmony among the needs of men. It appeared to Professor Skizzen, now, that reason was no more than an instrument of human appetites, the way our teeth and tummies are, precisely as some philosophers had suggested (though he had at first resisted them). The intellect was not the Columbus of ideal ends, the designer of legitimate aims, or the motivator of moral action. Instead, when it was not busy making money or in the inventive service of military might, or creating calcifying conveniences and debilitating amusements, it was being begged to justify envy's slanders, spite's pettiness, resentment's cruelty, power's enjoyment, and greed's greed, or asked to excuse lying, ineptitude, or brazenly manipulative ideologies, and sent to the aid of gross indifference or fashioned as a shield against pity, and support for a mercilessness exceeding any our boiling pots have for their lobsters or our guns for their game.

Each one of us shall perish. That is the good news. Our race, however, may survive. That is the bad news. Those who have perished will be beyond suffering and will not mind. That is the good news. Those who live later will care quite a lot about living and pay a great price for their desire. That is the bad news. The race shall survive for there are greater calamities to come. To die like flies is not how the flies will put it.

The first movement of Webern's symphony is followed by a second that is a candrizans of the first. Maybe that is how it will be. From Adam to Armageddon and back again. At the end of the world two humans will be left—so to say, standing—evE (whose palidromic name is perfect for the part), and madA, whose spelling is not so felicitous), and they shall live in a valley between mountains of slag and hills of reeking corpses, at first fully uniformed with passion aplenty to rape one another turn and turn about, and, only at the last orgasmic gasp, buck naked, sated, and ignorant as worms.

It occurred to Professor Skizzen that the problem with his sentence was: it wasn't a full twelve-tone row. What really obsessed him was the perpetual variation of a single idea that so perfectly suited music based on twelve tones.

First I felt mankind must perish; then I feared it might not.

Not quite. The right number of words, but he had repeated "I." How predictable. But he admired the *m*'s and *f*'s. Terse. To the point. Direct. Like a blow. Modest if it weren't for the pronoun. Semicolon though?

First Skizzen felt mankind must perish, then he feared it might not.

He had a feeling of great relief before he wondered what he might do with his wayward thoughts if he had no sentence to focus on. Would they dwell upon his coming confrontation and his almost certain ouster from the college? He needed to practice. He was rusty. His fingers were like stuck keys. When had he eaten last? Something green from the garden that Miriam must have mislaid. In F-sharp. No. There was no longer any key. Was "not" too unstressed for an end that was—well—another beginning?

First Skizzen felt mankind must perish, then he feared it might survive.

First	**Skizzen**	**felt**	**mankind**	**must**	**perish**
then	**he**	**feared**	**it**	**might**	**survive**

But were the "he" and "Skizzen" tones sufficiently distinct? As far as that goes, were "mankind" and "it"? Pronouns were merely pseudonyms trying to be names. He had gotten close, but the sentence's purity was not complete. It was not pure enough for Webern. Webern, who loved purity and order as much as the Führer did. The Inhumanity Museum was not pure because you would always find, in the neglected corners of these accounts, some helpless decency; and the evidence was not really ordered, only gathered in randomly disposed bunches and hung upside down like drying plants. Anton von Webern, he told his students, believed that the musical world his forefathers knew had dissolved and that a new order was necessary, one that would not tolerate cracks where weeds might grow. Wagner, who pushed tonality as far as Liszt would lead him, died, *Kinder,* in what year? a show of hands? Ai . . . In 1883, in the moment, I like to think, that Anton von Webern appeared. Tonality was *kaputt.* Adherence to the twelve-tone row was salvation.

Or so it seemed to Anton, since he got along quite well in the Vienna of the Nazis, where he taught (for a pittance) until the Americans began to bomb it; where he had his exquisite short works performed (to minuscule audiences); and where prizes (involving no money) were pinned to his chest like a general's medals. He was a von Webern, a German patriot, his soul grew as the territories of the state did; he dreamed, as did the Führer, of lands lapping at both oceans and admired the purity of some races. The frowns of the authorities and neglect by everyone else eventually silenced the sound of his music, yet his person and his position seemed safe. Ah, *mein Klasse,* reality is not a twelve-tone row, reality is a sly trickster, a Münchhausen, a femme fatale; because this mild mystical man, Anton Webern, this master of the minute, this Moses of the new commandments, he had a son-in-law, how could he help it? his daughter was not a violin, so (he thought) to prove to herself that she was not one of Daddy's instruments she married a cheapjack scoundrel, a man who, after the war, traded on the black market not like an ordinary person wanting a bit of butter but like an entrepreneur, making more money than his eyes could understand, buying this stocking, selling that cigarette, what could Anton Webern, good quiet agreeable follower of the Führer, do? anyway the war was over, order was everywhere disgraced, and the composer himself, fleeing American bombs, did I not say? had come to live with his daughter south of Salzburg, a city you, *mein Klasse,* should know admirable things about—and do you know any? show hands . . . ai . . . it's awful how you are; and there, in this little town of Mittersill, having dined with his daughter, her children, and this grievous mistake-making son-out-law, Webern went considerately to the porch for a smoke—a postprandial cigar—you will have read, heard, a cigarette, no no, a large cigar—and instead stepped into an ambush set by American soldiers for a black marketer who happened to be the very husband Anton's daughter had chosen to hurt the composer—you will have heard, you will have read, that there was a curfew Anton inadvertently violated, not at all, nonsense, and did he look brainy out there like Arnold Schoenberg? or willowy, beautiful, like Alban Berg? what a name, eh? Alban Berg! Anton Webern, Arnold Schoenberg, what names! no, he was a stoopy muddy-booted peasant who had a hangdog habit, very misleading, but just such a habit of hanging the dog nevertheless. The cigar did not glint, perhaps nothing glinted in the deepening dusk, perhaps it glowed, there was a gesture, a sudden turn, particulars are suspiciously lacking, and some GI, some Greedy Impulse, shot him dead when he turned with a pistol perceived to be in his hand, and this great man of minimal music died as if executed enjoying his last smoke, a picture that may be responsible for the cigarette it is said—you may have heard—he lit up.

Like fog, the professor liked to thicken his Viennese aura by addressing his class from time to time as *mein Klasse* or to employ unfamiliar word orders. This might remind you—no, of course not, it will not remind you, it reminds me—of another victim of horrible happenstance, one Bruno Schulz—you have had an acquaintance heretofore? how many hands? It was Skizzen's habit to ask such a question—how many hands?—and he continued to do so more determinedly after he learned that the campus called him Professor Namedrop, because it didn't hurt his enrollments to be a college character. Moreover, a few students were happy to make the acquaintance of some of these folks on whose behalf he called for a show of hands, as though he were arresting the answers, and even the scoffers loved the stories that followed the unrecognizable name in his lectures—incidents often full of gore and general calamity. They didn't mind being convicted of ignorance. Had every hand gone up, what would the professor have done with his anticipated and mock disappointment? ai . . . that no one had ever heard of the creature in question, ai . . . or knew anything about its name: the person some lout had shot, some loose lady had betrayed, some poet bitten by one of his own rhymes, some thinker clubbed by a thuggish thought.

Skizzen was also overly fond of the cute, riddling, or trick question. Do you know what the letters *SS* stand for? They stand for the Schoenberg/Stravinsky polarity. They stand for the opposition of the German musical tradition to Frenchified Russki danceatune music. Grinning, the professor would leave it at that—for the nonce.

So, Bruno Schulz—you wonder what is the connection?—he was a writer and a draftsman after all, not a musician—so you should wonder at my claim to relevance. He wrote great Polish prose. He drew nudes—you naughties would like that. One of his drawings depicts a dwarfish man and a hurdy-gurdy—that exhausts his relationship to music. As far as we know. And how far do we know? Anyhow, Schulz is another example of what happens to greatness in this world of ours. Like Webern—shot as a dark marketer by some stupid corn-fed pop-singing assassin who at least had the decency to drink himself to death during the years that followed, from guilt, we may like to imagine. Only the Pole's case was worse and more so. It happened—Schulz's life—the lesson of his life, our lesson for today—it happened in Drohobycz which was a small provincial town like Webern's Mittersill, but located in Galicia, not Austria—you know where is Galicia? nah, no hands—well, it is now the western Ukraine, a region also rich in composers, artists, scholars, and oh yes influential Jews including the founder of Hasidism, a movement of which you know? how many? show hands? *nein?* with a name like Bruno sewn on him you'd never think . . . of Jews. They slid slowly away from their faith, the Schulz family, in evidence of which I cite Bruno's mother, who changed her name from Hendel to Henrietta, though what would be the use? what? well, I spare you Schulz's low-level life, except he wrote wonders, pictured domineering women, drew men down around the women's ankles like sagging socks.

Misfortune would not leave Bruno Schulz alone. Early in World War One—eh? . . . many hands for World War One . . . ? six, twelve . . . congratulations . . . his house and the family store were burned, as they say, to the basement. In the middle of the thirties, his brother-in-law suddenly died, and Schulz became responsible for the welfare of a bereft sister, son, and cousin. But let us skip the merely syrupy third movement to enjoy the finale. In 1939 Poland is eaten by the two hogs wallowing in their sties nearby. The Nazis devoured the eastern half, and the Reds swallowed what was left in the west, including a little morsel called Drohobycz. This annexation ended Schulz's publishing career, as meager as it was, for the Soviet Union specialized in propaganda and hero worship, neither of which our writer had any talent for. Two years passed—one wonders how—and the hammer and sickle was raised to affront the dawn and claim ownership of each dismal day.

Then the Nazis invaded Russia and the Huns came. They were far worse for the Jews than the Reds had been because the Gestapo sat behind the city's desks and made dangerous its streets and corners. Among these minions was a man with a murderous past, a man alas from Vienna, a man named Felix Landau . . . one of many but one to remember . . . Happy Landau . . . called by some Franz, more acceptably German, Franz is . . . well . . . how fluid names were, then as now—people, places, identities, owners—no matter . . . whether Franz or Felix he was a man who eliminated Jews the way he moved his bowels. For a slice of bread and a bowl of soup, Bruno Schulz painted the walls of this art lover's villa, including the nursery . . . Landau had commandeered the house from another Jew . . . it was later known as the Villa Landau, isn't that—as you say—a hoot . . . and there he had multiplied himself, imagine . . . now his son had a room with a crib and a wall full of happy Felix-like scenes from the brothers Grimm . . . actually a princess, a horse-drawn carriage (Schulz had done a lot of those), two dwarfs (a lot of misshapen souls as well) . . . anyway, do not let the nursery be a surprise, they always do this—barbarians do—they go forth, they occupy, they consume, they multiply. Moreover, Felix bragged among his thuggish friends about the talented little slave who colored walls for him, a miserable painter who must have wondered what it meant to be actually a submissive man rather than a dreamed and drawn one.

Political criminals require accomplices—their power is based upon obedience, obedience upon dependency, upon bribes, threats, promises, rewards—consequently: so that his sister might live, Schulz acquiesced; so that her son would survive, Schulz said sir; so that a cousin could continue, Schulz kowtowed; and so that Schulz should gain a brief reprieve for himself as well, he took care to please his captor with his painting. On walls stolen from a Jew, another Jew depicted reassuring fairy scenes for the child of a man who murdered Jews and thereby earned a smidge of notoriety; moreover a man who, not as merely an afterthought, had a nice family he considerately looked after. Meanwhile, the Polish underground had not been idle. They provided the highly valued Bruno Schulz with forged documents designed to facilitate his escape from Galicia. He was to become an Aryan. His papers so described him. He was to leave Drohobycz, where he was known, and hide away someplace—someplace elsewhere—in the guise of a person of good blood and docile character who would therefore not write or draw or dream of washing a woman's feet. Meanwhile, a German officer—a genuine Nazi, too, another Gestapo goon, with his Luger handy at his hip, a man whose name we know as Karl Günther—unlike the GI whom the Americans hid in anonymity—had grown envious of Landau's gifted lackey, and, during a roundup of leftover Jews on November 19, 1942, shot Schulz in the head while he was bearing home a loaf of bread.

I have heard it said: All dead are identical. Do not choose but one to mourn. Broken toys are broken toys, and useless legs aren't legs.

Thus Bruno Schulz—born an Austrian, raised a Pole, and about to become a Gentile—though a freethinker—died a Jew. Shot in the street. Who, do you suppose, picked up, dusted, carried off, broke, greased, ate his loaf of bread? Hands? Hands now. Please show.

Cassandras have been misunderstood. They bring good news. That is why they are not believed. It is the liars who promise us salvation. We believe them.

23

Joseph brought his first paycheck home as if it were a turkey. He opened a bank account, acquired a credit card, and bought Miriam a shiny trowel to poke into her compacted yellow clay earth. Marjorie

Bruss had recovered her equilibrium after losing it during the Portho incident, though the process was more like finding your cat in a tree than discovering your keys at the bottom of a purse. Joseph and Miss Moss had reached, he thought, good terms, and he was teaching himself how to play the piano, as if he had never had a lesson, from a small series of books he had found in the library, one that was entitled *Theory and Technic for the Young Beginner.* He sat in his garage of an evening and thought, This is my room, my place, my lamp and chair. And nobody knows I'm here. Which wasn't altogether true. He was also delighted because he was driving a car without knowing how to drive and playing the piano without knowing how to play and generally living free of what others might think and see. It was true that the Bumbler was in such sad shape it sometimes drew remarks, and Joey would have to remedy that, but, on the whole, he had to applaud his degree of disappearance. His job, his car, his clothes, his room were part of a cordon sanitaire of which any diplomat might be proud. Here we go round the mulberry bush, he sang, so early in the morning.

Indeed, the air had a clean blue chill in it. Then Portho accosted him as he was turning up the walk to the library's entrance. Mister, sir, the bogey beggar man said from beneath the bill of his red BEER cap. You strike me, sir—no, you do not strike me, sir, of course, you are a gentleman who would not raise a hand—you seem, yes, to be—to me to be—a sensible and caring person, and might have a bit of change weighing in your right pants pocket because I have observed that you are right-handed and would put a quarter now and then down there without thinking, naturally enough, where you should put it. Had it been winter, Joseph's shoes would have frozen their soles to the bricks. Astonished, he thought: I am being panhandled. Then he thought: Beards moisten the mouths they encircle. Portho had very wet lips. His words seemed very wet. Joseph would not have recognized the voice. Though hesitant, it was clean firm smooth. He shook his head, ashamed of his flight and ashamed of his shame. He was annoyed, too, because this man had spoiled a good mood and a lovely morning.

I'll tell you something true, something true will only cost you a quarter. Joseph might have continued on up the library steps if he hadn't suddenly realized that Portho's voice did not seem to be the same one that had protested his expulsion from the library. Where was the man who mumbled? That lady—your leader—that leader lady screamed, Portho said with the earnestness of a boiling pot. That lady didn't shake me awake the time, you remember? when there was all the fuss. She's done that before—shook me, I mean. This time she screamed me awake. She screamed in my ear. I yelled, sir, but she screamed. That's my secret, the truth. Have you ever been screamed? Gave me an earache. Now I think, to be fair, you owe me a quarter.

The tone, the diction, the manner, the wet words, were unfamiliar. Sparrows, hidden in the boxwood hedge, continued chirping. Joseph put a quarter in a mittened paw. And how had Portho known he was right-handed? The man had seemed the opposite of anyone observant. Portho normally slipped inside the library to get warm. Then Portho slipped inside a magazine to nod off. All this was customary. But perhaps only in cold weather. It wasn't cold, early in the fall, but to receive that quarter a mitten was extended. Miss Moss had also insisted it was the Major she had heard. Was there such a thing as supporting—cor rob bor ay ting—witnesses? This was confusing. Inside, he hung his jacket on a hook and felt hung there himself.

Marjorie might have screamed because Marjorie had gotten fed up sitting at her desk to oversee a library full to overflowing with nobody, nobody but a snoring tramp. Marjorie might have screamed because Portho's nose, his roaring mouth, made the sole sound in a library otherwise silent as a tomb, with only the *tick tick* of her pencil stick to mime the clock. Marjorie might have screamed because Portho wasn't weary, hungry, cold, or lonely but drunk and smelly instead, defaming the purpose and position of the library as a public institution. Marjorie might have screamed because she wished to summon someone from somewhere, raise a ruckus, wake the silent books from their dull mortuary shelves. Marjorie might have screamed because she had already told Portho a dozen times not to doze, not to snore, not to smell up her house . . . Joseph went over to the stamp-out table and said hello and good morning to Marjorie.

Both hello and good morning to you, too, Joseph, she said, as chirpy as a sparrow in a boxwood hedge. He wanted to say—but he didn't say—he said that the sky was as clean as a scrubbed plate. Good boy, she said, now go and get some sorting done. We've been given eight boxes by the kid who lives with old lady Lawrence. I don't have a notion what's in them. What do old ladies read these days, he said as if his feet were frozen to the pavement. Find out and then tell me, tell me, tell me true. Marjorie smiled her wide smile of see you soon.

Joseph realized that he had been enlisted—enlisted for a cause—by Portho—for Portho's cause—at a quarter. Judas needed more. Was he to forsake his—what did beard-mouth say?—his leader, for a quarter? Did Portho want him to put in a good word? did he merely want to get even? or see justice done? the truth known? It could hardly have been to clear his name. Though he had used some tones of respect—some "sir"s—in his approach. In the middle of Joseph's wondering came another: why was he chewing a cud so lacking in nourishment? It was an insult to have been asked for a quarter, an insult to have yielded one. Admittedly, the expulsion was no slight concern to Portho who no doubt would need refuge from the coming snows. Joseph reminded himself that it was always interesting to open strange boxes of books. You could never be sure what might be inside. Sometimes a stuffed animal. Portho was a mystery, too. So, after all, was Skizzen's father. Joseph really didn't know why people did things. Were they keeping their counters clean the way he was? Perhaps homelessness had been his father's aim, free of precisely the cards of identity that Joseph had just acquired and was enjoying in a condition of self-congratulation—when the supplication came. Maybe he should have confronted this man, said to him, I understand that you are trying to embarrass me into giving you money, but what have you done to deserve anything from me? why are you due even a penny from my pocket? because you have suffered something from me? so have we all, all suffered something; the very air is full of poison, everyone has losses, has been bullied, has been forced to feel ashamed, has been beaten or is a beater, starved or indulged, until our souls are bent out of their shapeless spiritual haziness into a hard shard. Except the sparrows who continued to shuffle while hidden in the hedge.

A moist mouth is not a proper state for a man's mouth. Joseph slit the tape down the length of the flap where the box was sealed. Suppose he carried a knife—Portho—suppose he carried a knife. A knife fashioned from razor blades, blades wedged in the crack of a stick. A sudden slash followed by a lifetime of disfigurement, a lifetime of sympathy, a lifetime of pity. Pity even from people passing on the street. Joseph withdrew a volume an inch and a half thick. It said it was a biography of Anton von Webern. The front of the dust jacket didn't give him a clue to the nature of this person, though a picture showed an intense sharp-featured head with rimless glasses, thin lips, tight tie, lots of brow, an unashed cigarette, sour expression. In his other hand Joseph raised up a volume bound in lipstick-intense red cloth. It called itself *An Introduction to Twentieth-Century Music.* More rapidly, he pulled several volumes out until it became clear that this box was packed with books on modern music. Joseph began to feel an unpleasant physical excitement such as the apprehension that customarily preceded his first descent on a playground slide.

Could this be an old woman's reading? Joseph selected a book about a musician named Boulez who was pictured on the cover conducting with his fingers. He could no longer breathe easily when the pages fell open at a passage on the composer—for it turned out Boulez composed as well as conducted—a passage that described the artist's search for a father, a search that dominated his life. Moreover, he learned of the Frenchman's admiration for the subject of another of these books—an Austrian—an Austrian, Anton von Webern. Joseph read with thirsty eyes. Names he had not known before streamed by as if celebrating his ignorance, and paragraphs debating the primacy if not the tyranny of technique alarmed him, he knew so little about it, had so little of it. How could a score appeal to the mind, yet outrage the ear? How could one consider singing an equation? A entire generation of artists and composers were quarreling about chance and order while agreeing that whatever resulted, all the old ways had to be cast aside the way you would a wife who has put on weight and shopped unwisely. Composers were advised to depart from the "tonal world," as it was rather grandly put, by trashing all the old rules and regulations, seeking fresh sounds with special machines, and composing with rests rather than notes. A quote from the great man himself, which Joseph happened upon, indicated that Webern had once written a quartet in C major but bragged that the chosen key note was invisible and called the feat "suspended tonality." Another writer blamed "the crisis" (Joseph knew only that it was "dire" and "severe" and "catastrophic") on Abstract Expressionism, a combination of words that, to Joseph, created a label whose meanings went together like ornery dogs, and was, in any case, about painting, so let the painters keep their dogs from quarreling and let the composers pet their cats in peace.

But every few pages old friendships broke apart like snapping twigs: Stravinsky was praised past the passing clouds, or he was a treasonous reactionary fit only for shooting against a wall. Schoenberg was dead alas or a case of good riddance (though of course he was quite alive); no, he was dead because he couldn't compete with music that was being made by jazz musicians and alone beloved by the people; no, he was dead because he was impure and neglectful of rhythm. How was that possible, Joseph wondered, trying to breathe unevenly.

So you have decided to use the library rather than work for it, the Major said, with a smile like a slice of lemon. Oh, I am so sorry Miss Bruss, I got caught up in these books and lost all sense of time. It's "Miss Bruss" now, is it? Joey cowered by the boxes. I'm truly sorry. I didn't realize. These boxes are full of amazing things. As far as I can see, Miss Bruss observed, you've only opened one in the time you lost, which has been two hours. Yes, sorry. These can't be an old woman's reading, though. Suddenly Miss Bruss endeavored to be jaunty: Why not, pray tell, pray tell me true? Well, they are all about modern music, and they look difficult to me. Older women do not have the wit of young men, the finer interests? she pursued. Well, it just seemed to me unlikely—here—in this town. You have spent much time in New York City then, more than two hours even, to see us as the dull tips of the sticks? Joey said nothing without meaning to. First Portho, now this, he thought. Caroline Lawrence came back to her hometown to live after her husband, who was a violist in the Philharmonic, died, Miss Bruss said tonelessly. So the Major probably knew what kind of donation she was getting, after all, Joseph thought, without then daring to pursue anything quicker than his own panic. He managed to remain as still, though, as a library lion. Miss Bruss went away when her shoes did. And Joseph went on with the boxes of books as if unpacking them were everyday business.

Joseph remained at his post two hours past his appointed time so the muted tones of twilight were beginning to sound in the woodwinds when he opened Miss Bruss's front door. It occurred to him that he had a key, but he took small pleasure in it. On the left of the entry was a door for which he had no opener but its knob, and he went through this to the garage—his haven—like a cautiously driven car. Joseph threw his coat on the bed as if he were throwing himself there and said Wha . . . to a plate of cookies. Does this mean I have been forgiven? He bit into one. They were thin and wore pale yellow with a nice brown rim. Um. He let the crumble slowly sog. Buttered saliva. It also meant that the Webern biography his coat had been concealing could not safely stay in his possession. Why hadn't he noticed that his own door had no lock? Marjorie might come and go like one of its numerous drafts. Joseph had debated the ethics of his theft while sorting the contents of the other cartons—all musical. Who would ever feel the cost of an unknown loss? he was needier and could give it a better home; he worked for so little the book was nearly his due; and he could take it back anytime if he changed his mind, as he very well might.

Standing next to the cookies like a sentry was a glass of milk. What was the matter with him? why hadn't he seen it as soon as he saw the cookies? He had let Portho sneak up on him. And the Major, too. Had he grown dense as it seemed to him his sister had, so consumed with her own few plans, her body and her boyfriend, that she saw little else and cared even less for her loss. The milk was still cool. Good heavens the Major might pop in anytime then. And she would see how low the level of the milk was, and if any cookies remained, and the uncataloged volume that nevertheless belonged to the library wherever he hid it, thief of words that he was. Joseph looked around without any real confidence, crumbs in the corners of his mouth. He put the book back beneath his coat. He had been so eager to get to his room and read about Webern, said to be a innovative influence, and now the bio had to lie concealed like the lie it was a party to.

Joey swallowed rapidly and chewed the cookies furiously, possibly the way Portho might an uncommon tidbit, while sitting under the glow of his gooseneck to be interrogated by his conscience. Whom was he thinking about: Portho or himself? whom did he resemble? might the Major scream in his ear until afterward it echoed and ached?

Sure enough, shortly two knocks were sharply nailed to his door, and during the third beat the door opened for Marjorie in a puffy white robe. Oh . . . , Joseph responded. Then Oh . . . , said Joey. How do you like them cookies, Marjorie said, showing a sharp sliver of teeth. I love them. They go so well with milk. Milk and cookies for my baby. Joey laughed. After hilarity's brief life allowed him, Joseph watched the robe as if it were a ghostly assailant. Marjorie said she was about to have a bath, just stopped by to see how things were going, to say she was sorry she had possibly sounded a bit sharp this morning, but she understood and saluted his desire to learn more about his enthusiasm. Music was a constant comfort, alone as she was so much of the time, even at the front desk, because Miss Moss was far away in the basement, just as well though because she really didn't like Marjorie a bit after the incident of the twenty days and who could blame her, so a good good night to Joey then, she had just dropped in to see if the cookies had hit the spot, and she saw they had, so good night sleep tight don't let the cymbals clash. The door shut firmly behind her ghostly garment. And Joseph sat still as a library lion that has been frightened half out of its ferocity.

24

Howard Palfrey's niece, Miss Gwynne Withers, hoped for a career as a serious singer. She went to her knees every night as she'd seen it done in pictures to pray for a solo recital in Carnegie Hall. However, at the moment, she was preparing for a small soirée at the president's house, and, although she was hiring a highly regarded accompanist from Columbus for the affair, to practice properly she needed some suitable assistance nearly every day. By words of mouth that Joseph never heard, he had been recommended to her. Consequently a call to the cottage came while Miriam was in the yard unrolling wire mesh upon which her clematis might preen. (They were on a party line at last, though Miriam believed that she could ring anyone she wanted whether they had a phone or not and was miffed when Joseph explained that the only phone nearby his room belonged to Miss Bruss and that he was to be brought to it, or to the one at the library's main desk, only by matters of the gravest import.) Miriam was endeavoring to flatten the mesh with her feet and was consequently unable to reach the instrument before the ringing went away out of all hearing like a disobedient child. She felt that anything that came by phone, as unaccustomed to its trivialities as she was, had to have a telegram's vitality and, like it, bore bad news, so she fretted over having missed the message that could have been sent from Urichstown. From who else but her son? from where else but that town? If Joey had not taken a job in such a distant place, she wouldn't have invited the phone into her home. Now that it was there she heard its sound as a command or an outcry and felt tethered to it like a dog. So Miriam was reluctant to return to her yard again and after a period of anxious waiting went regretfully to her shift (as she put it) in the rubber dishpan plant.

The following day, a Saturday, the instrument rang again, this time as she stood in her kitchen where it clung to the wall, she felt, like a big black bug. The jangle gave her such a fright a porridge spoon flew from her hand to do its own ringing. Miriam was quite baffled by the high fresh voice she heard when she answered with her own. It was a woman wanting to hire her son for something. This was suspicious. Miriam explained that her son worked in Uhrichsville, five or more miles away, and could not readily be reached, then wished she had not given up that information; she promised to pass on the woman's inquiry and wrote down a number, then rued her promise the moment the phone was hung; she vowed to improve her ease with talking to a funnel, and considered making a number of calls just for practice—to friends who worked at the plastic plant and were familiar with the vocal manners of Americans; she debated whether she should really pass on such a seemingly innocent message to Joey who might not know how to handle it; she wondered whether the alarm clock might confuse and frighten her now that its rival in ringing had arrived in her home, and slept fitfully, as a boat bobs, in the direction of Sunday.

Monday morning Marjorie received the same call, and she beckoned Joseph to the instrument with raised eyebrows and a gruff wave to the row of new arrivals he was straightening. How did you get my name, he wanted to know but did not ask. This was especially puzzling because his caller wanted a library in Uhrichsville. They had reached Urichstown instead, Joseph explained. To the other end of the phone, this seemed not to matter. Miss Gwynne Withers needed an accompanist while she practiced for her recital. It could be done in the evening if that suited his schedule, but the need was urgent, the alumni board had been alerted and expected six songs at the very least. It was inconvenient indeed to have a different accompanist for practice and performance, most unwise, but it couldn't be helped since Mr. Kleger was the best available before you got to Cleveland, and the well advised, of course, did not look south in this state for anything honorable. Her explanation passed Joseph like most cars on the highway. How did you learn where I worked, he wanted to know but did not ask. It had to be his mother. From whom else but his mother? where else than home?

Joseph began to explain that the only piano available to him was in a church basement that echoed like a range of hills, moreover the choir liked to practice on the floor above, though there was a woman with rather a nice contralto who sang . . . she might enjoy . . . but Miss Gwynne Withers was in too great a rush. They would have to use the piano in the president's house . . . of Whittlebauer . . . where the recital would be . . . for the alumni board and various officers of the college's vast . . . Classical of course, he would be given the music when he came and could practice it in his basement if he needed to practice before their practice. But I, Joseph said and then thought better of it. The fee was handsome enough to kiss. What kind of classical? lieder? Ah . . . no. Good, but he didn't say that either. Mostly opera? good. What operas? Mostly Italian, of course. A few French. Joseph silently thanked the God he had forsaken and hung up. Bemused, going over the conversation, trying to understand it, Joseph drifted away from the front desk and Marjorie's quizzical look, now cast in plaster, and disappeared down the stairs to the Catacomb Room without a word without a word without a word to the Major.

Joseph managed to persuade his Bumbler to climb the considerable hill to the college whose buildings stood around a leveled knob like tired towers, ivy covered and slovenly maintained. The institution was done up in gothic armor except for the gym, which had once been—still was—a Quonset hut. Otherwise, just over the knob, immured among a few trees, a stately Georgian mansion stood, where the president hung out, entertained, and shook local hands. It had a view of the far valley rather than the town. When Miss Gwynne Withers had given Joseph directions to his destination, she added that President Taft himself had given a speech from the West Porch concerning, she thought, the need to bust trust. Although at long distance, Joseph and Miss Gwynne agreed: Bust trust? whatever for?

In a large lounge where many armless chairs rested next to the walls stood a very glamorous piano, its lid latched like a candy box, and next to it, in perhaps the position she would assume at her recital, posed Miss Gwynne Withers, slim and decorous in brown hair and a long brown gown. The music he would need was already on the rack. The piano was frightfully imposing and shone in the late light like dark chocolate. Joseph strode. At least he tried, but his nervousness made it more a stumble and a grab. He raised the key cover, but it slipped back with a clack. I am wearing something long to proximate any dress suitable for the occasion that I may eventually choose, she explained. Joseph sat down at the nearest end of the piano bench. He slid slowly into position. What was the music? "The Bell Song" from *Lakmé.* It was vaguely familiar, but one glance at the score told him he would make a hash of it. He struck a few keys: A . . . C. The notes thudded against the piano's closed lid. They sound like animals trying to escape. Miss Withers winced, whether at the comparison or the performance. He hit a few more. No. Tennis balls. Joseph propped the lid up, but to his considerable relief the piano remained disastrously out of tune. He couldn't play it even for her warm-up. Nothing musical would ensue.

When the young lady began to sing a few scales anyway, Joseph heard a pleasant light soprano that at least knew how to tra-la-la. Her hands were one fist. A shiver of strain showed in her voice. Joseph felt sorry for her and her situation. Is there a tuner in town? Perhaps in some city nearby? Uhrichsville? It's Urichstown. Anyway, he would try. She would try. Tomorrow it could be tuned. It would be. It had to be. Then they could proceed. They would take the necessary time, make the necessary effort. In the songbook, the chosen pieces were marked by torn strips of paper. Joseph made for the Bumbler. He would need to return to Urichstown immediately, although Miriam was expecting him. Perhaps the Major would know of a tuner, or perhaps Miss Moss might. He feared a flurry of phone calls. That would be inconvenient. And he had to practice that night in the basement of the church. When he left the lounge Miss Gwynne Withers was sitting in a side chair, her brown gown spilling down her thighs.

Miriam tried to be incensed while talking on the phone. Joseph apologized. He apologized for returning to Urichstown. He apologized for not being able to talk further on the phone. He apologized to the Major for doing family business on library time by talking to his mother on the phone. He apologized to the janitor of the church for staying so late and for using its phone as well. Miss Moss knew a man who did piano tuning and said she would phone him; then she phoned Miriam to tell her to tell Joseph that the tuner would turn up at the time desired. When Joseph phoned his mother just to check in and apologize once again, he got Miss Moss's message. Joseph then reached Miss Gwynne Withers with this information. Meanwhile, she had found someone in Woodbine by phoning everyone she knew to ask for help. Well, they thought, one of the tuners ought to make it. The next day. In the morning. It might take a while to get that whale to whistle. She would try to phone.

Neither of them showed up.

Two days of calling, begging, even beseeching by Miss Withers went for naught, and President Palfrey, now apprised of the situation, decided that the wise thing would be to call the recital off, since no one wished to have Miss Gwynne Withers be at less than her best, besides there would be other occasions, perhaps even more suitable, to showcase her lovely talent. The president was sure that the alumni board would be equally amused by some magic that Professor Rinse performed while employing in quite a unique way other instruments of the orchestra, even though many alumni might have witnessed a bit of it before because he was in considerable demand nearby—he would draw lengths of silk from his fist and use them to play something on the violin—well, the entertainments were scarcely at the same cultural level, and, yes, "amused" was not the right word for the effect of Miss Withers's endeavors; still, the problem could be solved best by abandoning ship, although only Miss Withers's father, Mr. Grayson Withers, put it that way, probably because he had served some time in the navy during the war.

Mr. E. J. Biazini was put out because he had driven to the college all the way from Urichstown per instructions received by phone from his old friend Miss Moss and was unable to find the piano; Miss Moss was peeved that matters had been mishandled after all her efforts, calling both hither and yon on the phone and sending her old friend Mr. Biazini to tune a ghostly grand piano; while the phones themselves miffed the Major, ringing, as she said, off the hook but not on library business. Miriam was now convinced that—traveling over wires for so many lots and even blocks let alone from town to town—Woodbine to Lowell, Lowell to Uhrichsville—a perilous passage—she was convinced that what one said at one end was squeezed into something quite other and quite else by the tortured time of its arrival. Think of what happens to toothpaste, she argued, with what relevance Joey did not pursue. President Palfrey didn't want to spend any money on the gosh-awful piano, he told intimates, not right now with the budget busted and the underpinnings of the West Porch in need of repair, so he wrote Joseph a nice note thanking him for his helpful efforts, as did Miss Gwynne Withers, though she sent her thanks by phone from as far away as Columbus, where she had fled to be consoled and advised by the master accompanist, Herbert Kleger. Joseph thought it was awfully nice of them to thank him, he was not lately used to thanks, more and more like scowls were the looks that the Major sent his way, and his mother was in an awful mood, unhappy at having to live near wires, even stretches of mesh that honeysuckle might one day embrace, perfume, and wither on.

He still had in his possession the very strange book he had picked up from the piano rack. It was old and badly shaken, the cover as loose as a coat, and contained the pieces Miss Withers was to sing marked by long slim inserts of paper; or so he had been given to understand, because the inserts did not jibe with the description of the program she had related to him over the phone, nor did the book itself, though it was called *Songs That Never Grow Old* and had at the front several pages of glamorous publicity photos of famous opera singers. Despite such initial promise, it was mostly a volume of "Polly-Wolly-Doodle"s and "When the Corn Is Waving"s. When an operatic aria did turn up, Joseph noted with a superior smile, it attributed "La Donna È Mobile" to *Il Trovatore.* Over the phone, just so, his mother said, You were misled, nothing goes honestly over those thin black droopy strings. I've seen them lining the roads like scratches on the sky. Joseph would have to return *Songs That Never Grow Old* to Miss Withers at the address of Mr. Kleger in Columbus, but he did want to learn a few tunes like "The Man Who Has Plenty of Good Peanuts" and "Bohunkus" before he did so. He had spent an evening on Wagner's "To an Evening Star," which was apparently a selection for the recital. "The Lost Chord" was also flagged, but Joseph didn't know what opera it came from.

Here I am, speaking to you, you are trying not to listen, but you are listening all the same, and you hear my voice no differently than you see my face, my dress, the lace you always loved, and how would you like it if my lace were taken from me, torn from my neck and sleeves? and suppose that is all you saw then, scraps of me, pieces and remnants that became me—your mother now is a rag of lace—well, that is what the phone is doing, cutting off your voice like the nose from your face, so there is no smile where your teeth show, no gestures; this rude tube is setting you adrift in darkness, only your voice is allowed to remain, a ghost like that cat in the story who is all whiskers. It is an evil business that black phone is doing.

Joseph did for a time believe it.

But the songbook was a good fairy. Or so it seemed. After three weeks Joseph still had not returned it, caught up as he was in its traditions, its ardent sentimentalities, its violent bravadoes, and its innocence. Most of all, though, he was charmed by its idiocies. He had singsonged the words of "The Low-Backed Car" for Marjorie between bursts of healing laughter. They debated what a low-backed car was and decided it had to be a kind of pickup truck or farm wagon because the lyrics began:

> When first I saw sweet Peggy,
> 'Twas on a market day.
> A low-backed car she drove and sat
> Up on a truss of hay . . .

Then they considered the copyright dates, which were 1909 and 1913, in order to calculate the age of the automobile. Since some of the songs were Civil War or earlier, the book's two birthdays weren't much help. The picture of Peggy perched upon a bale of hay was almost perfect, but as the song went on, its absurdities improved.

> Sweet Peggy, round her car, sir,
> Has strings of ducks and geese,
> But the scores of hearts she slaughters,
> By far outnumber these;
> While she among her poultry sits,
> Just like a turtledove,
> Well worth the cage, I do engage,
> Of the blooming god of love!

While she sits in her low-backed car,
The lovers come near and far
And envy the chicken
That Peggy is pickin',
As she sits in the low-backed car.

For several days Marjorie imagined herself pickin' chicken at her no-backed desk. Joseph blew her kisses as he passed. She responded by pulling imaginary feathers from her rolladeck. These fooleries were observed, but only once and at a distance, by Miss Moss, who was not amused and scurried off to her dungeon cell. Joseph had to arrive soon after with a request for glue and, by the way, letting her in on the joke lest she read into the kiss blowing more than was appropriate. The jealousies that lay between the two women were beginning to be more than an inconvenience that required delicacy and tact; their animosities were moving into Joseph's mind like raccoons into an attic.

Still, the days were endurable and came and went like breath with only a few deep heaves to harm the pace. Joseph scraped by though he often felt like a scoured plate, just a bit cleaner than he thought cleanliness required. Along Quick Creek the winds picked up. They bowled through overhanging trees, rolled leaves down streets and sidewalks, rattled loose shutters, and hurried the streams. Sometimes, toward evening when the day cooled, flakes fell like little announcements. Miriam's mums were rusty now as iron, and raindrops stung. They had been hail when they left their cloud. The Bumbler ran between towns with the sleepy regularity of the bus, while Joseph enjoyed Ohio's dippy hills—the sumacs red as a poison label as if warning the others of the colors' coming. Joseph became a regular at the church and frequently played on an old upright at its child-care center. He sometimes sang an old lyric or two in his thin, rather sharp voice. The kids loved "Polly-Wolly-Doodle" but, because of the congregation's racial mix, Joseph had to be careful, he explained to Marjorie, not to let them hear the third verse, which went "Oh I came to a river, an' I couldn't get across, / Sing Polly-wolly-doodle all the day. / An' I jump'd upon a nigger, an' I tho't he was a hoss, / Sing Polly-wolly-doodle all the day."

It didn't sound so bad when sung. Marjorie laughed, mostly in surprise, at the awkward rhyme. Is that what music did to affairs of the heart, to military anthems, to futile calls upon God, to sadness and loss? Even the most ordinary tunes could enliven exhausted sentiments and make acceptable some of the cruelest and coarsest of human attitudes. Things too silly to say can always be safely sung, he said, quoting some forgotten source. Joseph would play while softly singing "Tell me the tales that to me were so dear, / Long, long ago, long long ago; / Sing me the songs I delighted to hear, / Long long ago, long ago," and every time he did he felt a twinge, as if he had lost a lover once, as if he owned a black man he could mount, supposing him a horse, or even as if he had lived "long long ago," in a place called "yesterday," enjoying the golden haze of wheat-filled hills or corn-green fields, strolling amid sunlit houses, standing at the edges of placid ice-cold lakes. Polly-wolly-doodle—it's okay—do-dah-day—come out and play—hip-hip-hooray. Miss Withers would have sung her songs to chairs as armless as wounded soldiers. President Palfry would broadcast his beaming countenance without a fee. And the alumni would go away relieved of their savings for a rainy day.

Having had the experience twice already in his life, Joseph knew that on the next Fourth of July the national anthem was going to be bellowed by buxom ladies until it was as worn as the banner, and parades would feature survivors of foreign wars, limping along on roads lined by a national pride that waved paper flags stapled to brittle little sticks. Joseph's world suddenly fell into the blahs as though into a bucket. Or down a drain that gurgled as if it had a stomach. He had them, the twelve blahs of Christmas. Perhaps the unromantic truth was that painters made poverty picturesque and Christ's suffering grandly dramatic. He remembered how blood traced a graceful path down the Savior's speared side; how architects built great halls to hold the egos of tyrants; and sculptors made Lenin's ignoble nose look as if it deserved its own coin.

Joseph's mother loved "The Man with the Hoe." Maybe it reminded her of the farm life she had once enjoyed. Anyhow, it made her feel good, about what he wasn't sure. Salomé cavorting with the head of John the Baptist, flames consuming sinners, pre-Romans raping Sabine women, were all highly acceptable subjects. Congregations of good people still sang "The Son of God Goes Forth to War." "His blood red banner streams afar." He tried to remember that the Christian soldiers of the popular hymn only marched *as to* war, and, when they had to do it, dressed like the people who put out pots for pennies to help the poor. They did their ring-a-dings at corners and the doors of stores. Ho-ho-ho. Blah-la-la. Christmas—with the gifts neither he nor his mother could afford arranged around it—terrified him.

Joseph had lost a father once, long long ago. Was that actually so bad? Blah or ha-ha or ho-ho. He didn't know. But that little pang he felt as pleasure when he played and sang the long-ago song made him happy about what? It made him happy about loss. The dear dead days beyond recall.

> My little dog always waggles his tail
> Whenever he wants his grog;
> And if the tail were more strong than he,
> Why the tail would wag the dog.

Blah de blah ah ha, hurrah, ho ha, blah blah.

Pitches and beats, pitches and beats, that's all the blahs were, pitches and beats. It made him want to skippedy do dah. Hit it boys. That odd command meant: start together now. The words were all so violent: hit it, strike up the band, pick up or capture the beat. There was also stomping at the Savoy. Reading at sight from his hymn book Joseph sang

> My name is Solomon Levi,
> at my store in Baxter street,
> That's where you'll find your coats and vests,
> and everything that's neat;
> I've second-handed overcoats,
> and everything that's fine,
> For all the boys they trade with me
> at one hundred and forty-nine.

Now the chorus, boys, the chorus:

> Oh, Mister Levi, Levi, tra, la, la, la;
> . . . Poor Sheeny Levi, tra, la, la
> la, la, la la, la, la la, la,

My name is Solomon Levi,
At my store in Baxter street,
There's where you'll find your coats and vests,
and everything that's neat;
I've second-handed overcoats,
and everything else that's fine,
For all the boys they trade with me,
At one hundred and forty-nine.

This last, Joseph presumed, was the street number of the shop, not the price of the overcoats. One tra and ten las rollicked along after poor sheeny Levi like yappy little dogs.

His songbook had suckered him. He had a tune for his temper:

I think I'll go down in the dumps
'cause lately I've taken my lumps.
I'm feeling so low
I call myself Joe . . .

He stared at the keyboard as he sometimes had to, ordering the piano to play, willing it to anticipate his fingers. This exercise was not a Czerny, nor a Cramer either. He had to relax his fingers. They needed to be fluid, loose as cooked pasta.

Whats that you hummin?

Joseph had been singing just above his breath. It has no name. It's improvised.

You a real musician then, Miss Spiky said in some surprise. Her hair had been cut and combed out of its customary wrappings. It transformed her appearance, but she remained wide. Now Joey would have to find her another name. He might just ask for the present one.

Instead he said, No, not real. I'm just a pick-it-out, pick-it-up player.

Thats the best kind. You humm you is down in the dumps. Well thats what blues are for. Singin em brings the spirits up.

Yes, it does but that's what's got me down.

What?

Sometimes you deserve to be down in the dumps.

Hey, I own a dump, I dont have to live there. She sang "I gotta right to sing the blues, / I gotta right to feel low down."

Joey laughed. Music is cheap medicine.

Thats right. What else so cheap does so much good?

You really love singing in the choir, don't you?

Shurely do. We all go up together. We just rise up together like steam from the road.

May I ask what your name is? My name is Joseph Skizzen.

My name is Hazel Hawkins. People call me Witch.

25

The spring semester is almost over, Professor Skizzen said as he drifted from one side of the classroom to another, a manner he had just recently adopted; only a week, a week and a half, remain, and most of you will leave the campus, leave this community, for your summer vacation and your menial job in a burger palace. Then after a few months—to play the alternatives—those of you who haven't failed this class or some lesser subject, those of you who haven't transferred to one of the cheaper Ivies, graduated to the job market, or run away to Europe or the circus, those . . . those of you who remain will return. That means most of you . . . most of you will be back, for who fails at Whittlebauer? we are so built upon success.

Of course, in order to come to college you had to fly from your nest, bid bye-bye to your yard, your toaster, your elm tree with its tired swing—too many loved things for me in this crudely shaved hour to touch on . . . touch on or to name—and from that vantage point . . . hold on . . . correction . . . you may have brought your toaster with you—true—bags of clothes, toaster—yes, certainly—indispensable . . . anyway, from that perspective what you shall do next is fly back to your old neighborhood. Take your toaster if that pleases. Note this—you shall go home even if the elm is dying. Even if an aunt is. Even if you don't want to. This cycle—of departure and return—evaporation and rain—yo and yo-yo—will be repeated in one form or another your entire lives.

I beg your pardons, all . . . I used a misleading migratory metaphor—branch, nest, yard, garden—not wise, requires correction . . . why? because the migratory bird has two homes, its cool summer cottage and its warm winter cabaña. Hands if you see the difference. When you achieve physicianhood you may be able to afford it. But let me turn this inadequate image to account. Twin homesteads are not unknown to sociological research. Our earth has two poles. Such divided loyalties are regularly demonstrated by those in the dough, though one habitation is usually the castle while the other is a cabin. If you have too many homes, however, as the jet-setter presumably does, we are compelled to conclude that the jetter is really homeless . . . homeless as only the very rich can afford to be. They are on permanent vacation—not to and fro, but fro and fro. A woeful situation. So sad for them, you see.

Miss Rudolph, if you have a cough that bad, you should go to the infirmary.

So . . . yes . . . We start with your dorm room . . . a dorm room is your local habitation from which every morning, if you can manage it, you rise from your bed and wobble off to the Student Union where . . . where you'll crunch some sugar-laden biscuit . . . some processed wheat or exploded corn before it sogs in the bowl. I can see you . . . Professor Skizzen made an I-spy gesture with his hands. I can see you sweet-rolling your way to your first class. What a pretty sight! You dutifully follow your schedule throughout the day and return at the end of it to that same rubble of a room . . . to sit under a study lamp, perhaps to gossip with a friend, guzzle cola, or play guitar noise on the old Victrola before sleep . . . yes, before sleep takes you once again into its somber chamber of dreams and its crude simulation of death. That's how it is at your home—here. But soon you shall have to return to your home—there. Perhaps you will drive your own tin lizzie back, or your family car will come to fetch you—Father and Aunt Louise—or you will ride a bus with a bunch of strangers from another world—

What?

Ah, I see . . . We don't say that anymore . . . Too bad. "Lizzie" makes an appropriate sound and ought to be still in use. The car wasn't made of tin either. Anyway . . . while you are traveling, you will leave the car to fuel, leave it for relief, leave it to snack, to stretch your legs—candy, restroom, gasoline, coffee—leave, lock, carry out your mission, bomb the supply dump, make a safe return. The vehicle will seem in such moments to be your special place, your familiar surroundings where your guard can roll down like one of its windows, where your can of pop, wad of highway maps, or that sweet roll waits. Small cycles turn inside of wider ones, don't they? Every sentence has a subject to which its predicate must return. First establish a base. Then see to its safety. Embark on your adventures. Return to rest up. In relief if not in jubilation. Round as a gong. Wheels within wheel, you see. Like Ezekiel's, wheels with eyes, eh? fire filled . . . Ezekiel? Show of hands . . . Show . . . Ah, yes, no surprise to me . . . ignorance . . . ignorance is epidemic.

In my home my desk is yet another haven—for my pencils and the seat of my pants—and when my mother calls from her garden her sound will be one I go to as if it were a beacon. Meanwhile, noises on the street I shall ignore. They are not a part of the composition. They revolve about other suns, have other eyes and other axles. Yet you know . . . that when you arrive home—leave and arrive, yin to yang, come to go—this familiar cycle and its center won't roll sweetly on forever, because you expect to have a job one day, a car and dog and garage of your own, an office to go to, a kitchen to cook in, main and subsidiary bases like a diamond, to traverse—ball diamond don't you play on? bases to stand safely at, stages on any journey, on life's way, don't you say?—and so you expect the future will be full of places to return to. You expect homes to be here and there all over the place all the time. To spring up like spring does every year, and fresh blooms crack open, birds sing, new leaves hatch. Imagine. Homes to come home to, homes to leave. Everywhere. Imagine.

Who is imagining as you were instructed? Hands. Hands up.

Home is not just the last square on the Parcheesi board—oh, I beg your pardon once again—occult reference—shame makes my cheeks redden—I try again—it is not just the tape you break at the end of the race or the plate you run to to put your foot on . . . score . . . that's clearer for you? . . . But it is a set of things, habits of using them, patterns of behavior, met expectations, repeated experiences. Ho! Ho! Ho! makes it Christmas.

I know that in your dorms you call me Dr. Digress . . . do I do so? or am I a comet returning to tell on my tale?

Now then take notice, pay a quarter, will you? . . . for my voice and your attention: these homey spaces—so many—familiar voices, scents, satisfactions—comfort food, don't you say?—will be more important to you than other things, they can even dominate your thinking, monoply your feeling, they will be in the major keys, but there will be minor keys, too, lesser variations, hierarchies will appear like old royalty arriving at a Viennese café where there will be requests from the customers, preferences in tables, order in the kitchen, ranks throughout the staff, competition in the silver, even among the pots and pans, bowls fit for barons shall sit on peasant plates, an ordinance will promulgate itself, a sub ordinance will sound like a summoning to church.

How many of you knew I was speaking of music all along? its inherent higherarchies? show of hands, please. Hah . . . You are such good students. Why do I complain?

Because many of you have not turned in to me your analysis of that little tune I gave you. Such a simpleton task. A simpleton could do.

Where there is alter there is sub alter. Where there is genus please expect species. Order among the tones. Order among the instruments. There is no note born that doesn't have a lineage, a rank, a position in the system. The force of past performances. Imitations of the masters. Traditions of teaching. Centers of learning. Habits of listening. Among them who will rule? for someone must rule. The horns? . . . surely not the winds. Some particular view of quality and composition shall be current. This theory, instead of that, shall be preferred. Therefore the French style will be enforced, the German manner obeyed, the Russian soul—it is always the Russian soul—obliged. They also come and go like cuckoos in and out of clocks.

Where music is, Vienna is. The maestro is. You think music takes place in isolation, in some hermetic solitude? Cakes, coffee, gossip, and the gypsy violin—loopy swoons and much mealy schmaltz surround the violinist's form and dismal dress. Huge, too, the opera *haus.* High the hats. Gaiety. Flirtations. The hunt. The waltz. Vienna tuned out the terrifying world to listen to Strauss. To *Fledermaus.* A social round of balls. Yet there must be a leader or there will be chaos, all those instruments braying at once. There must be a home to come home to, didn't the Austrians at one time suppose, while longing for the Reich to envelop them like a mother's warm milk-white arms? *There* is a home for you.

The bosom of the family. The leader raises his baton, Stukas scream from the skies.

Did not Odysseus strive to reach his wife kid dog and palace—you remember him? ah many of your hands need washing, I can see—too few pink palms . . . through countless trials and tribulations, too, remember the delays, the teases—Sirens, enchanters, giants lurking—one two three ten twelve thirty troubles, trials, tribulations, did I say?—lures of ladies, comforts of creatures—in wait like rocks—to bring the wayfarer down, to sink his soul to his sandals. So, too, we depart from the tonic, we journey farther and farther afield—yes, we digress—until it seems we've broken all ties with the known world, we are farther away than anyone has ever been, we are at the edge of the earth, we can forehear . . . forehear the Wagnerian downfall, we stand at the brink . . . the brink that splashes into silence . . . when . . . lo, behold . . . magically . . . the captain, the composer, sees a way, steers us through the storm, and we modulate, do we not? sail ride walk to the warm and welcoming hearth again, the hiking path winds but takes us to our hotel in safety just as the signs said they would: what relief at what a climax . . . the sight of a spire, familiar stones at one's feet, the smell of a pot on the stove. Nice walk, good hike, healthy return.

Poor Miss Rudolph. Glad you're back. Nice of you to cough in the hall. No music there.

Or shall we let a cough be music? music made of cough and sniffle? chance and error? the music of the blown nose, the phone call, the unwrapper's annoying rattle? With our new instruments of bedevilment might we not record all sorts of sounds out there in the world that calls itself—that call themselves—real; where squeaks and squeals and screams are on the menu, where dins assail us by the dozens—the crinkle of cellophane, *whishiss* of small talk, the fanning of five hundred programs—where we fill our ears with one noise in order not to hear another . . . yes, record, preserve not only the roil of the sea but the oink of pigs and moos of cattle, the wind rattling the cornstalks like the hand of an enemy on the knob, and put them in . . . in the realm of majesty, of beauty, of purity, in . . . in music, let them in—poor Miss Rudolph's cough included—why?—why would we come to such a detrimental thought? or why should we learn to sigh at silence as if it were a sweet in the mouth, as if it were a pillow soft as a sofa, why should we order our instruments off! as if silence were an end? Only to invite the ruckus—of which we are the ruck—to rumpus us, to ruin our holy space?

[...]

Just then we had a silence, did you hear? a rest. Broken like a pane of glass by . . . explanations.

Because music has its holies, has its saints; because music has sounds all its own that no one else, no else like thing, no motion that the muck of matter makes: nowhere is one tinkle like them, these tones that musicians know. Pure tones, resolute tones, resonant tones, redolent, refulgent, confident tones. We have artisans whose ancient art is to fashion instruments so different from the heartless machines that now can capture a starling's idle clacks and chop the resultant cacaphones into eekie-screechie parts in order to blast them—these ultra audibles—earclapped, earboxed earrings—save us, save us, save us from such ruffians, yes . . . give us smooth-wooded polished fine-tuned bodies instead, that glow in anticipation of being played, shining trumpets proud of their purpose, soothing tubes from which much love emerges, and virtuosos who have devoted their lives to learning how, from these wily and noble objects, to elicit the speech of the spirit. Consider: a quartet of them: four men or women. Centuries of preparation will go into their simplest tuning—into a single scrape of the bow—nor will they be togged like Topsy or some ugly ragamuffin, but garbed and gowned for these rites, these magical motions that make truly unearthly sensations. Our costumes, our manner of bowing or blowing, shall not be upstaged by clown costumes or gyrations. Shut up, world, while we hear the sounds the soul makes. This is where we should worship if we had the wit. Today Köchel Five Fifteen will pray for us. Play on our behalf. Be our best belief. Besides, this C-major quintet is assigned. You will note how the apparently harmless theme sinks into C minor only to startle us with a chromatic passage meant to be stunning and achieving a vibrant numbness. That's the way to talk to God.

Now, children of our century, inheritors of what is left of the earth: calculate the consequences. Of a cough.

The musicians begin. After sufficient silence is imposed on the audience—for the slate is being wiped, a space cleared of all competition (note that, but return all the notes you've made before you leave, we dare not lose any)—then, and only then, they play. There are vibrating hides, vibrating tubes, vibrating strings. Vibrating air in vibrating spaces. Vibrating ears. Vibrating brains. Do the notes fall out of them like spilled beans? out of these instruments as if they were funnels?

By the way, did you know that "spill the beans" means to throw up? Hands please. You others may sit upon yours and be uncomfortable.

No, the notes do not have anything to confess. They emerge like children into an ordered universe; they immediately know their place; they immediately find it, for the order you hear was born with them. Did I not just say so? Hands? Every one of them, as they arrive in their reality, immediately flings out a sea of stars, glowing constellating places. As a dot does upon a map or grid. As a developer on an empty field sees himself standing on a corner in a city that's yet to be. For these notes are not born orphans, not maroons surrounded by worse than ocean, but they have relatives, they have an assignment in a system. Did I not just say so? do you suppose that this will be on an exam?

Relations . . . As you have in your family. Aunts, uncles, haven't you? oh, I dare say, and addresses, underclothes, honor codes, cribs. The whole equipment of the gang. Yes, for even gangs have their organization, their nasty-nosed bullyboy boss and the boss's chamberlain—First Violin.

But now . . . now remember the honest reality of that home—so sweet—a home . . . there's no place like it, just as the song says. Let us have a second thought about that collection of clichés . . . Those relatives—remember them?—arrived like ruinous news: they broke the peace; they ate the candy; they spoiled naps; they brought their own rules. Their kids cried. And you were punished for it. Sweet home? Dad is seeing his secretary on the sly, Mom is drinking long lunches with her female friends or shopping as if a new slip or a knickknack would make her happy. Sweet home is where heartfelts go to die. Sweet home is where the shards of broken promises lie, where the furniture sits around on a pumpkin-colored rug like dead flies on a pie. Home is haunted by all the old arguments, disappointments, miseries, injustices, and misunderstandings that one has suffered there: the spankings, the groundings, the arguments, the fights, the bullying, the dressings-down, the shames. Yes, it is a harbor for humiliations. A storehouse for grudges. A slaughterhouse for self-esteem.

Families are founts of ignorance, the source of feuds, fuel for fanatical ideas. Families take over your soul and sell it to their dreams.

[. . . . .]

That was not a silence but a hush, and a hush is filled with awe and expectation. It is a pause, an intake of breath, release of steam.

Somewhere during the slow course of the nineteenth century, the children of the middle class woke up to the fact that they were children of the middle class—well, some of them did. They woke one morning from an uneasy sleep and found they were bourgeois from toe to nose; that is to say, they cherished the attitudes that were the chief symptoms of that spiritually deadly disease: the comforts of home and hearth, of careers in the colonies, of money in the bank where God's name was on the cash, of parlor tea and cake, of servants of so many sorts the servants needed servants, of heavy drapes and heavy furniture and dark-wood-walled rooms, of majestic paintings of historic moments, costly amusements, private clubs, a prized share in imperialist Europe's determined perfection of the steam engine and the sanitary drain. Daughters who could demand dowries were in finishing school where they were taught to tat, paint, play, and oversee kitchens; sons were sent to military academies or colleges that mimicked them, where they would learn to love floggings, reach something called manhood, stand steady in the buff, and be no further bother to their parents. And in these blessed ancient institutions both sexes would learn to worship God and sovereign, obey their husbands or follow their leaders, serve and love their noble nation, and dream of being rich.

It was inevitable. It was foregone—the drift of the young to Paris. Where the precocious began to paint prostitutes; they began to write about coal miners; and they began to push the diatonic scale, and all its pleasant promises, like the vacuum cleaner salesman, out the door. They took liberties as if they had been offered second helpings; they painted pears or dead fish instead of crowned heads; they invented the saxophone. They shook Reality in its boots. Fictional characters could no longer be trusted but grew equivocal. First there was Julien Sorel, then Madame Bovary. Novels that undermined the story and poems that had no rhymes appeared. Soon there would be no meter. Though you would still have to pay for parking. Painters tested the acceptability of previously taboo subjects, the range of the palette, the limits of the frame. With respect to the proscenium, dramatists did the same, invading, shocking, insulting their audiences. Musicians started to pay attention to the color of tones. They pitched pitch, if you can believe it, from its first-base position on the mound. They fashioned long Berliozian spews of notes, composed for marching bands as well as cabarets, rejected traditional instrumentation, the very composition of the orchestra, and finally the grammar of music itself. Notes had traditional relations? they untied them. Words had ordinary uses? they abused them. Colors had customary companions? they denied them. Arts that had been about this or that *became* this and that. The more penetrating thinkers were convinced that to change society you had to do more than oust its bureaucrats, you had to alter its basic structure, since every bureaucrat's replacement would soon resemble the former boss in everything including name. Such is the power of position when the position is called the podium.

Who shall build from these ruins a new obedience?

They . . . who are they, you ask? they are the chosen few, chosen by God, by *Geist,* by the muse of music: they are Arnold Schoenberg, Alban Berg, and Anton von Webern. They chose, in their turn, the twelve tones of the chromatic scale and thought of them as Christ's disciples. Then they sat them in a row the way da Vinci painted the loyals. I don't want to convey the impression that this disposition was easy, no more than for da Vinci. Suppose out of all the rows available, the following was the order of the group—ding dong bang bong cling clang ring rang chit chat toot hoot—and that we found the finest instruments to produce each one, the finest musicians to bring them forth, and sent them—the musicians, I mean, but why not the notes?—to Oxford to Harvard to Yale to Whittlebauer, to Augsburg even—thank you for the titters—to receive the spit of polish.

Yes, it is true, this music will be keyless, but there will be no lock that might miss it. Atonal music (as it got named despite Arnold Schoenberg's objection) is not made of chaos like John Cage pretended his was; no art is more opposed to the laws of chance; that is why some seek to introduce accidents or happenstance into *its* rituals like schoolboys playing pranks. Such as hiccups. Miss Rudolph's cough. No, this music is more orderly than anybody's. It is more military than a militia. It is music that must pass through the mind before it reaches the ear. But you cannot be a true-blue American and value the mind that much. Americans have no traditions to steep themselves in like tea. They are born in the Los Angeles of Southern California, or in Cody, Wyoming, not Berlin or Vienna. They learn piano from burned-out old men or women who compose bird songs. Americans love drums. The drum is an intentionally stupid instrument. Americans play everything percussively on intentionally stupid instruments and strum their guitars like they are shooting guns. But I have allowed myself to be carried away into digression. Digressions are as pleasant as vacations, but one must return from them before tan turns to burn.

Imagine, then, that we have our row: ding dong bang bong cling clang ring rang chit chat toot hoot. Now we turn it round: hoot toot chat chit rang ring clang cling bong bang dong ding. Next we invert it so that the line looks like the other side of the spoon. Hills sag to form valleys, rills become as bumpy as bad roads: hat tat chot chut rong rung clong clyng bang bing dang dyng. We are in position, now, to turn this row around as we did our original. Or we can commence the whole business, as Schoenberg himself does at the beginning of *Die Jakobsleiter,* by dividing the twelve tones into a pair of sixes. Thus the twelve tones are freed from one regimen to enter another. What has been disrupted is an entire tradition of sonic suitability, century-old habits of the ear.

Then come the refinements, for all new things need refinements, raw into the world as they are, wrinkled and wet and cranky. The rule, for instance, that no member of the twelve gets a second helping until all are fed. They have a union, these sounds, and may not work overtime. Compositions, too, will tend to be short. Audiences will admire that. For instance, Webern begins his Goethe song, "Gleich und Gleich," with a G-sharp. Then follows it (please hear it with your heads): A, D-sharp, G, in a nice line before slipping in a chord, E, C, B-flat, D, and concluding F-sharp, B, F, C-sharp. You see, or rather, you intuit: four in a line, four in a chord, four in a line. Twelve in a row. Neat as whiskey.

What a change of life, though, is implied by the new music.

I hear a distant bell. It tolls the end of our unanalytic hour. The sound might have come from any bracelet in this room, from a bellflower that my mother's grown, a garden row, or from some prankster in the classroom. Shall we include it in our composition, ignore it, or tell it to shush?

Because this rustic buzz is as regular, dare we say, as clockwork; it is only half an accident, like those noises that Cocteau wanted to include in his conception of *Parade*—you know this ballet? . . . hands. They included the clacks of a typewriter, the stutter of Morse code, and a few wails out of sirens leased from the police, as well as the hoot of a railroad train, but Diaghilev killed each of these radical suggestions—shall we show hands for him? . . . who, you say? . . . a Russian, good guess . . . that's all you have? . . . so, no applause from up here. Sweet sweet deity, why have you put such ignorance into this world?

With this question I conclude my little history of modern music.

26

The autumn months marched into winter like a misled army into Russia. Joseph was now in excellent hillshape since he regularly walked to work, his Bumbler's rear wheels firmly blocked by two bricks where they sat on the steep slope of Marjorie's driveway just beneath the stare of the small square windows that crossed the face of his garage. Joey's routines established, he began to take in the town, to enjoy the slopes he strode or rode on. Some mornings mist collected above the creek like another stream, and he would gaze upon the tops of trees as if he were one of the local birds looking for a place to light. He liked to imagine he was living among some Alpine foothills, in an Austrian town where armies of the Crusades had camped, or legendary royalty had trouped, on their way to Vienna, say, or rested on their return, burdened with booty, from the straits.

[. . . .]

Fencing lessons?

Yes, Marjorie said. Three books on fencing are missing from the stacks. They haven't been taken out—not officially anyway.

What a memory!

I remember because we had a kid here—skinny kid with lots of stiff hair—who was giving fencing lessons—thin as a foil and just as devious, I don't doubt—who kept borrowing them—hardly usual takeout fare—but it was a way of impressing young ladies, I suspect. As far as I know they were returned. Perhaps you might see if they have been captured by the clinic.

The clinic?

Miss Moss, Miss Moss. She secretes them. Books vanish from view as if borrowed by a ghost. The way the dimes did during the twenty days.

Joseph had finally decided that he was somehow expected to understand this mysterious phrase, and he feared that if he admitted ignorance it would be held against him.

Ah, he said. The twenty days. And if they are very ill?

The books? If ill . . . ? That will be the end of my interest.

[. . . . .]

On weekends Joey drove to Woodbine to visit with his mother who had filled the room that he and his duds had formerly occupied with plants she wished to rescue from the threatening frosts. Saturday night now, he bunked with a ficus, a gardenia, and a Norway pine. One evening, after they had dined on *Würstelbraten,* in an expansive mood no doubt encouraged by one of his favorite dishes, Joey tried to describe the rocky but happy relation he enjoyed with his "three ladies," but realized almost at once that he wasn't clear himself about what it was.

He did worry about Miss Moss, who seemed a bit rickety to be climbing the steep slopes to wherever she lived, because windy wet weather had covered the walks with slick leaves, and in the winter—a few brief snowfalls had announced it—Joseph figured even he would need the equivalent of climbing gear—ice ax and crampons—to rappel those snow-smothered paths every morning or, in the late afternoon, to ascend once more the icy flanks that were their streets. Still, it was a healthy way to live. Joey drew the crisp air into his lungs the way householders let cleansing breezes into their bedrooms.

Never mind about me. Miss Moss dismissed herself with a wave of carbon paper. I am used to the winters. I am used to the Major. I have a cane with a spike on it. I know how to scale these ignorant pavings. The city salts them, and the salt eats your boots. So don't buy yourself expensive ones. But then you haven't any money, have you? I imagine you live on sweet cookies and milk. Or treacle at the bottom of a well.

Joseph tried to chuckle and managed a rhetorical cough. I guess they are good for the tummy. He eyed her waiting stacks of patients while wondering what treacle was. Nothing on fencing in any of the piles. Joey remembered one thin devious red-haired kid who he felt had a . . . what?—rap sheet—a history of making trouble, but that would be too . . . too . . . Miss Moss was looking at him crossly, so Joseph worked on a show of indifference. On behalf of that appearance he decided to say: You've got quite a crowd of clients.

So the Major sent you.

What? the Major? . . . sent? I wouldn't say sent . . . how did you—?

"Client" is her word. She sent you. To the clinic, she calls it, the sick bay, she says, the hospice, the ER, the laboratory. To spy. She insists I steal stuff. I am supposed to pretend that a book needs repairs, and then I squirrel it away down here. She says I stole dimes from the overdues—nickels and pennies, too.

I can't imagine Miss Bruss would say that.

Well, on your imagination . . . work.

[. . . . .]

It took strong healthy winds to pull the mud-brown leaves from their noisy crowds in the oak trees, and Joseph was fascinated by the way in which they whirled off toward the valley, spinning and dipping until a cul-de-sac captured them or a little windless area let them land at last on a distant road or lawn, each leaf having fled the consequences of its shade, each note running from its sound. He would watch one leaf setting out and try to guess where it might go, but he had no success whatever. They spiraled out of sight and were swallowed by sullen skies. Autumn leaves had inspired so many poems and pop songs, too. Dead leaves, Joseph thought, shuffling through them as he walked to work, people say dead leaves, but what is really dead about them? He was lonely. That was his cruel epiphany. These leaves chatter like monkeys in their trees. He realized it with a pang that was more immediately painful than its cause. They flutter just as moths do in the least breeze. Lonely, lonely. It bore repeating. Once they leave their tree they grow lonely as they once grew green. Blown about because they no longer have any connections. Some pretend to be children chasing one another through the streets. Nevertheless, loneliness made him observant. Leaves do seek piles, and they speak like crumpled paper to the feet that crush them. As if he and his own shed skin might be conversant friends. Joey imagined himself a released leaf. Wasn't it his dad's design to become disconnected? Loneliness should be a sign of success. He thought of edges brittle as old paper,

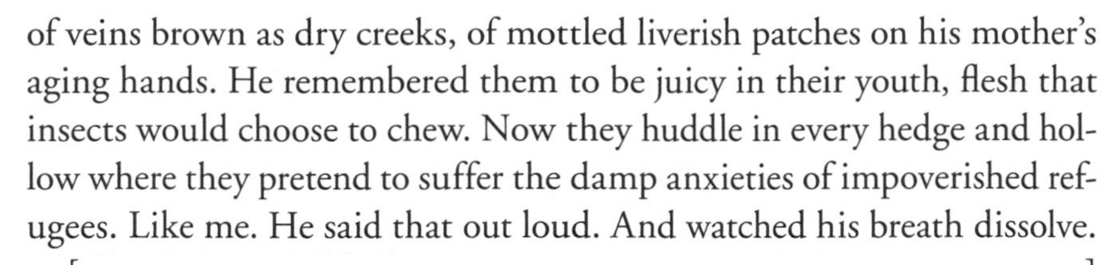

of veins brown as dry creeks, of mottled liverish patches on his mother's aging hands. He remembered them to be juicy in their youth, flesh that insects would choose to chew. Now they huddle in every hedge and hollow where they pretend to suffer the damp anxieties of impoverished refugees. Like me. He said that out loud. And watched his breath dissolve.

[...]

Portho? him I haven't hide nor haired. The Major excluded him with a wave of her pencil.

Portho is not likely to challenge you again—not anytime soon.

Portho knows I always forgive him.

Oh, have you had run-ins before? . . . with Portho?

He isn't important. Not that no-account. Not Portho.

[...]

He remembered having to memorize in school "If I could ever be the last leaf upon the tree . . ." Unlike the initial robin or cuckoo of spring, no one ever noticed when the first twig lost its cover or, during an attack, some unnerved soldier initiated the retreat by dropping his weapon and turning his back. Indians, he'd read, buried their dead on elevated platforms as if they were already halfway to heaven. The sun would bleach the bones the birds cleaned. Skulls could be used to frighten trespassers, he supposed, or warn of their owners' magical powers.

Fluff from the cottonwoods, as well as those released by milk- and bindweed packets—perhaps the souls of the Indians, too—sailed in the same errant way, scudding along like bits of cloud or bobbing gently at even the rumor of a wind, until suddenly a stave of locust fronds would spin like a dancer down the side of the sky and cause clusters of those seeds to waver out of the way like pedestrians maneuvering a congested walk.

[...]

Miriam said that she had read in the *Woodbine Times* of the death of an old and much-beloved professor of music. She thought the college would surely be looking for a replacement. Joey should let them know he was nearby and available. Joseph tried to explain to her the absurdity of her suggestion, but Miriam just grew angry and started blaming him for a lack of ambition. This failure was soon attributed to his runaway father and then, after a moment's reflection, pinned to most men because most men lived on the love of women like weevils in a biscuit. To conclude, she said: Debbie phoned; she phoned on that damned funnel. Really? Joey was surprised. It seemed to him that Debbie had run away as effectively as their father. Miriam's glower was replaced by a gleam. Your sister is pregnant. I'm going to be a grandmother.

[. . . . .]

On days of calm, Joseph watched white coils of smoke rise slowly from the coal fires still popular in a town so close to the mines. They were soothing, the way they grew, as if to hurry anywhere would be simply gauche. All over hillside, in icy air, the gray soot steamed straight as a palm until it cooled and gradually smeared the upper sky. The world was coming down with the cold.

Yes, there were so many causes for everything that nothing could be conjectured with any certainty. The apparently hollow firmament was a rush of rivers, streams, creeks, trickles of air, and frequencies of transmission, the earth itself was quietly shifting in its sleep, and through uncountable homes and firesides shivers of pleasure or apprehension were vibrating like the strings of an instrument. At twilight the intensity of every color became an outcry, and a step on the street an announcement as leaves rushed to be crushed by someone's feet. Every evening, Joey watched the lights come on in much the same order: first in the house with the widow's walk, then in the yellow cottage and the hired rooms of the bed-and-breakfast; door lights were notes in an expectant score, kitchens warmed the lower floors, while late at night bathrooms played at shining like a second sky. Yet the general scene was solemn, silent; the world went about its customary affairs as it had in other ages, other times. On the page of a picture book there could be peace.

[. . . . .]

You will never gain weight, Joey, even if I were to put you to bed and feed you *Würstelbraten* by the fat forkful, Miriam said. You'd kick the covers and fever your fingers pretending to play the piano.

If the sausages you thread through the beef were the size of *Faschingskrapfen,* I wouldn't need to sit stiller than my chair. Joey used the German to please her. She believed immobility encouraged one's body fats to cool.

Joey, you ought to practice curling up in cold weather like the squirrels and bears do. For Christmas I will fry you some fritters if I can find a brick of white lard, but here . . . in this country . . .

Goose grease, Mother, Joey said, is the answer to everything.

Ach, who can afford a goose . . . in this country . . . it is chickens, chickens, chickens. Frozen in bags. In plastic. Their guts in cellyphane like gumdrops. Here everything is plastic, my job is plastic, spoons are plastic. They pretend they've made them from beans. *Lieber Gott* . . . raincoats are plastic. Old days, we had deer from the woods, ducks from the lakes, grouse, is it? sheep. We had geese.

You had plenty of chickens, too, Mother, didn't you? dirtying the yard.

What would you know? hah! Britisher! we had chickens, but never chickens, chickens, chickens.

Well, dear, anyhow, the *Braten* was delicious.

It was all right, though the gravy could have used a plop of yogurt. Still, in this country . . .

[. . . . .]

Miriam was somewhat reconciled to the fact that her son had a job in another town, though she frequently complained of his absence and his enslavement to civic virtue, since Joey had presented his occupation as a kind of social work, a contribution to his adopted country. To Miriam they had been kidnapped by Arabs, held captive in a leaky hold, and were now slave labor. It was Joey's fault his poor mother had to be picked up Sundays like the sickly were and driven to mass. She believed that he had not tried hard enough to seek better-paying employment and accused him of finding a position that allowed him more leisure than work. I don't have enough education to get a good job, he told her repeatedly, but I shall remedy that in time, he assured her just as frequently. He now had a diploma that awarded him a bachelor of arts and another that gave him a music degree, though he thought that he would save such good news and make her a gift of it later. Then she would praise him and wonder how he did it—to be so busy and still devoted to his studies. He worked, he drove, he could go into debt because he had what they called a charge account: that seemed to Joey quite sufficient for the present. And in contrast to the way he spent his time at college, now he only listened to what he liked, read what he liked, looked at what he liked, consequently he had the skills he was willing to have and knew only what he was willing to know.

Weekend had followed weekend with happy monotony until at last

Miriam, who had kept her news in her purse for two months, as she confessed, told Joey he'd be—what was it?—an uncle. He hated the funnel then as much as his mother did. And the smug look of pregnant women. The contented pride contained in Debbie's swollen sweater. He could see Miriam skewering the roast and then slowly patiently pushing sausage into the soft holes she'd made in the meat and feel his own belly swelling—not with sympathy, not with something he'd eaten—milk *mit* cookies—but with a kind of living wind, a palpable pushy balloonishness. Entire buildings, his car, his library, grew larger; their sides bulged with unwanted life. And now, Miriam said, I shall need to go out—go out often to the country—to see her. To see how she is faring. To hear first movements. To feel the child kicking. To press the button and touch the baby through her mommy's belly. To press the button like you've come to call. It is all recovered to me now, you and your sister, how it felt when I was walking with you all the way to England, leaning back to stay upright, you, Joey, heavier than groceries. So your car needs to sit nearby me, Joey, and you can't live at the dark bottom of a funnel either, *nein* to that because now I must get out in the country to see Debbie and the baby, since she has been such a stranger to us, gone as if to another part of the world, across seas of soybeans and fields of potatoes. It's only a few miles, Joey said. That's far if you've got to walk. That's far if you're a granny.

She seemed so fine about the idea of being a granny that Joey wondered how she would feel when she actually became one, and the bell began its toll; for that's how she'd go to the grave, as a granny, wrapped in a shawl of mother-love, smiling up through the dark box, the thrown dirt, the stone post, at the next generation as if she were fertilizing its future and content to be manure. Joey was reluctant to change the image of his sister he treasured and kept safe as though by a locket: her body in the air, legs wide, her open mouth shouting Rah! And in the background, bleachers loud with cheers.

[...]

Sometimes, deep in the quiet shaded avenues of the stacks, Joey would lean against a row of books on finance or fishing with another in his hand that he meant to shelve and give daydream time to his desires, a rather new thing with him, since he hadn't thought a great deal about his future before. During so much of his past he had been helpless and in the hands of fate or strangers, always leaving wherever-he'd-been behind and taking a bus or a train or a steamship into some unwanted shelter or unknown port, inevitably changing his name and his nation, his language, his church; only the dry bagged sandwich or the thin soup and its tin spoon the same, his groaning mother carrying him like another sack, his sister eyeing his every forkful as though it should have been hers, and he eating with a reluctant show of hunger as if his food had been previously chewed by another set of teeth.

To his surprise, books had been a bigger stimulant than music when it came to fanning his fantasies, and when he put it that way—"fanning his fantasies"—he realized the image had its origin in an illustration taken by his memory from a Rubaiyat—of a sultan at ease in his harem—a picture that for him had Hazel holding a huge frond above her own broad person. He had imagined once a Christmas tree decorated with strings of variously sized—though all small—lights that would compose a score when read in a spiral around its branches—"Heilige Nacht," perhaps—a ditty tuneful, seasonal, and trite. He thought something like that was what astronomers must do, singing the night sky's song, their instruments like flutes through which far-distant spaces blew.

He had it in his head that he ought to complete his father's business—to escape the world's moral tarnish—because his father had most certainly failed, leaving his family in the lurch, running off with money he rightly should have spent on his kin. Of course there were extenuating circumstances, there were always those, in particular the fact that when he did disappear he had not been his real self but a Raymond Scofield, one of his characters of concealment. Abandonment, as well as the other charges, had to be lodged against this impersonation not its impersonator, just as you wouldn't arrest the actor who played Hamlet for the death of Polonius. In that case, though, the murder being made up, villain and victim invented, blame would have to be imaginary, too. Perhaps it was—all of it—theatrical. And the notices of harm that cluttered the papers were like reviews, recounting for people who hadn't been there what had happened in the play. "When I murdered my wife I was not myself." So all the world is a stage. That had come out of his book of quotations. Well, it was the library's book of quotations, which he must remember to return before the Major sensed its absence and accused Miss Moss of its detainment.

But if all the world were a stage, what was backstage, what lurked in the wings, and where were the actors and the actresses when they weren't on, and why did everybody talk all at once, and the people playing at war shout their lines while the people playing at peace were trying to read theirs, and why were only some shows sold out to an audience more often than not anxiously fanning their faces and drinking booze, because wouldn't they be participants, too? And would there be music coming from the pit? Backstage, to be sure, was a deity devising the lines, and a whole host of angels, devils perhaps, imps and fairies, raising curtains and dressing persons, contriving designs and prompting the forgetful. Every performance would have to be a play about a play within a play. It was a daze-inducing thought.

He did dream of strolling naked as Adam through a garden filled with music the plants made. No . . . rethink that . . . he would be more naked than Adam, leafless as a winter tree, untroubled by any companion, Eve or angel. Yes . . . he would be freestanding the way a column can't be because a column implies a building—the ruin—of which it was a part. No . . . re . . . rethink . . . he'd have no navel . . . as naked as Adam after all . . . he'd be born without parents like a god, even speaking a language only he . . . only he . . . the Adam of this figment . . . understood. He'd be free to do whatever he chose to do, to his blame or to his credit, but he would be relieved of the burden of worldly opinion by the absence of any mouth from which even praise might issue. Joey, Joey had hoped, would become such a released Prometheus. He would grow old in these surroundings, unlike ivy but like oak, sustained by his own roots in a soil that was silent about its disposition. After all, he had no father; he had had no sister; his mother was becoming an exotic plant that he no longer was expected to water; except that the sister had come back to life in someone else's service, and now his mother wanted him to shift the car she scorned into the sphere of her desires; by now the Major had him under her thumb; he was indebted to Miss Moss for help with things he should be ashamed of; and Hazel Hawkins took him for a laughingstock.

Yes. To be a good king you would have to forswear having subjects. The moment you moved to rule would be the moment of your undoing. Other people's flaws—and flaws were the yeast that let their loaves rise—would weaken your will. They would oppose it; they would cajole, they would seduce it. They would want so much—for themselves, for their families, for their friends and all those who they believed wished them well. Be good—to me, to mine—oh great and perfect Being. Joey believed Adam had eaten the forbidden fruit only as a favor. I have taken a bite, just as you begged me to, but only to make you shut up, so hush and let me be thoughtful now, alone in the peaceful shade. But Eve was busy getting pregnant.

27

Finally (after a few weeks during which Joey's blameless spirit grew a loincloth and knee-high stockings, and in an increasingly material form began to sit about like the most contemptible functionary), Joey readied himself for the first day of his employment as his mother's chauffeur. He winced when he recognized the romantic source of the resemblance. At whose court was he expecting to appear? He did not own a hankie, let alone a scented one, and the language of its use was truly foreign to him. So were Adam and Eve. So was the society of sultans, fans, and Negroes. So was the cultivation of crops.

Nor did Joey quite understand his aversion to Debbie's blessed event. Why had he hated the idea of her marriage in the first place? Why should he care if she reproduced her kind, or mind that their mother, whose love he should have expected to share with his sis but had never really had to, was so delighted by her role as a person of whom society unanimously approved. Perhaps it was precisely because of that approval. Still, Joey had not sensed much rebellion in his nature—a great deal of quiet grief, some self-pity, a touch of envy, and an attitude of passive endurance toward a wrongheaded world—yes—but . . . all right . . . some unearned feelings of superiority, which he had already decided he must mask . . . yes, but not as a reveler does at a dance, rather as a surgeon does, shrouding his mouth not his eyes, before he performs his rites.

He disapproved of her husband and their rustic life, her workaday world, her smooth and easy accommodation to American ways, her enviable disposal of the past, yet what sort of level of living did he enjoy? Was there any lock he felt he would fit? one whose opening would make him a pasha, a gallant, a piano player, even? He had never felt he needed a reason for his distaste of Debbie's showy ways, her saddle shoes, her short skirt, her letter sweater, her

beaux . . . .
her . . . .
her attachment to something so shallow as a school . . . .
her . . . .
careless glee . . . .

Debbie's soybean and potato farm did not enjoy a traditional white two-story clapboard house with its mandatory wraparound porch. Its managers had settled for a prefab ranch: low, sprawling, and painted a color Joey's mother had described as "dying daffodil." A concrete slab was its only connection with the earth. The front windows were as wide as the draw of their drapes and faintly bayed like a distant dog, though curtains clouded the view, such as the view was: of plastic chairs idling in the yard, an empty road in front of an empty field, a postbox lonesome as a sentry. With its requisite rusty grill, a picnic table rotted in the rear. Because of a heavy overhang, the house appeared to be wearing a hat and seemed to have strayed from a suburb that, in turn, had strayed from its city. Now it sat in the middle of a flatness that also belonged to another state, shaded by its one big tree and encircled by a lawn of winter-yellow grass that made it seem in the beam of a theatrical spot.

You reached this house down a gravel road. The road was accompanied by two weed-filled ditches that occasionally stopped altogether as if they had grown tired of running alongside and then, revived by their rest, took up the race again. A fence post could be counted, less often a cattail, and, almost as an afterthought, a thicket, a foolhardy shrub. The land on either side had been stripped of its crop and lay cold wet dark and fallow. Birds had fled to find trees. Joey's mood was morose; it was melancholy; it was angry; it was the mood of one who felt put upon, betrayed, discovered in the wrong, disturbed in his life when life seemed to be, for a change, proceeding properly.

The interruption was his mother's doing. Miriam could not understand Joey's attitudes and would not try to imagine why the prospect of Debbie's baby was not a cause for rejoicing and a feeling of fulfillment, as if some significant aim in life had been realized. Begetting was so inevitable, Joey thought, it was as routine as dying, consequently it could be safely left to nature, and otherwise ignored, the way Portho's presence was ignored even when he slunk indoors, even when he scattered magazines donated by doctors' offices on one of the polished tables, even when he dropped off, even when he snored. In due course people were born, in due course they managed to walk, they learned to talk, they attended school, they got a job, partied, married, had kids, sold stuff, bought more, overate, drank to be drunk, were relieved to be regular, labored in order to loaf, lived that way a spell—its passage sometimes stealing years—coasting down due's course—while they lost their hair, sight, hearing, teeth, the use of limbs, the will to live, until, in due course and as their diseases desired, they took to bed; they laughed their last; they said good-bye to the ones they said were loved ones—they curled up in a fist of aches—said good-bye to the ones they said were closest to them—complained about their care—said good-bye to the ones who came to kiss them off, said good-bye to comfort themselves with the sight of another's going, said good-bye while the designated goer complained, complained of neglect, complained of fear, complained of pain, and disinclined going, but would go, go over, cross Jordan, nevertheless. They uttered last words that no one could understand; they curled up like a drying worm; they cried to no avail because weeping begot only weeping, wailing was answered with wails; they repented to no one in particular; they died as someone whose loss was likely to be felt no farther than the idler's door, and dying, quite often, in debt for a cemetery plot, the service of a funeral parlor, in the pursuit of a false ideal. Joey didn't see much to interest him in any of this. It was what was done between times that fascinated him, when due course was interrupted by dream or discovery, murder or music, though wars were, he had to admit, due course to a faretheewell. And he thought, more and more, that death, assuredly dire, was also something due.

His attention, now and then, took to leaning in Portho's direction. He thought about those whose lives were so lean and broken there was no due course within them to enjoy, no lifeline to snap, for whom complaisance could never be a complaint about them, who didn't know a norm, could not experience even the average, reach a grade of C on any exam, would never bathe in tepid water or enjoy warm, whose lives were simply endless stretches of suffering, and numbness was a coveted relief, death a reward. Maybe Debbie was concealing herself beneath a blanket of middle-class comfort. Didn't she deserve both comforting and comfort? Didn't she deserve an American identity? Joey had felt its force, the lure of security. Didn't he also merit a little griefless good and his own soft harmless life?

Joey and his mother arrived still arguing over the use of his car, because, as he had pointed out more than once, Debbie and her husband had a car of their own, and why couldn't they, at least now and then, pay a visit to Mom, their martyr, so that she could size up her enlarging daughter and determine the remaining distance to the tape, the birth weight of the baby, its sex, the color of its eventual hair and eyes, the side of the family it would most resemble, and inquire of its name—had there been a choice of kinds? Hermann for a beefy kid, Hans for ordinary, or Heinrich if he was going to be tall, Gretchen if she was fated to be fat.

But Grandmother could not remember that the baby's name was Boulder, would remain Boulder, and that Hans or Hermann Boulder was not a felicitous combination—as if much went with Skizzen either—or plainly face the problem that would arise if the baby was a girl—Heidi Boulder? Gretel then? or Melanie? Melanie Boulder, for heaven's sake.

They sat in the drive for a moment to conclude wounding each other in a nice way before they knocked at Deborah's door like explorers who switch on their lamps when entering a cave: smiles like headlights, eagerness concealing caution in one case, apprehension in another.

After having stared at his sister with the requisite interest, Joey said, I don't see any difference; you look the same to me, cheerleader lady. Oh no, the roundness is easy to be present, his mother exclaimed, releasing Debbie from her first, wet-eyed embrace. Later, feeling a bit more welcome than she worried she might be, Miriam touched the cloth that covered her daughter's sacred stomach the way she might pat the head of a pet. You will be showing soon. I shall sew some skirts. With a maternity panel.

Deborah wasn't wearing bobby socks and a letter sweater. She was wearing an apron. Joey's remark had been both stupid and dishonest. He felt sorry for the first, ashamed for the second. She did look different. Her hair was no longer ponytailed but full of waves that fell to her shoulders, her face was fatter, too, and rosy, her eyes didn't appear to be looking into a mirror, no makeup was noticeable, no crimson nails. She was as matter-of-fact as a spoon. There was one positive outcome to this exchange of clichés. Joey had concealed his consternations.

Their further greetings were equally conventional and consequently cordial. Roger will be in shortly; he's at the barn repairing the tractor, Deborah said, he'll be along, and how about tea? They followed her into a sunny kitchenette. How convenient the machine proved to be, Joey thought, Roger didn't have to be here. The tractor could play broke and its driver miss the visit. Joey began to put words to their discussion of how important her husband's presence would be. To Miriam, only the sight of the unseeable baby mattered. Joey was green as a shriveled lime. But Debbie? Her attitude he could not discern.

The table was ready for them. A pot of jam, he saw, had been set on a robust red tomato, the largest among the many tomatoes that hung from several long thin inadequate vines inked into the cloth. The sun rollicked along the lips of the teacups, already put about. Lemon slices had been cut, and sugar cubes collected in a kind of square bowl whose odd configuration was meant to be moderne. No cake?

Miriam asked many questions, none requiring an answer, while Joey worried about Roger, who was in what barn? Joey'd not seen a barn, or any—what were they called?—outbuildings of the sort that usually sat around like ill-treated dogs and glared at the main house they were not allowed to visit. Miriam and Deborah shared a laugh as Debbie drew some buns from her oven. Sugar buns, well, what a treat, Joey said, though neither listened, except perhaps the stove did, despite having its door closed.

On a fan of fingers, Miriam counted the crucial months before the baby was due. Never had he felt so shut out, even when, on their various journeys, he was often excluded because of his age and inexperience. In those migratory days Joey was sometimes the very subject from which he was being shielded; but now, though as large in the room as they, he was noticed no more than the tomatoes that even several saucers and a trivet could not conceal from his eyes; even though each of these implements was being gay and prancy on his behalf, while sugar and sunlight were stirred into pourings of tea.

I don't see any barn. Where *is* the barn?

Does it fold up during the night and only appear when you need it?

I remember noticing that your car was gone, Deb, is your barn, then, a drive distant? That's unusual, isn't it? not to be nearby? I don't remember missing the barn when we were out here for the wedding.

It's a drive. I haven't been sick a day so far. Roger walks it sometimes. I feel the same each morning as I felt the day before.

Oh, that's fortunate. But it's early. I remember how sick you made me . . . ach . . . as sick as that evil English clotted cream that brought me to bed that time, remember? you were eight? No, it was the eight days running I threw up, I'm thinking of. You were how old?

Isn't it unusual for the barn . . . you know . . . to be so far away?

Gee, I don't remember. All that—it's as if it happened in another life. This house was built under the only tree.

I was very impressed by tractors when I was a kid. Well, the ones I liked were bulldozers really.

For me it's like yesterday, that other life, Miriam said in her serious voice. I see it plain as that windowpane. I hear it—the sirens and the plosions and the burning—I hear them in my head, especially at night. At night, you must remember, we waited for the rockets.

They kept shoving rubble into piles so trucks could cart the bombing off. Joey tried to hang this contribution in what proved to be a closet.

No flows for a while, no cramps. What a relief. I do the same things I always do.

That's fortunate, but that will change, oh my, will it. I swear I used to feel my skin stretch.

I always wanted to sit on one. You suppose Roger could hoist me up?

Joey sensed some wheels on the gravel drive—it was probably Roger—but then he heard an engine rev, and the wheels moved out of earshot. He fastened his gaze on a saltcellar made entirely of knobbles.

Is it red—the tractor, he heard himself ask. Is it red?

Miriam admired the tomato-covered cloth.

Coloring-book red, his sister said. I did it myself. The colors are fast.

Do you have pink things set aside, his mother wanted to know.

Plenty of time for that. Have some more? Plenty of time.

It's only a pebble right now, but it will be a boulder someday, Joey considered saying but wisely did not.

No hurry now, Miriam said, you'll be in a hurry soon enough.

All smiled. Including the cups.

The tractor? Is it . . . ?

Joseph informed the Major of his new duties, and even spoke about some of his misgivings, confiding in her, to his surprise, more fully than he had his mother. But of course the Major could ride free on his train of thought while Miriam wouldn't want to pay the fare.

My sister will bear a Boulder.

Marjorie didn't smother a laugh.

No, I mean her husband's name is Boulder. We've never mentioned it. As if it were unspeakable like God's. Or as if Deborah's husband didn't exist. We never used his given name either. Roger Boulder. Mr. and Mrs. Roger Boulder request the presence of a name at the christening of . . . Now . . . now that colony he calls his family is frantically trying to find suitable names for the coming kid. Like Nick. Or Rocky. Bad enough that Deborah's should end in—

While he's still a baby you can call him Pebble.

See, that's what I mean. In my heart I already have—made a pebble of the fetus.

Melody. No, Melodious. What do you think of Melodious Boulder? . . . or Carrie?

Barry Harry Downie.

I think Very Much would be a good pair. And for a boy—Clint—no—Cliff.

I have it. Izzy.

You are gifted. I dated a boy once whose name was Steve Sleeve. They laughed in happy unison as if they had just seen a bluebird.

28

Impatiens, or Touch-Me-Not, Busy Lizzie.

Professor Skizzen was sitting sidesaddle on an orange crate he had upended in a dormer of his attic. This leftover space had become his office because he could carry on business better from any cranny that refused to accommodate a telephone. Though hidden from almost all eyes, it was lit by a single high window that provided lots of southern sun and a good view of the distant trees. If Joseph heaved up the sash, he could peer directly down upon his mother's garden, upon the tops of hedges and low shrubs, and take in the outlines of her carefully laid out beds. In the middle stood the great vine-smothered beech, its bench, and a puddle-sized pool where Skizzen would often vainly search his reflected face for a tuneful line. Sometimes he would catch sight of his mother hunched over while wielding a hoe or, trowel in hand, sprawled upon the ground, her legs sticking out from behind a bush, her hat poking up through a forest of fronds. He had discovered to his horror (it had now dwindled to a small disturbance) that Miriam liked to sniff the earth, plus the low stems of her plants, precisely at the point they went into the ground. Where the living and the dead intersect, Joseph had observed, but his mother would have none of it. The earth is as lively as you or I, she said. I smell it, but I also listen to it breathe.

Only a brisk walk up a rising street from where he perched, Whittlebauer sat as steady as Stonehenge, and there his students gathered. He heard the college bells divide the academic day into equal and peaceful parts, but never felt the years as they slipped away.

If Joseph's seat was not very luxurious—even precarious, rudimentary—it was appropriate and would not encourage nodding off, which he was now inclined to do, although his customarily scrappy little lunch should have left him alert as a hunter. Two similar boxes elevated a drafting board to the level of his knees. Many years ago—oh, so many, Joseph thought—he had come upon this castoff in a salvage shop in Urichstown. Ancient ink stains, coffee spills, and the tracks of thumbtacks, collecting like boxers in neutral corners, made interesting this instrument's once-featureless face; and there the professor cut out columns of the latest calamitous news from the daily papers, labeled them as to subject, pasted pictures with their accompanying clips into scrapbooks, and emptied a handful of raisins nearby his glass of tepid tea.

So much had changed since he and Miriam had moved into the gothic "spookhouse," as he'd heard the kids call it while under the influence of Halloween. The college owned the place as they did many of the old mansions near the campus and let faculty members live in them rent free, awarding the houses like prizes instead of paying their occupants a decent salary. It was also a way of keeping valued teachers from seeking more-moneyed pastures. Joseph guessed that rich farmers had built these mitigations of their wealth when they retired to town. As homes, they were tall, ornate, whimsical, constructed from timber that was both local and plentiful, and band-sawn according to new techniques that made possible the extravagant filigrees of the Queen Anne style. Every such home was required to have at least one biblical moment pictured in art glass and positioned where the sun could strike a landing window: Susanna, clothed as though she were naked and ogled by the elders, Ruth in a swath of sentiment gathering grain in Boaz's fields.

Miriam welcomed the large yard with cries of ancient Austrian origin. There was no doubt that she was a different woman from the mousy cottage complainer she had been during their early days in Woodbine when she "sweated over tubs of plastic" and marched rows of unwilling flowers alongside walks and around borders, as if their modest cottage had to be outlined in petunias and forget-me-nots the way a Valentine sported its scallops. Vines had climbed about like too many squirrels, shinnying downspouts and masking lattice with wild rose and honeysuckle. Others lay in gutters like sunning snakes causing rainwater to shower along the eaves onto the sodden soil below and fill a number of the season's struggling tulips, as though they were goblets, until the petals sprang apart.

As a landlord the college was as much an absentee as God in the Deist's conception of him, and it permitted the property to run down in a manner suitably decorous and stately. Annoying as this was, for Joseph Skizzen it had the considerable advantage of his privacy, for no one was likely to wander unwanted upon his masterwork or even raise an eyebrow at his and his mother's living arrangements: neither the grand piano to accompany the potting table in the dining room nor the scatter of scissors and trowels would cause a snook to be cocked, neither his boxes of flypaper and pots of paste, nor her piles of muddy gloves or ranks of empty flower packets, already neatly sleeved over tongue depressors, waiting to mark, as though they were really graves, the place of some plant's birth.

Dicentra spectabilis, *or old-fashioned Bleeding Heart, will self-sow.*

Nowadays Miriam wore durable trousers that elastic closed at the ankles; she strapped on padding for her knees; fastened around her waist a carpenter's apron stuffed with tools and little sticks; drew over her coiled and braided hair a floppy broad-brimmed khaki hat, and encircled her neck with a kerchief soaked in insect repellent. Gardening was war, and like a professional soldier she also bore a firm stern face into battle, uttering hoarse cries (Whoa! or Woe to you, Joseph wasn't sure which) when, for instance, she removed an invasive violet from her carefully calibrated pools of grass. She would howl and slap her thighs whenever a stray cat came to poach, for she generally thought of the birds as her friends unless, like hawks or crows, they were predators or lazy sneaks who laid their eggs in nests not of their own contriving the way the cowardly cowbirds did.

Sometimes, momentarily defeated, she would burst into Joseph's breakfast kitchen. Ah, calamity! Where is my red currant jelly? I shall cook *Hasenbraten . . . Hasenbraten mit Rahmsauce* . . . how would you like that? I'm sure I would love it, Mother. Well, we shall have a year's worth. Joey, I suffer from an overrun of rabbit. They are eating all my petunias; they decapilate my zinnias; it is massacre season for my marigolds. Poor babies. Malignant *hassen! Ich hasse hassen!* They sit in the grass like city folk visiting a park and chew my clover. They fornicate in the nighttime and give birth by dawn's break. A root of ginger, I need, and some spoonfuls of jelly. I shall *braten* them for a year. Their big eyes shall become my buttons. Miriam laughed, surprised by her language. I am trusting their pitiful squeals will not disturb the music you are singing in your ear.

Miriam tolerated lightning bugs, dragonflies because of their beauty, bees because of their service. She granted butterflies a pardon even though the charming worms of the swallowtail were insatiable (she'd plant extra parsley the way she once would have set a dinner plate for a visitor); but hornets received no such reprieve because they tried to bite off frayed edges of her chicken when she enjoyed a leg for lunch.

Do not disturb the dew. Some nights the world weeps. Late-morning light, before the sun grew uncomfortable, was deemed the best time for gardening, and Miriam would, as she said, work hard on behalf of her friends, moving her ministrations from shade to shade. No longer were her enemies droning noisily through the night air, or—in her husband's language of fear—were they vaguely whispered to exist behind bushes, royal beards, or in government bureaus. And she had allies: ladybugs to eat aphids, lacewings to go after whiteflies. Some of these otherwise *züchtig Mädchen* carry parasites into the garden, she'd say—I have to watch out for that—but mostly they fatten on potato beetles and similar bad behavers. But you aren't growing potatoes, Joseph would protest, on behalf of the gorgeous black-and-gold insect as much as the welfare of the tuber or, choosing whatever the argument seemed to require, in defense of the onion's thrips or spinach's leaf miners, or any errant vegetarians that might come searching among the flowers, such as the squash's modestly gray bugs, cabbage's maggots, or the carrot's weevils. Ya, but our neighbors are. Better the nasty things should die here. The poor potato (or corn ear or bean pod), Joseph joshed, is born just to be eaten by somebody. God saw to that, Miriam said with satisfaction. God made aphids, too, *and . . .* ***—and*** (he said with emphasis, trying to prolong his indictment), but Miriam would break in anyway— . . . so that ladybugs would have something nice to dine on . . . —interrupting with redoubled pleasure because she had scored a goal. Joseph was then left to finish their contest by lamely naming codling moths and cutworms because God had also designed them. Each of us eats, and each of us is edible. Miriam made her pronouncements as if they were pronouncements. This irritated Joseph, who thought the tone only suitable to speakers with a certain status, a status that was due his professorial position.

Upon her plants she loosed a vociferous stream of advice. Pointing to the bleeding heart that was prospering in its place across the yard, she would address a flower in front of her that was flimsy and order it to do as Marlene was doing or Roberta across the way: Look at that stream of red hearts—like fat fish. Spend yourself on bloom! Do as Clem Clematis does: Be blue!

When Joseph wasn't meeting a class, he and his mother would sometimes exchange shouts about their business, pro and con and up and down. Joseph called his announcements "Reports from the Ruins of Reason." Miriam merely bellowed, as routinely victorious as any Caesar. She took her midday meal resting on an overturned pail and looking wan as a beaten soldier, sore-footed and weary, while Joseph munched his sandwich—lettuce and liverwurst—searching the columns for a story and flinging bread crusts from his window. More reports from the ruins of reason. This, he would cackle, is for the birds.

Digitalis, or Foxglove, impossible to duplicate.

Sometimes, when a gentle breeze made the blooms bob, and a cardinal lit on the top of their holly tree like a Christmas decoration, performing its territorial song, its tail pulsing with the effort as if it were pumping each note through some designated distance, perhaps as far as Joseph's even loftier perch, then the professor would be tempted to descend and walk about in the garden, though Miriam thought he did so like a health inspector, his hands clasped behind his back, promising not to touch but bending slightly to be nearer the fragrance of a flower or the wrinkled leaf that spelled fungus.

It was just that he worried over their welfare, Joseph insisted. How is Clem this morning? Miriam maintained that her son didn't believe she could do anything really well except cook and expected the garden to fall over dead of black spot, larval infestation, or webworm at any moment. That wasn't true, Joseph felt, but he knew that it was Miriam's habit to pick black-spotted leaves off her rosebushes one by one or routinely to rake them up from the ground around the plant if they had fallen and then to burn her collection at a safe distance from all things as if they were the bedclothes of plague victims.

Train the beetles to munch the black spots, Joseph suggested, whet their Japanese appetites, redefine their Asian tastes, but his mother was never in the mood to humor him when the garden was involved. Let them make nice lace of the leaves, was his final advice. Do you notice how they never eat the hard parts but leave the veins. Remarks of this kind would rile her, because what she got from her garden was not only reprieve and renewal but romantic transportation to the old days—by wagon back then . . . plodding horses . . . sing-alongs . . . cider . . . the redolent hay—when Rudi Skizzen had begun his love affair with her round wet eyes and when, as Nita Rouse, she had barely recovered from her childhood. They eat everything but the skeleton, Joseph said, and he was not alone in his opinions. They go clean to the bone, the way you eat a chicken's thigh. That's what, according to Mother Nature, they're supposed to do, he'd add in a tone of triumph. Miriam always threw up dirty hands as if to ward off his words. Am I then—your good son—evil, too? Because I chew my food? Professor Skizzen received a scornful look instead of an answer that might have been maybe.

I'd rather think about the good people, not the wicked ones, Miriam could be counted on to say. Look how that primula lies on the earth like a kiss on a loved one's cheek. She would smile then, because she knew such sentiments embarrassed him, and reach out with her arms in tribute to the flower's intense yet tender blue, its velveteen allure. They are as pure and innocent as I was before I became a washerwoman, when we lived in the low hills on the farm, ach, how the day would break, as clear as birdsong. Whereupon Joey would point to the shrill green leaves the primrose possessed, almost prehistorically indented. Miriam would agree that the plant was medieval and had been sewn into tapestries in order to stay in bloom forever.

Yet it was Joey who was the tenderhearted observer of the scene, worrying about everyone's health and suggesting remedies he had seen in old books for this or that perceived ailment; while it was Miriam who ruthlessly rid herself of anyone weak, ripping the plant from the earth, not hearing, as Joey did, its pathetic scream. It is not individuals we are growing here, but families, she insisted. I worry about the clan they come from, the kind of plant they are, not about this Hans or that Kurt or my Heinrich. Still, she named them all and lectured them all and threatened them with failure and removal very much as the professor was forced to hector and chide his students according to the system in favor with his college.

Joseph, who had cultivated snobbery as an essential professional weapon, was always surprised by Miriam's eagerness to learn the Latin names for the plants she grew and to insist upon their use, so that when Joey spoke about the primroses she would correct him with "*Prim yew-luh,*" emphatically broken into its pronounceable parts. If he complimented her Jacob's ladder, she would respond with "*Po-lee-mow nee-um.*" When he admired her patch of lilies, she told him what he loved was called *Lil ee-um* and that they were the belles of summer. Then it was Joey's turn to complain that there were too many "um"s. It's a Latin ending, she would say with a pleased growl of disgust, because she loved to correct her professor. As they crossed the garden on a grassy lane dotted here and there with the projecting ends of quite-white rocks, Miriam recited the names she had learned, halting by the beds where the named were flourishing: Hettie Hem-er-oh-kal is, Rudy Rud-bek ee-uh, Hortense Hos tuh, Gail Gay-lar dee-uh. Connie Ko lee-us.

This new learning was both gratifying and disturbing. Everyone ought to have a proficiency concerning which they could claim the honor due anyone skilled, the respect appropriate to every form of learning. For Miriam, as these proficiencies grew, the garden grew, and as the garden grew, she flourished. She became active in the Friends of Woodbine's Gardens, a group of ladies who met once a month to exchange enthusiasms, information, and neighborhood gossip—quite a lot of gossip if Joseph's ears were any measure. Nonetheless, he had to be happy his mother was finally a member of the community, had friends, as well as a familiar, much-approved, ongoing enterprise.

Yet Skizzen had no such friends, his connection with the college had become purely formal, he was close to no one and, if anything, moved farther away every day like the sun in winter. Was he improving his mind as she was? were his fingers more agile today than they had been a year ago? did he glow with pride when his students excelled or when one of his observations was published? no and no and no, the answer came. Only his madness progressed, along with the museum that was its most persuasive evidence. It was an advancement that came through accumulation not selection, repetition not interconnection or—he feared—any deeper understanding.

He had once thought that the many terrible deeds of men might be understood by positing some underlying evil working away in the dirt of each life like the sod webworm. Perhaps there was an unrequited urge at the center of the species, a seed or genetic quirk, an impulse, bent for destruction, a type of trichinosis or a malignant imbecility that was forever ravenous. It might be just possible that we were killing off the weak to make the species strong. The young men can shoot one another. Those left standing can rape and murder the enemy's mistresses, whores, and wives. Dead men cannot fertilize, or dead women bear. Then maybe our wars worked to keep our increasing numbers in check. But that hope turned out to be Heinrich Schenker's doing, who had put these ideas in Skizzen's head by insisting that for every harmonic composition there ought to be such a hidden center—a musical idea from which the notes that would be heard emerged, and were thereby governed, the way words issue from a mouth when the mouth moves on account of a consciousness that is formed, at least in part, by a nature as obdurate as an underground god at his forge hammering the white-hot blades of his weapons.

Nicotiana, or the Tobacco Flower, best in C+ soil.

Joseph enjoyed the progress of the seasons, especially that period in earliest spring when the trees showed the tiniest red tip at the end of every twig—just before they grew a furl of green. The color was like a tentative chirp from inside an egg until you turned your head a moment, perhaps to confront invaders—cabbage whites like tossed confetti or dandelions as orange and unacceptable as yolks where they disgraced the grass—only to find that while your attention had been withdrawn, the entire tree had burst into an accolade of bloom.

Music, above all, is what drew Joseph Skizzen to the garden, particularly on those days, as crisp as radish, when the birds were establishing their territories. The air seemed to sense the seeds and the seeds to grow toward the songs of the birds. Joseph thought he knew the plants that had sought out the twitterers, and those that had risen for the wren, or a fern that turned, not to the sun, but toward the chatter of the chickadee, so quick were the petals of its song, so sharp so plentiful so light, so showy in their symmetry, so suddenly in shade.

Astilbe, he said to his own ear. There's a name that could be played—uh-stil bee—a plant that could be sung.

But the robins wanted worms, and the whitethroats wanted grain; he had read of a hunting season specifically designed for doves; the honeysuckle was rapacious; one stalk of bamboo was soon twelve; and violets choked grass while looking cute. Miriam yanked weak plants from the earth and thinned the strong as if they were Jews, but Joseph could not tease her in those terms—not an Austrian. So he suggested that perhaps a little food . . . No, not worth the bother, she'd reply while troweling a plant that had prospered in its present position for removal to a place where it would look better. I need to force these to flower, she would say while wielding a pair of snapping clippers. Deformities were dispatched without remorse, as readily as the infected or those that reverted to their prehybridized days or whose blooms surprised her by being magenta. Creams and pinks that had been together several years were ripped asunder because they were no longer thought to complement one another, and poisons were planted in otherwise wholesome specimens to kill whoever might later eat a leaf.

Miriam wanted a dog that would pursue rabbits. Joseph reminded her that dogs were copiously indiscriminate poopers and adored digging in beds of bulbs while pretending to bury bones, when they really dug just for the hell of it. She then proposed acquiring a cat until Joseph reminded her of their poor rapport with birds. Their moon times are meant to be filled with another kind of stalk. Had she forgotten how they yowled at night? in the afterglow of ruins? after the bombing stopped? Miriam begged him to dispatch a garter snake that wore a streak of gold like a zipper down its back, because the snake surprised her hands when they uncovered its concealing leaves; but Joseph demurred, defending the reptile's reputation. I promise you, he said, this fellow is harmless and beneficial. Miriam responded with a dubious look. This Eden needn't be a haven for snakes just because the first one was.

You can't improve on God, observed the professor.

He worked before hybridization, responded the faithful.

I'm not a Saint Patrick for hire either—to scare them all away.

It's all *Scheiss* about him, Ireland, and the snakes. Anyway, I wasn't about to pay a saint wages. Saints work for nothing.

In lieu of larger help, Miriam released throngs of ladybugs from mail-order boxes. She also had to be persuaded about the virtues of spiders and praying mantises. Webs she abhorred, although she knew the results of their operations were desirable. These loud lemon-colored garden spiders think they own the plants they hang their webs from and pretend to be flowers themselves, as if suspended from sunlight and air.

In the alleged state of nature, Joseph would begin, it is said to be a war of all against all. I know you are teasing, Joey. No one can go against gardens. So let me be with my beauties, at peace with nature and all this world's tossing and yearning. Despite a pledge to cease and desist, Joseph heard himself repeat to his mother how unnatural gardens were, how human-handed every rose was, how thoroughly the irises were trained, how the prizes plants won in their competitions were like those awarded after a proud parade of poodles, each clipped like a hedge. She should not ignore the size of the industry whose profits depended upon fashions in flowers and fads that were encouraged by the press or those ubiquitous catalogs which provoked fears of diseases, worms, and insects that could only be controlled by the poisons, hormones, and fertilizers they recommended. Nor should she make light of the myths extolling the harmless healthiness of gardening, even alleging its psychological superiority to every other avocation. She should notice how the seed companies' bankrolls grew more rapidly than their marigolds, despite extensive artificial breeding; she should also admit the plants' reputations were puffed and as pretentious as their adopted stage names—moonglow, for instance. The garden, he felt compelled to suggest, was like a fascist state: ruled like an orchestra, ordered as an army, eugenically ruthless and hateful to the handicapped, relentless in the pursuit of its enemies, jealous of its borders, favoring obedient masses in which every stem is inclined to appease its leader.

Once he had aroused his mother's ire, Joey would repent his meanness and attempt to calm her by repeating what the great Voltaire had advised . . . Ya ya ya, she would hurry to complete the notorious sentence, I know, I know, I should fertilize . . . cultivate . . . weed my garden. So I do. But you, Professor, you do not. What do you do but stir me like a *Gulasch* with your smarts for a spoon. Play the day through with paste and snippers. As in the *Kinder*'s . . . ya, *dass ist* . . . the *Kinder*'s *Garten.*

Sometimes her scorn, only partly assumed, stung him a bit, but he had hidden his ego so far beneath the layers of his cultivated public selves that even the hardest blow was diverted, softly absorbed, or fended off. The truth was that he was proud of his mother's garden now. She had achieved a renewed life through her interest in it, and her mind had prospered as much as her emotions had, something rarely true, he understood, of love affairs. She would repeatedly disappear into its shrubbery, hidden on her hands and knees, planting and weeding, folding her fingers in a more fundamental form of prayer.

The garden had but one bench, but there Joseph would sometimes sit to enjoy a brisk breeze because these discouraged the mosquitoes that flew in from every point on the globe, he felt, to intrude upon his peace and spoil its brief serenities. The swifts swirled about like bats presumably stuffing themselves with pests, but there were always bugs and always would be bugs—leaf miners, fire ants, flea beetles, earworms, borers—his mother had taught him that—aphids, whiteflies, thrips, and spider mites—the way there would always be weeds—crabgrass, foxtail, purslane, pigweed—it was a wonder, she said, that anything worthwhile remained alive—as well as murderous diseases—leaf spot and brown patch, bean blight and root rot—*mein Gott!*—but the Good Lord made these things, too, to bore and spoil and chew, she would say, cursing them in her childhood German—the loopers, maggots, weevils of her flower beds and borders.

So her world and his were not so dissimilar after all.

Ilex, or Winterberry, Red Sprite, seeks Jim Dandy
for companionship and pollination.

From his attic window Professor Skizzen (feverish, he thought, with flu) patrolled the snowy ground. In a patch near the kitchen door, where Miriam had spread millet and sunflower seeds, numerous quarter notes swayed across a hidden score. What were the birds playing when their heads bobbed? three quick pecks, a pause, three quick pecks, a backward bound that Skizzen decided to characterize as a stiff-legged scratch (a cough), then another pause quite brief before the series was performed again. His chest felt sore, was it his ribs? It might be a dance peculiar to white-throated sparrows and their kind, if his mother's identification was correct, because the doves rattled off eighth notes like a rifle and then rested, the cardinals cocked their heads and bounded forward like balls, while grackles clacked on nearby wires. Skizzen turned away from the window to cough again, not to be heard by the birds. Suddenly a branch would sway, out of the side of his eye a shadow slice across the crust, or a jay caw; then the flock would flee as if blown into limbs and bushes, leaving the dove, a lone hoot from a horn, placidly putting its beak to the ground—*tip tip tip tip*—too stupid to be frightened, yet making the most of the moment's lack of competition by pecking solo.

Joseph's snuffy head stared at the sheet-white yard. Its dazzle did him in. A few withered rose hips, dark marks against the snow, a few bent dry fronds with enough substance to cast an insubstantial likeness, a few thin brittle sticks: they pierced the snow's sturdy surface to lead the eye over one stretch of death to another and encouraged the rabbits to bound across it as if it were hot, and the squirrels race to a tree, snippily flashing their tails. His own fly strips fluttered like kite tails when he coughed. Elsewhere, beneath the now-solid sod, where there remained but little warmth from a sun a month old, moles in dark runnels rarely moved, and bulbs that would later bloom so raucously kept counsel to themselves as if indifferent to entreaties from their nature. Skizzen, always perverse on Tuesdays, and made worse by phlegm and fever, let his thoughts seek those buried green blades that were so eager to push through the first wet earth offered them and flaunt their true colors. That's where growing went to winter. That was elsewhere's elsewhere.

Skizzen's present season wasn't winter. Winter in Woodbine was crisp and clear and cold and clean. The trees were dark-barked, even a sharp wind could not bend their stiffened twigs. His present climate was a stew of steaming fluids. What he saw leaked out of his swollen eyes like an overfull cup. What he smelled fell into a hideous hankie he wadded in his fist and held helplessly to his mouth. In front of him hung a column of clippings that warned against eating Chinese chickens. He stifled a sneeze and sent it to his ribs, which responsively heaved.

Spring's final frost would bite those bulbs for their boasting and bring their beauty, so fragilely composed, to a rude and cruel close, the way wily sovereigns tempt the tongues of their subjects in order to learn who might be bold enough to wag them and thus nip oppositions, as we customarily say, in the bud. Another human's warmth might draw him out and leave him exposed, Skizzen concluded, especially when occupied by discomfort as he was now and dearly desiring a nurse. He considered it a thought worth noting down for use when he spoke to his class of music's lulling little openings, childishly gleeful sometimes—"carefree" was the word . . . yes . . . sunny their disposition—strings of notes that did not pull a toy train clattering behind them as they seemed to promise but drew open suddenly the very door of war.

Once most of the birds flew away in winter, performing feats of navigation while on their many migrations that made the Magi seem novices at geography, since the three sages, at least, had a star; but now so many simply stay and tough it out, counting on the sentiments of humans who have for centuries protected those they couldn't eat, and even kept some cozy in cages most artfully fashioned for them, or prized them for their plumage, or pitted them in fights, or said they sang at night when lovers . . . well . . . so it was rumored . . . did whatever they do . . . counting on others like his mother's hand to feed them.

Hydrangea, or Lemon Daddy, the Fickle Bush.

Joseph tried to encourage the escape of the heat that built up in the house during the summer months by keeping the attic windows open, even if he risked, through one of his rusted screens, the entry of some unfriendly flying things, especially bats, which could hang as handily upside down as his flypapered chains of news clippings, the new group especially, strung near the opening of a dormer, that featured pederasts and their victims, a bunch he had with reluctance begun collecting because he had finally noticed the possibly suspicious absence of sex crimes and criminals—rapes, brises, and other genital deformations, gays and other aberrants, exhibitionists, porncones, sodomists, and other mysterious trans-mix-ups—an absence not to be pursued, but people and practices that nevertheless belonged in any proper inhumanity museum, the nutsy fagans and other detrolleyed toonervilles—others, aliens, weirdos, those were the words—the unlike and therefore unliked, whose unnatural acts promoted inhumane behavior in the species. It gave Joseph no pleasure at all to pursue these topics, in fact they made him queasy, but he felt it a duty to his dream.

Stir reet stir reet, he thought the wrens said, and then *stir reet stir reet* again. Not music, he suspected. Not conversation. Only pronouncement. *Cheater,* the cardinals insisted. *Cheater cheater cheater.*

Calamint, till frost, dainty of bloom and tart of odor.

A stinging wind brought tears to Joey's eyes when Joseph looked down on Miriam's garden filled with captured leaves. They flew just above the mums to be caught in hedges that had lost theirs and whose briars were now eager to seize any debris the wind blew in. I still have mine, Professor Skizzen thought, fly stuck and fluttery, though I'm not evergreen. Angered by the blurred vision in his watery eyes, Skizzen brought his fist down on his right thigh. The blow couldn't reach through the cloth to cause a bruise.

29

We giggle together, that's a good sign, Marjorie said.

•

She stole nickels, she stole dimes. That's no way to run a store.

•

She was the head librarian once, now she's just the basement dunce.

•

I don't know what I'd do without me.

•

That Portho person took out a dirty blue bandanna to wipe the chair he'd chosen as if it were the seat of a public toilet.

•

The pencil's point should not be too fine. Otherwise it will scratch the paper and leave a trail that no eraser can rub away.

•

I don't like weather you can't put a name to.

•

Nobody has worked harder to get nowhere than I have.

•

I hear that during the Depression famished poor kids used to eat library paste in their art classes. If you're hungry enough you'll eat earth. I wonder what sort of sounds they make, those inflated bellies? Do they growl? squeal? Can they catch cold? Can they cough? Not in the library. Of course anything you can hear in here I hear.

•

I'm told your concerts in the church basement are pretty pop, Marjorie said, with an inquiring smile. I'm told you play gospel, too, as if you were born to be black.

•

Good boy.

•

I'm not sure I like the way you listen, Joey. You let me talk about myself until I feel bad.

•

I never had it in for her, you know. My eye just caught her picking up the pennies and peering at the dates on them . . . or she was looking for Indian heads. So what, I thought. Until I caught her sneaking a dime from the overdue box. I bet she bought gum. We used to chew a lot of gum in here, we got so bored sitting at the front desk like an ink pad, you could have filled sacks with our yawns, but when I took charge I put a stop to it because it set a bad example for borrowers, you know, put ideas in their heads, we had enough trouble without aiding any of it, it didn't need any aiding, so I put a stop to it. Full stop. To it.

•

I hate Kleenex. If you blow your nose you put your blow in your purse. But no. Into a library book the soiled fold goes, stuffed between pages and infecting the words. Tissue with lipstick on it wedged between pride and prejudice. Pardon me, Joey, but you know what they can wipe with it.

•

Before me, nobody thought about things. She didn't. She sat here and smiled, stamped your book and smiled, said, Have a wordful day. Her smile was wan, though, with no conviction to it, not even a smile-filled smile, just a little twitch that widened the mouth, disturbed the lips. Wan, I would say it was. And have a wordful day was said in a whisper, as if it were between her and the book. Me—I have my great gray eyes. I look you in the face to say my say and I say sometimes, Have a nice day, okay, sometimes that's what I say, I remind the moms, the kids, the occasionals—This book is due the twenty-first, remember—but you never know, I might say, Go away and jibber your jabber elsewhere, babble to your chums of your little life and loves, make out in the car, Carl—was that the skinny redhead's name? who taught—would you believe it?—fencing.

•

I aspire for you, Joey. I have hopes.

•

I hate hairpins. I've got plenty of hair. People who come in comment on how plenty. No pins. Not anywhere. So where do these little wires end up? They end up keeping somebody's place in somebody's book. Put a crimp in the page. Scratch the paper. Ugly things to find in the midst of your reading like a fly in the ear. They don't own the book. It's not theirs. So what the hell, they think. No need to care.

• •

I took out a penny for a postcard. And that Marjorie Bruss slithers over and says, I saw you, I saw you take money from the overdues. I say, I need a penny for a postcard. Not from the overdues, you don't, she says. Just consider it, I say. Just consider what you've said—how silly it is, how childish, not to say cheap, how niggling, that is the word, niggling, petty, that is the word, how petty—and aren't you sorry now you've said it, because it shows off your soul, as if your soul were out walking and it were Easter.

But she says she's going to report my actions to the library board, so I inform her that there was only one action in question, but her plural suggested others. Well, she did have others in mind, plenty of others, my improprieties, to report. That's another reason why I call her Major. Oh, do they? don't they? will they? won't they? put people on report. They wear white gloves that hunt for dirt like pigeons peck crumbs. Have you a dossier, then, on me, I ask her, and she says right back and boldly in my face, Oh yes, I'm keeping accounts. That's in the plural, too, I remind her. Neither of us has ever married. Notice that, dear, I ask of her, which sets her back, back in surprise she is rudely taken. Her face starts to redden, and I understand reddening to be a warning. Everyone knows why I'm not married, why I'm a librarian. They look at me and know, but you, Missss Brussss are well made, have hair, and speak easily to the world. What could the reason be? For our joint chastity? I am a witch, Missss Brussss, as anyone can see, but you are a bitch, as everyone will learn. Well, Mr. Joey, at that she screams that scream she screams, and I know I have added one more rude word to her report.

• •

You think you know what the life of an old maid is like because we are well represented in commonplace literature, in commonplace movies, in lady mags. We are leftovers from the Victorian family album, the homely sister who never hears a marriage proposal, who sits at home for dances, at parties leans against floral walls, is always a help around a complacent house, hair in a net as if each strand were a fish.

Yes, well, we aren't alone there, most of us, at home sweet home, we are taking care of Mother, whom we have to dislike, it's tradition. Father always dies first, like the first-picked fruit, and Mother languishes for years in an upstairs chair while her virginal daughter sits by her tatting and occasionally chatting but mostly glumly waiting out the silence through which Mother dozes between jolts of blackberry brandy.

Well, I like my little lonely world where I can keep my secrets and my skirts and my scrapbooks to myself. I liked sitting at the front desk, filing for future reference what everybody in my community was reading and noting who is a sound loan risk and who is always tardy and who tries to escape the overdues even when only a few pennies are at stake. I didn't shush. The Major does that. I didn't stalk the stacks like a policeman on patrol. The Major does that. I didn't read the riot act to every moist-nosed grubby-fingered kid who comes within my hearing. The Major does that. I lacked a stamp.

I kept my wits about me, though. I kept my counsel. And in my apartment, just three rooms, one is reserved for concocting spells. I also make my own valentines, Christmas cards, and those that wish ill people well and those that anoint them with a curse, as well as little stuffed figures I pretend to puncture with pins. The pleasure is not major, but it is quietly lasting. It cools the soup spite spits in. But I am speaking far too frankly, more and I shall have to prick myself—ha ha—ha ha—you see I am not serious about any of this, none of it is really true. And these days, Joey, how are you?

. . .

I sing one language Mr. Skizzen, but I speak several, depending upon the circumstances, just as I hold down several jobs in several different towns. I speak teddy bear, just to cite an instance. I can make my words as white as marshmallows. I can niggerate so thick you'd think I was from Africa last minute or a tar pit in Haarlem. As well as all seasons of speech in between depending on the climate in which I find myself. Honey, you are a baby in this world and don't know how to howl yet.

. . .

We is a bod-ie. When we sing, we is one heart, one heart the shape of one lung, we make moves froms the movies, we sway, we shout it out, we clap the beat, we unison ourselves right into reality. We casts spells. And that's how I sells cars.

. . .

I know all about the geography of money.

. . .

People call me Witch Hazel. I sorta like that. I rub myself all over with the stuff. What a lot of me there is. You know, you play better when you just play. My husband used to say my ears looked like my head was melting. You hold your ears in as if you had just heard something alarming. He'd say, Hazel, you can sell anything. You have a nice dark-chocolate tongue. He died of his weight and I expect to die of mine.

. . .

I can be aggravated, but if I'm aggravated, I make sure, right then, that the causes are aggravated back. Even if it's a fender. Rusting when it shouldn't, like this morning in the wet air, overnight it seemed, and it was there, orange as the fruit, a wide patch like you'd sew on pants. Damn bad for business. Baked bad, the paint was, on it. So I scrape off as much of the color as I can with a finger file. I swear at it, too, a long complicated swear that would have peeled its paint if it weren't orange as orange gets already. Poop. I'm nice in front of you. You such a baby. But don't aggravate me by bawling about life. I'll send you to sit my teddy bear. My teddy bear, darlin, don't care.

. . . .

You just fuss and find fault, Joey, I know you from womb to past noon, from even when your father lay upon me, if you can bear the truth. Well, I bore you and so I know you. Maybe I'm the only one who knows you because people think now you are a mal—a malcontent—a malcontent man of middle age—well, when you are really old the way I'm supposed to be really old, you know how harmless your kind of malcontentedness is.

But your seed started me off down the garden rows, remember? Your packets of alyssum and other scrounged stuff you gave me for my birthday back when you hadn't a penny for a pinch of sugar even, well, who knew what it would lead to, me with the spoon digging in the dirt like a child, but it was the miracle of that gift that gave me the peace your father took away from us all when he—they say here—vamoosed, a likable word. You helped make that maternal me you see in the garden, caring for my little sweet things and my big shameless blooms on stalks thick as thumbs. Your father, God rot his soul, used to walk me through the city gardens when we were—when I was betrothed, and in the hillsides, too, he would say the names of the flowers as we passed, the little yellow flavorings that came up between the sharp white rocks like surprises in the spring.

My plants are fastened to the ground. I like that. There's no running off out of my garden except by the butterflies and bees, and they come back again as soon as they get thirsty. Then when all my beds are quiet—when there's no humming or buzzing or waving from the breeze—and the heat is even heavy as the past is—all my beds are still green.

So you should be nice to your sister, Joey, even if she's making a profit from potatoes because she is growing good things, too, or her husband is, since he's always in the fields with poison to protect them. He and poison do make a pair, don't they? Handkerchief across his face like a bandit so as not to breathe the foul fumes. But I say who can complain when it is beans and potatoes he is doing? who can put that profit down? so long as he's there to spoon his soup and comes to bed like a person prepared to sleep, because most men aren't like you, Joey, devoted to your mother the way you are, and I love you for it, God knows, though gardener you aren't, but a man of peace and steady as a broom near to hand. You've done well by yourself and by me, with an upstanding reputation at the college, yes, you've grown respect, and that's a splendid proud crop, Joey, no backseat to take there, spreading music around, too, like peat. Who knows what will come of it?

Then again it rains on sodden fields. Then again the rabbits make their meals out of my asters. Black spot and beetles, worms and rots and weevils, cut my yields. It rains on wet beds, on sodden fields. There is a sudden uncalled-for freeze. The daffs are snowed on till the stems bend, weary of the feathered weight of all those flakes. Then again the blooms brown beneath the relentless sun. Day after day goes by dry. Then again there's hail. I want to cry and you don't carry any sympathy for me because you think everything I do is futile, my trees and bushes fruitless as rocks. The weather will always worsen, you say. Due proportion is impossible, restraint, proper measure, are never nature's way; it's either heavy stillness or brief tornado. It's either rags or riches, you say, while I curse the four corners of the sky, each one a *Karlkrautkopf.* Ach, but then again, Joey, in every year comes May. *Gott!* what did I just say? In every year May comes.

30

Some of us used to wonder whether the human race would escape the consequences of its own folly, but now we worry that our species will somehow go on indefinitely regardless of how wickedly it behaves.

This world is made of three kinds of stupid. The commonest stupid is so stupid it doesn't know it is stupid but is content to be stupid; the second sort is the stupid who denies it is stupid and claims to be wiser than whiskey; the third bunch is convinced it is stupid, too, but knows it knows that much and wisely fears the worst. Among the stupidest of stupids, not knowing any better, a few will luck out because they won't have the wit to perish properly.

Once upon a time there was a professor of music whose best instrument was hypocrisy, and who pretended to be concerned about the fate of the human race, when, in fact, he hoped it would vanish from the face of the earth the way a fog dense enough to obscure the landscape slowly diminishes, rising like steam from a damp land, so that the earth could smile again as it must have once, in the days of simple cells, titanic trees, or even reptiles with necks grown long in order to reach the leaves.

Joseph Skizzen wanted to go into his mother's garden and shit upon the ground, but he realized that his shit would only aid the garden's growth. Moreover, what he wished for was impossible because he could barely think shit let alone say it let alone deposit it or even shush it before it became evidently present.

The crucial problem facing any parasite is the health of the host upon which it feeds, whose substance it steals, and whose balance it upsets, because on the day that the host becomes a husk, sucked dry as dust, the parasite must be prepared to live on small bites bitten from itself, something the tapeworm may not be prepared to do but which the human worm has practiced its entire span, gnawing on the sweet knuckles of its young, cutting into small squares many of the members of its presumptive community.

Professor Skizzen was a fretter, he just couldn't help himself, and if he was not fretting about this, he was fretting about that, because, in his experience, when things were looking their best, the worst would infallibly happen; thus it was that when he thought that the human race would come a cropper, a result it deserved and would be a boon for the earth, he fell to fretting that such a benevolent catastrophe might not occur, and if it did not, such a disaster would be, among dire consequences, the most dreadful injustice he could imagine.

Because Professor Skizzen, as he grew older and was more established in his work and community, found himself with increasingly large periods of time to spend as he pleased, he was now able to dream of improvising, while riffing the piano keys, a kind of music that would somnolize its listeners and render them serenely comatose until they quietly passed away from indolence and immobility, not having eaten any more of the earth's provenance or ravaged another inch of its land or consumed, in their scurrying about, any additional portion of its minerals; but alas these lullabies were made of dream chords too immaterial even for angels to sound, and there was nothing to be done, not even in nightmare, to relieve the planet of its deadliest denizen—every man jack a ripper.

Justice was never served, so why shouldn't the race of men get away with their crimes, since individuals did, more often than not, and the idea that ultimately each one of us paid the piper (by burning in hell if not through some type of anticipatory suffering) was no more than a comforting fiction promulgated by the same criminals who gave us God and the Holy Ghost and who offer us a few paintings of their Christ on the cross or one or two smug-faced Madonnas as proof that men are on balance better than weevils and have their hearts in the right place (see the Sistine Ceiling or Chartres in the moonlight) (contemplate the advance of science or our voyages to the stars); or, conversely, those who tell us that HIV is a man-made epidemic designed by puritans ashamed of our fleshly sins to get rid of us, ironically through the very copulations by which we come to be; and that this effort, when you view it from the right perspective, proves humans to be humane after all, and that they are trying their best to cleanse the world of their company before they do it irrevocable harm; but their best will not be good enough because hermits, honest priests, and ugly virgins shall survive; fat Adams, thin Eves, shall take up nakedness as nature's way, and, although they will look round then and see the world gloriously alive and lush and orderly, warning erections will not prevent the opportunity, and the formerly chaste will fall to fornicating with a glee the world before has never entertained.

The Inhumanity Museum made Professor Skizzen think of death a great deal—no, rather, of the dead, of the dead in heaps, of the dead in holes, in the forks of trees, of bones in Catacombs, of a body left like the remains of a blown tire in the road, and how the body goes back to being a mere heap of stuff that might have some nutritional value to fungi. It made him think of bodies less alive than plant stems, less alive than leaves, or even streams, oak smoke, a breeze, except when the cavities are filled with little nibblefish, maggots, or a greedy eel, or when the body simply ascends as stench or turns into its underclothes; and he would now and then stand naked in front of the mirror in his bedroom door to wonder why he was standing there, why anything—his wardrobe, his bed—was there, why he was so thin and why he had let a beard appear—oh vanity! because he wanted to be thought idiosyncratic by his students—and why his hair was unkempt—oh vanity! because he wanted to be seen as quite a character on the campus; but so naked now he couldn't look at everything that was shamelessly mirrored there disgracing any self he might have chosen as his public image; though in better moments he would argue that his reflection, apparently stripped of all subterfuge, was really a misleading appearance and not his real self, which was five foot eight and one hundred forty-two, muscular though not by much, absent his mirror's identifying marks—for instance, the rough patch on his knee where he so often picked off scabs, and that small mole like a dot of dye on his chest—really bare of body hair and so utterly ordinary no attentions would be drawn to it even if it stood nude as a statue, loincloth unattached, in a public square.

The evidence initially pointed in the direction of human extinction, but biologists suggested that, although no one would admire what they had become, a few, the most adaptable to execrable conditions (with their claws, fangs, and double stomachs), would survive.

A virus is the best bet. However, there are billions of people. A few of them are bound to be, by sheer chance, immune.

CON. No true human will survive—if any of us do—by being reduced to a species, by becoming a scarcely remaining member of a class the way there are some salmon left; because out of our species has emerged the individual like a flower from a dung heap, the self blooming as a unique person should, valued for her singularity, the quality of her consciousness, the gifts of her genius. This is our extraordinary, our miraculous achievement; it is the legacy of the great Athenians. When a genuine individual dies, he or she is not replaced. Every day, the individual has to be achieved anew. Appeals to the collective would return us to the evolutionary fold. It is true that the individual cannot survive alone; but what he or she needs is the help of other individuals not more loud-mouthed members of mankind; rather the community of those who are fully aware of the world. What a dream it was to imagine the universal kingdom of ends. That, Professor Skizzen would whisper to himself, is the moral imperative. It is totally impossible to realize. So Man may survive, after all, but only as a flock, a pack, a horde.

PRO. But every snowflake is unique, it is alleged; every salmon, petal, pinch of dirt, is as different as Mondays in Montana, Tuesdays in Tucson, Wednesdays in Waco. Fingerprints, retinas, DNA: they distinguish us. Besides, we can find the world in a grain of sand.

CON. Phooey to that hooey. Those distinctions disappear whenever we vote. Each of us becomes a number. The belief that we are special—you and I and he and she—is revealed as an illusion. Two thousand six hundred twenty-nine died in the April storm. Mud slides buried thirty-five. Shot while sitting on the porch swing, seventeen this summer. That's the norm, the average age of, the median for . . . Six miners were found alive. When the ferry capsized twenty-one Chevys drowned. Twenty-nine million cans of tuna were returned to have their engines tuned. Last year at this time he was batting .334. When Charlie died three people noticed and one cried. Most men have no more than six different sexual relationships during their erectile lives. The tornado caused 18 million dollars' damage. Christmas sales are up. The lottery

pays 60 mil to anyone holding ticket number 8210759364. That's my phone number at work.

PRO. Everyone I know is an unusual individual. Aunt Minnie does jig-saws for a living. She enters the most difficult contests under the stiffest rules: you cannot look at the completed picture or even learn its title; the edge must be completed first, not omitting the last, lost, little one; the fitting of forms must rise like flooding water from bottom to top, puddling is prohibited, etc.

CON. Harriet Hoff's time of fourteen minutes fifty-nine seconds, during the 1995 finals, was better than Minnie's by two minutes thirteen seconds. Women have won for the sixth straight year. Among the men, Frank Link had the best time but he still finished eighth.

THE WORLD comes in 1,500 pieces. Of this puzzle we have 1,250 in stock. A few of the boxes have nothing missing. At cost: $2.73. At retail: $9.99.

31

There were three sharp knocks, and Marjorie slipped in. She seemed zipped into a towel, her wild hair terrible to behold, and sat upon the bed with the familiarity of one who has made it. Joseph followed each movement, transfixed. White hands darted out of her sleeve like laboratory mice and just as swiftly were withdrawn. After a moment during which Marjorie inspected him for flaws, she rose and moved in his direction. Joey put down his milk. Good boy, she said. You deserve a nice surprise. To Joey no surprise was nice. The Major bent over, her palms shot forth and closed upon his cheeks. The holes in the sleeves were great dark ovals now. Unhand me, Madame, you forget yourself, Joey said, frightened from the world into a novel; and Marjorie recoiled as though struck by the book from which he had unconsciously taken the phrase. *Un hand me,* she shouted. *Un hand me,* she repeated, with renewed emphasis. Next she screamed in his face at the point of his nose. As if blown by the noise, Joey backed his chair away, causing a plate of cookies to slide across the tiny table, overturning the glass of milk, and knocking a heavy history of music to the floor near which the equally startled stream of milk had commenced its spill. Her scream was as sharp and high as a child's cry but lasted longer than the length of any blade and undulated as if made for a scary movie or the stage. Out of the room, whose door now stood open, Marjorie paused for breath before emitting a shriek that rivaled her first. Thoroughly frightened and utterly bewildered, Joey held one ear shut while trying to save his history. Finally he simply kicked the book to safety with a foot and released his ear, since the scream had wound down like the siren does for all clear. In the reverberating silence that followed, a few pellets of snow ticked the windows. He actually thought, Sleet; even: Oh dear. Finally Joey's heart could be heard rising to the occasion.

After a pause to prepare his body for its next move, Joseph found a towel to mop up the milk, although one edge of the rag rug had done a good job. A door bang brought him to his row of windows. Marjoric, in her white scuffs and terry-cloth robe, was kneeling by the back bumper of the Bumbler. She removed the blocks from behind the wheels of his car, brushing the bricks away with a sweep of her hand. Then, after a pause and a faint squeak, the emergency brake failed, and the Bumbler accelerated awkwardly down the steep drive, careening over the curb and into the street, where it narrowly missed a parked car but struck a utility pole with such force the pole acquired a lean and the car a dent in its trunk that looked intended. Standing at her door now, Marjorie yelled, Good-bye, you ungrateful piece of waste, and disappeared into the house. The door shut with a slam that sung in his windows. At the foot of the drive, blocking half the street, the Bumbler sat in a pool of shade or a pool of grease; it was hard to tell because of the way the light had to fall now to reach the road.

Joey peered at his car in disbelief. That good-bye had been meant for him. What had he done, he wondered. Then—what had she? He could not immediately find any meaning in this attack on him or his vehicle, but he knew he would have to leave at once, pushed into the cold and continuing sleet, evicted like someone who hadn't paid his rent. Ah, but perhaps his rent had come due just now. His mind refused to proceed in that direction. Somehow—the thought fell into his lap like a dislodged book—it was Debbie's fault. Fortunately he had very few things that he needed to gather. There were the documents that Miss Moss had helped him compose (those that they had done together as a joke), a knot of socks, and—lucky break—Miriam had most of his laundry. He had to get himself and that car on the road. Or off the road. Joey's eyes fled around his former room. His first fear was not that he would leave something behind but that he would meet her in the entry, ready to rescream and recurse and recriminate. Ah . . . the key. Should he leave the key. He fished it from a pocket and put it down by the turned-over glass. Then he snatched it back again. Suppose the car would not start. What could he do then? Where would he go? He had a library key, too. If he left the one he should leave the other. Or should he keep both and—Joey was surprised by his own train of thought, as if it had burst around a curve into its station—haunt the stacks, sneaking in to sleep like Portho might have, and in future years, in cahoots with Miss Moss, to spook the Major, visiting his thin presence upon a section labeled INJURED AND INNOCENT.

Joey decided to retain both and later mail them to Marjorie in a jar of silverfish. All of a sudden his head replayed her most recent scream. Unhand me, Madame, had he said? In a desperate hurry now, he packed his few things in a pair of pillowcases he pulled from those on his bed. These, too, he would send back to the library unexplained. After astonishment, shock, and shame came rage like a wind that's had a run from upriver. So what if he met her in the entry? she who said she was his friend, with whom he had shared amusing observations, and whom she had called "good boy" more than a few times; yet who had attacked him with unsheathed claws, causing him to knock over the milk, which was only a little milk after all, good to soften a butter cookie, and did no damage, but spill as in the proverb, which implied that shrieking about a little thing like that was unmannerly and, what's more, pointless and could have the most inconvenient and unfortunate consequences.

And calling his car a . . . a piece of waste wasn't a bit nice either, even if it was a wreck, because after all it did its work and kept its promise to turn its wheels and keep to the road—he was through the entry, out the door—Close it closely, he advised himself, close it softly, no horrid slam such as he—the neighborhood—had already had to suffer, and he was oops . . . slipping a little on the curved and dipping sidewalk as he made his way down the rise, a sack on each shoulder—some Santa—why had it happened? but—another thought made its presence felt—sleet showered him like rice—if the car wouldn't go for him now, it wouldn't go for Miriam either, when she wanted to call upon the baby rising in Deborah's belly and exchange recipes and give her daughter her gosh-darned advice. There is some sweetness in the sourest grapes.

He never locked his car, not the driver's door or the trunk, and he was grateful for that neglect now. The trunk, though, wouldn't open, deformed as it was, so he had to toss his pillowcases into the backseat. An onset of shivers overtook him. It was cold, the car was cold, the seat as cold as an enamel sink, his cheek bitten by particles of ice, and his ears were burning, maybe from her sounds, maybe from the wind. He felt keys heavy and cold in his pocket: house key, library key, car key, mom's key . . . cold, and he was scarcely dressed. His hands hurt while on the wheel. Its cold cut through flesh and bones that were no longer fingers. There was a laugh in the sound of the starting car—Witch Hazel's laugh—it coughed, she laughed, it ran, and he bungled the clutch into gear so the car lurched from its curbside onto the street and immediately began to wobble down the hill toward town.

Lord. Lights, he thought. One worked. It looked like one was working. He could see a house lunge out of the dark at him as the beam swept along the sidewalk. Joseph refused to drive at night. Before this, that is, he had refused. He pumped the brakes as he had learned he had to do to slow the machine on icy streets, and the Bumbler squeaked like a conversation held between rusty hinges. He knew one thing for certain: he didn't dare get stopped. First he drove below speed out of caution and then sped down the road out of fear and finally settled in at thirty-five as the safest. But the lone light was a beacon. The police would surely see it. And then he would be arrested for having an unsafe vehicle and no proper license and heaven knows what crimes the Major may have accused him of, for she was someone known and trusted in the town and would be believed. Without lights he could only crawl, and as he left the limits of the city the stark darkness of thick woods and plowed fields closed in until he turned his one eye back on.

A car came at him blazingly bright and blindingly haloed. Then blinked before it passed. What was that? what did that mean? Sometimes he saw the white line. Sometimes he saw a tree, a fence, a highway sign before the road turned, and he swung just in time to follow its course. He was too cold to know now just how cold he was. The windshield wept and the wipers weren't working. He heard himself say Oh God oh gosh as he drove, growing small and losing his hold on Joseph altogether.

Whoa. He was traveling up a hilly dirt lane. He didn't remember this. The road had gone the other way. Joey stopped and backtracked in a series of jerks and consternations as if retreating between deep ditches or climbing down a ladder leaning in a well, seeing only where he shouldn't go, since ahead of him was entirely behind. He realized, in the midst of this, that he needed to pee. His bladder, he believed, had shrunk to the size of a prune. Tears of frustration felt like frost on his face. He halted the car but left it running and relieved himself in a stream against the side of something. It was covered with weeds and wouldn't mind. Then he threw up, too. Mostly milk. Good boy, Joey said, wiping his mouth as far as his eyes. Good boy. The rest of his drive continued on the back of the night's mare.

The lights of Woodbine were reassuring. He stalled the car in front of his mother's house. Now it would have to be his house, too. It coughed as if killed. What next? What next? He dreaded the fuss that was about to ensue. Women. Major Miriam Miss Moss Debbie Miss Spiky Madame Mieux . . . Women. Mieux and Marjorie, Miss Moss and Miriam . . . Women. Mieux and Major, Moss and Mizz Spike, Debbie dear what have you done? He sat quite still in the driver's seat until he got the joke, got out, and walked with slow deliberation to the house. He had a key for that, didn't he? Which key? The cold one with the long cold barrel. In Woodbine, no sleet this night.

His mother actually put her arms around him. Poor Joey, she said in a tone meant to soothe. He had already thrown up so he didn't cry. He sighed. His chest shuddered so his mother thought he might be sobbing. Joey broke her hold to insist he wasn't. It's all right to be upset, she said, which ordinarily would have made him furious. He held her hands to his cheeks. See. Dry-eyed. Poor boy, she said. Joey ran to his room and stood near the bed in despair. The bed . . . He couldn't sit there. Eventually, he chose the chair.

During the next few days, Miriam got around to reminding him that she had always maintained the majorette woman was up to no good, had deep designs, even though Joey had not told her what had really happened. He wasn't sure himself. There was an unpleasant proportion at the bottom of this business. As the Major had screamed at Portho, Marjorie had screamed at him. And he had been kicked out into the street the way Portho . . . the way Portho had been . . .

with lowlife language . . .

kicked . . .

along with his car . . .

into the street . . .

actually, Joey had been booted

out of town.

Like a penny in a pudding, the truth sank in. The Major's yell had been intended to turn all blame toward him. No one else would hear his protest—Unhand me, Madame—they would only hear her cry as she defended herself from his . . . advances. Joey's innocence made him guilty once again. So Portho may have been innocent, too, asleep behind the fold of his magazine to be suddenly awakened by a familiar perfume or drift of hair across his cheek . . . the possessive cup of her hands felt through the fur of his face. Yet Joey had placed his mother's hands upon his frozen cheeks. Suppose Marjorie had simply been making a friendly, a comforting, a cheek-warming gesture he had then rejected in obnoxiously theatrical terms. That was another upsetting element in all this: the way the "unhand me" expression had apparently leaped from the page into some hole in his head only to pop from his mouth in a moment of startle.

How unexpected? Hadn't he viewed the milk and cookies with some apprehension? Why would anyone be suspicious of such a harmless gift? or his all-too-ready hire, the handy offer of a spare room, its more-than-reasonable rent? Or the friendly chats or the fond banter? Joey had to admit he had found the shelter of her wing pleasant enough. Looking back, however . . . Perhaps their relationship had been adding to a different sum. And he had sensed that.

On the other hand, had he ever been any good at sensing slight things? did he pick up small clues with alacrity or even look for any? Joey was too busy sending misleading signals of his own. Was that the right method? maybe to become motionless, scarcely to breathe? the rabbit's ruse. In contrast, Rudi Skizzen, his mentor in these matters, was a master of disguise. His false mustache was hidden by his beard. Mistrust was catching, though. The deceiver deceives the deceiver before he deceives the deceived. Ah . . . how about playing a role just for practice? To get good at it. Was Marjorie Bruss good at it? Well, he simply didn't know. Miss Moss certainly thought so. But Miss Moss called herself a witch. What did that mean? Mr. Kazan was certainly a man of multiple suspicions. Yet Joey remembered thinking Mr. Kazan feared what wasn't there—perhaps a good part of his obscure past. Still his store was robbed. Or was it?

There was a poet who had written about a word he liked—"presentiment"—the author's name would not come to his tongue—such an annoyance, a sign he was flustered—and that poet had said the word referred to the way a lengthening shadow signaled the setting sun. It seemed a gloom-soaked poem, a gloom-soaked word. The unanswered question was: did Joey have, regarding Marjorie Bruss, some sort of presentment? Oh dear, he realized suddenly that his mother had accused him of crying. She didn't know it was over spilled milk. Well, the cookies hadn't crumbled, had they?

32

Don't hang back. Come in, my boy. My name is President Howard Palfrey. These are my colleagues, Professors Morton Rinse—no, over there—and Clarence Carfagno, to my left. My left, yes. Have a seat. Oooh. I should say, have a chair, meet a chair, shouldn't I? It's more fitting a president. Well, one day we shall have a chair or two here at

Whittlebauer. I call these gentlemen colleagues because we are a family here at Whittlebauer, and I think of myself as a member, you see, of every department, therefore they are colleagues, QED. That one will be fine. You, sir, appear to be younger than you are, if we can trust your transcript and vita. Haha. But what else is there to a man but his CV, come to think of it. We are rich in CVs here at Whittlebauer.

Yes, sir. I guess I do look young for my age. My mother thinks I'm still in my teens.

Ah, haha. You have a mother. Of course. They always think so, don't they? Might be a problem, though, managing a class, keeping discipline, that line of things, what do you think, Mort?

Very possibly. Yes, sir. Well observed.

But now we are getting ahead of ourselves. Mr. . . . ah . . . Skizzen, this meeting is merely—. What sort of name is that, may I inquire?

It's German.

German?

Austrian.

Hear that, Clare, Austrian.

Viennese.

Viennese! But I know that, don't I, from your CV. What I asked was what does it mean?

I believe it refers to . . . means . . . is a . . . sketch, sir. Plural. Yes, the plural. Sketches.

There's many of you, then. Morton here we call Salty Wash. Out of our dear love, of course. The students are so fond of Mort, aren't they? of Clare, too, of course. You don't play the piccolo?

No, sir. The piano. Only the black keys.

Rich . . . only the black. Haha. That limitation isn't mentioned here . . . in your CV. Nooo. So we know it's been thinned, not padded. Haha. Haha. You find me in a good mood.

I thought Mr. Skizzen mentioned the organ in his dossier, Professor Carfagno ventured. In addition to the piano.

Oh. I did. Yes. The organ.

We have a wonderful organ here at Whittlebauer when it works, the very thing angels would play if it was light enough for them to carry around. Though I guess they find all things easy.

We need an organist, and somebody who can do choir. Professor

Carfagno spoke to Joseph's knees, pressed together like a girl's should be.

But we mustn't rush things, mustn't let need hasten us into error. Yes. I mean no, we mustn't. This meeting, for example, is wholly preliminary. We shall cast our net wide. Our trawlers shall plow the seas. However, since we could see from your CV that you—surprise! eh?—live here in Woodbine . . . well, we thought we might speak to you first.

I'm glad of that.

How long have you been living in Woodbine—it seems such an unlikely spot.

Oh, now, Clare, don't say that. What is unlikely about our little piece of Eden?

For someone born in Austria.

We all come from somewhere else, here, in America.

I understand you studied music in Graz.

No, sir, Professor Rinse. My studies were in Vienna where my father played a second violin for the philharmonic.

Quite an accomplishment.

Thank you, yes, but a second violin. To be only a second. It broke his heart.

I should imagine. Rinse's eyes had now risen to Joey's belt.

The symphony has a school. I studied with the great Gerhardt Rolfe.

You don't say. Rolfe?

A very demanding man. I was very young, of course.

How precocious!

I might have been called that if I had been four or five, but I was ten.

It seems to me I've heard your name. Bruited about, you know. Morton's eye was eye to eye with Joey's finally, under a wrinkled brow.

My mother lives in town, too. And I did do some substituting at Saint Agatha's Church.

Ah, yes, that . . . must . . . be . . . it.

I must see to the welfare of my mother.

Is that on your CV? I don't remember that being on your CV.

It was just a little substituting. I didn't think it significant.

For what were you a substitute, may I inquire?

The organist.

Nice crowd at the Saint Agatha's. You read our ad, I suppose, and know what we need. Here at Whittlebauer we are a different denomination, of course. So many children . . . in their world of belief . . . destined for the service of the church. Great advantage. They are aimed like an arrow . . .

No, I'm afraid not, sir. I didn't see—didn't read—

But they are as prolific as herrings!

Yes, sir. I meant that I learned of the position from my mother and she from friends before I called the office here on the Hill and got the information.

Oh, too bad. We had a fine ad . . . in all the major journals, too. We even considered the *Times,* the ad was so fine.

The *Woodbine . . . ?*

No, no. *New York.* The *New York Times.* But they wanted entirely too much. Who do they think they are? We are not a wealthy school. Just rich in CVs. Haha. They take advantage of our Middle West, our size. We select, of course, as carefully as any good greengrocer. Our students. And our faculty, too, as you can see.

Professor Rinse, you might have heard my name—I just remembered where—you might have heard my name in connection with President Palfrey's niece, Miss Gwynne Withers, who—

Gwynne Withers! she's my niece. How is it you know her?

—whom you once substituted for—music and magic, was it?—when she was unable—

To get my piano tuned! yes! I remember that. You remember that, don't you, Mort? the piano she was going to use—well, the piano belongs to the college, of course, but it is located in my—

For the Board of Trustees? yes, she was quite distraught, as I remember. So I stepped in, Mr. Skizzen, as it happened, yes, music and magic, stepped in with Music and Magic. I play the violin, sometimes, with my tie.

They couldn't find a tuner in time. Was that you? who was to accompany—?

Yes, but I found a tuner. He just couldn't find us. I was to accompany her in preparing for her recital. A man from Columbus was to have—you know—come for the occasion from Columbus, it was indeed Columbus—

There is a story there, Mr. Skizzen, with a moral. Or an immoral—haha. I *am* in good spirits. Whittlebauer is in good spirits.

A Mr. Kleger, it was, wasn't it, sir?

You are right, Rinse. Miss Gwynne . . . It is the Welsh blood, you know. Can't otherwise account for it. She's married now.

How so?

To that Kleger fellow. Herbert Kleger, that's it. Married his pupil. There was hanky-panky, sir, you can believe me, and it reached the Columbus papers. He accompanied her right up to the altar. And a child should be along any day now.

Well, that's news.

Kleber—Kleber—never liked the fellow, though he was said to play well. So you were to—well, you should have accompanied her. Why didn't we do that?

The piano wouldn't have accompanied us.

Ah yes, of course. Did we ever get the damn thing to play?

Clarence?

?

Mort?

?

What, Mr. Skizzen, is your principal area of interest, Professor Rinse asked after enduring his own silence. You realize that we are a small department and must cover the musical globe.

Well, sir, I have many interests, modern music most of all, I suppose. While studying in Vienna I became fascinated with the work of Arnold Schoenberg, especially the pieces he composed during his transition from tonal to atonal music. I am about to publish a piece on *Style and Idea.*

Professor Carfagno cleared his throat. Everyone paused to listen. This throat is going to kill me, he said, between moments during which his face turned an unaccustomed color.

Clare, you should have that looked at. You can't help the chorus with a throat like . . . Lozenges. At least lozenges.

Frederick Delius, Joseph was in a hurry to say. I like his music, too.

Oh yes, delicious.

Perfectly charming.

Though his C-minor piano concerto isn't much, Joseph dared to add.

I've heard some say so.

I didn't want you to think I was stuck in the present.

Oh, no. All the great music, Professor Carfagno said, has already been composed.

So then when did you leave Austria for America? Morton Rinse leaned forward as if this question had particular importance.

My mother and I—oh, and my older sister, I have a sister, not musical—we fled to London on account of the Nazis.

Ah, yes . . . the Nazis. The three interrogators nodded sympathetically.

Terrible!

Awful!

Monstrous!

Oh, yes, hideous creatures in red armbands and black uniforms.

And your father, poor man, playing second fiddle . . . well, not precisely that but—

He couldn't leave his seat in the symphony. He sent us away to safety. Not sitting in a first seat broke his heart. I cannot imagine what losing his second seat would have done.

I see. Devastating.

Yes indeed. Calamitous. It would be—

I quite understand the struggle in his soul. And then?

I studied some with the great Raymond Scofield. But only a little. Because of the bombs—V-shaped rockets, you know.

Terrible!

Awful!

What a time!

I thought the rockets were round. Pencil-shaped and pencil-pointed. No? Thermos bottles hurtling through the sky.

They had V-shaped fins and they growled.

Ah . . .

Then after a bit we were able to get passage to America.

Oh yes, the government had quite a plan for rescuing you people, and relocating them. So, here in Ohio?

Yes, sir, they relocated us all right, but not because we're that sort, because we're not. We were under the influence—no, inexact—there was a welfare organization—well, my father was influenced by Luther, and he opposed the *Anschluss*—I mean my father opposed it. My mother comes from a good Catholic family, but later she sort of veered toward Presbyterianism—

Ah . . . Howard Palfrey's eye lit with approval bordering on hallelujah. A happy veer!

It looks like it. Anyway, we never saw or heard from my father again.

After our perilous journey to England. Hiding in cellars from every sound. Living on rinds.

How distressing!

So sad! What a diet!

For your father, such a loss! no doubt his seat in the string section, too.

I like to think, when I hear recordings now, that I hear his instrument in among the rest.

A charming idea. Though you couldn't actually do that, could you? I suppose not. Nothing will bring them back—our lost ones—because why should they wish to leave Elysium and return to our sordid world with its secular vices and cheap popular enthusiasms?

I think you should understand, Clarence Carfagno dared to say, that European—that is to say, Germanic—methods of instruction do not suit American students very well.

Yes, Clare, you are so correct. Too harsh a hand when one longs for the loving touch, the understanding ear, the—were you struck?

Wha—

In your Viennese institution, were you flogged—those dire old days are gone—were your hands hit or were you berated for idleness in front of the class?

Oh dear, no, oh no, never was any such force employed, though my teachers were stern and strict and expected the fullest effort in all we did. The great Gerhardt Rolfe could freeze you with a look, and sometimes described your playing with considerable scorn, but he never stooped to violence.

His reputation has carried across the seas.

Oh yes, his name is a magnet of respect.

His teachings are indispensable to our profession. How many books did he write, all told?

I hadn't been aware he'd written any. He said, you remember, the beauty of music is offended by words.

Oh yes, words don't quite come up to it.

My favorite of his extraordinary maxims is: The notes of the piano ask nothing for their hire and pay nothing for their keep.

I quite understand.

One would rather love that.

I could use such thoughts in my next address, which is, by the way, to the State Board of Education.

That Rolfe was quite a guy.

I'd love to see his CV.

33

After four years and two publications, the college offered Skizzen a house. That meant a home for Miriam, with a side yard that went on till it reached the outskirts of Forever or otherwise met an inviting fork in the road, one tine of which led straight to the college, whose peaks and spires could be seen from the main porch, while another went slowly west along the brow of the college hill. A professor of bacteria (the students had so named him) had retired and left town, so the big gothic shambles stood (if "stand" was the right word for what it seemed to be doing) empty except for some meager furnishings dating from before Christ or during the residence of Frederick Maine, its first owner. When students referred to a large building on the campus as "Old Main" they thought it was called that on account of its size and age and former function, but it was really named for one of the college's earliest donors, a wealthy farmer who lived in a wraparound—which is how locals referred to any house with a nearly circumnavigating porch.

Miriam moved them out of her ivy-covered cottage (or *die Bretterbude,* as she commonly called it) with remarkable alacrity, delighted that their belongings, which were beginning to elbow them out of two of its five stunted rooms, disappeared into their huge new dwelling without a sign of crowding. The house had a cavernous basement with rough dark damp stone walls and an attic that ran for a long way on empty, as dry as its counterpoint was wet, both attic and basement as bleak as uninhabited country, both inviting adventure and boasting an atmosphere of mystery. Miriam greeted her cellar with a cry of joy. I can winter over!

I can winter over! And Joey believed that it was the new house with its dark battery-lit cave, its porches and wide side yard, that transformed her from an idiosyncratic and bungling amateur into a master gardener. This time, she promised, she was going to do it right. No more of that *gottverlassen* alyssum! No more military marches, rather beds that gracefully swelled as if they were buds themselves, a garden with the contours of the soft-lobed white-oak leaf.

Although the house leaked like a colander, with some windows that refused every request made of them, and was disfigured by two woodshed walls warped by weather, it also had floors whose boards were warmly gleaming though unwaxed, paneling finished in fine-grained maple, a bay that puffed out like a blister, and still other windows that pictured long-necked moon-eyed ladies who had apparently grown up entwined in elaborate vines that paid the maidens no mind they were so vigorously climbing toward a delicately tinted heaven. Lighting was hit-and-miss. Ah . . . but the closets were many and vast, the grand staircase spilled from the floor above like a shawl on sale in a shop, rippling between a sturdy border of rails. As for the two porches, one was the wraparound, while the second—elevated—acted like a bridge between two dormers. As cute as it once must have seemed, the span's paint was peeling and looked scroll-cut now—a porch for a paper doll. Miriam deemed it unsafe for sitting and forbade Joey even to play I spy from the advantage of such height.

Most of the older faculty avoided any commitment to these funeral homes, as they were discreetly maligned, so they did not envy young Skizzen's capture; but a few felt overlooked and more deserving, since he had taught at the school for only four years and had no sizable family to house or feed. Such sourness as flavored their attitudes did not last. For most, the feeling was: Here it is and welcome to it. The house's noisy steam radiators were so inefficient that some rooms had to be closed up for the winter. Coal costs were substantial. On a walk around Joseph noticed many torn screens where the copper had corroded. Two outside spigots that Miriam would run her hoses from had drips that would form icicles in winter, but in the summer their leaks encouraged the weeds beneath them to be especially prolific and as coarsely green as an immigrant. The few fireplaces had a tendency to smoke and were, Joey thought, inadequately fendered. An old pump still pled its case in the kitchen sink. The hinges of the cellar door needed replacing, and neither Joey nor his mother were handy. Miriam marched about the house counting its deficiencies. The porcelain in the bathroom had stained, and the sink was rimmed by rust. Still, for the Skizzens, the feeling was: All of this is free.

Skizzen and his mother disappeared into Mr. Maine's quirky spaces, rarely entertaining anyone. They were not in the habit of making ostentatious improvements they could then parade before a community constrained by good manners to admire them. And every passerby enjoyed Miriam's garden, a pleasure the strollers had to regard as a gift. The house might look run-down, but the garden was glorious, and this constituted an acceptable compromise.

The two papers that Joseph Skizzen believed were responsible for obtaining them the house, and retaining him his job, had been written at the kitchen table of the cottage, despite the strain of a dim light, during evenings of the first three years of his tenure. Joseph felt that it was essential for his future that he define himself as an au courant guy, someone hard-edged and up-to-date, as well as a bit menacing. If he had correctly gauged the level of scholarship at the school, the publication of even a few papers would put him high on the list of productive people, and if he had read the intellectual thermometer properly, his choice of specialty—Arnold Schoenberg—should be effectively frightening. Such intimidation might keep people at a distance, and output of any kind should give him a secure income.

Since Joey's career depended upon the ignorance of others, and their natural reluctance to make that condition public knowledge, he had to select material that would be sufficiently musical to establish his expertise, yet not so technical as to exceed his limited understanding: in short, something historical or biographical, something on the edge of the subject the way a fringe completes a shawl while at the same time remaining a lot of useless yarn. He was taking a big risk, he knew, but he chose a topic for his first essay that would immediately advertise him as a person in the "know." Its title would intrigue, confuse, and frighten simultaneously: "Max Blonda's *Von Heute auf Morgen.*"

What is scary about today having a tomorrow, Miriam wanted to know, after he had boasted about his choice. And who is Max Blonda?

Exactly. Who is she?

She?

Yes, dear, it is an assumed name. Arnold Schoenberg's second wife wrote the libretto for his light Viennese opera, *Von Heute*—

She was a Blonda? what sort of name is that? did she bleach?

I have no idea.

Well, why "Blonda" then?

I have no idea.

Ach, so you are writing, why?

To find out. Oh yes, and to get ahead.

After some months, the essay, which had ripened like a fruitcake soaked in the sherry of its own neglect, had an even more angular title. It had become "Max Blonda's Saxophone." The editors of the little music magazine he had in mind wouldn't overlook this one when it arrived in their weekly slush pile. Finally, however, needing a prominent name up front, he went with "Schoenberg's Saxophone." That would shake them up.

Like everything else, from table silver to lines of nobility, the instruments of the orchestra constitute a kind of country club and possess a rigorous social hierarchy. So before you can be consigned to a life next to the wooden clappers in the percussion group, you have to be accepted by each of the orchestra's sections. Many instruments, including the piano, which appears as a soloist from time to time, aren't fully permissible precisely because they can stand so easily alone or, like the harp, are too limited in their range or peculiar in their quality to be called upon often. Alas for the piano's social ambitions, it was fatally bourgeois, and unattractive ladies played it. There are a few noisemakers that belong entirely to the folk, to their jokes and hokum, such as the tin whistle, banjo, and kazoo; others, like the xylophone or bottle organ, appear to have been created mainly to show off the player's dexterity and might have been invented by a juggler; while many are just too weak to make their voice heard—the Jew's harp and wax-paper comb, even the recorder or lips' whistle—puny as dwarfs among giants; or those that have been harmed by their close association with one sort of music and consequently called for only when their sort is about to be performed, such as the guitar and castanets; or there are those whose tones are coarse, vulgar, untrue, or mechanical like the electric organ and amplified guitar, as well as the accursed accordion that has too many fatal shortcomings to list. Some simply were born on the wrong side of the clef like the saxophone and trombone, associated first with military and marching bands and ultimately with jazz combos, cigarette smoke, and syrupy dance kings. Gadget instruments occasionally had music written that included them just for the hell of it. Foghorns, whistles, sirens, typewriters, telephone bells, and the glass harmonica were sometimes placed in an experimental composition for amusement, shock, or surprise. The saxophone, sounding like a hound baying at the moon, its notes too full of air for refinement, was a particularly bad joke. To prove that Arnold Schoenberg was one of the boys and could write operetta with the best of them—no doubt also seeking vainly for a popular success—he included this instrument in one of his few efforts at levity, *Von Heute auf Morgen.*

His new wife wrote the libretto, but Krenek's, Weill's, and Hindemith's successes spurred him on. The saxophone may have jazzed the tunes, but a twelve-tone row created the main alignment, contrapuntal variations were the order of its march, and canons memorialized its end—the heaviest light opera ever penned. In books about Schoenberg, *Von Heute auf Morgen* was lucky to get a line, which made it perfect for Skizzen's purposes.

Schoenberg was incapable of the middle-C mind. He was unable to sustain mediocrity. Skizzen thought he probably never understood the bland, the ordinary, the neutral, because it is as difficult to strike as oil. To be the man at the party whom no one remembers is easy for the guest who can shrink into the woodwork without trying, he is so inherently shy; but to be a person who disappears because he is so like everybody else as not to count; who is neither the least lively nor the most; neither the designated driver nor the drunk; neither the most drably dressed nor the most flamboyant; who is as unidentifiable as a glass someone has emptied two drinks ago and left upon the tray like keys mislaid on purpose and subsequently lost: to pretend to be such a one when one is not such a one is to undertake the circling of the square.

During his preparations, the paradox inherent in his plan became increasingly obvious and embarrassing. Joseph Skizzen had chosen this subject and this theme in order that its author, who would have to be Professor Joseph Skizzen, would be noticed. It was desirable for the professor to be impressive so that the real Skizzen—Joey—who really didn't care much for either Schoenberg the man (a tyrant) or Schoenberg the musician (a romantic at war with romanticism)—who, when the maestro's atonal music washed over him, felt as if his head were being held in a toilet Polly who found these serenades and songs beyond him Wolly quite over his head, his hair, his head of hair like a sudden shower Doodle who recoiled as the land does in front of distant mountains Polly-Wolly for whom Liszt's *Transcendental Études* were about as adventuresome as Skizzen could bring himself to be Doodle as he could bring himself Polly-Wolly-Doodle yes, so the real Skizzen might fade like a figure a flower in the wallpaper a wall of paper flowers a pattern whom familiarity ignores, paint obscures, or the sun fades Polly-Wolly-Doodle all the day.

Both Joey and Joseph dreaded the tenure struggle; however, Whittlebauer pretended to be a part of the academic publish-or-perish world, so they had to make believe they were citizens of it, too. Alban Berg Polly Anton von Webern Wolly with the twelve tones they had to work with Doodle the twelve disciples that Schoenberg (Skizzen, too) had to seem to teach Polly-Wolly-Doodle even to prefer, Joseph had now to embrace as well. All the day. What was the farm and family music Joey was able to play good for alongside this cacophony, this opulent mystery of mathematical music? Jolly Polly secrets he could no longer confess to his conscience Wolly those Arnold S. couldn't confess to either: Doodle that he hated the system he built Jolly Polly Wolly Doodle hated anything named Stravinsky all the day because Igor (a Russian and representative of everything lax, borrowed, and overlush) Jolly Polly Wolly Doodle had triumphed by giving in to the past Polly openly Wolly as if it all were a kind of party instead of a struggle Doodle whilst he was fed up with Wagner and Zion, Brahms and Dvorak, Jolly Polly Wolly sweets his tongue begged him to swallow Jolly Polly Wolly Doodle calories his mind told him to avoid Polly-Jolly Jolly-Wolly Wolly-Doodle he was a Joey and a Joseph, too, Polly Wolly Doodle all the day for Joey had begun to expect Jolly-Polly Polly-Wolly Wolly-Doodle all the day as he placed obstacles in the path of the paper's preparation Polly Wolly Doodle in order to make any thought's smooth and orderly development impossible Doodle Wolly that Joseph was proud of his choice of Schoenberg as a subject Doodle Wolly Polly because he had an arrogance of his own Polly Doodle Wolly a tendency to make difficulties if there weren't any Pilly-Dilly-Dollie disliked what was proper and loved to overstep bounds

Pilly-Dillie-Doodle-Dollie knew words Joey professed to have no knowledge of Pilly-Dillie Doodle-Dollie Woolly-Wolly was angry Doodle-Dillie Doodle-Doodle-Doo not always without cause Doodle-Oodle at the idiots who were the largest element of the population Doolie-Doodle Doodle-Doody Doolie-Dilly really wished he could play Bartók instead of Joey's favorite for the moment Dollie-Doo-Dollie Doo-Dilly-Doo, which was "Bohunkus," and began: *There was a farmer had two sons,/ And these two sons were brothers;/Bohunkus was the name of one,/Josephus was the other's* . . . polly . . . wolly . . . doodle . . . all-the-dooly-dilly-day.

Joey had no more Miss Moss to call upon, which he regretted now particularly, because he would have liked to discuss with her the weakness that had undermined him as he approached the end of his essay, since it had seemed to him a weakness without any other symptoms, one that fit the nature of a magic spell suddenly cast upon him the way a shadow falls upon the ground, with nary a squeal or an ouch, so that Joey became, to echo that popular phrase, gray and unsubstantial, unable to move at will, no longer his formerly vigorous self, not even with the depth of a reflection. Fortunately it was Easter Week (to President Palfrey) or Spring Break (to the students), consequently Joey missed no classes, as he otherwise would have, because he could barely sit up, let alone stand, refused food, and stared into space as if even his seeing was asleep. The problem was, as the patient was reluctantly compelled to admit, although only to himself, and only for a moment in the final morning of the pall upon him, that both Joseph and Joey were equally ill.

Miriam at first thought he was just being metaphorical, tired of it all, fed up, the way one is tired of filling out forms or shucking oysters, but shortly she came round to agree with his pale face, weak groans, red ears; then she grew worried, forced broths and compresses upon him though he had no fever, had no flush, no stuffy wheezy runny nose, had no rash or bump or swollen node or pimple (only lobes so red they seemed listening for a train) while finding a pain was like chasing the bug itself vainly through his body. Wet paper held its old ink better.

What is called good fortune had done this to him. Every social rung he placed the simple shoe of his climbing person on put him in greater danger; every pittance he gathered meant more of gather was expected. For his mother's sake he mustn't be a failure; for his father's sake he mustn't be a success. His image in her eyes, though she scolded him as if he were still very young or soon would be older than she, had to be sustained; Joey was the most valued plant in her garden, if it wasn't the beech tree. His image in his father's eyes, though those eyes were his eyes now, of a boy whose exodus from Austria had saved him from damnation, had to be maintained—mustered as for war—if the past was to matter. But what was his merit, where were his credits, during his illness, to either of them—so meagerly distilled, so dimly disgraced?

During his studies, Joseph had run across reproductions of Schoenberg's paintings: there the great composer's soul was, as it couldn't be shown in music, naked as if flayed: furious, frightened, intense, unforgiving. If he honored you by doing your portrait, at the end, there *he* was, staring out of your eyes, glaring with every wild strand of hair, each vertical line like an asylum bar, each curl a coil, and Schoenberg himself behind the painted face just far enough not to notice his sitter's terror and chagrin but certainly hoping for it. Even in his wife's portrait, where she is surrounded by a swirling halo of hat or hair, his temperament reddens the lips of her almost soft mouth. But the painting that followed Skizzen from chair to bed like a guilty conscience was called *The Red Gaze,* because it was that formerly obscured face, with its bullet-eyed look, brought out into the open, as if the pulp of a fruit had taken the place of the rind.

34

To fill their silence, Miriam said: Tonight we are trading plants. Ah, it's that time of month again, Joey said, joining her in filling it. What do you mean, Miriam pretended to exclaim, don't talk smart and don't talk *schmutzig* to your mother, who, by the way, is well past that point and doesn't need you to poke up my *monatliches* like the cinders of a fire. I meant . . . , Joey said, pretending in his turn to be perplexed, that it's your meeting with the girls of Woodbine—Don't do *spitzige,* I said, she said, we are women and women of one mind, not a one with childish curls. Does it take that many of you to make one mind, replied the smarty, now too young to be in pants. She threw an empty crumple of seed packet at his head. What is this month's subject?

Weeds, Miriam answered, laughing at something, possibly a thought. Who weeds are. What weeds do. Why weeds are so hateful. And therefore why weeds exist. Finally, how to rid your lawn and garden of them. How to pull them from their dirt. Root them out. They've grips like fierce fists. *Ausrotten ihnen!* And how to poison their progeny, kill their kids. She wagged a warning finger at Joey. Don't give me your racial-cleansing speech.

I was admiring your cruelty. And your speaker is?

A former weed—now reformed—making up for an evil life with warnings to the rest of us.

But don't you have all this information already? Ladies and gentlemen! In this ring, introducing Weed Number One! from Bulgaria! It is the Aster-Eating Rabbit! Who will perform death-defying hops! Ta-da! Weed Number Three is . . . is the Bed-Digging Dog! An Austrian breed!

Who does number two?

Number Two is when—

Ach. You have tricked me. Your *Mutter.* You made me ask of it.

What I was getting at . . . well . . . what I meant was . . . Don't you know all about weeds already?

Not just any weeds . . . they are not the topic—*nein*—but invaders. Multipliers. Chokers. Carriers. Carnivores. *Fremde.* Seedy intrusives.

Immigrants, then, who arrive unasked and take the space of native Austrian primroses; immigrants who multiply like rabbits, inconsiderately sucking up nutrients and choking the natives in the throats of their stems—

You are uncorrectable. A naughty smarty. They pretend, you see. They wear pretty leaves like sheep's ears, or win you over with nice blooms like violets and such, deceive by smelling sweet—honeysuckles humming in the heat—or the way that *grosse* bamboo grows, faster than bean stalk, and including what they call here bind, or bishop's weed, because it is so relentless and uncorrectable a sinner it would make even a bishop curse.

Joseph realized with wonder how well spoken his mother had become.

He was trying to add Austrian to his speech while she was *Ausrotting* hers of most things foreign. English with a twist of pepper. Her German had become a sneeze. Today her sneezing was nostalgic. Instead, he said:

Just the same, dear, don't you know everything about them already?

Most of it, I imagine, but we like to listen, like children, to the story told samely and samely. It warms me, anyway—like mulch—with memories of summer, now it's winter.

Well, you should be careful going, the paper says it may be snowing. Whose house is it? where you're meeting, I mean?

Maybelle's.

Maybelle. Do I know a Mrs. Maybelle?

Wife of that fat professor of geography. You know, the one with the watch chain. Oh yes, and the three chins. His ears are wattles. Well, when we meet at Maybelle's he sometimes sits in. Sits down. Smooooch. You can hear his rear when the air leaves the pillow. He sits not out of the way in a big chair you'd think had been built for him but in a rickety ladder-back you worry is going to break and stick him like a roasting pig. Sits right in the middle of the living room and listens most attentive to everything.

The club has never met here has it?

Not yet. I go in fear of when it will be my turn.

We'll have to beat some neat into this house. I shall accompany the buffet on my *pianola.*

You shall be banished to the belfry.

Does Maybelle do anything?

Nails. She does nails. At that beauty parlor on High Street. She also marcels, perms, and trims.

I meant about her heavy husband.

He is immovable.

They can afford to live around here?

Oh, the fat one is well-off. He owns the furniture store—Leonard's.

The store that's always going out of business?

Derselbe.

My goodness. Which house is it?

The one with the glads.

A welcome mat?

The red front door. Her garden is a confinement for *die Gladiole.* She's in business for them, too. Sells armloads to funerals. In bunches—one for every sorrowed friend.

Ah . . . Bouquets that once seemed a measure for sorrow.

She plants them in military rows the way, you remember, I used to arrange my plants—all of them from bulbs to bushes—in her big backyard behind the house, fenced in and everything. There are kinds and kinds of kinds. They look pretty big and brave lined up against the boards, but I don't like that icebox lover much. A glad stands stiff as a soldier and flowers like a ladder.

Icebox lover. Yes, I imagine he is.

No, *dummster.* The gladiolus . . . gladiola . . . gladioli . . . They are always in the florist's icebox.

So Maybelle has a week of big bloom, and then it's bust for the rest of the year?

You can plant some, wait some, plant some more.

Stagger?

Ya, and they don't all grow at the same speed either. Lots of various. Kinds, like I said . . . of kinds.

Aren't they all orange? I seem to remember—

Nein, mein Kind. It has cultivars in all kinds of colors.

"Cultivars," Mother? what a word is this? Incorrigible? Confinement? Cultivars?

I never uttered a word of incorrigible.

Uncorrectable.

You lack all education, Joey. You snoozed while you were being—what do you say? "self-taught." A cultivar is a new plant from an old plant taken. A various. Is what it means.

Variations on a theme.

Your mother is even on a committee.

Is that what has made you nervous? There's more German in your speech when you are nervous.

Which is it going to be—too fine English or too much German?

I thought you said this Leonard taught geography? . . . sells furniture? Maybe he's living in a gift house like us.

That's what Mr. Three Chins said when I asked him. He said he taught geography at the college and owned the furniture store. Nothing from him about free rent. Three Chins knew the exact number of miles from here to Columbus, anyway. It came up in conversation. And how far our speaker will have to come from Urichstown. She is staying overnight with Maybelle. Old friend maybe.

Not Gwynne Withers.

I have no idea.

Gwynne Withers sings. It was she who wanted the piano tuned, remember? Well, how many miles is it to Columbus?

I am a member of one of our committees.

Funny. I've never seen or heard of him. Odd combination—fat, furniture, and maps—maps and manicures. I shall have to look into it. Maybe he was just leading you on. I don't think we even teach geography anymore. At the college, I mean. That's what he said?

So . . . ah . . . Your club has committees?

What club doesn't have committees? They're the reason for clubs.

Well . . . I just thought . . . your society is so small, couldn't you conduct all your business as a committee of the whole? The twelve disciples were enough for Jesus.

They made a mess of things. They needed a few committees.

Wasn't the great flood supposed to wash away all committees.

I admit, when we meet, we mostly gabble, but we aren't replanting the earth. Noah went by twos, we go by threes. I am on the plant exchange committee. They honor me with that. I know how to trade.

Do you dicker then?

We are the flowers' friends. When we have overachieved, we are ready to harvest, so it is easy to give one to get one. I have too many iris, I think. I'll know those weeks they bloom. So when I dig up the corns I can set some aside for trade. They go in plastic bags labeled VIOLET or WHITE.

So Mrs. Maybelle will trade her extra glads for what?

No "missus" to Maybelle, ninny. Maybelle Leonard. She is double trouble. No one wants the glads because they are too hard to grow here. You have to dig them every fall, winter them over, plant them again, and what do you get? flowers for your funeral. Their kids—what do they say . . . offspring?—feed on their moms. I bet you didn't know that. That's how they grow—not in their moms but on them. Like goiters. It gives me the shivers. Glads are picky about soil, glads freeze easy, they want full sun. Want want want. Sniff one—you smell nothing but your own air.

What do you mean? all moms feed their kids.

They do not. Not all moms are as milky as your sis.

------------------------- I guess, but that's the intention of nature.

Whoo! Look who knows the intentions of nature. No one knows the intentions of nature. Nature does everything ten tons of times. Nature runs in all directions at once like a blown bomb.

-------------------------------------- Okay, Nita, you win. ----- What is it I don't know?

The newborn corn sucks the old one dry. The mother dies of dryness in an earth of plenty.

I believe that's corm.

---------------------------------- Sometimes there are more little corns than one. Then they take two years gnawing on her before growing off on their own.

You could think of it as the old body fashioning a new one for the same mother who just steps from one incarnation to another.

---------- You could think. But not is the fact of it. So everyone offers Maybelle their plants for free—a one-way swap—

I think it's called a gift.

Like this house? -------------- Anyway Maybelle's feelings get hurt because of all the excuses she has to hear—you know—excuses: Sorry, I have no room for big plants like glads—or Sorrry, I'm no good at wintering over—or Sorrrry, I can't compete with your garden, you are the glad-growing lady among us—*und* so she thinks we don't like her.

And do you like her?

No. We dislike her like a tight shoe. All ten of us toes.

Is that the double in trouble?

Or treble. I lose count. She cheats. She has free brown paper bags of bulbs to hand around like jelly beans, but they are rogues and she knows it.

Rogues . . . ? Colorful idea.

The use is special for gardeners. You wouldn't want to understand. Her corns are scabbed. She is giving us her diseased stuff. Mrs. Maybelle? *Nein.* Mrs. Stingy, maybe. We like to be nice so we say, Thank you very much, Mrs. Leonard, some other time because I am devoting myself totally to peonies or—I don't know—to bushes of lilac, to Chinese lanterns, I need dry sticks to stake my peas.

Veggies? Snap peas?

Nein, nein. Sweet pea, not snappy dragons either. Just a flower. Ha, as she is—May belle—herself . . . a flower . . . her daughter wears dandelions braded in her hair, and Mrs. Hursthouse, too, my, what a lady she sells herself for, bosom like a river bridge, she moves about on all fours among her tea roses looking not so grand from the rear and not so nice neither. She says she studied to be a gardener and has a little framed brag-and-lie certificate to prove it. Probably got it by coupon from a catalog, I would bet a posy on its purchase through the post, I could smell violet ink when she held it under my nose, still she has to crawl around like the rest of us, naturally not looking too lovely when dirty-kneed and not dressed in big hats and heavy dresses. She likes to hang strings of things around her neck. I must say, though, her roses are lovely resting in their fancy vases with just a shot or two of fresh mist glistening from the petals on the bouquet that's always glorifying her buffet when we have meetings at her house—slide shows sometimes, Millicent has a machine, Hildur has the screen—quite a grand place, true as glue and stuck up too, with enough colored glass for a cathedral, including Jesus in a long white robe and upraised palm so serene in the stairwell bidding us be good and peaceful or else. Hursty has a rose in her garden that looks so like one in one of her windows she has to show it off, but she is right in this particular to be proud of the pure light-filled pink petals it has as if lit even in the dark, how did they do it? the workmen? how did God for that matter? always a wonder.

Hild her?

Hil durr. Nice lady most of the time. Unless she feels thwarted. But then, most of us are like that—angry—when things don't go our way. She is a skinny blond lady who teaches, too, at the high school, didn't know you, though, came after, teaches numbers of some sort, the ones made of letters, *x* and *y und* so *weiter.*

Does she have a specialty?

Most of us just do our gardens, bit of this, bit of that, a bush, a potted plant, a bed beside a fence, a few vines, more columbine than we need—but I shouldn't say so—such a lovely flower, columbine. I also believe in the bleeding heart.

I think that is a chapter of the Catholic church.

Order, smarty.

Order is good.

------------------------------------ You called me Nita just now.

----- I guess.

----------------------- You haven't called me that in years, since you were a *kinder.*

It's okay, Mom. Don't cry.

-- I wish I were the Nita that I was.

35

Professor Joseph Skizzen had learned the importance of the chalk tray. When he first took his instructorship he had been handed, like keys for a city, a claw made of chalk sticks held in place by wire that could draw the lines of the staff with a swift swipe across the board. This implement now sat flat on his desk like a symbol of his subject. It took a steady confident hand, though, lest the lines wiggle instead of the notes. In the chalk tray, along with small mounds of white powder, were scattered bits of chalk too small to be of use any longer and a box the size of a pack of cigarettes, full of fresh pieces, as if at leisure, resting in it. Two erasers that badly needed banging lay in the tray as well. Whenever the professor leaned back against the blackboard there was a strong chance that chalk dust would form a line on his bottom. This line, when he turned around to write something important, could provoke a good deal of mostly silent amusement in his students. It proved him a ridiculous old fool and a figure that deserved their snickers. But to be a ridiculous old fool was not entirely a bad thing. The students might not remember his lecture on the mental deficiencies of notable composers, but they were certain to recall the humorous white line he always left behind when he drew conclusions.

And always good for a chuckle were ole Skizz's cloth cap and white dice. These were his most recent props, and a great success. The cap could have come from a Fitzgerald novel and looked most at home on the golf course. He kept it wadded like a hankie in a jacket pocket. On the dot of the hour, the professor would position the cap on his head so it shaded his goatee like an eave and enter the classroom with a look that said, I am listening to distant music. He would put down his books and perhaps a record album; then remove the cap, tossing it onto the desk with a negligent gesture. After a moment for a stare around, he would retrieve it, probe under the brim with his fingers, and extract, as smugly as a magician, one pair of bright white dice. These he would roll across the desktop as if shooting craps. Then he would bend forward to see what he had shot, pause to take in their dots and appreciate their significance, and finally begin the hour by saying: Today, it seems, we shall study the passacaglia from the first act of Alban Berg's opera *Wozzeck.* Instead Professor Skizzen would proceed with a lecture on Mendelssohn's symphonies . . . as the students expected.

That was how Joseph Skizzen created his Herr Professor, and a beloved one to boot: by doing silly, often inexplicable, hence memorable things, and in that manner developing, he thought, like a blooming plant, into a charming character, the subject of many an amusing collegiate story. He was a sketch, students said of him at first, but his classes were difficult and music of this elitist kind was . . . oh . . . so out of it. He had grown a goatee, purchased a pair of funny trousers, and affected a slight accent. But none of these oddities was sufficient to sustain a semester's interest.

Life, he had learned, was mostly made of themes and their variations. Skizzen would open by explaining how little we knew about the music of the Greeks. He usually dwelled on the different modes distinguished by Aristotle. He would play a few snatches of this and that. Could the students pick out the military from the dirge, the sad song from the energizing march? They could. The students and their professor also reexamined Albéniz, requested Bach, rethought Chopin, requeried Debussy, every semester. Joey rolled in at ten. Joseph rolled out at six. Joey immersed his face. Joseph packed his pipe. Joseph boiled an egg. Professor Skizzen read the news, saw an item to be scissored, searched for his equipment. Joey complained until he found it. Professor Skizzen walked to school. He put on his cap to enter class and then entered. The professor tossed his dice; he fingered his chin; he stared out the window; kids coughed or whispered, giggled or shuffled their feet; fell asleep. Repeat. They were never dumb in different ways. Well . . . almost never. They almost never were dumb in different ways. The important thing was: Joey never left the house.

Another great truth was that Skizzen's sniggering pupils became alumni despite his low regard for them. They would be sure to remember the time Skizzen brought Saint-Saëns down a peg by quoting Berlioz about the precocious genius, namely that "he knows everything but lacks inexperience," and it won't matter much if they get it wrong or its point is lost during recollection. When the little game of reminiscence was played with alumni friends, they would still have a few high cards. Really? you don't say? a white line like the equator around his rump? Sure, as big as the track of a sailing ship. Actually, for a music teacher, old Skizz wasn't half bad. Yup . . . jeez . . . those were the days.

Even Skizzen thought the classroom seemed a strange choice to represent his professorial career, for he had never been comfortable in one, and certainly wasn't now, even after many years of playing the part of an offbeat prof renowned for his sharp ear, his clever tongue, his demanding standards, and, with regard to practical everyday matters, habitually bumbling. He could remember in terrible detail how he had taken his first step in local collegiate history. That step had to do with chalk, too, and taught him an important lesson even if his students had learned nothing from it. He could clearly recall the scene and situation, but they were likely to remember only the cloudy outline of an image they now prized like one of those brooches with the faded picture of a parent, girl, or boyfriend closed up inside like a corpse in a casket. Such mementos were occasionally to be peekabooed, and then passed along from one generation to another in place of an honest heirloom.

It was taken—the first step—during Skizzen's third year as an instructor. He had by this time learned academic routine as well as his ABC's; that is, he could recite them but do little else but spell out a few elementary admonitions. One was, unfortunately, that his students should listen with their third ear. Among the lads this had somehow become an obscene joke Skizzen otherwise refused to understand. Moreover, he had advised his few piano pupils to "make love to their instrument" when he knew nothing about that either.

It was spring term, and he had eight students in his Introduction to Music class. This was the department's bread-and-butter course, yet enrollments had declined from the thirty he had on his baptismal day, a number that had leaked like a rowboat until now, his sixth go-round. At the department's last meeting, held at the Mullins Hall urinals during a break in the student recitals, Professor Carfagno had called it their bread-and-water course, and then did so. Skizzen had responded, last into action because he wore buttons, by describing it as one of bread and wine, but Morton Rinse had trumped that with tea and biscuit, just before releasing a stream that outlasted the others, at least in noise.

Skizzen's career hung in the balance. He thought he had lost some students because of an obsessive use of clichés, common sayings that he adopted to hide what he knew was incompetence. And he stole opinions from any book that lay open. He really had to stop describing music as food for the gods or boasting, on Mozart's behalf, that the little brat was penning symphonies at the age at which the rest of us were struggling to learn our sums. His point was: music is easy; see, a three-year-old can play, a five-year-old compose; but his pupils thought what the hell they had no chance. Then, instead of trying to encourage them to admire nobler things, Skizzen would scoff at genius. After all, what else could Bach do beside fugues?

The young professor never took the right tone with his material because he didn't know the right tone to take. You have no tone, he scolded himself. You have no real beliefs. Of what, about your subject, could you say you were sure? if you were put to the lie-detect? if you had to swear before a court? Perhaps you could believe with some confidence that, although Saint-Saëns and Mendelssohn were both more prodigious talents than even Mozart or maybe John Stuart Mill, their careers were made of promises they didn't wholly fulfill. But what sort of promises did the cliché require? that they would surpass Liszt. In what? In his sum of seductions? In the length of his trills? Skizzen's native skepticism was no help either. His students simply were discouraged by it. They couldn't handle opposing points of view or any war of wills. All the same, Skizzen did believe music was easy. He had learned to play the piano by ear, and that showed he had promise, didn't it? but he could only play honky-tonk and pretend it was Chopin. Though he had skills, these tiddlywink abilities would never pay the bills.

If you are terrified of being a bore you probably are a bore and terror should be on its way. But Skizzen had become bored by himself, even alone in the urinal, so what must he be to others? Was terror transferable? He believed it was—contagious, like panic. There were books that argued for it. If you could not hear what you were about to play before you played it; if you could not measure the intervals to come, had no grasp of the constellations that notes and not-notes formed; then fear would fill your fingers as though they were sucking straws. When he faced his first class, he heard his words toddle from his mouth, their sense of conviction tied to a string for handy retraction. He would look in wonder at his notes, notes both musical and expository, that suddenly meant nothing to him. Now, of course, he could pronounce his judgments with the bully's bluster—"Wagner has taught the tuba's pomposity to the flute"—and he could formulate intimidating opinions—"Late Liszt is as atonal as autumn"—that meant nothing whatever; but it took Skizzen five years to get glib. He had to forget how he mucked about at the keyboard, didn't have his material in hand, couldn't teach the sea to roil or trees to leaf. He had to believe in his brilliance, he told himself with some sternness: Be proud of your knowledge, and confident about your mastery. Let superior assurance win the day. Ah, he immediately thought, there you go, winning the day. You must stop seizing or winning or greeting or wasting the day. You must be original even while sucking on an orange. But, when he tried to hear in his head the sound of a conch shell blown like Poseidon might toot it on a stony beach, the best he could do was imagine a whistle that signified to a grateful group that gym was over. Everybody got to shower.

He took hold of a stick of chalk, pulled it from the pack, and held it like a cigarette to steady his nerve. "I'll smoke it later." The chalk absorbed the sweat of his palms and then emitted a terrible squeak when rubbed across the slate. Did he remember how to spell "Tchaikovsky"? Tchaikovsky, he said, steadied his head with one hand when he conducted so it wouldn't fly off. His head, not his hand. Skizzen knew how the conductor felt. The conductor felt his head was a hat. Maybe it was the composer who worried about brisk winds and the conductor who kept a tight hold on the brim. Skizzen heard some signs of amusement from the boys in the back. In fact Tchaikovsky gripped his chin and waited for wobble. Sometimes, when Horowitz played, members of the audience climbed up on their chairs to watch his fingers run an octave like a deer. Skizzen found he felt better if he turned his back to the students and spoke to the board. Well, what was he going to say about Tchaikovsky beyond that joke? That his symphonies were soap operas?

Dates. He posted Tchaikovsky's dates. Oops. Wrong decade. He wiped the mistake away with the side of his left fist. Aware of what he'd done, Skizzen tried to rid his hand of chalk by rubbing it on a cuff of his coat. Then he dropped the piece he was holding in a trouser pocket. A bit of discreet riddance. Let's try to get on. Think nothing of it. Say nothing about it. As he took a step, he felt something run down his pants leg onto the floor. And then, starting nervously, he stepped upon something that caused a sound of crushing to come from his heel that had to be admired by the toe. Miriam hadn't repaired that hole in his pants pocket. Don't look down, you'll fall. Ignore it as you would a smart remark. Skizzen thought that by the time he strode to the other side of the room he might have an idea. Vengeful grains of chalk remained stuck to the sole of his shoe; they squealed when he walked; and, though he dare not look down, were probably leaving lines on the floor. All I need, he managed to say, is to write out the bass part.

Joey dared not look at those rows of grins. He pretended to be contemplating the lawn outside. He remembered nothing of what he was supposed to say. A man with a red kerchief wrapped around his head drove a mower closer and closer. Bless that man with the red kerchief. Bless that grass, all noisy mowers. He said: How can we be expected to speak of music with racket like that in our ears. It's dis-tracting. Skizzen slowly wiped his chalk-covered fingers on the front of his shirt. Turning back to the class, he put a forefinger in his mouth and made a face. Then what did he hear?

Applause.

36

From the same post that delivered the professor's daily *New York Times*—three days late but with admirable regularity—he received a valentine. Out of an envelope whose lacy getup made him reluctant, he withdrew a handmade watercolor that his past identified at once as by the brush, hand, and careful purpose of Miss Moss. The realization produced only apprehension, since his mother had celebrated the holiday's sentimental occasion weeks ago with cupcakes and a cartoon movie chosen to amuse Nephew. Perhaps Miss Moss's wall calendar still hung open at February, as he had once observed. The card was built like a triptych. You saw, first, a bright red apple out of which someone very hungry had taken a bite, although tooth marks were not visible. The apple, when you opened the cover, was sliced to disclose a length of worm as wet and dirty as might please a bird. On the left side was a hand-printed greeting: EAT THIS APPLE ADAM. On the right was a message in bright blue ink: Dear Joey: I am being poisoned by the Major. I shall soon die. Good-bye. Not immediately, but after a brief bemused study of the image, Joey guessed that the biblical serpent was represented by the worm. Across the bottom from side to side, in the smallest of hands, but clearly in the same one, was written: *I have stuck a pin into her quim. Though thin as a slot, the pin went in. I thought her dead but she is not. Who would miss that mean old twat?* He could not acknowledge the words his eyes at first fled over except with a shiver of aversion. This was followed by a rereading that incomprehension and disbelief prompted, and to which a prolonged hiss of disapproval put period. I do not know what this portends, Joey said almost audibly, as if whispering an aria. He had almost immediately broken out in something. It appeared to be a sweat.

First there was fear, fear of the sort he would experience at any reappearance of his past, especially a piece torn from one of his months in Urichstown: a fear of old unaccountable angers, and the possibility that at any moment he might be unmasked by the simplest mischance. Even the Scarlet Pimpernel was eventually found out. Joey did not take Miss Moss's contention about the Major seriously—at least not in terms of its reality—but as a concern of Miss Moss's, he knew the threat was worrisome enough. He was certain, too, that some Raggedy Ann had received a puncture wound, with serious intent to harm.

Of no minor seriousness was the knowledge, verified by Joseph's repeated examination of the evidence literally at hand, that what had seemingly delayed this letter was not an incorrect address or a redirected journey to his present residence from an earlier one or a passage through the slow-motion screenings of his college, because its labels were all in order and, from what its postmark said, the apparently laggard valentine had been recently mailed, so that it had, like cupid's reputed arrow, delivered itself with promptness to its target, stirring his heart, if not with love, with love's equal—alarm.

Then another memory arrived like a late guest—one Joey had allowed himself to forget. Just the other day—no more than a week ago, it was—perhaps two . . . Joey thought he saw the thin carrot-topped back of Castle Cairfill sauntering along Main Street as skinny as you please. Joey jumped into Schafley's shoe store like a frightened bunny and then had to pretend he was considering a purchase. He didn't know his shoe size, but he knew he had a hole in his sock large enough for the flight of a heel. Cairfill had been suspected of theft . . . back when? Cairfill had failed to return several volumes on fencing . . . was it fencing? so unlikely . . . but what was likely anymore? Gossip said Cairfill had been caught playing naughty games with girls. So unlikely. But what was . . . likely?—what was . . . Caz doing?—these days. How might he have greeted the scoundrel: Well, if it isn't . . . Good gracious, it's . . . 'Pon my word, where did you pop from? Wait a minute! It was Joey who had been accused of stealing. Shame reddened one cheek, anger the other. To think he had been suspected if not accused! Police had come to his mother's house, bursting with impatience; they had rummaged in his bedroom closet, annoyed by their defeat. Even for a moment, his mother . . . might have doubted . . . She was certainly angry about the fuss.

Skizzen had never fooled with the surfaces of his pupils either, or with that French teacher—horrid notion—though some people might have gotten ideas. Suddenly he had a picture of the Major thrusting a foil through the chest of a rag doll. The doll screamed, Mum-eee, Mum-eee. And bled . . . . red thread.

Women. Joey and Joseph and the professor were vexed. Major, Miriam,

Miss Moss, Debbie Boulder, Miss Spiky, Madame Mieux . . . Women. It wasn't fair. There were only three of him. Mieux and Marjorie, Miss Moss and Miriam . . . MM and MMM.

The professor had been putting off the thought, even when it followed him home like a stray, that someday his real-life history would be exposed. While sauntering happily along he would stumble over something, the most unexpected thing, a small stone in the road, a buckeye that turned an ankle and overthrew a throne. Or a gust would blow a tattered poster from a public wall to reveal Skizzen with his head mummified in swathes of toilet paper, but otherwise, skinny-naked . . . then the wind would blow again to disclose a skull covered with shreds of newspaper, a hair of headlines . . . before his exposed figure became a boney bust of death with teeth made from yellowed piano keys . . . His heart beat against the nature of what his imagination dreamed: the professor should be shown to be a smiling boy, sweet-featured, a bit coy, modest about all things, quiet, unobtrusive, innocent, though not naïve, and although young and small and weak, fixed in a determination as strong as those of religious faith: Humanity, thou shalt not enmesh me in your horrible history! The sweet smile was supposed to stay until it became the last bonbon in the box, and the rest of his ideal qualities had been eaten by enemy eyes.

Suppose Skizzen were the one who remained; suppose he were the aftermath, the *i v e* of "survive." He had finally unlocked the word! Properly rearranged, it read: "I've served." The laugh that fled his throat left it sore. He sat for some time in a silence scoured by that passage of amusement.

What he really wanted the world to see, were his lifelong ruse to be discovered, was the equivalent of Moses's tablets before they got inscribed: a person pure, clean, undefiled, unspoiled by the terrible history of the earth. So he could rightly say to his accusers (and accused he would be): When you were destroying yourselves and your cities, I was not there; when you were debasing your noble principles, I was not there; when you were fattening on lies like pigs at a trough, I was not there; when you were squeezing life from all life like water from a sponge, I was not there. So see me now! Untarnished as a tea service! I've done nothing brave but nothing squalid, nothing farsighted but nothing blind, nothing to make me proud, yet never have I had to be ashamed.

My father's son! After all . . . after all . . . I *could* be proud.

Yet Joey had been ashamed just now. Or was it just Professor Joseph Skizzen? He had been for a moment uncertain. Yes, it was the prof who had faltered.

Many of his colleagues had seen a travelogue about turn-of-the-century Vienna at the local cinema and began to ask Joseph about it: where a certain square was, relative to his lodgings; had he sat in the pews of the cathedral; whether he had known this man about town or another; had he ridden on the Ferris wheel that had been erected in the Prater, or enjoyed a Sacher torte at the Sacher Hotel? And, of what, exactly, was such a cake made? These questions had quite unnerved him. He said, truthfully, that he was too disturbed by the past to discuss its leaner features. Since that moment of emergency—heavens, it was some years ago—Professor Skizzen had taken care to read up on the period of his residency. Now he knew all the names of Vienna's points of interest and a bit of the bios of its main men. And of what a Sacher torte is made: chocolate cake and marmalade. As the thirties there drew on—which meant the deepening of his civic reading—he felt he could occasionally catch something of what his father had said he smelled: the aggressive odor emitted by an increasingly fragile smugness—in sum, rudeness heated to the degree called brutality.

He had now the habit of rehearsing some of his more elaborate stories, whenever he had a free moment, so that he would not forget the facts he had alleged or mix their circumstances. After a while there were so many anecdotes, vignettes, and reminiscences he kept a card file for them where he noted all the salient details by means of keywords: whooping cough (when and how serious), the stormy voyage across the Atlantic, close calls during train travel, funny things that happened to him while learning how to play the piano, ditto for the organ (very chancy, that one), the arthritis that limited his present performances so that he could no longer give Chopin or Liszt recitals (as he once had done, to great acclaim), the makeup of the legendary Vienna Philharmonic—its death and resurrection—the fat content of the local cuisine, what he learned in Vienna from the esteemed Gerhardt Rolfe, the noble nose of a character he called Father who smelled catastrophe. About real people and actual events—his sister and his mother mostly—Skizzen possessed a reluctant tongue.

What had once been difficult to utter—falsehoods that weren't just social lies and lame excuses or little trivial elaborations—in time became a custom and a challenge. The satisfaction he felt at being to the world an artifice was the deepest he knew. All the world was a stage. But not for all the world. Over time his tales became so much a part of his public self, he could eventually remember, as he recounted them, how he felt, for instance, when, nearly naked, he ran after his Rambler as it coasted backward down a hill into the highway. In the snow, remember, in the snow. This part of his history had such a brilliant shine that, like a diamond, it had to be rather regularly reset. Where had his car been parked? Why was he wearing a towel? Better make that a bathrobe. And because so many of his stories made fun of their source, they were, he surmised, readily believed.

The persuasive element was always the same: why would anyone tell such a tale if it hadn't happened.

Miss Moss had sent him an apple, a bitten apple. Its significance hit him with the shock and the shame of a slap. He was the Adam addressed; he was the Adam commanded: Eat this and swallow my message, swallow the truth, digest your guilt, let your appetite worm its way through every self you own. And bring you down.

So—now that you have eaten from the tree, what are you going to do about what you know? Here was shame showing again on his open face. For he would do nothing. That was foregone. Eat the apple and welcome the worm. However, Miss Moss's threats were surely idle. No one was going to kill or be killed. Rhetoric was rhetoric . . . and the worm was painted paper. Ah, but how artfully, amid the creamy white pulp, had she depicted that almost living length of moistened brown. Still, how could Miss Moss accuse or threaten when she had helped him take his first steps toward a duplicitous self and its misleading life. Miss Moss would recognize at once what he had done. Lordy, she might even approve. She *should* approve. Bravo! what a joke on the school, the town, society itself. Of course she would approve.

Okay. From the garden . . . from the garden he could be expelled. He and Eve, fig leaves in hand. Miriam would find nothing funny, nothing clever, nothing admirable in his masquerade or the solemn leafy departure they made, even if it became a theme for artists to enjoy the way they once rendered the positions of the cross. There were so many cards to watch fall from their delicate embrace of one another: Professor Skizzen's name defiled, his position, its status, its income; his house, its landscape, taken from him; Joseph's standing as a musician too, respect—right down the line—lost, Miss Spiky's hearty warmth cooled by contempt; Joey's moral purity dirtied by inevitable leaks—seepage was certain—Professor Skizzen's great project—his obsessive sentence, too—made laughingstocks, the condemnation of mankind they represented turned into a simpleton's idiosyncrasies.

He had to laugh anyway. Miss Moss had sent an angleworm to do the devil's business. Who, among that holy bunch, was supposed to be a fisher of souls?

Joseph, when he entered the garden, always sought shade. The beech tree's trunk had been trimmed of its lower branches so that early and late light would flood easily under the reach of its leaves, even as ivied as they were. Consequently he would sit where the house could shield him, where the faucet was, and a weathered chair that had been positioned to let him feast on the flowers from a vantage bees might have envied. The wood of the chair was of a pronounced gray because flying ants and other insects had meticulously licked off the inner resins that the sun of several summers had lured to the surface. In June, after the season's first heat had deeply warmed the earth, the garden burst into bloom the way, during the hot evening of the Fourth, the sky brightened and smoked with homemade stars. Now the beds were lit by daylilies during their brief bright lifetimes; buddleia and penstemon beckoned the butterflies and hummingbirds while daisies, monarda, rudbeckia, stood steady for weeks on end, when, every fortnight, the grass paths were cut by the mower's roll. Sometimes he dozed till his sweat, like the sap in his chair, drew insects to him.

Skizzen had read about posthumous people—those whose real life begins long after their death—but he was equally impressed by prenatal folk who live before they live and are made of fear or anticipation—people whose promise is fulfilled by the promise itself—when one cleans the house in case you might hire a maid—or those villains in books who hiss: I live for the day you die—because its realization is invariably disappointing and often dimmer than a bulb that has never seen soil or emitted light. His father, he liked to imagine, understood how future conditions drew upon present desires to ready the field and plant the earth, scour cities and hills for next year's pogroms; how the masked ball that has not yet been held brings about its preparations: an engraved invitation, a new dress, a novel disguise, a fresh date. And there are all sorts of details that "flesh out" these dreams: the corsage that a boyfriend sends ahead of himself, the dark car that whisks you and your young prince away, the bright lights that dominate the party rooms, the music of Mozart, the glitter of silks, skins, and jewels . . . ah, he had let his mind flee into a fiction . . . he heard hunting horns, hooves, and baying dogs.

For the young prince will become a poor printer, the bright lights will be those of searching beams, bomb sounds will follow sirens, and sometimes screams will even precede. But he, Joey the Joseph, will have no actual past; he will be safely out of the stream of consequences: I was not here, I was not there, I was not noticed anywhere.

So: was Miss Moss seeking safety from the Major by fleeing to the imaginary welfare of his arms, or was it revenge that motivated this menacing greeting—but for what sort of oversight or failure?—for forgetting, when he left the library, to free her from her dungeon room and restore her like a deposed queen to her rightful place at the front desk, next to the day's overdues? How could he have accomplished that? And the scurrilous verse—he guessed it was—what was he to make of such words and their worse thoughts? that Miss Moss was a witch, too, like the Major and Miss Spike? Hawkins, she said it was . . . Hazel Hawkins.

How long had it been since he'd worked in the library, since he'd sat like a young squirt in front of the Major and worshipped the whirl of her hair and the swirl of her laughter, too? Thirty years? Good grief, none of these ladies might be alive. Yet here he had a note from the eldest of the trio. Joey had thought of her as old when he was fetching wounded volumes to receive her ministrations in the basement of the Carnegie. Good grief, the library might be gone as well, torn down, its contents scattered to the six winds, though the winds of heaven were unlikely. People, nowadays, liked old brick. They might have stolen its walls to pave their patios. The town itself might have slid into the river. But he had heard of things going on down there . . . faint aromas had floated up the map . . . a person passing through from that direction who reported a severe season of bird flock or leaf fall. Yes . . . signs that said they were there . . . as we were here . . . and the world was still at war.

Professor Skizzen disliked mystery even more than Joey, especially mysteries whose clearing up could not be kind, like clouds that part to reveal rain. Was he also old by now? old in an old house, practicing an old trade—not in the teaching of music but in the arts of deception. Was he older then than his mother? Fear-filled will be his nights, when his curtains blow the way they do in the movies, accompanied by gasps from terrified strings. Skizzen, sheet drawn to his chin, shall lie stiff as a stick in fear of the denunciation that his father foretold and his mother described: darkly dressed creatures, caped and cowled, uttering imprecations while they form a hounding circle around him. Fake. The word could not be hissed. Fake. Fake. Evenly spaced. Tock. Tock. Tock. Until he heard his alarm. At which time, his accusers would flap their cloaks and fly through the window. Good grief, Joey admonished Joey, I now remember rightly: the Urichstown library was not built of brick, it was built of stone.

What to do about this *billet-dure,* this piece of poisoned pen? He remembered Maurice. If you were waiting for the worm to turn, Maurice would keep you waiting until you walked off arm in arm with your impatience, whereupon, leaves eaten, the twig to which his freshly finished cocoon was fastened would sway a little in the wind. A moment ago Maurice had barely had a name. Marjorie marched into view, looking mad. For practice in screaming, she screamed. Sheets of music were hidden in Mr. Hirk's piano's seat. On the cover of one song a woman in a widespread dress stood by a bicycle composed of one huge front wheel. A silly thing to wear, he always thought, when cycling—a widespread dress—especially if you were a woman with only one song. How did Maurice arrive to trouble Joey's consciousness? Not by bicycle. Even standing stock-still, Maurice sidled—sidled in a circle—as if searching for the center of the sky. You have a fake social security number. No, sir. My number works for my taxes and is busy being genuine in the bursar's office. You have a fake license plate. No, sir. I no longer own a car. I no longer drive. My sister's husband drives my mother about now, and to the farm to see the child . . . occasionally . . . once in a while he does it . . . all right—only too often. To see—

—his first steps in the making of a duplicitous self . . . Wrapped like Gandhi in nothing but a diaper, the kid totters toward his mommy with enough glee on his face to cover toast. Debbie wears her pride like a pullover and the fingers that beckon her son are so full of eagerness as to take years off the age of her wedding ring. She is cheering for her team again. She kneels as if ready to spring up, as she will when her son reaches her arms: yes . . . there . . . the feat has been accomplished, and up the child rises as gleeful as any victor. Good-oh, Joey cries, clapping his hands hard enough to sting. I picked my way through rubble, he thinks. I brought back pieces of broken homes and watched them get flung away as foreign to our ruins. For my first steps—well, they weren't my *first* exactly—there was no applause.

You do not have any advanced degrees, Rector Luthardt said. I have publications that identify me as a Ph.D. Fake. You fake! The word could not be qualified, just multiplied. What difference does it make? A fraud occurs when a fake is used to mislead. You fraud! Oh my God, oh my God, oh my God! The words could not be qualified, only multiplied. You don't like Schoenberg. I do so, and with great determination. Your enthusiasms, your loyalties, are pretenses. Anyway, his early work is okay. Nice of you to admit that much, but what a condescending thing to say. A lie too, by the way. His painted self is your bogeyman. He fumbled his own faiths the same way you have . . . fumbled them. No, I admired, I longed to imitate, that change of heart. You are accustomed to your dodges after so many years, with every day and every lie, the same old lie, repeatedly woven like a friendly sweater. The maestro led us all astray. Would you say: like shaven sheep on a midsummer's day? Well, that's what you might pray to the God your mother worships. But you would be . . . A Fraud! I put in a good word for Alban Berg. Your life is a lie from earth to sky. I am better at my business, though you call me a fraud, than my colleagues, whom you call genuine. You are a cartoon. I believe in what I say. Cartoons do. I don't really mislead for gain. Repetition is your reality. I try to give the right change. You think you are Professor Skizzen? My students all address me in that way. Your students are frauds, too. That's right. The furies—for whom this voice is a spokesperson—give you frights. That's right. You don't know a damn thing about music. In all things necessary, I know how to get by. That's demonstrable, I admit, you are right. I played it smart. That's right. I took no part in affairs of the heart. That's right. But now, obnoxious noise, did you notice? "right" is on my side. You are an infant Adam all the same and can only complain of fate and your mistake. In a song composed for my piano? In a stolen key.

Adam's Lament

He had not played it smart, she was just a tart, though she sang like a lark; but it was no way to start, he'd taken no part in such affairs of the heart, even if he'd been struck by cupid's dart, and kept in the dark where the cars were parked; because his love lacked art and would make small mark on her hardened heart: oh, she'd played it smart, for her it was only a lark, those affairs in the park, when she'd offered him an apple from a vendor's cart; well, she'd keep no part of his broken heart because he was getting over the shameful smart of the affair in the park, where he'd bought her a tart from a vendor's cart, and carved her name on the compliant bark of a birch.

37

All this furniture comes with it?

I guess so. That's what I understood.

Miriam was alarmed. It doesn't sound very permanent to me. As though we were hoteling and were planning to stay only a few nights. No need to change the sheets . . . We shall be so swift as not to soil them . . . The cream commode, the chifforobe—can we move them if we can't paint them? And such appointments . . . Are we renting these pots and pans, this dirty sponge, these spoiled mirrors? This drawer—here—is full of chipped knives and bent spoons. How about the dampness in the basement—are we being lent that?

You said it might be good for plants.

I don't want to move anymore. I want this sink to be mine, not on loan. You know High Authority will visit one day and say, Look: that scratch is new; is that scratch yours? are you harming this establishment with your foreign fingers?

Really? Do you honestly think a supervisor has ever inspected this building? do you figure on entertaining some busybody of the sort you ordinarily deal with at work? or coping with a landlord huffy behind his outstretched hand?

No, I guess not, because nobody who lived here lived here long. You got a contract, do you, Herr Sonny, from this college?

Yes. I thought you liked this place. I guess we didn't have to move. We could have stayed where we were, in that itty-bitty box all covered in vines like an arbor, buried in bloom, a butt of jokes, a place that passing cars slowed for, but it seemed to be a big saving . . . to be rentless . . . to be rich for a change . . . in property.

In London, my lad, we were rentless.

Gee, I misread you once again. I thought you were pleased with this place.

You want to misunderstand. I am delighted for the space, such an old distinguished house, my goodness, I'm standing on a floor furniture is made of, in front of a staircase big enough to bounce a ball down . . .

And a Steinway.

Ach. That old piano, too. It was born in a *Bierstube.*

Now, Mother, be fair. We could never afford a sofa with three pillows or a piano as pedigreed or rooms so warmly paneled as this house has.

That's my meaning. It exceeds we minor mortals. The building is too big for you and me to take proper care of—too vast, too costly, *Grössen,* too much in the movies. It has gobs of history we are ignorant of and foreign to. Besides, the house is falling apart. You can see it. I can sense it. Creaking to a halt. This place is full of groans. Clear to the eaves.

It's windy out.

Drafts. I share twelve paths of air in the morning when I make my descent of the stairs. In the afternoon, when I take my nap, we go back together like a bad smell. And the radiators knock.

That's a sign the boiler is working.

They sound like that dreck you're still driving.

The house, the car, go bravely on.

You always make excuses when I want to see Debbie. The Rambler is . . . in op—what do you say?—it's fragile as tissue is to a snort's nose.

Debbie doesn't need looking after. I do. What's for dinner?

I have noticed that in recent years you are always here at mealtimes.

I notice that in recent years there are fewer of them. Breakfast and lunch I have to fix for myself—

—open a box, stir a spoon in a bowl—

—yeah, open a can, drag a spoon through some soup—

Don't I do dinner for you?

Now and mostly then. What happened to the *Würstelbraten* and the *Faschingskrapfen* I love so much?

Oh, ya, then you are prompt as a cold at Christmas. When the pots steam. You remember sometimes to pour me some wine. You smile and lie about your day. It's nice. You are going to pretend the *Faschingskrapfen* remind you of Vienna.

Impossible.

Ya. Indeed. Impossible. You have never been there. Many times. But you like to pretend. When you talk to people at parties sometimes, I see you cycle the streets.

I never do that.

Like a newsboy. You know addresses.

I have never memorized a number or cycled a sidewalk. My tires are flat. Besides, your *Faschingskrapfen* aren't imaginary. They are merely missing. Along with *Krautfleisch* and that *Steirisches Schöpsernes* you used to make.

I used to be invited to your parties.

Everyone was eager to meet you.

Now *nein mehr.*

You don't like being given small bites of things. You complained, at the beginning, that all the parties were the same.

They were little and round. Gossip on such crackers as break in the hand. In every drink, small sunken olives. A grimace of cheese spread on office news. *Mein Gott!* Carrots leaning like oars in a water glass. I tell you, Joey, chitchat about people you don't know is boring as celery.

When the first wave of greeting is over, it lies quiet on the sand awhile. Anyway, celery is famous for being celery. Perhaps you should teach the faculty wives how Austrians cook.

In the kitchen, you can't make a living with just drippings. That's my lesson. Did you ever find a nice white brick of lard in that place Americans call a butcher's? This town! how badly equipped it is for life! Or see *Beuschel* or *Kalbskopf* or a handful of *Hirn* or a plump *Huhn* either?

What a town, I tell you! Lamb maybe you can find but not mutton. Now what is *Beuschel* in this dreadful language?

Lights.

So you say. Who's heard of "lights" in such a dark and barren land! The lights they refer to are a kind of cigarette.

Close. "Lights" means lungs.

At least you don't smoke.

No, I don't do that. I cycle down dark hotel hallways.

The common folks of this dreckish and dismal country don't eat hoofs only haunches, shoulders, and flanks but not kidneys or brains. They are strange. Odder than Amish. Everybody in town drives a truck.

I can't argue with you there. These locals prefer only the visible parts of their animals. They devour the outsides of things.

Jews love liver.

They aren't American.

They don't eat hair or eyes or ears . . . Americans. No noses . . . not Americans. Spit out nails.

Who eats hair?

People eat the fruit in scrotums.

Mother!

I could say more about what gets eaten.

Mother! You have become coarse like one of your graters.

While I grew old, you were supposed to grow up.

It's my skimpy diet.

You can't have drafts in the kitchen when you are preparing *Krapfen*. Or cool instruments—you know—bowls must be as warm as your hands, hands you have briskly scolded, and the pastry board should be in the same state, and not gray with the dust of old loaves. You will need knuckles to knead flat those sneaky folds of air, and you must give the dough a few swats with your scrubbled palms. Whap! Like you slap the cheeks of an ass pincher. The skin of the dough will contract. And have the palest lard nearby to fry your dough's nut in, like some saint—I forget—he requested—you know—he chose the oil that would make him a martyr.

I can seal the windows with putty.

So. All these rooms, up and down, over and back. We shall rattle around. What a racket! Which one have you selected?

For what?

Arguments. Which one is the argument room?

Do we argue, dear?

Incessantly.

We sometimes disagree.

Incessantly. We argue about whether we argue.

You complain. That's not the same.

You oppose me only to oppose me.

No. I try to reason . . .

Haw! You grew to fit into a cartoon of your father.

That's not fair.

You stayed inside his lines.

Compared with him I have crayoned the sky.

At dusk I could mistake you for him. Ach. I'm glad he's not here.

So am I.

Then Joseph and Miriam went their separate ways, gradually laying claim to this space or that by making various deposits (clothes, books, other obvious belongings—he coffee cups, she tea—on whatever was flat—sills, floors, tables, radiator covers); or with more deliberation declaring a proprietary interest in a sewing table by covering its cherry top with chess pieces positioned in the same brink-of-checkmate configuration as Capablanca, playing white, had cornered Nimzowitsch during a Mannheim match. Joey didn't play chess but he possessed an *International Herald Trib* that mentioned the game. He said the simple wooden figures gave his (patrolled) zone in the sitting room class.

Miriam, for her part, might arrange on some shelves the beginnings of her seed catalog collection or on a fireplace mantel settle a bowl holding only two Christmas cards both from Woodbine's one and only bank or perhaps upon a hassock pile issues of a magazine devoted solely to knitting. Empty LP sleeves did the trick for Joey until they slid under newspapers still awaiting perusal. There remained, in every room, a need for chairs. Perhaps the most peculiar of their proprietary signs were those that lay claim to a prized window-lit space—even when it had no rocker handy in which to deposit a claimant's body—such as a saucer into which Miriam had spit tangerine seeds or a sausage saved from maceration by somebody whom neither tenant admitted being, and no one consequently would remove, or several pages torn from a copy of the magazine *Modern Musical Notes* with its damaged cover depicting an augmented guitar and a player piano. Oddly, no one would confess to having planted that marker either.

The problem, as even Joey was able to discern and Joseph to define it, was that neither mother nor son seemed capable of putting anything back where it belonged. In this house, with its ample rooms and many floors, there were few spaces that could be clearly marked as home for a specific implement, object, or activity, like a toilet, closet, or sink, so that the idea of a possession that was utterly impersonal in its demand for order remained to the pair more foreign than French: that the crayons belong in their box, that pins should be put in their cushion, that plates need to stack in a cupboard; or even that states of affairs had their initial conditions to which they should be returned: drawers once drawn open should be shoved shut, doors ditto, shoes kicked off need to be replaced upon their owner's feet, a book, having been read or fingered to some sort of finish ought to be returned to its gap in the row; and lights switched on should not be left to glow uselessly and wastefully over empty chairs and blank walls or flood vacant rooms with their pointless scrutiny; that beds must be made before they are messed again, perishables put back in the icebox to perish there, the eggcup in which Miriam intermittently keeps her wedding ring scrubbed clean of egg before its next use, or that Kleenex tossed in soiled wads should be responsibly aimed and safely reach a wastebasket: otherwise all will be lost in jangles of clutter and scatter, deserts of dust that will stultify the eye, and piles of partly experienced, and only faintly understood, previous behavior will lie smothered by puddles of past time like uneven sidewalks after a very gray rain.

Several days later, Joseph had polished his reply: "I'll bet he's also glad he isn't." " . . . Isn't here." But what good is a retort if it comes a week late? and has, as he immediately saw, no originality, no snap. "I'll wager, he's glad, too." Oh, dear, "wager" was the wrong word. "Wager" would bring them both back to Rudi and his winning ticket. All the words were wrong. Short ones and long. They arrived too late, like callers who just drop by to say good night. His choices were as bland as blue milk. They lacked zing. Presence, pop. He had made a mouse trap that had sprung for an ant.

Joseph had also learned to let Miriam have the last word, as if she were still the martinet mother who had borne him out of London in a boat. Nevertheless, in the attic where he had begun to accumulate clippings, he imagined several versions of what he thought might be his father's response and practiced some appropriate performances. He often assumed the voices of others and presumed their points of view. To speak for Marjorie Bruss he donned her long blue frock, its white buttons marshaled from neck to hem. As the head of the library, she could not countenance confusion and utterly disdained those who, she said, danced the dillydally when they should be marching in squares like members of the military. The Major's world, of fonder memory now that months of reruns had rubbed Joseph's embarrassed role in it to a high shine, kept standard library time as it had to keep if it were going to carry out its functions efficiently. Everything in Tidytown, including the paraphernalia and litter of visitors, not just the overcoats, lunch boxes, and handbags of regulars and staff, had a place appointed for it, and there, each morning, like cadets, they answered the roll call: books in their comforting ranks, magazines in their appropriate displays, newspapers rolled on the right sticks, stands for umbrellas and racks for hats, bulletin boards whose out-of-date notices had been harvested, light that had touched, like an old friend, its customary patches of floor, and the fresh hush that a nighttime of silence had delivered to the reading room. Soon the clash of the push-open door would be felt right up to the front desk where the Major would take her first drag of the library's consoling atmosphere, just as Joey had seen smokers inhale their early morning smoke.

The first cigarette, whose life would be abruptly snuffed in an urn near the entrance, normally belonged to Mrs. Harley Stuart, who arrived shortly after nine with a volume recently read or recently rejected, both now to be returned, almost always with an energetic "whoof" for works deemed difficult and/or heady. Now and then she would share a naughty giggle with Marjorie Bruss, which was customarily followed by her wish for "a novel that's daring, a story that's new." This request would occasion more laughter—screened by Marjorie's white cloth gloves, her fingers pretending to be modesty's fans—a sodalike bubbling that the lady gave off when her cork was pulled, and who otherwise never seemed, even during such stretches of snickering, to be a woman that in bed, as it was said, drank, smoked, and read, though she did, and did, she sure did.

At the end of a day, Marjorie would note with satisfaction the number of cigarette ends sticking out of the sand like projectiles from a desert war, counting them with glee, because they each represented a bomb that had failed to go off or a bullet that had missed its mark.

"I'll bet he's glad . . . I imagine he's happy . . . I'm sure he's pleased . . . to be absent too . . ." "I'll bet he's also overjoyed." "I'm sure he's relishing his absence." "I'm glad he's not here," hadn't she said? So he could say, "Now I understand the reason for my father's disappearance." That last would hurt her. Was hurting her wise? Why be wise when stupidity was so readily available?

Visits of son with mother were easy, generally pleasant, when Joseph was a student at Augsburg or working in Urichstown, but now, with Debbie pregnant, Miriam's affections, formerly pointed at him, had been recompassed. And his usefulness around the house had been put to the test, another exam on which he'd performed badly, having no gift with the pliers or the wrench, and his experience as a handyman limited, when a small boy, to banging against a heap of concrete a shovel whose flat wide blade was expressly made for shifting rubble into trucks and wheelbarrows. It rang like a dinner gong and would be, in short order, taken away from him. The noise is too much like my hunger, his father would say to him, trying to be jovial. Joey did not understand the connection, even now.

After its second rising, Miriam rolled her doughnut dough slowly, lifting the entire mass from time to time so that the softer sides would sag back toward the center and folding its edges in the careful way Joseph folded up his copy of the *Times*. For *Fasching* she added a bit of beeswax before fast-frying the floating balls in a very hot pot of pure lard. It wasn't long before the dumplings took on the color we call gold. His mouth didn't water when he thought of how they smelled or how they tasted, but his soul yearned for the agreeable times these preparations brought back, because the kitchen was really the heart of any house. He would sit quietly on a stool in the warmth of its occupants and marvel at the magic his mother made.

The house would have enjoyed the company and function of three substantial fireplaces had Joseph been able to persuade them to draw properly; however, as it stood, they smoked like Mrs. Harley Stuart. Of course, had they drawn with relish, and greedily eaten the woodpile already in place, Joseph would have been expected to replenish the supply without hurting himself on the blade of an ax. Although fresh fuel might be a necessity, his injury would be a certainty. So while Joseph felt the behavior of the fireplaces to be quite benevolent, Miriam found them cruel and obstinate. She never failed to exit their rooms without an insult.

Joey had always admired, and desired to possess, even to be, one of those little boxes that swallowed still smaller ones of the same species until almost nothing was left to be the last bite eaten but a grain of atmosphere. The result of this clever storage would be a cube of cubes, secretly multiplying, at least mathematically, and kept, in Joey's case, in a cigar box papered by exotic young women in hoods for hats and plastered with official seals that proved someone had paid an appropriate tax just to open it. But with his new residence's gothic vastness confronting him, at first he could not successfully cope. Counter to everything he had heard about romantic styles of building, this house did not seem willing to contain a series of secrets in descending sizes. Everything one did or privately thought stood about like the furniture for sale at Mr. Hursthouse's shop. There were closets galore; there were back stairs, attic stairs, and a stairway that took you to the cellar; but there were no secret spots where mirrored evaporations might take place or dark corners where bad behavior might go to hide, be by curtains engulfed, or in crawl spaces lie concealed. Perhaps if he were still twelve, the house would feel, by turns, surprising, sinister, and melancholy, but now that he had reached the last cruel stages of his thirties, the college's loaner was repeatedly threatening to creak (and in that way verify its age), to leak (and in that way call out for repairs), to squeak (and in that way complain of its neglect), to crack and break (and in that way give evidence of its abuse).

Joey had initially looked forward to carrying plates of succulent sausage and creamy potatoes, sauerkraut, or—most particularly—Wiener schnitzels the size of a breakfast pancake, golden like a pancake, too, with three or four thin slices of lemon languishing on top, from a—to be sure—ancient kitchen into a dining room so woodworked it astonished its chandelier; but Miriam had—in effect—announced an end to her stretch of mothering in this life and made it known her present baby had been the unintended consequence of—okay—her son's gift of seeds, whose subsequent plants had spectacularly surrounded their cottage, slowing most cars and stopping some, and that she would now expend most of her nurturing energies in gardening, because—even Joey would have to admit it—their new yard, though oddly shaped, was the great grand thing about their borrowed house, and it simply yearned to be farmed.

Joseph had his own field to plow. The idea of a museum that would remind its visitors of the vileness of mankind—not its nobility and its triumphs but its vulgar greed, stupidity, and baseness—had taken hold of him; but he was already realizing that many aspects of its subject would have to be left for others, since there were facets of human behavior so persistent and enduring as to defy any enclosure: daily criminalities, vandalism, elementary embezzlements (from local banks, charities, or schools), small-money muggings, corrupt police, neighborhood whoring, disease, drugs, drunkenness, the theft of cars, break-ins and home invasions, every family's choice of its method of administering cruelty, the repetitive landscape of the obscene, going postal while in possession of guns. If Joseph were to include everything that counted toward his general indictment, he would have to pitch the entire daily paper into his disgrace case: just look at this . . . and this . . . and this . . . and this . . . and this . . .

38

The Catacombs contain so many hollow heads:
thighbones armbones backbones piled like wood,
some bones bleached, some a bit liverish instead;
bones which once confidently stood
on the floor of the world:
footbones anklebones shinbones,
bones a boneless mind moved many times
from its home in another bone;

a bone where it lived without being anywhere,
without misplacing the eyes in their eyeholes
or the nose in its slit or any ear's aperture either;
these skulls had a hollow in their hollow
right where the brain brimmed.
Somewhere nearby, Paris built those bridges
for the river to run under;
there were riveted towers and girls with likely limbs,
and all those trees, all those flowers,
streets, sky shops, and sidewalk vendors,
filling the head where the brain brimmed
without spilling a drop.
What a lot, what a lot of bones
dug up from their last homes:
coffins caskets boxes catafalqued
hearsed or wagoned to the grounds they'd go in.
Dug in, dug down, but not for long
—as afterlife goes—before being dug up again;
so many many bones where high-rises are wanted,
where houses libraries turnarounds should be,
more bodies coming all the time,
each one with thighbones armbones backbones
arranged like furniture in a well-kept flat:
ankles knuckles elbows knees
none of them—footbones anklebones shinbones—
what they used to be,
but roughly like the Great Lakes,
where they're supposed to go,
now needing lowering away into a sea of soil.
Down down down down
into a ground groaning with the dead,
crawling with cadavers corpses stiffs,
and a lot of rot a lot a lot;
so dig them up, sort them out:
armbones headbones toebones ribs
into armpiles headpiles toepiles cribs,
washed with a strong hose—hosed—
down down down down,

and then left out to dry—
catch some rays, eat some sky—
because we don't want wet bones in the Catacombs.
It'll be damp enough down there:
down down down down
in the tunnels we'll have runneled for them
where they'll be piled as high as the heads
of the tourists who are bringing their bones
down down down down
to see these bones through eyes,
eyes set properly in their sockets
just to see, only to see, not to smell
wet earth around them: heavy deep odiferous dirt.
Down down down down
all those steps, those stairs
lit by yellow light, lit by bulbs in pairs,
into halls which hold the transferred bones:
dongbones ballbones bustbones,
on and on and on and on and on,
sorrowbones terrorbones bitterbones,
liverish in the light, gray in shadow, offwhite;
tempting the memento mori in us
to pilfer one, an armbone maybe,
pop in purse, stick in sack, slip under shirt,
look good on mantel coffee table desk:
chitchatbone talebone pickbone
wishbone tomorrowbone smightbone,
one's own homebone,
and treasured chest.
After all those upstep stairs
up up up up up up up up up up,
toward day's light, let us rest awhile,
with the dead awhile
and try to smile the way they smile.
Up up up up to smile into fresh airs
a show of teeth, sigh of relief,
where the flics are waiting
at the backdoor, the exit of the Catacombs,

to peer into your purse, look into your bag,
pat your ribcage breastbone neck
in case your cunt conceals a bone,
or the boner's in your pocket.
They must fish in them for that:
to retrieve your souvenir of death Almighty,
return it to its pile stack proper aisle;
for these bones have another body now,
the body of the buried they belong to—
long long long long to—
down down down down—
through the comb like teeth,
straw in a broom,
teeth in a comb,

in a comb,
a comb,
comb.

Professor Skizzen thought it should be sung. He planned to compose some music. If only he knew how.

39

The Bumbler coughed but caught fire anyway. Like the shadow of a cloud, a moment of sadness, brought on by nostalgic thoughts, passed over Joey's other, more energetic, even malevolent, plans; yes, the way the shadow of the car passed over the road when the car was running smoothly; and its passage softened his anger toward the old heap, because, right now, its existence was a nuisance. This was going to be, Joey vowed, the Bumbler's last voyage. Miriam was in her own foul mood. She yelled orders at him as though he were refusing to wear his overcoat or go quietly to the dentist. The Rambler is out of commission, Joey lied. Do you want to spend the money it will take to get it fixed? His mother cursed in German as if he could not possibly understand . . . . *Verstehen?*

Joey had parked the car alongside a vacant lot a few blocks away and well out of Miriam's customary lines of sight. There it had sat for some weeks, out of commish, he insisted, to smooth out the scowls of doubt from his mother's face. It really was a field of metal weed. The car's soft tires demonstrated fatigue; its pale orange color had the pallor of weak rust. It did seem abandoned, and Joseph hoped the neighbors would complain, so it might then be towed away by the city to serve as spare parts. More than once he had dreamed of the organs and other elements of his body being distributed like prizes among the maimed. A shoulder here, for someone to cry on, a liver for an alcoholic writer, a spare ear for a tone-impaired musician, a tear to repair a dry eye, each part and appendage arriving promptly at their posts, ready to take up, anonymously, their new duties. These were pleasant dreams, the sort his mother once nightly wished for him as he began his brief encircle of the earth.

Was he not a criminal and the Bumbler his getaway car? In answer, Joey had left behind nothing of himself. He imagined he had wiped the seats and dashboard free of any previous owner's mischief, and the wheel clean of incriminating prints. Maps that might have given away habitual routes, grocery lists, and other trash had been removed. A soda bottle that had been thrust into a door pocket, because Joey couldn't bear to touch it, remained until Joseph, with a gloved hand, achieved its extraction. Despite these precautions, an umbrella lay neglected in the trunk. The Bumbler's slide backward into a humiliating dent had made it very difficult to retrieve the jack. There was no spare.

The days when the car was of great service were over. It had allowed itself to be driven between Woodbine and Urichstown for nearly a year. The word "driven" seemed supremely appropriate. Joey felt the need to remind his mother, when discussing their vehicle's parlous condition, that the Bumbler had been backslid

down a hillside

over snow and ice

during the early edge of night

by a screaming Major,

only to return

to Woodbine, its tail in a crook. Subsequently it was compelled to journey in petulant jerks around the county over a period whose conservative measure was several college semesters. Joey claimed to have lost count of similar treks the Bumbler had bravely undergone, its body full of fear, its engine of trepidation. Why did we risk mechanical failure or suffer the threat of arrest, my dear mom? To visit the smug new weds and their freshly harvested seed? To run errands of no need and less import? To satisfy selfish and sentimental wishes called love? Of no need because the Boulders had a far better car than the Bumbler and could safely make the required round-trip. As for weekly duties, the grocery store was an unimpeded downhill walk and, in its pleasant old-fashioned way, filled orders and made deliveries in the grateful light of late afternoon when its boy was out of school. So it needn't be driven to. Or in parallels to park. Of less import because grandmotherly visits to their last offspring will scarcely alter the spin of the planet. The kid will grow up in a nation perpetually at war and indifferent to the safety of its citizens. Cars will carry guns and fly flags. The kid is going to be an important part of my world, Miriam said firmly, as if she had already thought about it. Even if he is a Boulder, the boy is the best thing that has happened to our family since we arrived in this country. We shall never know what the best thing is, Joseph declaimed with an emphasis that stepped equally on every word. Are you going to ferry me to the farm so I can hear this baby talk and chortle, to see him walk, or not? Why do you speak of "world," Professor Skizzen replied, when your glimpse of it is like that straw mat of hall light that sneaks under your door at night. Hah! Miriam scornfully said, we inhabit a hotel now, do we? What of the world I don't see I shall ring for! DO NOT DISTURB hangs on all our hearts, Joey shouted, shocking both of them into laughter. As a consequence of Miriam's bullyraging, the Bumbler's humiliating servitude, dangerous to itself, its driver, and the road, lasted two years longer than anyone expected. Despite that, the poor wreck was cursed instead of praised, its wounds scorned, as if, again, it had fought in the wrong war.

Now his sister—*his* sister—had a baby big as its bellow. Joey called Debbie a cow to draw attention to her milk-heavy breasts, but his mother put an outraged stop to that. Honor the mother! honor the sister! older than you! properly married! suitably respected! And my small pleasures should receive your smile! No more of your excuses! Don't you forget

I mothered you! held my breasts to your greedy mouth! You weren't a baby when you were a baby—your father took away your childhood and gave you war instead—but you've grown into one—that's right, an infant—spoiled as last year's apple—to be jealous of your sister's sweet sunny cuddlesome cutie. Miriam's tone had slipped into a croon but in a moment recovered itself. He sleeps through the night. Can you say the same! I've heard you scratching about the house for something missing. Miriam would bring in her voice for a landing and then, without a gear newly engaged, go on to boast of the boy's fat legs, his rolling eyes, and squeals of astonishment.

Joey had visions of his car going conk in the middle of a cornfield. He drove in fear of the police and his own lack of education at the wheel. Every year he grew more apprehensive about the day—in every other way quite ordinary—in which Authority would come and take him suddenly, in shame and chains, to the clink. The cause would be an accident, an arrest, an account overdrawn, a signature faked, a vengeful pupil, a person from his past, a colleague, out of curiosity or suspicion, who had researched his file, an innocent clue . . . a . . . who knew? He had once wanted bank accounts and credit cards; to have ID was a victory; but now he saw the wisdom in cutting as many connections to the Machine of Modern Life as he could sever. Sometimes Joey dreamed, not of dismemberment (he'd let that happen in his sleep), but of jollity and a little peppy music set to a rhyme relentless as sirens—

> The Machine of Modern Life
> will insist you have a wife,
> will demand you vote for strife—
> the bomb the gun the knife—
> but especially wed a wife
> with whom to spend your life,
> and tho with troubles rife
> continue to be blithe
> in the grip of modern life.

These lines should be repeated incessantly but each time accompanied by a different solo instrument. And animal illustrations of the text held up for listeners to see: a muskrat running from a potato peeler.

Joey's plan, which had gradually matured until it received Joseph's okay, was elegant in its simplicity and design. He would drive the car back to Lowell and to the scrap yard where he'd found it. He would seek out Miss Spiky and ceremoniously return the Bumbler to her with his thanks. Then he would pop on the bus that passed that point on its way from Urichstown to Woodbine. The car would thus, like a South American protester, disappear. This escapade, as he saw it, would be a big step back, but the step would take him even more deeply into anonymity and its protections. It would also force Boulder to fetch and carry Miriam on her grandmotherly visits. Better yet, it would lessen the need for his attendance at these deeply humiliating gaga occasions.

Once the Bumbler decided to move, the trip to Lowell went without incident. That, to Joey, was a minor miracle and the car's last gift to him. At Lowell, however, matters began to sour. The yellow oil drum had a deep crease across its middle that made it bend as if kowtowing, and rust had eaten through its base. A wire fence had been planted along the front of the yard, but in places its stanchions danced perilously close to the ground. The Airstream still stood on its cinder blocks, but it appeared to have been idle for a long time, and ignorant of company. The side screen door hung from one hinge, while the wooden steps to the entry had sagged and seemed suspended now from the few tougher grains in its board. There was no line of cars to face the highway, only untidy patches of resilient weed and puddles so filled with oil they couldn't evaporate. They gave the sky an iridescent leer. With a groan Joey drove Bumbler over a low point in the fence and left the car where it stalled.

One thing went to Joey's satisfaction. Once enmeshed, Bumbler looked at home.

The scrap in the scrap yard seemed scrappier than he remembered; the large piles of metal were now small and ate slowly at one another like couples in a lengthy marriage. There were still a few gatherings of running boards, bumpers, and grilles, as well as melted cardboard boxes from which spilled wipers, hinges, and latches. What a desolate place, Joey and Joseph thought. Unlike buildings after bombing, these remains had no dynamics, inertia was their god. Rainbow-colored water was that deity's substitute for incense. Professor Skizzen rapped on some tinny-looking pieces, but there was no spring in their response, no music in this mess of messes. All things have their demise, even stone its catacomb. Of Miss Spiky there was no evidence. Professor Skizzen had saved up a sigh appropriate for cemeteries, and he used it now. He did not regret missing Miss Spiky in this place of her business, though his intent had been to see her, because she made him uneasy and ashamed of the feeling. Where did you stand, he wondered, to expect the bus.

While he waited, wishing he had brought a suitcase he could sit on, Joseph Skizzen suffered several sorts of reverie. Cars would rise over the nearby hill and rush down toward the spot he had chosen. Drivers must think him an odd hitchhiker, with his funny cap, his young goatee, and his black-and-white knickers. Joseph's vacant gaze rose for no reason toward the ridge. Traffic was light and shot indifferently past Lowell, whose old church spire you could barely see beyond the trees that formed the rear of the junkyard. He felt slightly chilled and quite alone. Wasn't this what he had feared: to be broken down, inappropriately dressed, on a country road far from any viable town? The light for that day had realized its age, and was feeling its weakness. Most bushes, trees—all feisty replacement growth—were leafless now, revealing their skeletal configurations. Joey, Joseph, and the professor stood in their own puddles of stupidity and noted the time between trucks. The still air had some heaviness though the shadows through which it passed had given it a slight bite. Wasn't he sporting his best duds just to impress Miss Spiky and elicit her laughter? There were other hints of winter, he observed. Cars raced their reflections up and down the hill, the shadows shrinking or enlarging as they ran, and seeming faster, to Joseph's eye, than they really were—always ahead, never behind—so that when the highway emptied, he felt he was being painted into his posture.

Professor Skizzen imagined that beneath each heap of wheels or side-view mirrors or backseat springs there lived a singing spirit and that during the earliest edge of dawn any unlikely visitor could hear them, as a chorus, making a mournful moaning punctuated by Miss Spiky's contralto—she the secret conductor of these ritual performances—in an oratorio of the discarded, the used up, the forgotten, those standing alone at the side of an empty road always just before dawn . . . always before or, at twilight, always after. What would that stack of tires behind the Airstream contribute? or that pile of bruised bumpers near the collapsing shed? because these were, after all, pieces that once composed the American dream—the automobile—that freed us to leave, move, travel, get around. Should these stacks sing of the speedometer that had made us equal, the backseats that had offered us sex, the accelerator that had given us power, the wheelbases that had conferred prestige? Or should they complain of their fate, like the Bumbler who had been left pinioned in a tangle of wire, the driver's window not quite closed, so a bird might fly in, an animal enter?

Leave them to their fate, the professor said, and tried to mean it, because, were all the pieces in these piles reassembled, what you would display here would not be an advert for used cars but a quite ordinary murderers' row.

Joseph thought that the highway needed repair. The asphalt, without a good curb, was being slowly squeezed thin at the edges, and places where pots would form by next spring were visible, even from where he was standing. This stretch, at any rate, needed work, its no-pass yellow line as faint as a cola straw; but roads like this one only trickled from town to town so the concern for them was equally meager and intermittent. You could tell he was marooned in small farm country because of the frequency of light trucks, many of which looked as if they were ready to be returned to this dump where they might have been bought. Debbie's husband (Joseph forced himself to think "Boulder") doubtless had a red one parked in his potato barn.

Joey dreamed that he ran to the middle of the road like an old-time highwayman, flagged down a truck with a (providentially provided) wimpy driver, whom he dragged unceremoniously out of his cab, to drive the rig to Woodbine at reckless speeds with whoops of glee. He wanted out of this place where he was presently cold, had the need of a pee, feet that were tired, a heart that was fearful, and a revulsion for scrap yards, cinders, and fat people. When the light failed he'd have to shortcut through the lot to reach the road into Lowell, and there he could expect . . . what? I've never been there, he thought, but it is hardly even a dot upon the map, a dim dot, at that. The warehouse that lived a vacant field away had burned some time ago and was only now a dark smear; the gas station had gone up in the same fire; and the nearby store was boarded and apparently abandoned. It was altogether not a nice spot for a picnic. Yes, here he'd put pee before picnic. The sign for the trailer farm remained, however, like an old-fashioned storyteller who never tires.

An hour passed. One-half more. A quarter. Minutes at the last. Skizzen patrolled the yard briskly to keep warm, reaching miserable conclusions about himself before turning around like a sentry to repeat the excoriation. Now and then a car would appear with dimmers lit. He might have to repair to Lowell, poor sanctuary that it doubtless was, because he was beginning to feel the cold change in his pocket. Also true: he was a mite scared. And he felt utterly out of place, lost, disowned, discolored, used up by misuse: just what he had been told would be the fate of the Bumbler if he continued to ride the clutch.

Oh hell he'd have to go. Why hide? Pretend you are in Paris. Skizzen stepped nimbly across the short drive into the junkyard and darted behind the trailer where he peed copiously and in a worthy stream. You are excused, he said aloud to the place where the propane was once attached. The return to his station was leisurely. Perhaps his anxiety had been nothing more than a bladder problem.

More cars had their eyes lit. He felt seen.

Then the bus was upon him. Now numb, he had stared at it without recognition. It was not gracious about pulling over, but the bus stopped. Its door opened with an exaggerated sigh. He slowly climbed the steps toward the driver, his fingers familiar with the rituals of the fare. He thought it would be pleasant to sit awhile before a nice fire. But none of his chimneys drew. There were no Miss Spikys among the passengers who were few: two asleep, one a-chew. There would be no place to spit. Please God, make it gum. Joseph sat in the rear near a high school kid with a book bag and immediately closed his eyes. He wanted that Greyhound to drive him away from his past, but his past had assumed the shape and function of the bus.

40

He was about to be denounced. Joey Joseph Skizzen, Associate Professor of Music, was certain of it. He would walk to the college as he always walked. He would try to stroll, to regulate his breathing. His briefcase would hang from his left hand. So would all afterthoughts. For this tribunal, he should be dressed in his imposture. Why not wear the golfing knickers that made him seem so Viennese, with his little goatee combed and his cap firmly settled upon his head. He'd bring with him an occasional verb at the end of a sentence to attach, and a soft guttural sound to release from his throat as quickly as a cat from its carrier, so that his inquisitors would have before them the complete creature and object of their suspicions.

He had pulled the brown envelope out of his postbox at the college; saw that it was one of those reserved for interdepartmental use, with lines along one side where multiple senders and receivers could be scribbled in—discipline here, name and rank there, office box the only address, day's date no longer the day's date—and where old routings waited for reuse; so he stuffed it calmly in his case, as he stuffed every bit of academic business, to wait its time—banality in a velope—and enjoyed his calm and measured walk home where he could untrouble himself at leisure with a few wedges of apple and the perusal of one of his beloved newspapers. Yes, by this time in his researches, he realized he relished bad news. The world grew every day more obscene, more cruel, more painful to endure. Now and then a leaf went to pieces beneath his shoe. It had been a dry autumn. Most trees were still green, though a few had grown somber. Somber had been the daily news, but Skizzen had found the normal climate of his life quite temperate these recent years, now that he had reduced his courses to a habit, had respect from every eye he thought counted, and administered his health in happy doses.

In the early years of his tenure he had regularly stood himself up against the wall; he had imagined the day of denunciation; he had rehearsed again and again his defense; he had hidden himself in one of secrecy's smaller closets. He began to realize that repetition was a principal element in his nature. He was constantly revising the habits of his life, his thinking. It was like learning to play the piano. *Anfang* . . . Beginning is difficult, but practice makes perfect. Turning doorknobs, climbing stairs, tossing upon the table before every class his little hat, setting down his briefcase, rolling his big toy dice—always working the room for laughs. Before he began . . . *Anfang ist* . . . hard. Practice . . . Then when the time came . . . and it would come . . . he would be ready; he would be indomitable. He would polish the expected until it disappeared. Yet . . .

He was unprepared for the message he withdrew. Its tone was rather preemptory, even for a dean, and now that he had taken the message's first blow, he thought that its address was very formal, "impersonal" might be the most accurate word, and its brevity—one that left its occasioning as dark as a locket snapped shut upon a once-loved face—in the neighborhood of rude. In a matter of extreme academic urgency and concern, his presence was requested at the office of the dean on . . . the call was only a day from his receipt of the paper he had in his hand . . . short notice indeed . . . for a party . . . even for . . . a demand; yet it said—what was it? was its form the form for a note? its shape the shape of a routine letter? its brevity the brevity of a memo?—it said—let's see—it said that his presence was requested, not required; it described its subject as one of academic urgency, not criminal misrepresentation; it was a matter that needed no preparation; its subject was to be kept, indeed, from any possibility of private pondering or public gossip until the topic sprang from the dean's agenda, which was probably not written down—anywhere—off in the air like an arrow from its bow. It was he it was aimed at. He was sure of that. The shadow of his fingers showed through the paper. Yet now he could see that its contents had multiple addresses, and these might account for the impersonal tone. Morton Rinse. Mort was there. Why? The dean, Franklyn Funk, whose name should have been on a five-dollar bill—was said to be the author, but why should he address himself?—good God! Hazel Hazlet, the librarian! whose formidable face had incited many a schoolboy jest—Andrew "Kit" Carson from history, with his heavy mane of white hair—and Steve Smullion from biology—a group chosen to travel quite across the board—but no coach—was that significant?—no college president; well, the dean wouldn't, would he? address his boss as he might a subordinate. Palfrey could be present. Palfrey might have used the dean as a cover. That would explain the strange address. Why else would you include yourself? though it might be the way Joey wrote imaginary notes to Joseph. Skizzen felt Palfrey would be Palfrey, and when the president entered the seminar room, his jowls sagging still farther toward his throat because of the sadness and concern they bore, Joey would know the final score.

What were these happy doses, these swigs of happy times, he would prescribe for the healing of his soul? Joey would sit at the piano in the downside of afternoon and play what he loved—pieces he could skip through without effort or mistake—and whose words he would robustly sing as he went along: "Believe me, if all those endearing young charms, / Which I gaze on so fondly today, / Were to change by tomorrow and fleet in my arms, / Like fairy wings fading away . . ." When he sang he imagined Professor Skizzen to be assuming the voice of Fate, so Joey had to possess the boyish charms referred to. But Fate's firm boast of fidelity was futile. Although the sunflower, as the song said, turned its face to the twilight wearing the same devoted look it gave the dawn, when Skizzen was seen to be other than he had been, the expression would be anger and scorn.

As for Miriam, who already suspected something, and might not be terribly surprised by a little misrepresentation, the situation would nevertheless be as disastrous as could be imagined, because Miriam would have no more friends, could count the trials of her life as having accomplished less than nothing, and now would be compelled to face winter without hope or happiness or funds, hence to live on ingratitude as well as she could, since that was all there seemed to be an abundance of.

Upon his confession, Joey could hear her speak like this, as an outraged victim to a judge, not facing him, rather addressing the world or some god who had been brought in to preside at the catastrophe. Joey could only stand there: mute, helpless, enraged on his own behalf, ashamed, a destitute. Her manner of life, as well as his, would go up in such smoke as their suttee could summon: a bonfire of house, furniture, and garden, a consummation devoted to nothing: no degrees, no licenses, no number for a name, no father, no background, no learning, no love.

No guilt.

That would be his defense, and his explanation. Joey was innocent. He had not stolen the diamond-pointed needle from Mr. Kazan's store.

He had not given Professor Ludens the least encouragement. He had not had evil intentions when he accepted Madame Mieux's invitation, or succumbed in any way to intoxicating smoke in Mieux's nest of cozy pillows. He had not made sinful overtures to the Major or taken advantage of Portho's poverty. He had not conspired to defame or overthrow the Lutheran church whatever Rector Gunter Luthardt might say. He had returned all his borrowed books to the library. He had persuaded the college to feed the school's emaciated collection of recordings until it was plump, if not fat.

But you stole garden seeds from the school's shed.

And he had paid in cash for his car. He had not struck any human being with it either.

You stole garden seeds from the school's shed.

I was poor and needy. It was a gesture worthy of Dickens. It was my poor mother's birthday. They were cheap seeds.

You had no license allowing you to drive. You have never paid a penny in taxes.

I was . . . I was a misregistered alien, a victim of violence and dislocation; surely that must be seen as a plus, for it meant that I had never supported one of America's wars or failed to carry out the duties, like voting, expected from the ordinary citizen, since I wasn't one and was under no obligation.

But you lied to President Palfrey about your age, education, and academic qualifications.

Is it my fault if I had no training and had been denied by circumstances the tutorial skills of the great Gerhardt Rolfe? or that arthritis had slowed my fingers so that I could no longer perform my favorite Chopin? I drove my mother to see her daughter when Debbie was in labor. And again when the little pebble was born.

You got rid of the car so that you wouldn't have to do this favor for your mother.

I rarely eat her food anymore. I rarely see her through so many doors. She gardens as regularly as a tap drips. Debbie drives in from the farm now and then. She even brought the baby with her once. How loud it was in the walls of that house.

You spent hours of your lying life obsessively rearranging the words in that sentence you wished to pronounce upon humanity.

No, no. Not a life. It cannot have been an obsession because **I finally got it right.**

First Skizzen felt mankind must perish, then he feared it might survive.

First	**Skizzen**	**felt**	**mankind**	**must**	**perish**
then	**he**	**feared**	**it**	**might**	**survive**

Twelve tones, twelve words, twelve hours from twilight to dawn.

I furthermore collected evidence for my fears by establishing the Inhumanity Museum. One day the library will give over one or two of its rooms to my achievement. Perhaps the very authorities that accuse me now will establish in my honor the Twelve-Tone Chair or fix upon a bronze plaque the sacred words: FIRST SKIZZEN FELT MANKIND MUST PERISH, THEN HE FEARED IT MIGHT SURVIVE. At Augsburg College, Luther had his door of wood or block of stone, why can't I have mine?

Luther said you couldn't buy your way into God's good graces. It would come, if it came, free in the mail. You are the soul that needs reformation; right now you are made of nothing better than ballyhoo. For instance, wasn't the museum designed to the specifications of your pleasure, and your pleasure alone?

Did I not establish a yearlong course in the history of music? Was I not mentioned—twice—for most distinguished teacher? My students may have, but I never skipped class, was never late, and rarely ill. My oddities helped sustain the dignities of my subject. Compare me then with my compatriots. Pull them from the line! Send them to the rear! So I had no pretty papers to make my existence authentic, and—yes—I had to learn my trade by pursuing it. So what! Compare me. Compare me. Then fire us all. Our crimes vary, but our guilt defies dry-cleaning.

There is a system of certification, designed to protect students from incompetence and misinformation, whose rules you have broken irreparably. Even if you have done all you say, you do not merit special treatment. Serious students must learn many things they do not wish to learn, but you have learned only what you liked to know. You licked the chocolate from a candy wrapper. You are a clown, a pratfaller fellow. Selling snake oil from a pregreased bottle.

Joey did not dare to explain to the president of his college or his colleagues or his dean that he had an aim in life they might not understand but one that their suspicions were defeating: it was to pass through life still reasonably clean of complicity in human affairs, affairs that are always and inevitably . . . envious, mean, murderous, jealous, greedy, treacherous, miserly, self-serving, vengeful, pitiless, stupid, and otherwise pointless. My father fled the Nazis before they were the Nazis, because he knew our nature. He tried to remove himself from blame, from complicity. Had he not done so, would he not have been, in some small way, responsible for the behavior of the Austrian state, greeting their cheapjack little Führer as if he arrived with lunch? Nor do I belong to America. I am without number. My money, meager as it is, cannot be spent nefariously. I have not contributed to the tricks of high finance. I live simply, out of the reach of ambition or conspiracy. You see, Professor Skizzen is not me. I send him forth to represent me, you might say, to be the man who has to do the business with the devil that must be done.

Then why is—

Then why is his face still floating about the base of the dish, though it's been emptied of soup and every other info?

. . . puff and bray . . . puff and bray . . . puff and bray . . .

Professor Skizzen is only a memory. He is a disguise. His nose, his cheeks, his eyes, are made of a broth that others spoon into themselves. Hear that sound as they suck in bits of carrot and some peas. So I pass into their lives. I become them. I contrive what they shall see: me me not I, no not I. I guess you have the right to devour me, because you have made me possible: you picked me out of a basket, a mere folder, a sheaf of assertions; you saw fit to believe each lying page; you gave me a contract; you seasoned me like a stew; and you gobbled up much time in my life—committees, classes, study, civic service; you ate with your eyes closed. If I am a fake, so are you. If I am ignorant of some things, you are unaware of more. To you, a counterfeit is more acceptable than a real bill, the shade of a shade more important than the tree.

. . . smirk . . . bluff . . . heat . . . wash . . .

You never liked Schoenberg. You play the piano as if your fingers were broken. You live with your mother. You read the wrong books.

Think of the hours I devoted to my other selves: how often I had to dodge dangerous questions; commit to memory enlargements of one myth or other, rehearse sequences, qualities, effects; practice timing as though I were playing a concert, disguise my incompetence in that regard; pick a professorial wardrobe, choose a cap, grow a goatee; keep calm in the face of disclosure, which I cannot say I am doing very well right now . . .

. . . cheat and bleat . . . bow and scrape . . . preen and prate . . .

Okay, fire Professor Skizzen, for he has deceived you; erase Joseph from your memory since he has surprised you; Joey will teach the class, meet alumni, attend meetings, earn the livelihood. I have no more "me." I have my mother I must care for. You won't find a trustworthier chap. She is the only *M* left in my life. When asked, I recommended to the Woodbine Literary Club the best books about opera, even though one of my colleagues, whose name I will protect better than he will mine, warned me that the club was but a coven of old hags. I talked to little clouds of high school students about coming to Whittlebauer College even though they would very likely be better off elsewhere. At committee meetings I nodded when it was hoped I would. I didn't steal coffee cups from departmental offices, and I showed up for the stuffy lectures of dreary invitees; I made my bow before other notables and attended the performances of safely out-of-date plays. Oh, yes, and to chapel went I now and then, sober as the hymnal.

This is the way we smirk and sigh, lurk and spy, favor buy
this is the way we smile and lie
to prepare for the faculty meeting.

Oh dear, no, I can't beg Palfrey to be kind. Joey must not soil himself with the academy's hypocrisies. Your face, Prez, is not otherwise fat, but you have the jowls of a hound dog. Your handshake is an impersonation of a spit rag. You play with the emotions of widows. You constantly pretend to be concerned for the welfare of one, the forlorn status of another, and continually broadcast your love of the Lord, because that's what you are paid to do. Why should I be singled out for scorn? I lie small-time. No door squeaks when I slide by. Whose life was damaged by my subterfuges? What harm did I do teaching music? Just a little art and less craft to enable my girls to pass a leisure moment of the day:

such as a bit of knitting, threading a needle, brushing watercolor flowers into bloom, rendering a dear old tune. Yes . . . yes . . . I taught mostly future's ladies. Ditto your classes in French. It's said you love sinners. My small sins were made for forgiveness. Like forgiving a twenty-nine-cent debt.

Here, in this place, Schoenberg could not have begun the least measure of a career. Here, no one minds if you prefer Delius, a man who caught syphilis in Florida where he tried to grow oranges, and with whose work Thomas Beecham insisted on waxing the public ear. Once, when I pretended to be a fan, one of my colleagues, whose name I shall protect better than he will mine, followed me into this absurdity like an antelope fleeing danger with his flock, grateful to believe I had finally given up on Maestro Twelve Tones, because, had I maintained my interest, the copycat would have had to sustain his . . . an unpleasantly taxing fate. Was not my Delius period a generous gesture?

You never liked Schoenberg.

My life has been full of generous gestures. I never put myself forward. I loved background better than Romeo did Juliet. My opinions, sirs, were used merely to warn trespassers away. To secure myself from quizzers and their quizzes. Even so, with my colleagues I was able to play touché.

To steal cheap seeds. How low to stoop.

I must say the college is a lousy landlord. It let that small mansion become a big shack. You bribed me with its formerly grand piano. My mother and I are not responsible for the mess you might find if you ever examined the premises, for your neglect encourages ours. I could give you a list, given a little time, of the ways in which it's wanting, the repairs that need urgently to be made. I can't afford to make them at the salary I'm paid.

Your mother had to garden with a screwdriver and a spoon.

And the piano is a bad joke. Keys are chipped. One is silent. The rest are out of tune. I think faculty should be allowed to take recordings home. The library doesn't carry Jacques Barzun's book on Hector Berlioz. In the winter, the damn steam radiators clang and clatter in the midst of my class listening to "Clair de Lune." By the way, you don't have David Oistrakh's violin version.

You never liked Schoenberg.

I did so. At least two-thirds of me did. That's more than most people.

You hate humanity. You are an opponent of man's natural way of life. What have you finally to say?

I don't know if beauty is still possible in this world.

41

It was not strictly kosher, but Professor Skizzen managed to run off thirty copies on the college Xerox machine of the following list he had, over years, composed. Although he was, himself, in no hurry to advertise the existence of the Inhumanity Museum, in case of death or injury he might change his mind and allow a few special friends and respected visitors limited access. All of his careful notes, literally hundreds, were on small, easily filed, but not easily copied, cards. Whenever he undertook to classify all the ways human beings have killed or injured one another, he felt dizzy from the impossibilities that faced him. If wars were human necessities or at least habits of long standing, how could he call them unnatural, inhuman, or basically unethical. Could the inevitable be immoral? It would be like saying it was wrong to have two arms.

A SELECTION OF NEWS ITEMS ON 2 X 5 CARDS

416 b.c. Athens besieges the island colony of Melos, an ally of Sparta, during the Peloponnesian War. Melos is chosen for its particular weakness and to prove to others the power of Athens. The Melians refuse to surrender because it would look bad on their résumé (they were a shame society) and result in slavery for their citizens. The Athenians decimate the population by killing the men and boys, taking the women into

service, and later repopulate the place with their own kind.

149–146 b.c. Weakened by its victory at Cannae during the Second Punic War, the Romans, who simply outlasted their foe, burned Carthaginian ships, the pride of the sea, in their own harbor, then murdered the men, raped the women, and rampaged each street. Fifty thousand were sold into slavery, although, with such a plentiful harvest, prices could not have been advantageous. Emptied of all contents, the city was razed and left in shards and shatters, but scholars (the pen exceeding the sword once again) waited until the nineteenth century to salt the very earth the city once stood on. It made for a better story. I can only agree.

339. Because, among the Jews and the Magi, the number of Assyrians was, in clear evidence, multiplying, a firman was issued (possibly called a fatwa now) that doubled their taxes. Mar Shimun, head of the Assyrian cities of Seleusa and Ctesiphon, refused to enforce this levy, so it was carried out by collectors of particular violence and brutality in the hope that the Christians would abjure their religion in order to escape taxation and mistreatment. Just in case they did not, on the morning of Good Friday, 339, he had Shimun arrested for treason, all Assyrian vessels seized by the government, priests and ministers put to the sword, and churches torn from their moorings in the earth.

1200 et passim. Genghis Khan carried out mass murders in many of the cities he conquered, Baghdad, Samarkand, Urgench, Vladimir, and Kiev among them. Afterward, he appeared in several inferior films I have been forced by my mother to see.

1850–1890. Having infected the natives of America with smallpox, pushed them from their hunting grounds, thrashed them thoroughly in small engagements over many years, broken numerous treaties and agreements, the colonists resorted to death marches and emaciating dislocations over a period of nearly fifty years (the Trail of Tears that followed the Indian Removal Act in 1830 rid us of four thousand). Feeling a bit ashamed about collecting more scalps than the barbaric tribesmen, the white man made amends with bad booze, attic rugs, and baby rattles. The final indignity, in our present age, is permission we have given to the tribes to oversee and profit from tawdry gambling casinos erected on their reservations. Liquor and various drugs are available at cut rates, especially near borders. Speaking of borders, Dominican dictator Trujillo ordered all cattle-rustling Haitians, living close to the republic's legal edges, be eliminated. Twenty to thirty thousand were—more than the number of cattle. Haitians speak a sort of French, Dominicans a pretty good Spanish, but the nationalities may otherwise be indistinguishable. The test chosen by their murderers was to require their suspect to identify a sprig of parsley: what is this? Instead of our present choice of curly or flat, Haitians would either say *persil* or *pèsi* instead of the Dominican *perejil*. Nazis were no doubt similarly inspired to inspect their prey for circumcisions. Australians treated their indigenous populations rather as Americans did. They began with measles and smallpox, concluded with sabering, burning, and shooting. Tasmanian aborigines were nearly exterminated, but, like the buffalo, have since made a comeback, so all is well. Some claim our pacification program in the Philippines (1902–13), using cholera to do most of the damage, killed more than a million Filipinos, some of whom were actually dissidents. Nazis were no doubt similarly inspired by these advances in germ warfare to encourage families of malarial mosquitoes to set up shop in the Pontine Marshes where they produced ninety-eight thousand cases in only two years. Nazis were no doubt similarly inspired by their own example in German South-West Africa. They gave to history its first case, it is claimed, of state-organized genocide, led by a man perfectly named for it—General Lothar von Trotha. Two ethnic groups made up the colony's population. The general removed 80 percent of one but scarcely 50 percent of the other. [Required two cards]

1639–1651. Cromwell's army invaded Ireland to deny Royalists their farms and to put many of these properties in Protestant hands, at the same time preventing them from serving as a base for the return of the Crown to England. Colonization was indeed a British habit. When the French explored the New World they built outposts to facilitate trade; when the Spanish did so, after the initial slaughter, they settled in among the natives, often marrying them; but when the British arrived they drove the Indians away and built houses for themselves and handsome sideboards for their manners. This was not a new strategy but a successful one, except in Ireland's case. Nazis were no doubt similarly inspired to repopulate Poland, as the Israelis to enlarge Zion. The Irish were encouraged to remain bitter by British behavior during the potato famine of 1845–49. The Brits outpaid the Irish for their own crop, vesseled the potatoes away, and left the people to starve. Stupid, stubborn, slippery: the British do not own these qualities, but in England's case, they built an empire with them. The Irish moved to big-city America where they became cops. In their spare time, some rioted with German immigrants over saloon hours.

> 1793–1796. A part of France called Vendée was a persistent arena of religious conflict. It is difficult to separate the killing and maiming that takes place during a war with the sort that qualifies for the Inhumanity Museum. They didn't want to pay taxes. (I've heard that before.) This time the tax was to be paid by their church. Economics and religion will always set a place blazing. At first, supporters of the church and Crown prevailed, the insurgency seemed on the point of success; but the new bloodthirsty Republican state sent a huge army to "pacify" the region by killing most of the people in it. Until these ruffians arrived, there was not enough "inhumanity" to qualify it for membership. Women and children, houses and municipal buildings, flags and symbols, were all equally eradicated. Beliefs had sharp queries run through them, but beliefs, however stupid or foolish or bizarre, have no more material a body than God himself. They cannot be so easily destroyed, and always outlive their believers, if only in quaint volumes and old tomes. There they lie until some half-wit gives them animation.

What was truly shocking about his collection was not how many humans were reported murdered, but how many murderers were humans. Some of their victims were shot by revolvers in the safety of the home, others were run over by cars, still others knifed when knives were the instruments of choice, or poisoned by fouled water because feces were as popular as mustard. A special salute was due those who were allowed to lie down in the rows of their infertile fields and left to starve. How about the accommodating who hung themselves in closets—quite a few—both victim and victor, hardly fair. Rope should be forbidden, the pistol people felt, in order to prevent the advantage hanging has, but bullets can be bitten, even chewed, when triggered by a resolute finger. Walk into a pond with rocks in your pocket. It is a laundered death. Best of all, a few pills in a water glass can be counted on to shroud consciousness with a milky cloud. You die of kindness. Millions of us seem to find ordinary life so foul we must soften our sorrows with drugs or drink or acquisition, perhaps Madame Mieux's pillows were her condolences, kept nearby like pets whose silk purrs when stroked, or her stashes of grass that comfort when smoked with their smoke.

Skizzen really had no room or time or inclination to record the assaults of man upon his environment, as deadly as his pacifications. How busy we are with our days: felling forests, shaving hills, overgrazing, overfishing, setting fires, and causing floods, drilling, mining, bringing fresh infestation to local flora and native fauna, polluting the earth and air with fire and water; and how deserved will our pain be when our host rebels, and we do return to dust or slide into the sea. The professor would sometimes crumple a helpless strip of such reportage into a pill of futile rage. I will enjoy it. I must. Justice at last . . . in the form of rust.

I am *your* judge, he would believe during rarer moments, you are not mine—not mine—not mine—and with his inquisition scheduled he needed to collect righteousness like provisions for a voyage; for what would happen to him when they tossed him out, homeless and poor, into the very cruel and soiling world he had tried so valiantly to avoid?

> 1915–1923. It is estimated that roughly 1,500,000 children, women, and men were deported to their death by the Ottoman Empire. Those missed by the first sweep were later kicked out of their houses. The Turks claimed the Armenians started it. Young Turks took advantage of the First World War to massacre 275,000 Assyrian-Chaldeans and hundreds of thousand of Greeks. In 1938–39 Turkification was completed with the removal of 65,000 Kurds and a scattering of Jews.

> 1932–1933. As if stealing a page from the Brits vis-á-vis the Irish, the Russian government confiscated an entire harvest in the Ukraine causing 7 million to die nationwide. I especially like the name for this solution: the Holodomor. Ukrainian fields were borrowed by the NKVD in 1940 as sites for the murder of 20,000 Polish officers at Katyn (in the same fashion that the

> Germans were exhibiting elsewhere). Chechens often enjoyed the attention of Russian executioners. Future archaeologists will be able to find bones almost anywhere they shove a shovel.

Skizzen had recently read that a famous fellow named Bertrand had confessed: "Sometimes, in moments of horror, I have been tempted to doubt whether there is any reason to wish that such a creature as man should continue to exist. It is easy to see man as dark and cruel, as an embodiment of diabolic power, and as a blot upon the fair face of the universe." No, Russell. Russell, it turns out, is unable to persevere in this judgment.

> GERM WARFARE. Japanese Unit 731, operating between 1932 and 1945. The germ inflicts people with rotting-leg disease—ulcerous sores that killed between ten and twelve thousand of Chinese prisoners, and later three hundred thousand to five hundred thousand civilians. I have labeled it rare and little known in modern times, but one of the triumphs of my researches.
>
> These days. Backed by the USA, the Pakistan army, according to a customarily conservative scholarly estimate, killed, during 1971 alone, one and a half million Bengali citizens of Bangladesh, who happened to have an unpopular religion. Elites were the favored target. Germans also picked on Polish intellectuals and after killing both of them (the joke ran) turned their attention to washerwomen. The wounded are never counted as carefully as the dead, but it has often turned out that being wounded was the worse affliction.

On many cards, Skizzen had entered no more than a place-name and a date, intending to get back to those notes later with the estimated sum of each subtraction and to pencil in his personal comments. The work was routine but numbing. On the back of a card, he would occasionally paste a photograph of corpses looking like heaps of laundry, piles of skulls with their wide black eyes, or vaguely located mass graves and other places from which human consciousness has fled. Bodies that have been left out in the rain appear especially soggy and therefore more lifeless, as are the limbs, wet hair, and cotton blouses when examined separately. In winter one doesn't need to hurry with any interment. If, on the other hand, graves are not dug deeply enough, the ground is likely to heave as the bodies rot.

Skizzen repeatedly fingered through the cards, pulling one out and then, after a glance, pushing it back in place again as if looking for a specific entry; but his fingers had a case of the nerves, and his eyes were possessed by a series of startled blinks, while moisture had begun dampening his goatee. Might he be jailed? Would they dare do that? Or would they be satisfied if he quietly disappeared. A flick, a wave, begone, strangely beset man. Isn't that what you say when, after the play, you find a ghost still mooning about on the stage? He saw his mother's few belongings swept into the back of a truck . . . to be delivered where? at whose expense? There, too, was his mother, squatting among her pots and trowels, scowling at the sky, bidding bye-bye to her . . . well . . . life's work . . . Suddenly, to be forced to leave her palace of petals, as she was fond of describing it, and, most mornings, her so lovingly cultivated pearl-wet leaves . . . It was too painful. What moment of realization might finally overcome her, so that her tears could extinguish her anger?

Oh, good heavens, he'd forgotten. He had Debbie to deal with. Debbie lived nearby. Surely Debbie would take her mother in . . . She'd enjoy having her mother near. They could both watch Debbie's pebble grow beyond rock to boulder. Perhaps Miriam could take up a little gardening at the farm. At the farm they grow potatoes underground like so many of the dead. Though potatoes' eyes are multiple and small, their skins do resemble a mummified head.

What a stupid thing to think. Debbie might enjoy her mother's company now and then, watching her make goo-goo eyes at the tot, and Miriam might like to hoist the kid up into her hug, proud she can do it, proud she is a grandma, proud of her kin; but not, no not, as a regular thing, like every morning before breakfast, before five in the bloody morning when these folks were inclined to get up, outrising the sun, no not as a daily, hourly occasion, moment-by-moment event, like tick begets tock, until a hungry growth on Grammy's arm appears, one you can see swell when her heart beats blood through the swelling.

Skizzen admonished—he cautioned—he lectured himself. Skizzen, he advised, should concentrate on the good years he had enjoyed. Skizzen, he realized, had finally become comfortable in the classroom. Skizzen, he confessed with some pride, had improved the record collection. There were now two versions of Béla Bartók's *Concerto for Orchestra.* The college no longer used the mimeograph. While he lived, Carfagno treated him like royalty. Skizzen had his own office, he admitted, with a window that framed a view of the chapel and the quad, pretty as a postcard: all this from a building made of limestone scrap and healthy ivy. Skizzen, the professor, no longer scorned the rituals of conferring degrees or laughed at the happiness that graduation brought to parents. Skizzen, he had to draw the conclusion, was A-OK.

Fate had it in for him. It would grin—to suggest "not yet"; it would wink—falsely to promise "coming soon"; it would lead him to suppose success was as slow to release its sweet as a caramel in his mouth, he had but to wait—not yet—coming soon—only to find his sweet turn tacky each touch of his tongue; to find each succeeding moment rough. Although his first weeks at the High Note had been a bit awkward, he had adjusted finally, absorbed his duties, and had begun to enjoy the store's piano. He was swimming in music; he heard glorious voices; he saw melody in the movement of the light. Then the carrothead had set him up, Joey was certain. Castle Cairfill had plotted a plot and made Mr. Kazan suspicious. Cairfill's musical tastes were deplorable. Joey was free of blame, although his taste, then, rose no higher than the "Moonlight Sonata." Despite his superiority in every particular, his opponent had won that round. There hadn't been another, had there?

But wait. What an imbecile he was! Skizzen struck his brow a blow that he'd seen first in the movies. He should mark and measure his head, think like a yardstick. Yes, what an imbecile, Joey was. Professor Skizzen could count on the cowardice of these people. Oh yes. They would do anything to avoid scandal. He could threaten *them* with exposure. Oh yes, oh yes! He was in the driver's seat. He smacked both cheeks tenderly. Oh . . . oh dear. No, he wasn't. Yes, he was.

Miriam might find shelter at the farm. Nor did he think he'd be turned away, but would he be welcome? What could he do there, hoe beans? buy a banjo to play while setting fire to the hay? Her high school sweater would not rise up to cheer him, and in the stony glare of her husband's eyes he would merely be seen as an impediment to the plow: a rock to be turned over and tossed from the field. He had come to love his position at the school. He enjoyed his nice April walks across the quad, exchanging nods with the friendlier students, Professor Skizzen as dignified yet as interestingly odd as his station demanded, yellow daffs arranged in applauding rows along the path, tulips turning to watch him pass, a brisk wind asking the treetops to prance. What was left now but a life of crime? by setting the flypaper danglers afire! casually watching the cuttings curl up in the flame. HUMAN CRUELTIES, IN A PANTOMIME OF HELL, CONSUMED BY OVERLY DRY ATTIC AIR, reports the *Woodbine Times.* He and his mother had flown solo through life. It had never mattered to him that he had no friends. Nevertheless, he must try to die with decency. He'd be marched to jail in manacles. What did they call it? the perp walk—not the name of a dance step. It had actually come—that fearful moment. Friendless. Motherless. Fatherless too. He began to cry.

> March 16, 1968. My Lai Massacre. Nearly five hundred people in the Vietnam villages of My Lai and My Khe were murdered by members of Charlie Company. The Americans demonstrated their skill in such matters (although for some it was their first time) by dropping many victims, like a line of cardboard targets at a carnival, into a handy drainage ditch. Babies were dispatched by gun and grenade, animals and women as well. There were no plants in pots or they'd have been shot. This riot of killing was observed by helicopters. The helicopters snitched.

42

I shall assume that you have each listened with full attention to Béla Bartók's *Concerto for Orchestra.* Anyone like it? Hands. That's nice. Several. We are blessed. This concerto is one of the major musical achievements of the twentieth century. Bartók was ill with leukemia and low on funds. His friends passed the hat behind his back in order to offer him their charity in the guise of a grant from the Koussevitzky Foundation. Koussevitzky was the conductor of the Boston Symphony Orchestra. You may have heard the results of his direction on some of your recordings. [. . . um . . .] This support enabled the composer to spend the summer of August 1943 at the spa at Saranac Lake—that's in New York State—a spa is a health resort—where his illness momentarily improved. [. . . . . .] Apologies. His illness did not improve, he did. His illness weakened. [. . . . . .] The German poet Rainer Maria Rilke also died of luke. Lots of people do. Lots. It is cancer of the blood, cancer of the marrow of the bones. It should be the disease of duchesses and counts, but it isn't. Of blue bloods, you see. But it isn't.

The concerto had its first performance, naturally under Koussevitzky's leadership, in Boston during the winter of the following year. The audience's reception was "tumultuous." Critics were less excited, but performers liked the many opportunities the music gave them to blow their own horn and excel. Listeners were warm. Why shouldn't they be? It was a wonderfully romantic nineteenth-century piece, with swelling strings, pounded drums, and plenty of trumpets. With a climax worthy of the movies. You can hear the music running into the arms of happiness.

Koussevitzky was a faithful and genuine supporter of the music of his own time, an almost reckless thing to be, especially if you were the conductor of a significant American orchestra, because patrons were customarily twenty-five years off the clock and, like the busy noses of the bees, went for nectar and its sweetness, not newness however savory. For further information on the numbskullish nature of audiences and the even greater tin eardrum of critics, try to remember my earlier lectures. [. . . . . .] *Das Lied von der Erde* may have opened the door for Bartók and Schoenberg—it took some pushing and shoving to hear who would get through first—but it was melancholy—a downer, do you say? [. . . ya? . . .] We did "Das Lied" two weeks ago. Remember? "The Song of the Earth." Maa . . . ler. He died of a sore throat. I find it interesting that Mahler, Bartók, and Schoenberg changed their religion, not quite the way we change clothes, but as the occasion dictated nevertheless. Something for you to file away. Surprise the mind on a cloudy day.

All right, class, we return to our sheep: who is—Koussevitzky—did I call him: commissioner? [. . . . . .] I call him the Commissioner because he suggested and funded compositions from contemporary composers: for instance he asked Maurice Ravel to orchestrate Mussorgsky's piano suite "Pictures at an Exhibition." Listeners have forgotten that it was originally scored for the piano. For most folks only the full orchestra version answers to the name. Ravel's version is a wonderful piece to test your loudspeakers with. Sorry. It is a good piece with which to test your speakers. [. . . um . . .] As colorful as Joseph's coat. [. . . um . . .] A few good musical jokes about Jews. Listeners have forgotten about them, too.

You have to drive these gentlemen—Mussorgsky—Ravel—Koussevitzky—into the same corral, get them used to the smell of one another. Koussevitzky, Ravel, Mussorgsky. Up hands! Come on, don't you remember the Great Gate? Cymbal crash! [. . . . . .] Palms aplenty? Well, several. We are blessed. *Mein Gott.*

The Commissioner badgered work from Ravel—a piano concerto, not just the aforementioned orchestration. He encouraged a couple of operas: Douglas Moore's *The Ballad of Baby Doe,* and Benjamin Britten's *Peter Grimes*; then squeezed from Copeland, let's see, Symphony no. 3. Next, what? [. . . um . . .] He gave Olivier Messiaen's T-S symphony a push into the light of day, as well as Bartók's *Concerto.* [. . . . . .] No, it doesn't mean what you gigglers think. [. . . . . .] TS to you, too. It stands for *Turangalîla-Symphonie.* I shall write the title on the board. It is not easily spelled. [. . . . . .] The news about Koussevitzky is not all positive. He led the Boston boys in one of the earlier recordings of Ravel's *Boléro.* [. . . . . .] I'm disappointed none of you groaned. Orchestras in those days were largely made up of scowling old men. Normally they didn't like to learn, rehearse, or play new pieces, but the *Concerto for Orchestra* was bait too appealing to refuse.

Words as always fail to convey the power and beauty of this composition. Even Bartók's own description doesn't approach that kind of success. I am quoting from the composer's program notes for the debut performance: "The general mood of the work represents, apart from the jesting second movement, a gradual transition from the sternness of the first movement and the lugubrious death-song of the third, to the life-assertion of the last one."

Jesting! Jousting, rather. You heard the bray—the hee-haw—the yawp—and then the fairgrounds music? pretending to be a rodent running down an alley. Now, just because the second movement is designated, by the composer, "a game of pairs," we mustn't confuse it with boarding Noah's ark—you know—bassoons two by two, oboes as twins, clarinets a pair, next two flutes, and, lest they be too overbearing and brutish, trumpets with mutes. Nor should we allow ourselves to be misled about the seriousness of these blurts. I was told that, while Bartók was composing the concerto, he heard a performance of Shostakovich's *Seventh Symphony* on the radio and laughed when one of its subjects announced itself. He said it sounded like a Viennese cabaret song. This theme was so vacant of any real energy or significance that Bartók promptly borrowed it to use for an interruption he might ridicule. Why would he do that? Hands. [. . . . . .] Hopeless. In the middle of a serious sermon, why would the preacher stick out his tongue? [. . . um . . .] Rather, my young friends, why would he stick out someone else's tongue?

What was happening around him when he wrote this work? Sorry—when he composed this work. [. . . . . .] Well, yes, he was ill. He was dying. [. . . . . .] Okay, he was also a pauper. But he had more important things on his mind. [. . . . . .] What? His family I suppose. [. . . . . .] Nothing more? [. . . . . .] The world was at war, sillies. Everywhere. It was a very large war, deserving the name of "World." It contained countless smaller ones, and the smaller ones were made of campaigns and battles, deadly encounters and single shootings, calamities on all fronts. But history can hold up for our inspection many different sorts of wars, and World War Two was made of nearly all of them: trade wars—tribal wars—civil wars—wars by peaceful means—wars of ideas—wars over oil—over opium—over living space—over access to the sea—whoopee, the war in the air—among feudal houses—raw raw siss-boom-bah—so many to choose from—holy wars—battles on ice floes between opposing ski patrols—by convoys under sub pack attacks—in the desert there might be a dry granular war fought between contesting tents, dump trucks, and tanks—or—one can always count on the perpetual war between social classes—such as—whom do you suppose? the Rich, the Well Off, the Sort Of, the So-So, and the Starving—or—the Smart, the Ordinary, and the Industriously Ignorant—or—the Reactionary and the Radical—not just the warmongers for war but those conflicts by pacifists who use war to reach peace—the many sorts of wars that old folks arrange, the middle-aged manage, and the young fight—oh, all of these, and sometimes simultaneously—not to neglect the wars of pigmentation: color against color, skin against skin, slant versus straight, the indigenous against immigrants, city slickers set at odds with village bumpkins, or in another formulation: factory workers taught to shake their fists at field hands (that's hammer at sickle)—ah, yes—the relevant formula, familiar to you, I'm sure, is that scissors cut paper, sprawl eats space—*Raum!*—then in simpler eras, wars of succession—that is, wars to restore some king to his john or kill some kid in his cradle—wars between tribes kept going out of habit—wars to keep captured countries and people you have previously caged, caged—wars in search of the right death, often requiring suicide corps and much costly practice—wars, it seems, just for the fun of it, wars about symbols, wars of words—*uns so weiter*—wars to sustain the manufacture of munitions—bombs, ships, planes, rifles, cannons, pistols, gases, rockets, mines—wars against scapegoats to disguise the inadequacies of some ruling party—a few more wars—always a few more, wars fought to shorten the suffering, unfairness, and boredom of life.

Bartók never carried a gun or felt the shame of defeat on the field; but you should remember that Béla von Bartók was a Hungarian whose birthplace had been cut from its country like a side of beef from its carcass, and, by its political butchers, given to Romania to devour in 1920. In protest, he dressed like a Hungarian, however that would be. He vowed to speak only his native tongue. Hungarian isn't easy for anybody, so if you know how to speak it, you tend to brag. He dropped his "von" like a third shoe. He wrote a symphonic tone poem about Kossuth, a popular political figure. Bartók's interest in local music, and eventually his loyalty to a generous variety of Balkan folk songs and dances (Hungarian, Romanian, Ukrainian, Slovak, even Bulgar) is demonstrated by the composer's lifelong effort to record, protect, and encourage the survival of native styles while integrating their contributions into the more prestigious and demanding international movements. [. . . . . .] I see you writing. Should I repeat that?

In the Great War . . . Surely . . . surely . . . you are acquainted with this conflict . . . ? [. . . . . .] May heaven help me to the door. [. . . um . . .] Oh yes, many of you, I see. Well, I shall not embarrass you by demanding a definition of "Axis." [. . . . . .] A significant part of that worldwide confrontation—"on sea, on land, and in the air"—was the struggle between Germany and Russia that took place on what was called the eastern front. Why east? [. . . um . . .] Because, on maps, Poland is depicted as east of France. [. . . . . .] When World War Two began, the Russians were profiting from the German invasion of Poland to scoop up a few hunks of the smaller eastern countries—Baltic and Balkan—for themselves. At the same time that this was going on, the capitalist countries (including Germany) were the Soviets' . . . that's Russia's . . . antagonists in a noncombative, or "cold" war, as well . . . it was called a cold war, not because it snowed throughout, but because there was no shooting . . . because the Russians were Communists . . . and we—especially the U.S.—were at words if not at swords against the Reds . . . Left-wingers are still called Reds . . . No, it is not a gang name. [. . . . . .] I hope this isn't too confusing for you. [. . . . . .] The fact is that through World War Two, the USSR was first an enemy . . . because, as I said, it was a Communist country . . . the Union of Soviet Socialist Republics . . . then it was an ally . . . because it was also fighting the Nazis . . . N A Z I s . . . and then an enemy again when the war ended because it was still Communist. I mention this—yes, the Germans were called National Socialists. Yes, they were capitalist and socialists. Yes, they were fascists, too. I am trying to explain that a friend, while remaining a friend, can be a foe, and as a foe, a greater foe than if it had never been a friend. You see? a dissonance heard in one place can be harmonious when heard in another. What would two mirrors, facing each other, see? The Soviet Union and the Third Reich. A theme and its inversion. "Monstrous" spelled "suortsnom." [. . . um . . .] Something like that.

A theme will meet its match and be momentarily banished from the flow, only to return later to sing in harmony with that early enemy as though nothing bad had ever happened between them. By reopposing, end it. If you wish a crude but commonly employed example, think of the "1814 Overture" of Tchaikovsky, played to death, so that it only appears in performance as a zombie. It is partly built upon a battle of anthems. Some idiot fires a cannon. Ah, hands at last. So good of you. 1812. [. . . um . . .] Yes. "La Marseillaise."

This is not a course in military history. Yet I do not digress. Music, too, has its necessary opposites, ripe peaches that relish their worms. Don't scrape your chair. I might mention Rimsky-Korsakov and Mussorgsky—in fact, I have—they represent nationalistic fervor, while pretty old Tchaikovsky suits up for the cosmopolitan high hat. Hah. I know a secret about him that you must hunt for. Nor can we ignore the snobbish claim of superiority made by the Bach-to-Beethoven Teutonic Club over the Polish-French connection established by Chopin and Liszt, or the pronounced lack of enthusiasm of the followers of Berlioz toward the person, work, and partisans of Wagner who persist in thinking that the *Ring* is more impressive than *Les Troyens.* All right—you should say at this point—but what about that fellow Liszt, wasn't he transcribing both Mozart and Wagner for the piano? [. . . . . .] Oh, Liszt needed to be a leader of every movement. He had to do well by all and sundry, even Bellini. These transcriptions were once ridiculed by critics but now they are widely appreciated and admired. [. . . . . .] This proves nothing, one way or the other. [. . . . . .] Liszt was handsomely paid in money, fame, and sexual favor. In all things the fellow was an accomplished performer: so affected when he entered the chamber, such a show-off as he sat before the keys, and what a virtuoso with his fingers. I've been told ladies fainted as a consequence of the close salon air, their cinched waists, and alleged emotion. Liszt was a womanizer who became religious just to see how it felt, I'd like to think, and to be on God's good side when he died, but even in childhood he voiced his desire to become a monk [. . . . . .] okay, a priest [. . . . . .]—both ridiculous—and, although during his life he sinned repeatedly, in his old age he demonstrated his devotion to the Catholic church, in the laudable sacrifice of his talent, by offering to its altar many sacred works. The pope who was Pius at the time made Liszt an abbey. There is nothing unusual about this combination. Members of the Sicilian mafia love their mothers, their murders, their boys' club, and their God. So Liszt can be both a programmer—ideal for bourgeois tastes—yet a darling of the avant guard. [. . . um . . .] Now I remember why we are here. Well, I am here at least. Liszt, a fellow Hungarian, was an enormous early influence on Bartók. The man traveled the piano, coast to coast, like a coach. Late Liszt, my young friends, anticipates almost everything including the whole-tone scale. [. . . . . .] Did you know one of his kids, Cosima, married Wagner? [. . . . . .] She was a notable bitch. Isn't that how you say it? Liszt made an enormous contribution to the very notation that composes a score, but I cannot take time for that here, or offer you juicy stories about his girlfriends though there is a shelfful, along with a lot of books.

Now listen to what he says—von Bartók, I mean—the words he uses: "The outcome of these studies was of decisive influence upon my work, because it freed me from the tyrannical rule of the major and minor keys." "Tyrannical rule" indeed. Blame it all on the diatonic scale. Worse than an electric fence. What was at stake? Freedom, first off. From an imaginary limit. From the tyrannical State of Music. [. . . . . .] Got that? Equality, second. For the composer, the instruments, the notes. "This new way of using the diatonic scale brought freedom from the rigid use of the major and minor keys, and eventually led to a new conception of the chromatic scale, every tone of which came to be considered of equal value and could be used freely and independently." I won't let anyone tell me that music isn't political: this is the dictatorship of democracy. Down with the subordinate clause.

You all know how the freedom sought by the French Revolution—revolutionaries take note—or was it carnage? revenge? was it bloodlust?—was usurped—was reversed by Napoléon's emperorship, and [. . . . . .] ah, you don't know, do you? [. . . . . .] Well, good for you, you have nothing to forget.

So now we have to cope with the smarty-pants atonalists—Schoenberg, Berg, and Webern—Schoenberg, Berg, and Webern—Schoenberg, Berg, and Webern—who opposed the very romanticism that energized them—Schoenberg, Berg, and Webern—it's only a scratch—to deal with their more specific dislike of Stravinsky's eclectic modernism, et cetera. Lastly, nearing our station, we observe how the music of the folk as espoused by Bartók and Kodály got handballed from wall after wall of indifference: by the romantic music of Mahler, the intellectual regimens of the Viennese crowd—Schoenberg, Berg, and Webern—the turncoat classicism of Stravinsky, and the clangorous pauses of Cage and his crew. [. . . . .] You may make notes but not pass them. This isn't kindergarten.

I could say simply that the *Concerto for Orchestra* is an appeal for peace, but that would make it sound simpleminded, and this piece is anything but. It is a mingling and clashing of competing kinds of music, the instruments that play them, and the totalitarian contexts within which large ensembles necessarily require their musicians to perform. A violin or cello concerto brags that, for a change, the rest of the world revolves around this one violin or cello and its simplest string. [. . . . . .] This is only true of the genre, of course, instances vary. [. . . . . .] So, in the *Concerto for Orchestra,* various instruments enjoy their moment in the sun; turn and turn about, they are allowed to lead; and an ideal community is, in this way, imagined; one in which the individual is free, has its own unique voice, yet chooses to act in the best interests of all others. [. . . . . .] The problem is: how to save Difference without making its members only frivolously different, like taking your tea in a glass instead of a cup.

The materials of a work of art, my dears, appear first as simple differences but then begin to migrate into oppositions and into pairs. For instance, the cleeks and buzzes of insects in the night, each with their own scratch on the face of darkness, sidle alongside the clarinet's happy candy like ants to a melt of chocolate—apparently an enemy of our pleasure. No matter how pure a note is, when singly sounded, we realize its man-made character and its preordained place in that confectional box, the musical scale; whereas we trace nighttime's clatter back to the cricket, who is broadcasting its lust, first in one direction, then in another, with sharp chirps like the crepitations the locust makes by bowing its legs vigorously back and forth upon steadied wings to signal its presence and advertise its need. [. . . . . .] The action is called *crepitating.* I shall inscribe it. [. . . . . .] These little wails of music, or bits of ragged scrape, are seeking a companion, a connection, even if only momentary, but always so they may give more sense to their sounds and make more of meaning's music. Bartók composed many such dark concerts; arrangements of notes for a time as lonely as we fancy we are when we wake suddenly to find only "middle" occupies the night.

Now cast your eyes upon the palette that modern circumstances have placed before the composer, all pertaining to the nature of any singled-out sound or insect's whir. There is the instrument that is its source, as the cricket's is of its, and any messages that may be traced to it, for instance, the call of a bullfrog or the whistle given girls; there is the placement of the instrument in the pit, on the platform of the concert hall, or for solo or ensemble performance in a historic chamber; there is the choice of size and shape the musician must give his note (fat or thin, loud or soft, crisp or slurred) and the qualities of sound that can be expected from each of a hundred sorts of instrument; moreover, to be accounted for, there are the relations this note has with other notes (those that precede, those that follow, those that suffer or enjoy simultaneous existence); consequently the sounds collected in polychords, clusters, skeins, runs, motifs, themes, as well as all the other groups of notes that are treated as an entity—clouds of notes, cascades, fistfuls, snivels of notes—and all those with whom it shares rhythmic relations; repeated notes, notes that have been given a dominant position, those who satisfy subordinate roles, compositions in keys and styles and size, that have historical associations, reflect common customs, or reveal well-known intentions. Cast eyes and cry: too many and too much; take away this hive of opportunity, this surfeit of choice, and let us retire to simpler times when such a plethora was not recognized, our eardrums were not African, and our serious intentions were pious.

The next time you enjoy—say—a kiss, think of it for a moment as a moist slur of notes, and the experience showing up in your consciousness, as well as that of your companion, when your lips touch, is a chord of a chorus in a world of cacophony. All that laughter? That bad? I had to say "kiss" to wake you. How about a spoon in hot soup? Opposed palms coming together in a clap. Anyway, when Béla Bartók composed his celebrated concerto he was taking a musical world, like the warring one outside his studio, in all its prolixity, conflict, and chaos, and trying to resolve those factions in a triumphant chorus for a triumphant close.

Listen to that. We have arrived at our station. The noon bell rings across the quad. You may scuffle out. Our time is up.

43

I haven't seen Mother. I haven't seen her anywhere—Joey said not quite aloud because he no longer wanted to hear his voice—her face must be hidden in her flowers; but I shall have to see her soon enough, and suffer her shock, and the scorn in her speech: anger before despair. He felt he had a cork in his throat. A sweat, this early in the day, that wet his underarms, served to oil his apprehension.

There were several scenarios that would fit this faculty meeting, and he had endured them all. Why bother with this one, played out in the provinces? It ought to close before opening, since all its conclusions were foregone. Joey had no curiosity about which version would most match the performance the ticket holder had purchased.

Joseph walked slower than slowly; you might say he waded up the street toward a pickup truck that always seemed to be parked in the shade of a tall fir tree, night and day, all seasons the same. It reminded him of the Bumbler; how it had served him, as poor at the wheel as he was; and how steadfastly this example sat in front of its house, ready to run, but never asked. Lucky wheels that no one wanted turned.

The Bumbler, exercising its associative powers, charmed him by returning Miss Spiky, her mullet, and her Billy Bear to his consciousness. He heard her voice—he always heard the singers, it seemed, since Mr. Hirk introduced him to them—she who was one of the good witches of Urichstown, and he fondly remembered—he always heard the high notes, it seemed like, since Mr. Hirk played them on his machine—her brazenly advertised attachment to a child's toy. Hazel Hawkins—that was she. Maybe, just maybe, Billy Bear was a substitute for a child she had lost. He hadn't thought of that. But should have. Funny, he felt genuine with her, precisely because she was also putting on a show. To his surprise, he laughed, then snatched it back, as if he'd let fall a naughty remark. How much astonishment could this hour entertain?

It must happen every day: men, women, boys being taken between officers to a judge; or men, women, soldiers, sent to their death, cameras catching them now that the police had, or victims of gunfire spewing from a speeding car, or simply the shower curtain that's drawn upon a rain of shame. He now knew what fear was: strings of feeling tied into a numbing knot.

Professor Skizzen labored past a piece of broken curb that always marked, for him, a point halfway to or from his classroom, night and day, all seasons the same; except that when he returned, on the other side of the street, it was a cluster of telephone poles weathered to a pale gray that gave his position away. The clump had a slight lean. The way they might have grown in their original woods. The professor felt he had worn this path and won its naming, now that it had become the last half mile of his academic life, and was otherwise unpleasant only in the worst snows and a few winds. A little sign might be enough: Fake's Walk. The real difficulty was that after his arraignment he would still be alive. To have your name on something beside a shop, you had to be rich and probably dead. And even death would not prevent people such as President Palfrey from his calamities: the short path between Languages and the Science Building was called Snow Way.

Why should this crumble of concrete, returning itself to pebble-speckled sand, be an emblem for his colleagues at the college and always bring them to mind? What would they think? You guys remind me of a broken curb. True, run over and abused, dust to dust was that situation's ultimate design. Joey's youth, his energy, his need to succeed, had been a weight upon their collective weakness. For them, the department was serene if not strong because it was never tried or tested.

A few steps beyond Joseph, there were familiar views that never seemed to matter much: a postbox, faded to a sickly green, where he occasionally dropped a missive (that would be Miss Moss's station); followed by a forsythia bush that leaned out over the sidewalk with no justification but its early blooms, yellower than a banana then, but always badly pruned; a pair of bay windows, like great gray-curtained eyes, came next; however, no one seemed to be alive inside, no one seemed to be in the yard, raking the leaves or otherwise meeting the seasons—the house of the No Ones, he thought of them—and no one came to the door on Halloween; then came the Leffingwell House whose huge columns held up a porch roof no bigger than a party hat, yet whose cumbersome façade actually seemed welcoming. This mansion was featured, despite an outrageous collision of styles, on those occasional tours of painted glass the ladies of the Garden Club organized, not only for the many religious motifs to be seen in its windows, but also because of the dwelling's exceptional size. Not last, but for continuous company, there was always the hush of the street beneath pair after pair of spanning elms. Skizzen inspected their diseased boughs with genuine sadness, and tried to accept the death of which their droop was a sign.

Professor Skizzen, good day to you, sir. The greeting sprang on him from ambush like a movie Indian. Didn't mean to startle you, sir, just getting some air myself. It's going to be a beautiful morning, I can tell. Musn't waste it, eh? Off to work, are you? That case is full of musical knowledge, I imagine. Will it be lighter on the way home? I dare say it will. Skizzen got turned round. Ah, there, Mr. Leffingwell, isn't it? You surprised me. Well, it's my home we are facing. Leffingwell's arm swept into a wave. I see you pass nearly every day. As regular as the post. Except Sundays, Skizzen said, desperately. He hardly recognized this man who seemed to know him well enough for casual jollity. Oh, I match your favor. I often go by your house on the way to town. Good for my health, you know. I'm sure the walk to school is good for yours. That corner garden gives every passerby a lovely sight, it is so open on that lot, not hidden away, and well tended, a credit to our little community. I imagine it's your wife's work. My mother's, yes, Skizzen said as matter-of-factly as he dared. Be damned to you, he thought.

Ah . . . You are looking reasonably hearty, a bit pale today maybe. Full of vim and vinegar, I am, on such a morning. Thanks to God. I love it crisp as the crust of good bread, don't you? I always ate my crusts, Skizzen, a beaten man, managed. Good boy, Mr. Leffingwell replied, good boy. Skizzen stood as if tranced, hearing her voice; recalling how thoroughly he did enjoy that voice once, until her shriek scared him with its accusation. How he liked their amiable banter among the books, the deep pleasure they both took in the slightest exchanges, the quiet that surrounded their conviviality, until their giggles rose like bubbles in a glass.

I'm glad to see you bring some culture to the college, Mr. Leffingwell said, as if to encourage Skizzen's efforts. I've thought, for some years, that it was neglecting the arts, don't you know, for those courses in fashionable social issues. Not enough emphasis on basics—religion, music, the higher things—these kids need some polish before their insertion into civilization, I'm sure you agree. Teach 'em how to play an instrument. Read a map. Understand geography. Basics. I hear they've been running a distillery up there. It's those fraternities. Evil influence. If we teach geography, Professor Skizzen said, it's news to me.

Maybelle Leonard's husband . . . he does . . . teach geography. Part-time, I think. A rather large man. Of overflowing disposition. You would have seen him had you visited his furniture store. He sits there and rocks to prove how reliable the recliners are. Doesn't get up much, even for valued customers. But that's neither here nor there. It's somewhere, though, I suppose, Skizzen offered. I remember geography class. The Tigris and Euphrates Rivers. Right? Third grade, I think. Made an impression. We had to outline their course. The rivers, I mean. Locate Eden or something equally sacred God set down between them like an oasis. Not much doing there these days, I guess. Whatever God did. Skizzen's doom looked suddenly better to him. He took a step toward the school. I sell shoes, Leffingwell blurted. I don't think you've ever visited my shop. It used to be Schafley's Styles. I think I hid there from someone I didn't want to run into on the street, Skizzen said with a small smile of satisfaction. I'm enforcing improvements, Leffingwell said, continuing on his own train. Woodbine is ready for some daring designs, don't you think? Schafley was a bit of a 'fraidy cat. Well, I won't hold you up any longer. You must have a class to teach. Play marches for the kids, why don't you. Ha. They're no-nonsense. Brisk. Instills rigor in the mind and gives a thump to the boot.

Skizzen would soon see the tops of the taller buildings. He took time to flick some lint from his coat. He brushed a shoulder. He brushed another a bit more fiercely. It was as if he had never seen the coat, its shoulder, its collar, before. Not like a friend lost sight of, but familiar beyond recognition. So he sighed. It allowed him to cease flicking. They were just fixtures, too, these dear reassuring associates of habit and silence, who tracked his steps for him, and were normally smartly met like that robin to which he spoke kindly, the way he would to a comrade, or that neighbor whose name after years he still didn't know but whose nightshirt was as familiar as the mail it appeared for, as he made his progress up this small-town hill where nothing changed much—night and day, all seasons the same—except the color of the leaves and the state of the lawns; past the fronts of houses whose drapes were always drawn as if darkness made every interior more visible; and past porches where the daily paper usually came to rest or the gutter where one issue lodged after an errant toss, to dry in the sun then sog in the rain before drying in the sun again; or the persistent shadow of a holly tree, its red seed quarreled over by the birds, that now he addressed quite crossly as if the tree were she: no need to follow me anymore, to see if I'll be safe, remember, Mother, when you first walked me to school in grade school days—oh yes, it was another street—yes, ma'am—below High, downhill, on the other side of town, where we had a cottage cut into small rooms like a quartered orange. The things that stayed were things that didn't matter except they stayed, night and day, all seasons the same, and were peaceful to a fault and boded no ill but thought well enough of themselves to repeat their presences. Right now, Joey disliked everything that asserted its existence. He longed for only those pieces of the world's furniture that weren't flattered by attention or fearful of attack, just were, without guilt or accusation; that was what he wanted now; how he felt, seeming to slow his walk, yet increasing its speed. No need to tag along, Mom, my God, we're almost there.

At least I have no father who will blame me. Buck up. He would approve me anyway, for acting bravely in support of his fears. Put yourself in Carfagno's place, my boy, he'd say . . . on the day he went to the village doctor, whom you and Mort maintained was either a man half taught by a Guernsey, or a Guernsey half taught by a man, to be told he was dying of cerebral tumors. Remember what you said to yourself, and almost said to others: that they had to be the first ideas his head had held; remember that unkindness, and the pain of the doctor's announcement, and how we all tried to buck him up by putting the doctor down: Oh get another opinion, go to someone in Columbus, what does a Woodbine doctor know? It is just a stubborn headache. Remember how much worse that was for him than anything that can happen to you today, even if you think you'd rather die, because I know you wouldn't rather die. You would rather get off scot-free.

Now to cross the quad. Not too slow. Not too fast. Easy as whistling. But not whistling. Nice little breeze. It blew Joey to a halt. Joseph surveyed the scene. Professor Skizzen remembered to swing his briefcase slightly next his knee. One of them, they didn't know which, shoved off. When he first stood at the edge of the green, its diagonal walk was clear and clean; however, now there were three, approaching. Two students were already sitting in the grass. Where was the usual dew? Good morning, Professor. See: he was recognized; he was greeted; he was awarded a wide smile. He belonged. He was accepted. Now he was about to lose everything but recognition. He would become a figure of story if not of song.

Skizzen could still pretend to forget the order he had been given by the High Command. Morning, spoke the person passing. This "morning" was perfunctory and a bit muffled. He could be anybody to be greeted with "morning." In that spirit he would receive and return the customary acknowledgment. Friendly. But briefly friendly, the length of a flicker. He could still pretend to forget the order he had been given. Joey was all for forgetting. Joseph inclined in that direction. Professor Skizzen, however, insisted on pressing on. Hi, Professor, fine morning isn't it? What she offered was more like a grin. Her walk was almost a skip. She was gaining on the others and would probably pass them before the quad was crossed. Did that matter? Not a whit. That's why it was important.

Admin. The dean's domain. Skizzen pushed his way in. Wait a minute.

Wasn't Leffingwell the fellow who bought the High Note a while back? Started stocking it with heavy metal? Schafley, too? And living now in that huge house only steps away, having purchased Skizzen's past, keeping it close, and indisposed in an unattended upper room. Ah, how he would love to get rid of it all, and go to the conference table with a case of amnesia's euphoria. If you say so sir, I don't remember. I only remember that my sister showed me how to tie my shoes. Okay, I also remember I asked her twice to show me the inside of her sweater, but she refused to do so, I wasn't a howling crowd nor did I have some senior's inquisitive fingers. She is not a generous person, my sister. I remember that much.

The hall to the left, just before the office of the admin is the conference table I shall probably have to sit at. Everyone will sit around. The prisoner will be brought before. A protective smear of glass will cloud the grain. A thin strip of duct tape will no doubt be still holding together a crack sustained quite long ago by Professors Emphasis and Anger. A voice said: Please come in. Joey wasn't ready yet. Joseph realized that his figure could be seen through the door's tortured window. Professor

Skizzen recognized the voice. A bit stiff, it nevertheless flew through the transom. It was Palfrey's all right, but not limp or liquid as it usually was. It was in a cast as if protecting something broken.

44

Well now, is everybody here? Dean Funk?

My God, Skizzen thought. He is calling the roll.

Professor Carson?

Skizzen had entered the room with a face as frozen as custard, which meant that at any moment his nose might decide to slide toward his chin. The room was somber because the window blinds were half drawn, and shadowy because light was leaking in above the shade rolls.

Miss Hazlet.

Here. Her voice was bright and slightly metallic, as though it had been made by machine. She would be in bliss right now. She never did order that two-volume life of Berlioz. Or the Liszt *Letters* either.

Professor Rinse? Palfrey looked over the top of his glasses at Rinse who faced him across the table. Mort drew a tiny smile, swiftly erased it.

Professor Skizzen?

Skizzen congratulated himself on managing an almost imperceptible nod. However Palfrey didn't look in his direction, a bad sign. Skizzen now saw that in front of all the others, who had arrived here before him (another bad sign), stood a Styrofoam cup, a small pad, and a pencil. Skizzen had not been offered either cup or pad or shorty-sized pencil (a bad sign). These utensils all stayed untouched in their place. A bad sign. He entwined his fingers.

And not least, Professor Smullion.

Why "and not least" for him? Had Smullion published another *Biology for Babies* book?

[. . . . .] I thereby declare this meeting of the Whittlebauer Ethics

Committee to be in session. Palfrey had a manila folder that he now opened. Miss Hazlet, would you do the committee the favor of keeping its notes?

I shall be happy to, Miss Hazlet responded, but she gave her paper tablet a skeptical look.

Well you can record that our members are all present and prompt. Miss Hazlet wore a blouse covered with small green (leaping, were they?) leaflike abstractions. Her fingers scrambled for the pencil and the pad.

President Palfrey let his eyes rove, assuming the domination of the room. When this committee meets, he said, it is always a most serious occasion, since, here at Whittlebauer, ethical problems rarely arise. We have our by-laws for most issues firmly in place so that normally we have but to consult them. [. . . . . .] We have, however, in my tenure here, and as well as my memory serves, never had a case like this one, and that is something we can be grateful for and proud of. When we hire new faculty our procedures are thorough and severe. Each of you, at some point in the past, has undergone them.

What about . . . Professor Skizzen thought, while watching Palfrey like a mouse a hawk. He once more observed that Miss Hazlet had a blouse bearing leaflike figures (on the run?). This wasn't tracking Palfrey as a mouse does a hawk. Run, that's what a mouse would do. Find a slice of light beneath a door and vanish with the light when the light fled.

It seems, however, that, concerning the situation before us, there has been a slipup, an instance in which we, needing help in an area, failed to meet our standards of scrutiny and care. Now this imbroglio is the result.

"Kit" Carson cleared his throat as if he were preparing to speak, but, of course, he wasn't.

We can take our mistake to heart and learn. That's what the college is for, isn't it? Palfrey laughed rather openly, not, as was his custom, with one hand held girlishly in front of his face. We thought we had found what seemed to be a simple, very handy, solution. Instead we let our standards slip. So now we must decide what to do.

Smullion looked perplexed. So he wasn't in on it. Smullion had a suspiciously fancy CV, himself.

Dean Funk opened a dossier. The color for dossiers was green. Where had that file folder come from? He hadn't had it a moment ago. The color was an exact match for those things on Hazlet's blouse. Now there were two folders on the table. Not a good sign. [. . . . . .] The issue, in brief, is this: we hired to teach our students a man who provided us with an educational history that has proved false. We have it from Ames that no such person ever received any degrees from Iowa State let alone a doctorate. He was never even enrolled.

Good heavens, Skizzen thought, what does this have to do with him? Iowa State? Who was Ames? A secret informer? Or a city of some sort?

We felt we needed to offer geography. Kit Carson had intervened. We felt that without geography our seniors should not be released into the world. Fast trains, the superhighway, the airplane, have ruined geography. My students, Carson said, wouldn't know where Ames was. For them, distance is minutes in the car or hours on the plane. Where is Belgrade, where is Vienna, where is Ames? They are next to their airport—two, six, seven hours from here.

Ah, now we are getting round to it. Vienna. Sneaky. Skizzen didn't have a cup. Hazlet had picked hers up, but all of the cups were empty. Empty. What in the world?

So for them, the world is flat—car, plane, train, flat—Smullion said, not round, but flat, like the map says in the glove compartment.

We used to have a good softball team, but intramural play is too costly. We were supposed to play Rochester. As if it were another frat house, you know, next door. Mort's pencil had been pressed, point first, through the side of his Styrofoam. Now he slowly removed it.

Had he a cup, he would have begun to crimp its rim. But no cup had been set for Skizzen. Not a good sign.

"Geography" doesn't mean geography anymore, Carson said. It's all about the cultural atmosphere of a place—who it is, not where. Its classes used to teach climate; they used to teach soil; they figured addresses—lat. & long.—for entire countries, on a ball made for soccer. Now the geographer doesn't much care where rivers go or even what sort of boat sails on them. A barge of coal, salt, or ore. It cares, maybe, about how and when our rivers turned into canals, how they were made to behave—commit no floods in future. Oh, and they are interested in the people or organizations that profited from the traffic or who grew money from the former marsh that now sports corn.

Smullion wondered whether the committee was supposed to be deciding what geography ought to be.

I can tell you: it's all about the anthropology of places, not the place of a place; not raindrop amounts but the numbers of men those drops wet. Once "location, location" referred to sunlight and water, elevation and soil, now it means subways, saloons, and schools. A verdant valley has no place until we turn it into a colony. What counts: whose colony is it, who lives there, how many miles of suburb can it boast?

So Carson, the way he was carrying on, must have been appointed to that hiring committee, Skizzen thought. But what was this all about? Flood control? That wouldn't be a problem for Woodbine, Urichstown maybe. Ah . . . that's it . . . that far back . . .

Clearly, President Palfrey said, we have someone in Professor Carson who could do the job, but he has kept his light buried beneath the basket. The president's tone suggested that it was a little late for the history department to step in. But what happens now, when we have a fraud in the stirrups . . . I should say a fake in the firehouse . . . a cheat in the chapel . . . that's it, a cheat in the chapel.

What did he do, exactly? Brave Mort asked this question.

He misrepresented his qualifications. Wildly.

Who?

Hursthouse, of course. Who else does geography?

Do we do geography?

Part-time.

Why would he want to teach geography part-time?

To wear the honorable colors of the school.

You joke. What a courageous fellow Mort was, Professor Skizzen decided.

Not for a moment. It is an honor, I say, to teach here. Don't you think it is an honor?

He owns the furniture store.

That's somebody named Leonard.

Hursthouse bought him out.

The fat guy?

Why would we hire someone so heavy he has to have help getting around?

We are an equal opportunity employer.

You are thinking about the shoe store.

Part-time is hardly opportunity.

What about the shoe store?

How long has he been on the mound?

What?

Pitch—teaching. When did he start?

Three years ago. Three years of shame. On us.

All we can do is fire him.

That damned newspaper will love this.

All the Styrofoam cups had been damaged beyond use by this time, Skizzen noticed. He'd never have one of his own. You could draw on the side with your fingernail. His blood was slowly returning to him. What a dastardly deed, he said amid the hubbub. Skizzen trusted no one, and nothing is what he should have said.

We look bad, whatever we do.

Wait a minute. The term isn't over yet. How many are enrolled?

Four. The dean seemed flustered.

Four? Is that all? Four? Palfrey shook his wattles. I was told the course would draw dozens.

It did a bit better at the beginning.

In that case, just wait until the semester ends and tell him you have to close down the class because of too few funds, Miss Hazlet said. She seemed quite sure of herself. He won't know he's been found out; he's not likely to complain; nothing scandalous has occurred; no breach of our hiring rules has been broken; the fat caucus can't complain. A lack of students . . . a lack of students is a legitimate excuse. Even a tenured person can be got rid of without fuss if you eliminate their subject. And there won't be any story.

I don't know, Joey heard himself saying, despite his silent vow. I think we should throw the book at him, set an example, use this bad situation to reaffirm our principles, and advertise them. This guy took advantage of our goodwill—society's, too. Who knows what guff he has been stuffing in the students' ears. He probably doesn't know where Ames is.

Well, there is something in what you say . . . Palfrey paused. [. . . . . .]

Whittlebauer exposes a mountebank. That doesn't make for an embarrassing story.

It's still pretty hard to explain.

It might hurt his furniture business.

I was hoping he would be of assistance with our town/gown relations. And there are members of our board who thought we ought to have geography. Palfry released an unhealthy sigh.

What kind of documents did this man profess to have? It might be worthwhile taking a look at his application.

Skizzen believed that Smullion knew exactly what he was suggesting.

No need, no time, for that. It was, I assure you, in apple-pie order. Palfrey put his palm down on the papers before him. His entire weight assisted in the gesture. It fairly flattened his cup.

Who cares about his furniture business? Would you want to buy a sofa from a guy who pretended to have approval from . . . what was it? . . . Ames? There Skizzen was, participating again, inviting scrutiny. He tried to chastise himself but even the spears of fear that struck him intermittently did the trick. Like . . . like Saint . . . Saint Sebastian . . . A vow of silence, made silently, is not worth a librarian's psst. Could this be the trial of someone else?

President Palfrey, Hazel Hazlet said, addressing the president directly, in forming this present committee, its balance must have slipped your mind. There are two people from music. Isn't that a bit many for such a small group—if they are to represent the entire faculty I mean.

I formed the committee, Dean Funk said with some asperity. I deemed it a good one. After all, I appointed you to it, and you aren't even a member of the faculty.

I might only say, Professor Smullion said, that any order an apple pie has, is not likely to be found in nature.

I chose the image because it is American. Do you, sir, have something against that? The president pushed his little pad and little pencil into the center of the table, pocketed the sorry remains of his cup, and rose. I have now been properly advised by the Ethics Committee, and I shall proceed as it has recommended.

No one asked what that was.

The president shouldered his way from the room, followed by the dean who, at this moment, did not appear to have any.

Mort said to Skizz: Boy, do I feel foolish. I was afraid I was going to be in the dock for something I did with one of our secs. A transgression just coming to light, a kind of bolt from the past. Pretty dumb, I guess.

That's what happens when you carry around a guilty conscience. Even without reason, mind you.

Kit Carson said, to no one in particular: I thought Palfrey was going to carve me up. I was on the committee who let this guy perform his sleight of hand. He used his size like a chef with bacon. Mine was the only no vote. There was pressure on Palfrey from someone—maybe on the board or a rich alumnus—to hire this tub. Well, that's over. What is a no vote worth around here?

Hazel sat inside her blouse. Her leaves were of the stillness one sees before storms.

Smullion was from science. He merely smiled.

And Skizzen made every elation wait till, out on the quad, he let his relief expire the way a champagne fizzes some delighted skips ahead of its wine.

45

Joey's joy swept him up, bore him home, returned him to the nursery . . . the nursery he might have longed to have if he'd ever had one . . . A line that lived in the nursery—"Here we go round the mulberry bush"—took up an orbit about his thoughts as tunes do, penning them in the way he wanted his students to corral names for memory purposes. Mussorgsky! Ravel! Koussevitzky! But Joey had had his struggle with an obsessive sentence, and he didn't want another tussle. He determined to play a few good old stompers, and that way drive the nonsensical strain out of hearing. He rushed about the house hunting for the place he had put *Songs That Never Grow Old* so he could claim the area as his territory, the way space was staked when he and Miriam, awed by the vast emptiness of the house, began playing the territorial game. He found the book resting tableside a single bed in what must have been a servant's quarter. Then he thought: would a farmer, retiring from the fields to a tiny town, have servants? Weren't they an urban vice? In any case, why had he wanted to mark this spot? What did former occupants store up here? If this was to be a gold claim, it looked a washout. When he gave its back a negligent push, an awkward rocker, which had come with the house, squeaked like a frightened mouse. Ah-ha. Miriam was contesting him. He saw, on a windowsill, utterly out of place, an empty clay pot sitting in sundust. "The further into the self I go, the less and less of the self I know." What was that from?

"Never grow too old to dream . . ." Joey seldom sang, but his voice sounded loud and harsh in this unpleasant room. There were no panels of animal-covered paper on the walls—leaping eagles or soaring deer—no sheep, chalets, no interlacing ivy, to entice anyone to hum an old favorite or prance to a frolicsome "here-we-go" romparound. He would remove his book and cede the territory. The dining room with its many wide windows was the real nursery in the house, and there Miriam tolerated ogling only if it was directed at the plants. Large cookie-deep trays of moist peat covered in Cling-Along crowded up against the windowpanes and soon made their own atmosphere, droplets clinging to the inside of the wrap the way water is drawn to plastic. At first the soil refused to stir. He could never catch a thrusting spear. One morning, the seedlings would suddenly appear, thin-stemmed, tiny, pale green against the dark dirt, a nub of leaf beginning, imperceptibly, to unfold. His fingers were too fat to work the rows. Miriam would warn him every time that these seeds had been scattered, not planted in lines; which left each barren patch still a possibility or an empty chamber. Chance was Lord. Why was that spot unwelcoming, Joey would ask. Wait and see . . . delicately . . . it may come . . . wait and see. Maybe a blade will be drawn. Who knows about those fickle primula . . . ? A few more pushes, as the nurses always say, and perhaps we can persuade a nasturtium stem to show. But don't play lullabies for these babies. They get no sleep. They have to come up for air. They have to leave their sheath. For them this dirt is deep.

As he raised the book toward eyes that now needed a little help, it came open upon a piano score for "Good-Night, Ladies." From that opening a scrap of paper slid its yellowing self onto the tight coverlet. Upon this single leaf was carefully inked what appeared to be a poem. Joey felt an immediate pang of recognition. He immediately denied it. He had not written these verses, nor, out of embarrassment or shyness, stuffed them away in this harmless old compendium . . . had he? He had never rested his eyes upon such a neat and centered sheet. Of course, in the past, he had picked about in this ancient volume like a hungry bird, without care or method, only curiosity and need. Then he wanted to know where Miss Gwynne Withers's recital choices were. The book classified its contents for easier use under headings like HOME SONGS, LOVE SONGS, HYMNS AND SACRED SONGS. "Good-Night, Ladies" was called a College Song. Which meant it went with beer. On the folded paper, already turning color at the crease, there was a college song indeed, to be sung to the tune of "This is the way we wash our clothes . . ." It was titled "The Faculty Meeting."

Admittedly, something about the paper was familiar. But the lines were too orderly for Skizzen unless he was copying a final draft onto a clean sheet. The paper was a bit brittle. Cheap. He did borrow the school's stock. But only occasionally. The Major had warned him how readers left all sorts of things between the pages of their books. She said: Shake them. Hold them upside down and shake. A toothpick may fall out. This book, though, had an already shaken spine. Had someone hid a message or simply marked a place with whatever was handy?

How totally appropriate to this blissful moment its title was, Joey thought, still breathing heavily from his search, and from his hurry home. My God, he still had his position, his house, his good name and station. At least, Professor Joseph Skizzen did. Just as it had seemed about to be taken from him, and Miriam's garden wrenched from her while she held it to her breast like a grandchild. How cruel that would have been on top of everything else: a loss of face, of future, of income, then of one's beautiful creation. O but he had pulled it off. Old fat Hursthorse may have been caught and possibly hung out to dry, who knew what Palfrey had in mind; but he, Professor Joey Joseph Skizzen, the pianist, composer, scholar, teacher, had prevailed. O now he would stride the length of his classroom like the head of a marching band, and he would teach these kids a musical thing or two. He might let on about his true thoughts, as well, if he could get clear what they were, he'd been so long in his roles, his postures in the world.

He'd have to keep his guard up, maintain the caution appropriate to an animal in the wild, no doubt about that, but every moment he lived now he cemented his presence to this agreeable place: he fastened his figure to an airmail stamp. What did these lines say?

"This is the way . . ."

He didn't want collegiate rowdy, he wanted home sweet home; he wanted drink to me only with thine eyes; he wanted red sails in the sunset, which wasn't in the book. He wanted no hymns either though the book was full of them. God was always getting the applause. A show of hands for Joey the music professor! Then something odd occurred to him: the makeup of that committee was strange. Where, in an ethics investigation, was the parson, the Sunday sawyer who hung on Palfrey's every non sequitur, a yea verily man if ever there was one? He'd appoint no lawyer, Palfrey wouldn't want to take a chance on someone in town. Those people blabbed as regularly as the chapel's bells. Joey began to dance, something he called "twist that torso." Or: the President Palfrey waltz.

This is the way . . . this is the way we way we . . . flop our mops . . . blow our tops . . . learn the ropes . . . tell old jokes . . .

Miss Moss warned him not to read what he had found. The Major urged him on. Go ahead. I dare you. But it must be out loud. Miss Spiky laughed at him but her bear turned his head away in shame. Why in the world . . . all that love for a tubby little bear . . . why? He had not needed to give up his seat on the bus. There were plenty of seats. She—Hazel—had chosen to sit beside him . . . all of her—heavy arms and heavy hips. The road was slowly filling with snow.

How totally appropriate to this blissful moment was the labored screed he held off mouthing as though it were the last chocolate in the box. So what if one of him had done it. Bless this blissful moment, O hurrah for his team. Perhaps he could now enlarge upon his Viennese years—oh carefully, oh cautiously, memorizing, scrutinizing, taking notes; and perhaps he should let his hair grow, get a new cap. Miriam didn't care for clothes anymore, just equipment: knee pads, trowels, a little bench to carry about and kneel on. To pray to her god the garden. Saved through her son's sacrifices. Made possible, she would have to admit, by his gift of seeds and security: this house she now disdained and ignored, it was its land she loved and labored in. Miriam filled no rooms with light, sweet air, or vases filled with blooms. After they had gotten their starts, most of her plants grew up every year in the garden, giving their color to each passerby. Flowers were meant to live and die where their roots did, Miriam repeatedly claimed. Like them, she was meant to remain in Austria at her family farm. Beneath her skirt she hid something called "roots." "This is the way we wash our clothes . . ." soften blows . . . count our toes . . .

Our house rises from this ground too, shouldn't it be allowed to flower? Joseph could hear her laugh at "our."

He scarcely remembered his return down that familiar path from the college, he flew along so fast, his limbs elastic. How many knew the satisfaction that occupies the soul when the labors of a lifetime—yes, it was true, labors of a lifetime—have been justified. His worries were never needless, and even after this terrible threat has been removed, and its terrible scare survived, he must tread cautiously down a trail of traps; nevertheless, he felt ensconced, glued in place, a piece upon the board that refuses to be moved, though knights die beside it.

The authorities had never caught his father either. His father had received an unexpected benevolence after several years of trial and suffering, just as Joey had now gone scot-free in following his father's lead. "Scot-free." Why does one say "scot-free"? What was this poem doing here? Perhaps, like Schubert, he would set it to music, over and over again. The same song. Only faster and faster. This is the way we cheat at play . . . he felt an anger that was normally foreign to him, and he read aloud, as if in his attic, as if he knew the words that were coming. How did that academic bunch, as though hidden in dark gowns, dare to inflict their ignorance upon him, their incompetence, their hypocrisies . . . employ travesty after travesty . . . because that meeting was a comedy . . . it had worried him so . . . a joke . . . with its situation, its load, its cock and snapper too.

The Faculty Meeting

This is the way we smirk and sigh, lurk and spy, favor buy,
    this is the way we smile and lie
    to prepare for the faculty meeting.

This is the way we bluff our way, fluff our way, gruff our way,
    this is the way we puff and bray
    throughout the faculty meeting.

This is the way we cheat and bleat, bow and scrape, preen and prate,
this is the way we obfuscate
during the faculty meeting.

This is the way we wash our hands, beat our bands, call our clans,
this is the way we hatch our plans,
at the faculty meeting.

This is the way we tip our hat, smell a rat, bell the cat,
this is the way we take a nap,
in the midst of the faculty meeting.

This is the way we clear our throats, burn our boats, turn our coats,
this is the way we change our votes,
in the faculty meeting.

This is the way we hatch our plots, cast our lots, pick our spots,
this is the way we get our gots
by steering the faculty meeting.

This is the way we kiss an ass, lick a dick, turn a trick,
this is why we get quite sick
to learn what the dean is scheming.

So this is the way we'll buck the trends, fake amends, forget our ends,
this is the way we'll fuck our friends
by the end of the faculty meeting.

This is how our tenure concludes, in pissy moods and platitudes,
a career of complaint and attitudes
in the course of the faculty's meetings.

This is the way retirement starts, with a chorus of jeers, and a volley of farts.
They're the true heart of academy sorts,
who depart the faculty meeting.

This is the way to the grave we chose, the eyes we close, the nose we lose,
this is how each faculty goes,
when the worms attend our meeting.

Yes, Skizzen thought, my sentiments exactly. I cannot but agree. However there were a few words in among the rest like bugs waiting for a bite, that wouldn't suit Schubert's style. They certainly didn't suit Joey either, but he wondered sometimes about his own blandness, reticence even, in a world of obscenities and curses. He refused to join them, but he had to admit that from time to time a loud "fuck you" might be just the thing. When he first encountered that overused word it had been splashed in red on a shattered wall. He still associated bad language with London. Miriam said she didn't give a damn where they put such sentiments so long as they weren't in German. For her, they had no weight as words in a foreign tongue.

How would he dare approach her with his plate of joy, so he could share his happiness with her without his information? Perhaps they could celebrate the occasion with a nice Austrian stew. After which they might tidy up the place. He would sit down at the keys of an evening, great music in both his hands, while a loving twilight tiptoed across the piano.

Ach du lieber. He laughed as he supposed an Austrian would. *Ach du lieber.* What a funny phrase. Alas, he didn't dare mention his—he supposed narrow—escape to Miriam: not his worries, not his success, because she hadn't known of either. She had eyes only for her flock. And a few vague suspicions she didn't want cleared up. As her flowers moved in a breeze, she moved. She found her future in these stems, in their transformations, their blooms, and, like them, burst into a celebration of petal color in her old age. Instead of receiving his good news as good news, she'd take it as bad. For her, it would be like hearing that a bridge she had just safely crossed was expected to fail, when she knew she'd have to go over the same bridge next day.

Oh but Joey was planning some picnics, no need to say why but simply to salute the autumn, she might like that, and, of course, he would have to facilitate visits to his sis and her lot, the pebbles, rocks, and boulders. It meant so much to . . . to his relatives. My God, he had relatives.

"I'm a careless potato, and care not a pin
How into existence I came;
If they planted me drill-wise or dibbled me in,
To me 'tis exactly the same."

He'd never understood what families were for beyond bearing and raising babies. They carry you away from what you were hoping to become like leaking boats. Bail, boy, if you want to stay afloat. You'll die with a can in your hand, family man.

Ah, there was a line worth working over: you'll die with a can in your hand family man. Like Moore's "If they planted me drill-wise or dibbled me in." It had a lilt, as if it were asking for more of its music. Perhaps it wasn't as strongly regimental as "this is how we wash our clothes," but that might be an advantage. And it wasn't quite as universally threatening as "Formerly I thought the world might go up in smoke, but now I'm forced to give up hope."

His father had a dream: to keep his hands forever clean. Joey wasn't clear whether his father had ever understood that it takes a lot of digging in the dirt to do that. But he knew his students were now actually his, and that what he was giving them was his own hard-won lie-soaked example of fathering. That strangely exhilarating roundelay was wrong about committees too. This very day Skizzen had participated in one that didn't turn out so badly. Palfrey would probably do nothing and wait for the fat man to go away.

Joey was sorry he couldn't share his happiness with anyone. The world should be sorry; but you didn't burden friends with your own good luck. In no time, he would find himself relieved of his relief. Those bursts of celebratory energy he enjoyed would be replaced by the weariness left within their scorched shells. Already he felt his elation make a few farewell waves. As far as his mother went, silence was surely the better strategy. No need to know—that was the popular expression. He returned the songbook to its place on the bedside table. This time, reverently. Perhaps he would contest Miriam's claim after all. What did she want with this dreary leftover room? It occurred to him that he hadn't seen her in . . . what? one, two, several days. She must be in the garden, digging like a dog, quite out of sight. He felt like a little piano practice, a return to more virtuous days. The museum had regained its voice, and also demanded his presence. He knew a can that deserved kicking. Skizzen pled guilty of neglecting these duties. Newspapers were accumulating in sliding piles. He needed flypaper, and would have to go downtown in a day or two to fetch some. Last time, the kid in the hardware who served him exclaimed, "You must have a lot of flies." You hadn't noticed? Skizzen should have said. There *are* a lot of flies. The professor also had a few things to say to the assembled . . . Joey laughed—call them to quorum—Joseph winced—are there enough to have a hearing?—this is an assembled multitude? Be more forceful with your speaking. No more deliver a simple "say." As for your vocal level, exhibit more gradients than a shout. He ought to instruct his imaginary multitude about the virtues of marching bands. Then they will understand what has here been achieved. No need to search, some late afternoon, Miriam might turn up of her own accord. She couldn't cultivate her garden forever.

[- -]

A NOTE ON THE TYPE

This book was set in Adobe Garamond. Designed for the Adobe Corporation by Robert Slimbach, the fonts are based on types first cut by Claude Garamond (c. 1480–1561). Garamond was a pupil of Geoffroy Tory and is believed to have followed the Venetian models, although he introduced a number of important differences, and it is to him that we owe the letter we now know as "old style." He gave to his letters a certain elegance and feeling of movement that won their creator an immediate reputation and the patronage of Francis I of France.

Composed by North Market Street Graphics, Lancaster, Pennsylvania

Printed and bound by Berryville Graphics, Berryville, Virginia

Designed by Maggie Hinders